FLYAWAY SWEEPS

This month's destination:

Exciting ORLANDO, FLORIDA!

Are you the lucky person who will win a free trip to Orlando? Imagine how much fun it would be to visit Walt Disney World**, Universal Studios**, Cape Canaveral and the other sights and attractions in this area! The Next page contains tow Official Entry Coupons, as does each of the other books you received this shipment. Complete and return *all* the entry coupons—the more times you enter, the better your chances of winning!

Then keep your fingers crossed, because you'll find out by October 15, 1995 if you're the winner! If you are, here's what you'll get:

- Round-trip airfare for two to Orlando!
- 4 days/3 nights at a first-class resort hotel!
- $500.00 pocket money for meals and sightseeing!

Remember: The more times you enter, the better your chances of winning!*

VOR KAL

FLYAWAY VACATION
SWEEPSTAKES
OFFICIAL ENTRY COUPON

This entry must be received by: SEPTEMBER 30, 1995
This month's winner will be notified by: OCTOBER 15, 1995
Trip must be taken between: NOVEMBER 30, 1995-NOVEMBER 30, 1996

YES, I want to win the vacation for two to Orlando, Florida. I understand the prize includes round-trip airfare, first-class hotel and $500.00 spending money. Please let me know if I'm the winner!

Name _____

Address _____ Apt. _____

City   State/Prov.   Zip/Postal Code

Account # _____

Return entry with invoice in reply envelope.

© 1995 HARLEQUIN ENTERPRISES LTD.   COR KAL

FLYAWAY VACATION
SWEEPSTAKES
OFFICIAL ENTRY COUPON

This entry must be received by: SEPTEMBER 30, 1995
This month's winner will be notified by: OCTOBER 15, 1995
Trip must be taken between: NOVEMBER 30, 1995-NOVEMBER 30, 1996

YES, I want to win the vacation for two to Orlando, Florida. I understand the prize includes round-trip airfare, first-class hotel and $500.00 spending money. Please let me know if I'm the winner!

Name _____

Address _____ Apt. _____

City   State/Prov.   Zip/Postal Code

Account # _____

Return entry with invoice in reply envelope.

© 1995 HARLEQUIN ENTERPRISES LTD.   COR KAL

"I don't like being stuck with you any more than you like being saddled with me,"

Jed growled down at her. "I was on my way to something really important before I got sidetracked into coming after you."

"Important? What was it?" Victoria cooed. "Drinking yourself into oblivion or crawling into some unfortunate woman's bed?"

"Never you mind what it was!" he barked back. He'd had enough of this blue-blooded filly prancing around with her nose in the air.

"For God's sake," he started, once more surprised at her ability to ruffle him. "If there's one thing I've learned today, it's that you're the most exasperating, distracting female I've ever had the misfortune to meet."

"Distracting!" Victoria protested indignantly and slid gracefully from her saddle, affording Jed an unobstructed view of her gauze-encased thighs. The word *distracting* suddenly took on new meaning....

Dear Reader,

For those of you who like adventure with your romance, don't miss this month's title from the writing team of Erin Yorke, *Desert Rogue. Affaire de Coeur* gave this story about an English socialite and the rough-hewn American soldier of fortune who rescues her a five ★ rating! And *Rendezvous* called it "…five star reading." Don't miss this fast-paced story of danger and desire that is sure to keep you turning the pages.

Also this month, gifted author Deborah Simmons returns to Medieval times with her new book, *Taming the Wolf*, the amusing tale of a baron who is determined to fulfill his duty and return an heiress to her legal guardian, until the young lady convinces him that to do so would put her in the gravest danger.

Ever since the release of her first book, *Snow Angel*, Susan Amarillas has been delighting readers with her western tales of love and laughter. This month's *Scanlin's Law* is the story of a jaded U.S. Marshal and the woman who's waited eight years for him to return. We hope you enjoy it.

And with *Cecilia and the Stranger*, this month's WOMEN OF THE WEST selection, contemporary author Liz Ireland makes her historical debut with the charming story of a schoolteacher who is not all he seems, and the rancher's daughter who is bent on finding out just who he really is.

Whatever your taste in historical reading, we hope you'll keep a lookout for all four titles, available wherever Harlequin Historicals are sold.

Sincerely,

Tracy Farrell

Senior Editor

Please address questions and book requests to:
Harlequin Reader Service
U.S.: 3010 Walden Ave., P.O. Box 1325, Buffalo, NY 14269
Canadian: P.O. Box 609, Fort Erie, Ont. L2A 5X3

ERIN YORKE

DESERT ROGUE

Harlequin Books

TORONTO • NEW YORK • LONDON
AMSTERDAM • PARIS • SYDNEY • HAMBURG
STOCKHOLM • ATHENS • TOKYO • MILAN
MADRID • WARSAW • BUDAPEST • AUCKLAND

ISBN 0-373-28885-9

DESERT ROGUE

ERIN YORKE

is the pseudonym used by the writing team of Susan Yansick and Christine Healy. One half of the team is married, the mother of two sons and suburban, and the other is single, fancy-free and countrified, but they find that their differing lives and styles enrich their writing with a broader perspective.

For Tracy Farrell—with sincere thanks for all your encouragement in this roller coaster of a business. You make it easier to ride the ups and downs.

For Marion Willoughby, and all the other women who trudge across the treacherous sands of life without a hero to guide them—may he be waiting just over the horizon.

Chapter One

Cairo—1881

The whoosh of a clenched fist traveling past Jed Kincaid's ear momentarily drowned out the exotic wail of the snake charmer's flute as it mingled with the usual chaotic noise of Cairo's *medina*. Raising a questioning eyebrow, Jed spawned a lazy grin that didn't quite reach his hard green eyes, and turned around to face his attackers.

"Damn, you really are angry, aren't you? And here I had just about given up hope of finding any more excitement tonight... at least before I went to bed. But if you boys want to fight, despite the fact that I told your little sister she was too young for me and sent her on her way, then I'll be more than happy to oblige," Jed drawled. Knowing these Egyptians didn't care about explanations, he stretched his long, muscular frame so that he appeared even larger, his stand obviously taken.

Senses heightened, he noted a sudden absence of noise in the bazaar. Even the snake charmer's melody was silenced. Most of those who had been outdoors only a moment before had sought refuge from the impending melee behind the shutters of the small shops squeezed together along the narrow, twisting alleyway. Absently, Jed brushed back a wayward lock of dark brown hair from his forehead and raised his fists, readying his body for the onslaught to follow.

He wasn't disappointed. All at once, three men clad in *gallabiyas* charged at him, and Jed's powerful forearms made contact with the midsection of one Egyptian before he whirled to face another.

Though Kincaid's stance was easy and graceful as he delivered blow after blow, his steps swayed slightly, a result of the *zabeeb* he had been imbibing rather than any damage he sustained from the brawl itself. After all, there were only three of them, and Jed Kincaid had oftentimes discovered himself in much worse scrapes.

Somehow, trouble usually managed to find Jed, and when it didn't, he went looking for it. While others not born in Egypt might spend their time sequestered in their own sectors, which were nothing more than transplanted slices of their homelands, the dark-haired American preferred to experience everything foreign shores had to offer. In fact, after two grueling months in the desert, Jed had yearned to avail himself of the sweet pleasures of the Middle East. But even he hadn't hoped for an evening as entertaining as this promised to be with its drinking, its brawling, and his still undaunted intentions of finding some passionate desert blossom to share his bed.

Prodded by the one appetite he had yet to satisfy, Jed savagely thrust his elbow to the rear and was pleased to hear a grunt. Fights like this one reminded him of the constant tussles he and his brothers had indulged in while growing up in the woods of Kentucky. Steeped for a moment in boyhood memories, Jed barely managed to evade a lethal blade before he cautioned himself that there was one important difference between this and the scuffles of his childhood. These boys were playing for keeps.

The realization didn't sober him. He was a man who thrived on danger, and he decided not to allow the deadly attitude of his opponents to detract from his own enjoyment of the moment. After all, they were the ones missing out on all the fun, needlessly angry as they were. It was just a damn shame that most people didn't know how to enjoy life and its many challenges.

That thought foremost in mind, Jed threw himself with greater abandon into subduing the three Egyptians. After a few more minutes of exertion, one man lay groaning at Jed's feet while another was heaped over a pile of baskets. Two down and one to go, Jed noted with satisfaction. If the third assailant had any sense, he would learn a lesson from what had befallen his companions. But as the man lunged at him with renewed rage, Jed concluded that this fellow was no brighter than the other two. Couldn't the idiot understand that he hadn't approached the girl, that she had tried quite unsuccessfully to solicit him?

Now that the first blush of excitement had worn off, an impatient Jed decided to dispatch his remaining attacker quickly. Heaving a sigh, he sent the Cairene a wallop that had to have loosened some teeth, and received a blow to the jaw in return. Crouching and coming in suddenly under a fist meant for his head, Jed grabbed the Egyptian, wrapping his hands around the unfortunate man's throat while he heaved him against the wall of a small brassware shop. The *gallabiya*-clad villain landed heavily, scattering neatly displayed brass plates, tables, vases and coffee sets with a loud clatter.

Satisfied that the Egyptian wouldn't be getting to his feet for quite a while, Jed wiped the dust from his hands and turned away. Now that the fracas had been settled, he had no intention of being in the vicinity should the local police arrive anytime soon. After all, he still had one very pressing need that remained unfulfilled.

Setting forth with a determined glint in his dark green eyes, Jed had gone no more than a half-dozen steps when he heard an excited voice filling the narrow alleyway.

"English! Wait! Wait, English!"

Jed kept going. Whatever it was, it had nothing to do with him, and he had things other than curiosity on his mind at the moment. Yet, as he made ready to round the corner of the twisting street wending its way through the middle of the bazaar, the voice became louder and more insistent, until suddenly it was punctuated by the sound of rapidly approaching footsteps.

Muttering a curse, Jed readied himself for another fight, be it with recovered assailant or arresting police in pursuit. Damn! Didn't these people have better things to do, he asked himself in annoyance?

But the sight that greeted his eyes when he turned around was neither constable nor thug. It was, however, one very irate Egyptian, a shopkeeper from the looks of him.

"English, I will have a word with you," the man demanded indignantly when he reached Jed.

"Say, you're not talking to me, are you?" Jed asked with exasperation as he sized up this newfound obstacle to the pleasure beckoning him like the song of a siren across a turbulent sea.

Of Bedouin extraction by the look of him, the man was almost as tall as the American he confronted. From the expression of his sharp, angular features, the merchant was agitated about something, but Jed had neither the inclination nor the patience to find out what it was.

"Yes, you, English. I am talking to you. Where do you think you are going?"

"Now, see, that's where you make your mistake. I'm an American, not some overly civilized, staid Brit, and I guess I had better warn you that I don't play by their silly rules of proper behavior," Jed growled softly, angered that he had been mistaken for one of the sedate and unflappable Englishmen who had overrun the Land of the Pharaohs. "And as to where I'm headed, it's none of your damn business."

"But it is," the man insisted in spite of the formidable picture a scowling Jed Kincaid presented. "I will not have you run off without payment for the damage you did to my wares. I am Ali Sharouk. It was against my brass shop that you threw one of the men who had challenged you, ruining an intricately wrought coffee service in the process."

"Challenged? It was more a bushwhacking they had in mind than an open and honorable challenge," Jed said with a snort of derision. "As for damage to your coffeepot, get the money for it from one of those bastards who started the fight. I'm certainly not paying for it!"

"But they appear to be poor men. Where would they get the piasters to pay me?" the shopkeeper asked plaintively. "No. It is you I hold responsible, you who heaved my countryman into a pile of my lovely brassware."

"If they don't have any money, take it out of their hides," Jed suggested, turning to walk away once more. "From experience, I can assure you that you might find it real gratifying to do so."

"I am not excessively violent by nature," the tall Egyptian asserted, dogging Jed's footsteps as he dismissed the situation and set out on his way, "yet neither am I a fool. I will have my money from you."

"Like hell you will," Jed promised in a dangerous voice. For emphasis, he brought his face within inches of this latest nuisance, a man not much older than his own twenty-eight years, though by all appearances, a hell of a lot more domesticated. "A decent man walks down your street and is attacked and you expect him to pay for the goods you had heaped at your doorway? I don't think so. In fact, my friend, I know that is not going to be the case. Now, leave me alone before I lose my temper."

"Your temper does not mean as much to me as recovering the price of the goods that were damaged," the Egyptian replied with more persistence than Jed would have given him credit for.

"I said to forget it, Ali," Jed pronounced, lengthening his stride so that the other man was finding it increasingly difficult to keep pace with him.

"I will do no such thing," the Egyptian replied, reaching out a hand to slow this argumentative American down if not stop him altogether.

"Listen, I suggest you take your hand off my shoulder," Jed whispered fiercely, "and go back to your shop. That is, unless you have a hankering to wind up like the last men who touched me."

Ali involuntarily released his grasp but planted himself in Jed's path and kept up his harangue. Finally Jed Kincaid had had enough. The muscles of his lean jaw clamped tightly, and he shoved Sharouk out of his way with such force that the shopkeeper found himself sitting in the midst of refuse strewn across the dust of the alley.

Without another thought for the man, Jed left him there, ignoring Ali's shouted promise to track him down and recover what was rightfully his.

But to Jed's aggravation, the recent events in the *medina* had befouled his mood, robbing him of the euphoria he had found in the bottle of *zabeeb*. With an exasperated sigh, he decided to attempt to recapture his good humor with a few more cups of the native liquor before continuing his search for a woman. He had enough control to postpone his gratification awhile longer, and he had no wish to bring anger to his bed that night, wherever it might eventually be.

The estates of wealthy foreigners were a far cry from the poverty and exotic life of the Arab quarter. Behind the gates of the British and French dwelt beauty, great wealth and an ordered grace, if not the actual comforts of home. At least that was how Victoria Shaw viewed her world.

The sultry heat of the Egyptian sun hung oppressively over the Nile, the air visible in the shimmering distortion of the land across the river. Though Victoria had dressed in as cool a manner as was proper, in a loose-sleeved white chambray blouse edged with piping that matched her blue skirt, and had long ago dispensed with corsets and stays, the twenty-year-old was frightfully uncomfortable. Indeed, ladylike behavior or not, Victoria Shaw was actually perspiring in the early twilight.

Wearily tucking yet another errant curl back into her rapidly dissolving coiffure, the petite blonde sighed and moved further into the ineffectual shade provided by a nearby palm. What wouldn't she give to be under a true English oak, or even a walnut tree.

Over the years since the family had settled in Egypt, her father's servants had struggled assiduously to turn the Shaw property fronting the river into a small oasis of refreshing greenery, but, attractive as it was, it could never compare to the cool grassy meadows of Warwickshire that Victoria remembered so fondly from childhood. Even ten years of living on the outskirts of the Egyptian desert hadn't erased her vivid recollections of running barefoot across the dewy lawns of the Shaw holdings in England.

"Mother," the young woman said thoughtfully, removing her straw bonnet and using it as a fan in a vain attempt to stir a sympathetic breeze, "do you know, the experience I'm most looking forward to on my honeymoon is feeling cold again, being truly and properly frigid from my head to my toes."

"Oh, surely not, Victoria," gulped Mrs. Shaw, horrified that her daughter should entertain such a notion. She had thought Victoria adored Hayden and wanted marriage; whatever had come over her? Before she could express her dismay, however, Victoria laughed gaily and explained herself.

"For heaven's sake, Mother, don't look so grim. I don't mean with Hayden. I expect to be kept quite warm learning the ways of husband and wife," she admitted, recalling the embrace he'd caught her in the night before. "However, I am anticipating English weather with great delight, even if it will be November when we dock. As warm as I've been lately, I cannot think of a single discomfort to be suffered in a real English winter."

"What about that raw, damp chill that penetrates your bones, no matter how well banked the fire, how warm your gown, or how much tea you drink?" asked Grace from under her parasol, a concession to her fair complexion and the strong Egyptian sun. "That is nothing I would choose to experience again. Your father and I are quite content here in Cairo, but I suppose it will be different for you if Hayden moves up in the diplomatic corps—"

"*When*, not *if*, Mother," corrected Victoria, immediately indignant at the implied criticism of her fiancé. "Hayden Reed is invaluable to the British Consulate and soon they'll recognize it and give him a more prestigious posting. You wait and see how quickly my future husband advances in his career."

"Of course, darling. Hayden is a fine young man and your father and I are pleased you are happy with him." Idly playing with her parasol, Grace chose her next words carefully. "As much as we appreciate Hayden's sterling qualities, we had hoped you would marry a titled Englishman."

"Mother, Hayden comes from an impeccable family. His bloodlines are nothing to wince at," said Victoria with a pout.

"Nonetheless, society is much more pleasant when others must curtsy to you, my dear. Still, eventually your father might be able to arrange a title of some kind, baron or viscount, perhaps. Cameron does have Gladstone's ear on foreign affairs, you know."

"Hmm, Lady Victoria Reed. I like the sound of it already," the bride-to-be said with a smile, sinking down onto one of the small benches near the fountains replicating those found in the Shaw gardens in Warwickshire. "Perhaps we should postpone the wedding until Hayden receives that title."

"Victoria, you are scheduled to marry in less than three months. It would be highly inconvenient to alter our plans now. Since you were the ones who wanted to be married quickly, you should dispense with such foolish notions," chided Grace, impatient with the heat and wishing she hadn't mentioned her husband's hopes. "Come along, now. We have written barely half the invitations. We must get back to them."

"I do wish the British community in Egypt was not quite so large or that you and Father didn't know everyone."

"As the representative of the bank holding the notes on a major portion of the khedive's debts, it is your father's duty to invite almost everyone with whom he is acquainted," sniffed

Mrs. Shaw. "Besides, a good number of invitations are for your friends and people Hayden wishes to impress."

"Mother, I promise you, if you permit me this half hour until dinner, I will produce beautiful copperplate from the moment we finish eating until my hand falls off—or until you grant this prisoner a pardon."

"Such flippancy is hardly necessary—"

"All right, until we have finished," corrected the young woman with a winsome smile. "Just let me enjoy the air. Even if it isn't cool, looking at the water makes me feel better. See, there's even a *falucca* on the river. I don't recognize it, but someone else is appreciating the charm of the Nile."

Mother and daughter watched the graceful Egyptian boat gliding downriver, its occupants invisible as it barely skimmed the water, making the motion seem effortless. Used for hundreds of years, the design was timeless, and one rarely knew where the crafts were heading or from where they originated. Only one's imagination could attempt to solve the mystery.

"Very well, but don't make me send the servants to collect you for dinner. I expect you at the table when I sit down. With your father in Constantinople, I detest eating alone. I always feel the serving girls are waiting for me to spill something."

"Thirty minutes, Mother, I promise," agreed Victoria, inordinately pleased at her precious few moments of privacy, time to dream of Hayden and their upcoming life together.

Her fiancé was so much an English gentleman that it was difficult to remember that he had lived in Egypt nearly twenty of his thirty years, she mused, leaning back and closing her eyes to picture him at his desk at the consulate.

His chin was square, his features finely chiseled, so he appeared aristocratic even though he couldn't lay claim to nobility. Indeed, Senior Consular Agent to the Vice Consul was the only title Hayden Reed owned, but if Father could really influence the prime minister, life would be sweet, indeed. Marriage and a title, what fabulous treats were in store for her in the months ahead!

First, of course, was the ceremony, then a honeymoon voyage home to England, shopping in London, walking the estate in Warwick in cool, crisp country air. Images of bliss cascaded through Victoria's mind, the blessed promise of tomorrow making her oblivious to the heat of the evening until unwelcome noises called her back to the river.

The sudden sound of feet landing heavily on the quay and subsequent running awakened Victoria from her daydream. Rising, she was astounded to see two natives hurrying up the landing while a third man secured the *falucca* she had noticed earlier.

"This is private property," she announced sternly, waving her hand at the men in dismissal. The audacity of the Egyptians was unusual; everyone in the area knew the Shaw lands were not available for public docking. It could be that the men were from upriver, but she'd send them on their way quickly enough. "There is a landing site about two miles from here."

Still the men approached, moving even more rapidly toward her. Maybe they didn't understand English.

"I say, be off with you now or I shall be forced to notify the authorities that you are trespassing," she cautioned. "My fiancé is connected with the consulate and he won't deal with this matter lightly, I warn you. Now go."

Despite her urgent commands, for the first time in all the years Victoria had spent in Egypt, the natives did not scurry to do her bidding. Instead, they kept coming closer and closer. The distance between them was barely a few feet now, and, for a brief instant, Victoria felt panic and wondered if she should cry out for the old man working in the far gardens.

But why should she cause a fuss, argued her common sense, when they hadn't threatened her? Maybe they were heading for the house to deliver a message for her father. They were somewhat scruffy-looking, but that didn't mean they were intent on mischief. Perhaps they were only lost. Supremely confident of her position once more, she spoke again in an authoritative tone.

"If you have a message to deliver, one of you may take it to the house. But the others will have to wait with the boat," she insisted, raising her arm to point to the *falucca*.

"You come with us," responded the shorter man, grabbing Victoria and yanking her to his side.

"Don't be ridiculous," she said, laughing, wresting herself free and stepping backward, losing her hat in the process. Yet, despite her evasive tactic, Victoria found herself captured by the rock-solid arms of the second man. "I am a British citizen and Hayden Reed's fiancée. Neither he nor my father will stand for my being treated this way."

All at once a coarse rag was shoved in her mouth and she began to choke at the unpleasant taste. Trying to breathe in such a way so as to avoid the foul flavor of the cloth, Victoria felt herself being lifted and tossed unceremoniously over the tall Arab's shoulder. Horrified, she worked feverishly to free herself from his grasp, kicking her small pointed shoes toward the man's stomach with as much force as she could deliver.

Suddenly she knew success and failure simultaneously as her flailing feet evidently hit a sensitive spot. With an anguished cry, her captor dropped her on the riverbank, just yards from the moored *falucca*. Quickly she scrambled to her feet, but before she could pull the rag from her mouth and begin screaming for help, the smaller man had pinned her arms behind her back and was busy tying them tightly together.

Realizing that she might not be able to free herself from their company for a while, Victoria composed herself enough to notice that the shorter one had a small scar on his left cheek before she was dumped facedown into the *falucca*.

As the craft began to move, she knew only frustration at her unexpected predicament. To think she had protested writing invitations tonight! Any moment Grace would be sending the servants to find her, but they would be too late. Still, there was Hayden. Once he knew she had been kidnapped, he would have both Egyptian and British forces out searching for her, stopping at nothing until she was found. Of that she had no doubt.

Unwilling to consider the possibility that she, an English woman and the only child of a wealthy banker, could actually come to harm, Victoria felt little more than aggravated at the thought of the waiting invitations that would now have to wait that much longer. But then, Hayden would rescue her long before breakfast, certainly.

Lulled by the boat's forward motion, she concentrated her thoughts on Hayden's coming to rescue her, her blue eyes hardening at the memory of the villains' touch. For surely death awaited them for their unpardonable crime!

Chapter Two

Though Ali had moved off quickly in pursuit of the American through the narrow winding streets of the *medina*, he had lost his quarry. He refused to give up, however, and began a methodical search of the Arab Quarter, a hunter stalking his prey.

Twice he had found himself tossed out into the street for daring to demand information, but the man seemed to have disappeared. Ali could think of only one place to look for him, the brothel district.

Determined to see justice done, he directed his steps to this neighborhood and set up a vigil, telling himself that if he did not catch sight of the man he sought within the hour, he would go home to Fatima.

Suddenly, a hundred yards ahead of him, the lanky foreigner appeared, turning unsteadily into Nadir's brothel.

Ali hesitated outside in the alleyway. If Fatima ever learned that he had visited a house of pleasure, she would leave him and return to her father's house. Still, there was the matter of the five thousand piasters he was owed, nearly a month's income from the shop. He could not afford to forsake such a fee, regardless of Fatima's disapproval of his methods. With any luck whatsoever, his beloved wife would never learn the details of this evening's activities. It would be enough to go home and show her the American's money.

Dismissing the doubts that plagued him, Ali lowered his head to his chest, intending to remain temporarily unnoticed while he surveyed the brothel. When no eruption followed the American's entrance, Ali decided it was safe to pursue him inside.

A deep breath calmed his racing heart as he crossed the threshold into the shadowy recesses of Nadir's front room. Looking around surreptitiously, he spied the villain already moving up the stairs to the small cubicles above.

"No, no, you cannot go up to the girls without paying," protested an overweight Egyptian behind the table, holding up a paunchy hand as Ali started for the staircase. "It is not permitted."

"I am not here for pleasure. I am with the American," lied Ali, sidestepping the proprietor and beginning the upward climb. "I stand outside his door to guard his privacy while he enjoys the sweet treats you provide."

"Oh, room six, then," agreed Nadir, not wanting any trouble. The American had already paid for the girl's services. "Just stay in the hall. The girls get more money with an audience."

Room six was the last in the corridor and Ali stood quietly outside. He would give the man a few minutes to become so involved that flight would be the furthest thing from his mind.

Then it was time for a quick tap on the door, followed by a pause and another staccato tattoo.

"I bring message," he called. "Urgent message."

The flimsy door opened abruptly and Ali pushed his way into the shadowy room, its only light provided by a few half-burned candles. A slender, half-clothed Egyptian girl stood by the door while the bare-chested American lay sprawled on the rumpled pile of cushions on the floor, a bottle of whiskey in one hand. Taking a long swallow, he held it out as if to offer it to Ali and nodded casually.

"Here, have a snort and tell me your message. Another job waiting, I suppose, though heaven only knows how you found me."

"It is simple, sir. You owe me five thousand piasters for the damage you did to my shop," announced Ali solemnly. "Pay me at once and I'll leave."

"Oh, it's you, you filthy dog," Jed growled, trying to make his eyes focus. "The brass merchant from the bazaar! It seems your merchandise isn't the only thing that's made out of brass. Get the hell out of here!"

"What? I do not understand."

"You interrupt my pleasure to present me with a bill?" yelled Jed, struggling to his feet to confront the Egyptian. "I was never in your shop. It was the fool polecat I tossed against the wall who did the damage."

"Your memory fails you because of the drink. I told you he had no money," Ali explained rationally, refusing to be intimidated. "You must pay."

"Pay nothing," bellowed Jed. "Woman, get out of my way. I'm going to toss this ragged shopkeeper out on his ear and then we can get back to business."

Ali, however, was lighter on his feet and swifter than the drunken Jed and he effortlessly sidestepped the other's lunging motion. Extending his arms to harness the American's momentum, Ali used it to propel his opponent headfirst into the corridor, where Jed made contact with the wall and slid to the floor.

In an instant, though, the American was back on his feet, spoiling for a real fight. No one had ever knocked Jed Kincaid to the ground so that he stayed there, and no scrawny Egyptian peddler was going to succeed now. Uttering a screaming war cry, Jed lowered his head and ran at Ali, butting him in the stomach and thrusting him into the adjoining door.

The impact of two flying bodies crashed the thin panel without warning. Suddenly Ali and Jed found themselves on an already-occupied mattress, its occupants none too happy.

"What is the meaning of this intrusion?" demanded the man on the bed as his companion sought to cover herself.

"He struck me without cause," protested Ali, moving quickly to his feet, preparing to strike back at Jed. But as fast as he regained his stance and swung, so did the American.

Unfortunately, however, while Ali's fist swung wide and hit only air, Jed's connected soundly with the stranger's jaw, at the same instant Ali spied the jacket of the Egyptian police slung casually over a chair. Groaning, he turned hurriedly toward the door, hoping to escape even as their victim rose to tower over them. Muttering angrily to himself, the officer snatched up the manacles intended for another purpose and grabbed Ali's wrists while calling his men from nearby rooms to block Jed's escape.

"Constable, it wasn't my fault," the shopkeeper protested, already dreading the scene to come. "I apologize that we disturbed you, but—"

"Constable?" echoed Jed, a dull pain beginning between his eyes. Somehow he doubted the manacles were a good omen,

especially when a second set appeared and clamped his own
wrists together. "I can explain everything. I was simply having
myself a good time next door when this wild man interrupted—much the same way he, ah, we barged in on you—"

"Enough," the policeman snapped, donning his uniform
jacket. His evening's pleasure had already been lost, but he
might as well get credit for an arrest or two, he decided, herding the prisoners toward the stairs.

Disturbing the peace, disorderly conduct, attacking a constable, and probably another charge or two to begin with, he
mused gleefully until it dawned on him that the foreigner had
been speaking to his Egyptian opponent in English. How could
he arrest someone who was possibly a subject of the British
Crown? Giving in to such folly without consulting the English
authorities could put him in jeopardy of never being able to
patronize Nadir's again.

With a heartfelt sigh he adjusted his uniform and ordered the
felons to be taken to the office of the consul general.

Grace Shaw had lost count of the number of circuits she had
made of Cameron's study, pacing to and fro, but feeling somehow closer to her husband in this room though he was miles
away. She had endured dinner alone when Victoria hadn't returned, stubbornly refusing to send the servants after her errant daughter. But when darkness fell, the worried mother
capitulated and dispatched the household in search of her. Yet
Victoria was nowhere on the grounds and Grace was very
frightened.

What would Cameron do? she wondered as the clock struck
midnight. If she worried Hayden and it turned out Victoria had
merely slipped away to visit a friend in order to avoid address-
ing those blasted invitations, the Englishman would think ill of
his fiancée. Still, if she didn't tell him and Victoria was in
trouble, he would think her a fool or worse.

It was more than four hours since she had left Victoria on the
riverbank, where the old gardener had found her hat. But the
girl was impulsive. Many was the time Grace had seen her toss
her bonnet aside because she found it bothersome in one activity or another.

If only Cameron were here, fluttered the anxious mother. He
would know how to avoid scandal, and the longer Victoria was

gone, alone and unchaperoned, the more likely it appeared that would be necessary. Perhaps if she sent a note to Hayden, deploring the hour and asking him to escort Victoria home? That was it. She would dispatch a message as if nothing were wrong and the girl had planned to visit him tonight. If Hayden sent word that he hadn't seen Victoria, then Grace would have garnered his assistance without directly asking for help.

Relieved at having made a decision, she sat at her husband's desk to compose the note, only to be interrupted by the houseman.

"This was just delivered, Mrs. Shaw. The boy said it was urgent or I would have left it until morning," he explained, handing over a heavy envelope sealed with wax that bore no imprint.

"Thank you, Ahmet. I shall need you to take a message to Mr. Reed for me shortly. I will ring when it is ready." Her hand shook only slightly as she slit the packet, her unacknowledged fear finally taking hold. Victoria was missing, a young white woman in uncivilized Egypt. What else could this be but a monetary demand to guarantee her safety?

With icy fingers, she turned the envelope upside down, spilling out a crudely drawn map, a page of irregular print and the brooch Victoria had worn that evening. Her fears were confirmed.

Scanning the poorly spelled missive, Grace Shaw expelled a slow breath and, leaning back in Cameron's chair, uttered a prayer.

"Oh, Lord, I don't often ask favors of you, but please take care of my dear girl. I vow I'll get the money these devils lust after, but let them be satisfied with that," murmured Grace. "Surely if I do as they say, they won't harm her. Hayden will know how to handle them. He's good at problems and he cares for Victoria. I know he'll see the ransom paid if I give him the money. And then Victoria will be home safe and sound."

But after she had been abducted would Hayden Reed still wish to claim Victoria for his bride? With a strenuous effort, Grace concentrated on the matter at hand. There would be time enough to worry about that later; until then, emotionless efficiency must be her goal. First the message to John Thomas, Cameron's assistant at the bank, asking him to discreetly release the funds to Hayden. Then the letter to Hayden himself.

* * *

Hayden Reed, consular agent, finished buttoning his trousers and passed the back of his hand across his sleep-laden eyes. Struggling to attach his shirt's stiff collar, he wondered what emergency it was that would call him from his bed at two o'clock in the morning. He hoped that whatever it was, it had nothing to do with him and his work. Yet no matter the situation, the tall, slim Englishman vowed he would handle it. With unperturbed movements that belied his nervousness, he applied pomade to his hair, and a few swift strokes of his silver-backed brush soon had every golden strand impeccably in place.

He rinsed his hands and wiped them fastidiously, then checked his appearance in the mirror. Should the matter now demanding his attention call for the appraisal of his immediate supervisor, Hayden wanted to look every inch the proper British government servant. And if it was, indeed, his superior who had summoned him for questioning, a flawless appearance would not be amiss.

Easing into his expensively tailored suit jacket, and gently tugging the end of each sleeve so that not too much shirt cuff was exposed, he opened the door between his temporary bachelor rooms and the long hallway that led to the government offices at the other end of the building.

His inordinately fine leather shoes softly tapped out his progress as he trod along the corridor, happy that marrying Victoria Shaw meant he could leave his rather Spartan quarters behind and move into a house in a fashionable area of Cairo. A private residence would be so much more useful to a man in his line of work, and he looked forward to taking possession of it two days hence, a full three months before his wedding day.

When he reached the door that led to the office, Hayden straightened his tie and shoulders before making his entrance, his left eyebrow cocked to a suitably inquisitive yet critical degree.

Prepared for just about any crisis, the tall, wiry Englishman had never expected a sight the likes of which greeted him. It caused him to breathe easier. There standing on the costly, intricately handwoven carpet before his desk were two of the most bedraggled human beings Hayden had ever seen in the company of a common Egyptian constable, who appeared to be tempering his own irritation toward the pair with obsequious apologies for disturbing him at such an odd hour.

The unlikely duo was a study in contrasts. One was Egyptian, of obvious Bedouin stock, yet his demeanor and clothing, shredded though it was, proclaimed him to be a man of business rather than a nomad. But it was the other man who commanded Hayden's attention. A Caucasian, the fellow was nonetheless one of the scruffiest-looking specimens Hayden had encountered in quite some time. Dressed in the sort of well-worn kit one might don on an archaeological dig, the man sported a heavy brown stubble of beard and, judging from his arrogant grin, an attitude that struck Hayden as even more prickly.

"What's all this, then?" Hayden asked condescendingly. The question had been directed to the police official, the two men apparently in custody being, of course, beneath his notice.

"Most honored sir," the constable began, "a small problem has arisen."

"If it is so trifling, why bother me with it?" Hayden inquired, not troubling to offer the policeman a seat. This was merely a civil matter and not his own actions being called to task.

"Please hear me out. You are aware, of course, that the Egyptian constabulary is autonomous," the officer began, his spine straightening and his chest puffing out with importance. "It is only as a favor to you that I bring these two men here, and certainly not because we are subordinate to Britain."

"Yes, yes, get on with it," Hayden brusquely commanded with a wave of his hand, knowing as well as the uniformed Egyptian that the police force was independent in name only.

"My presence tonight concerns these two," the policeman stated with a nod, his tones made more deferential by Hayden's obvious impatience.

Hayden studied the pair in question, noting the apprehension in the Bedouin's eyes and the casual nonchalance of the other man. The one was obviously contrite about his part in whatever had occurred, while his companion appeared to be merely amused, a sentiment Hayden did not share as he thought of his comfortable bed at the opposite end of the corridor and the upset he had felt when he had been awakened.

"These criminals were involved in a most dreadful altercation, *mudir*. But since I suspected that fellow there might be a countryman of yours," the constable said as he gestured toward Jed Kincaid, "and despite the fact reports show this is the third fight the fellow has been involved in today, I thought it best to learn your wishes in the matter before I placed him and his opponent in jail."

"I tried to tell him I'm an American and not English," came a casual drawl from across the room, forcing Hayden's attention.

"Your nationality is quite evident," the British official replied in clipped tones. The man, with his sun-burnished skin and raw strength, was all too primitive for Hayden's taste. There was very little that was civilized about him, from his clothing to his manner. Dismissing him, Hayden pointedly turned to the portly constable once more. "As far as I am concerned, you can throw them both in jail for as long as you wish."

"No, most respected sir," the Egyptian in custody protested, his concern for Fatima overcoming his natural cautiousness in dealing with British officials. "I am not to blame. I was merely trying to recover money from this villain for the damages he did to my humble shop during one of his rampages. I asked him for payment, and that is when he set upon and attacked me."

"And with good reason," Jed growled, remembering the dark eyes and soft femininity of the woman employed at Nadir's establishment.

"There was nothing to excuse your assaulting *me*," interrupted the constable, his pride as bruised as his jaw.

"I wouldn't have had a chance to hit you if you hadn't been in that brothel," Jed replied, his low, husky voice ripe with insinuation.

"I—I was merely con-conducting an investigation," sputtered the squat, little police official.

"Yeah? Maybe you should ask him just what it was he was investigating," Jed muttered skeptically to Hayden Reed.

"Never mind that! Let's get back to the original issue. Why did you attack this Egyptian?" snapped Hayden with a nod in Ali's direction.

"He asked for it. Besides, he deserved a good pounding for retreating into his shop when those other three jumped me. Is that what the shopkeepers in the *medina* do when an innocent man is beset by cutthroats?"

"I am nothing if not a law-abiding citizen. I do not become involved in common street brawls," objected Ali. Never, in all his years in Cairo, had he called himself to the attention of the police or the English authorities.

"All that effort to recover a few piasters for some cheap tin and copper? I doubt that. It could be that you're associated with the men who tried to rob and kill me. Maybe it was your job to see that I didn't get away," bluffed Jed coolly. He'd be damned if he was going to spend a night behind bars while the fellow who had interrupted his pleasure went free.

"My only quarrel with you was to recover the price of the goods you had ruined. By Allah, I swear it," Ali maintained, casting a nervous glance in Hayden's direction. One never knew what these foreigners would believe.

"This doesn't concern me," Hayden stated with the exasperation of one of the upper class forced to deal with inferiors. "Though I thank you, Constable, for your intention of allowing me to help decide the fate of one of my countrymen, what you do with these two is your concern. For all I care, you can lock them up and lose the key."

"Whoa, one minute, Mr. Hayden Reed!" Jed shouted over Ali's moan of despair. "I happen to know Great Britain runs the show here, and if you think you can turn your back on this Yank and wash your hands of me, you people are going to have another damn revolution on your hands!"

When Hayden replied, his ice blue eyes had turned frostier. "Is that a threat, Mr.....?"

"Kincaid. Jed Kincaid." He'd dealt with men like this before, Jed thought, long-suppressed images of his stepfather coming to mind after so many years. And he'd see himself in hell before he surrendered to propriety and played by this stuffy Englishman's absurd rules. "And it's no threat, Reed. It's a reality."

"See here, you colonial clod, your blustering has no effect on me," Hayden retorted with disdain, half wishing that he had grounds to order this upstart American's execution. Looking at the restless energy of the man before him, he doubted many jail cells had been built that could contain this powerful thug for very long. To imprison him and then have him escape would only feed the American's already considerable ego as well as give the consul general cause to reassess his junior aide's performance. The possibility made Hayden decide he *should* set-

tle this matter—thoroughly frighten the man and then extract
a promise from the bloody bounder to leave Cairo immediately and not return. As for the merchant, he would lecture
him, as well. It wouldn't do to have the natives think they could
do whatever they pleased.

"I will tend to this problem," Hayden began, waving the
policeman out the door. Then he turned to Jed Kincaid.
"Someone has to teach you proper respect for authority."

"Many a man has tried," Jed retorted, a dangerous glint
lighting his emerald eyes, "and not one of them has succeeded."

"Obviously," Hayden replied dryly. "But now it is my turn."

Concerned with their confrontation, both the American and
Briton had forgotten Ali, standing quietly in the corner, view-
ing the escalating tension with growing anxiety. Hayden was
determined to bend Jed Kincaid's will to his own, and the
American was just as resolved not to comply. As the two proud
males squared off against each other, Ali feared that no matter who won, he would ultimately emerge as the loser.

But before either man could take any action, the door to the
office burst open and one of the *fellaheen* entered quickly,
carrying a message for the person in charge at the moment.

"Put it on the desk and then get out," Hayden Reed ordered brusquely, not sparing the native Cairene a glance.

"But, *mudir*, it is most important!" the fellow protested vehemently. "This is from Mrs. Shaw."

"There's nothing so important that Mrs. Shaw would feel
compelled to send me a missive at this time of night," Hayden
replied, the servant's insistence filling him with uneasiness all
the same. Then a possibility emerged, ladening him with dread.
Could Cameron Shaw have died, gone to his Maker before he
could use his influence to procure a title for his future son-in-
law? Reed paled at the thought, forgot the disturbers of the
peace and whirled around to confront the Shaws' employee.
"Nothing has happened to Mr. Shaw, has it?" he demanded
anxiously, "or to Miss Victoria?"

"It is the young miss, to be sure," the servant replied while
Hayden tore open the seal and scanned the letter addressed to
him.

Its contents all but undid the consular agent's practiced reserve, and he sank into his seat, an upset and bitter man. Life's
greatest treasure had been stolen from him. Yes, of course he

was worried about Victoria, she was everything he could want in a wife, and he had grown fond of her. But along with his fiancée, it was his own rise to power and social position that had, it would seem, been abducted. He slumped down further into his seat. Wondering if it was Victoria's link to him and his own profession that had precipitated so tragic an event, he threw Grace Shaw's letter onto the desk and rested his throbbing head in his hands.

Sensing that he and Ali had been forgotten, and curious as to what could visibly move a man of Reed's reserve, Jed drew closer to the desk to read the decidedly feminine scrawl on the proper, watermarked stationery. The first few lines caused his lips to curl in a grim smile. It would seem Hayden Reed was in for a long night.

"Is this Victoria anything special to you?" Jed asked the benumbed British official.

"*Miss Shaw* is my fiancée, and I will thank you to refrain from mentioning her name. It should not be uttered by a man of your ilk," Reed snapped before turning back to the servant.

"Five thousand pounds! I can't possibly raise such a sum in time."

"The money is no problem, *mudir*. The mistress has sent someone to Mr. Shaw's bank to fetch it."

"But even given that, do you think we can get it to the oasis south of Wadi Halfa in five days' time?" fretted Hayden.

"Wait a minute!" interrupted Kincaid. "I can't be hearing right. You aren't planning on paying the ransom for this girl's return, are you?"

"What we do is none of your affair, Kincaid," growled Reed.

"But why don't you just ride out and get your woman back?" a truly puzzled Jed asked.

"Don't be ridiculous, man! Difficult as it might be for you to comprehend, I can't even begin to consider such a tactic," Hayden protested. "The bastards are taking her to a wadi in the Sudan outside the realm of British authority. If I took it upon myself to send troops out after her, I could set off an incident that might cost thousands of innocent people their lives."

"Oh, I can understand that part, all right, Reed," Jed said, a taunting smile playing around his mouth. "What I can't understand is why you don't go after her yourself. If it was my fiancée, no one would be able to keep me here. It makes a man question your devotion to the lady."

"I'm an official of the British government! I can't be caught doing anything of the sort." Perspiration was beading on Hayden's brow. "It might very well involve my country in an intolerable situation that would only result in international confrontation. As for devotion, how dare you speak to me of my feelings for Miss Shaw? What does an uncivilized clod like you know about real love? After all, the constable did find you in a brothel!"

"I might not be on a first-name basis with true love, I'll grant you," Jed said with a chuckle, "but before this idiot interrupted me the lady I was with was loving every minute of it."

"Uncouth lout! This is not the time for such crude bragging."

"But, sir, what could you expect of a man like this?" Ali ventured to say. He had no wish for Kincaid's reference to the circumstances of their arrest to remind Hayden Reed that he still had two lawbreakers with whom he must deal. Now more than ever, Ali Sharouk wanted to disassociate himself from the troublesome Jed Kincaid. And so, he went on to say more. "Unfortunately, I have become acquainted with his temper. However, he and I are quite different. He is a drifter, whereas I am a family man, a businessman of good standing in this city. My people have lived here for generations, and recently I have been fortunate enough to wed the daughter of a rich man who has no sons. I have ties to this community, while this ruffian has none. I care about the consequences of any action against the Sudan, though he does not. Do not listen to his goading. You can send a messenger and expect him to arrive at the oasis within the appointed time, *if* he makes use of the Nile."

"Lord knows where I'll find a reliable, experienced man," Reed reflected aloud as his long fingers tapped out a perfect rhythm on the polished surface of his desk.

"Look, if you insist on going through with this ransom business, and I hope you realize that payment is no guarantee you'll ever see Victoria Shaw alive again, I can offer a simple solution," Jed said, recognizing the fact that trouble had found him once again, though he was willing to concede he had gone halfway to meet it. "I'll take the money there for you."

"You!" Hayden snorted in surprise. "You can't go anywhere. You're under arrest."

"Then release me," Jed persisted. Though he didn't know her, he wouldn't feel right walking away and leaving the woman's safe return in the incompetent hands of Hayden Reed. If nothing else, Abigail Kincaid Bradshaw had raised her boys always to help a lady in distress, and it sounded as if the Shaw woman needed all the aid she could get.

"If you do let me go," he continued, "I'll track down the men who stole Vicky and get her back for you."

"It's Miss Shaw to you. And I would never allow such a thing as you are proposing to occur. You would only make a muck of it. Miss Shaw would be killed before you ever came near her abductors."

"Really? Maybe you don't realize you're talking to the man who recovered Sheik Abdul Nabar's stolen amulet, the symbol of his sovereignty over his people. Tell me, who else could have done such a thing and returned to tell about it?"

"You? You're the one who went after the amulet and helped avert a tribal war among the Bedouins?" Hayden asked, cocking his head to one side and studying Jed Kincaid anew.

"One and the same," Jed asserted to Ali's dismay. Stories of the amulet's savior had circulated through the bazaar, celebrating the man's ruthless cunning. The idea that he had unknowingly tangled with him did not sit well with the tall Egyptian.

"You almost make your harebrained plot sound workable," Hayden stated wistfully, his hopes for the future once more taking flight. "Still, I'm not willing to put Miss Shaw's fate in your hands."

"But you can't sit by and do nothing," Jed said with derision. "You've said you can't undertake your fiancée's rescue, and neither can anyone else in your department without putting Vicky's life at stake or chancing this international incident. Me, I'm an American. If something happens, you can write me off as lost."

"You and the five thousand pounds," muttered Ali.

"What! Are you casting doubts on my honor?" a hotheaded Jed shouted, ready to begin a fight with the Egyptian all over again.

"Stop it! The two of you!" commanded Hayden Reed, coming to stand between the two men, the Egyptian's words echoing in his head. "You had better start being civil to each other, because you're going with Kincaid to the wadi."

"By Allah, no!" the Egyptian objected vigorously.

"Like hell he is," Jed growled simultaneously.

"There's no question about it," Hayden replied.

"But we hate each other," Jed grumbled.

"We would kill each other," Ali added hopefully.

"There will be no discussion on the matter," Hayden Reed reiterated. "You may have the ability to get the job done, Kincaid, but I am not such a fool as to trust a man of your caliber with five thousand pounds, when Miss Shaw's life depends on every shilling of the sum involved. As for you, your claim of indissolvable ties to the Cairo community and your family assures me that you will not run off with the ransom. You are going to see that Kincaid does as instructed. And that means merely delivering the money, with no dabbling in heroics."

"And what makes you think I'll allow Ali to go along?" Jed asked, his voice as bellicose as his tightly drawn features.

"Quite simply put, Kincaid, you are a man who needs his freedom. Refuse me, and I'll turn you back over to that constable and see to it that you are put in a cell and forgotten."

"How do you know I won't agree to your plans and then get the hell out of Egypt?"

"Because Ali will not allow you to abscond with the funds when I am holding him personally responsible for your actions. Should you disappoint me, his family will learn just how bad business can be in Cairo."

"And if I decline to become involved?" Ali inquired.

"Then we take you home and tell your wife that we found you tonight brawling in a whorehouse. Will she be pleased by those circumstances? I doubt it," said Hayden in an incongruously pleasant tone of voice. "There's really no need to think about it, gentlemen. You have no other alternative."

Jed scowled in Ali's direction, visions of the Egyptian's constant carping in the otherwise silent desert almost more than he could bear. His only consolation was that the shopkeeper appeared no more pleased than he was. Damnation! Jed swore silently before nodding his head in assent. This was going to be the most difficult job he had ever undertaken.

Chapter Three

Almost two hundred miles south of Cairo, Victoria, deposited as she was in the lowest part of the *falucca*, could feel the boat turning. She twisted her slender frame until she could look upward and see the sky beginning to show signs of evening, the sun cooling off to trace soft lavenders and blues across the heavens.

In the bottom of the boat, protected from sight and any possibility of a cooling breeze, the young Englishwoman knew only suffocating heat and discomfort.

This morning, though, just before dawn, the men had drawn the craft into shore in an uninhabited stretch of the Nile, beached it and allowed her a modicum of freedom, if not privacy, to care for her needs before resuming their rapid flight upriver. While they did not pamper her, neither could they afford to have their prisoner die of thirst or malnutrition.

As hard as Victoria tried to keep from surrendering to her fear, concentrating instead on Hayden's inevitable pursuit, every mile they sped from Cairo increased the apprehension she sought to bury. Had her mother recalled the unfamiliar *falucca* she'd pointed out that night and associated it with her disappearance? If she had, was it not possible that the authorities might overtake these villains at any moment?

Straining her ears for unusual noise, the slender blonde was disappointed to hear only the rustle of rushes against the boat and the soft scraping of the sand as its hull touched bottom.

A heavy splash sounded suddenly, accompanied by a violent rocking. Someone jumping overboard to pull the boat in, she supposed, hopefully the tall, foul-smelling fellow.

Then the movement stopped altogether and the pudgy Arab
loomed over her, reached down and grabbed her arm, pulling
her awkwardly to her feet.

Unable to voice her disgust at being manhandled, Victoria
shrank away from the man, her muscles stiff from being in one
position for so long.

"Soft lady," muttered her captor, supporting her weight
against him as he ran his callused hand over her hair, bringing
coarse fingers up to stroke her cheek.

Had Victoria been able to, she would have spit in his face.
Who did he think he was to touch her so freely? No one, not
even Hayden, touched her without permission, and that was
something she did not often give.

"I wager the rest of her is just as sweet," said the odorous
one, stepping forward to pull open her blouse. He'd been too
long without a woman and here was this one, available, if not
willing. "Let's have a look at her."

Unwilling to tolerate his impudence, Victoria didn't stop to
think, but swiftly wrenched her body free of the first man's
grasp with such force that she lost her balance, falling sideways against the hull and banging her head in the process.

"What are you ignorant dung-eaters doing?" bellowed a
voice from outside the *falucca*. All at once the boat shook as
their leader regained the deck, coming to stand between his
men, scowling at the fallen Victoria. Even in a fit of temper, he
spoke in English for the captive's benefit. It was time she knew
her destiny. "We have strict instructions. She is not to be
touched or you will pay with your lives."

"And you as well, Muhammed, not that you haven't been
wearing out your eyes staring at her curves."

"But I am not jackal enough to use the merchandise before
it is sold. English or not, unless she is pure, the slave market at
Khartoum will not get top price, and our master Zobeir's
scheme will go awry. Remember, we will share the profit yielded
by his cleverness. No bothering her!"

At the others' reluctant nods, he relaxed his hold on the
fearsome knife at his waist and motioned toward Victoria.

"Lift her carefully and bring her ashore to relieve herself.
Farouk, fill the water jugs. Hurry so we can sail again."

A short while later, when her gag was removed and Victoria
was seated beside the apparent organizer of the group, she had

prepared her arguments. Ignoring the goat cheese and dry bread he placed before her, Victoria chose to speak for freedom.

"See here, you said you were taking me to the slave marts at Khartoum. My family will pay you handsomely to take me home instead. You saw their lands. You must know they are wealthy," she pressed. "A thousand pounds . . . two thousand. How much can a slave trader offer you?"

"Much more for a woman with blue eyes like yours, especially if she keeps her mouth shut," he snarled, spitting out the pit of an olive. "Eat now or you will go hungry."

"If you insist on selling me, you should know that you will never live to spend your fee," said the blonde, refusing to consider the possibility of such an occurrence taking place. Hayden would come to rescue her long before they ever reached Khartoum. "Whoever your master is, he cannot possibly escape Queen Victoria's forces."

"The good Queen means nothing in Khartoum. It is outside her province," chuckled the native, briefly tempted to take the woman's money. Still, he would die more painfully and much more slowly if he disobeyed Zobeir, the slave trader. No, the female would be delivered as ordered. Rising to his feet, he looked down at the girl. "Money is the only power in that city, and you cannot pay what Zobeir will receive for your lovely white skin. Eat now. We leave in five minutes."

Biting back her disappointment, Victoria took a sip of the wine he had provided. The fool had rejected the salvation she had offered, so there was nothing to do but wait for the British army to overtake them or at worst to invade Khartoum. It was regrettable an international incident could not be avoided, but she could do no more. There was absolutely no doubt Hayden would rescue her.

On the fourth day of their forced excursion out of Cairo, Ali could see no reason to celebrate. Instead of holding his head up proudly, running his shop and bringing honor to his family, he had been ignominiously linked to this rowdy foreigner until the ransom for the English girl was paid, an issue that never should have involved Ali Sharouk.

Where the American viewed this journey as merely another exciting chapter in his quixotic existence, Ali sorely missed his own bed, his loving wife, and even the tiresome chores associated with his livelihood. His only consolation was that since they had begun their pilgrimage, Kincaid had become a man whose only vice was dedication to his mission. Yet the foreigner's very intensity made him as fearsome sober as he had been drunk.

Still, they had made excellent time on the Nile considering the current, one sleeping while the other maneuvered the craft. Now, however, the overland trek was about to begin.

"Enough sleep, American," he announced abruptly, using his foot to nudge the dozing figure, successfully resisting the urge to kick more forcefully. "It is time we must go."

"The only thing *you* must do is to quit telling me what to do," snarled Jed, thoroughly aggravated by his unwanted companion. He wasn't a native to the Egyptian desert, but Jed had spent enough time in it to learn the tricks of survival. Besides, being bred in the city of Cairo, Ali probably knew less than he did. "I've told you a dozen times already, go home and let me see to my business my way."

"Our business, Kincaid, much to my misfortune."

"But it was my idea to deliver the ransom. Hell, without me, you'd be rotting in jail—"

"Without you, I would have no reason to be in jail. *You* started this whole sorry mess by landing on my coffee set whose design took weeks to hammer—"

"We've already been through this—"

"And then you tried to escape responsibility—"

"All right. I've heard it all at least a hundred times—"

"And struck a police officer—"

"I'm going to beat the tar out of you if you don't shut your mouth," yelled Jed, jumping to his feet. To his amusement, the other man stood his ground. Giving the Egyptian a look of pure malice, Jed laughed and began gathering his gear. "Let's get one thing straight, Sharouk. I am no happier to be stuck with you than you are with me. In fact, I'm a damned sight unhappier—"

"Impossible," muttered Ali.

"I told you to go home and wait for my message, but you wouldn't hear of it."

"That is not the honorable thing to do."

"But it's a hell of a lot more practical! Without you, I could have been halfway to the oasis already, but you insisted on wasting extra hours packing supplies—"

"It is only prudent to be prepared. It makes a long journey safer," retorted Ali, folding the canvas shelter he had erected against the sun.

"It makes a long journey longer," snorted the dark-haired American, running a hand across his ever-increasing beard. Ali was a novice at this, Jed reflected, mounting the larger of the horses Ali had hired near where they had traded the *falucca*.

"Enough talk. Let's ride," Jed ordered, determined to reach the oasis as quickly as possible now. The thought of surrendering five thousand pounds to unknown villains with no guarantee of the girl's safety still irked him, but perhaps another option would evolve. It would depend on the situation south of the wadi. If the girl was there, well . . . No man would say Jed Kincaid couldn't accomplish what he set out to do, regardless of the wishes of the authorities or puppets like Hayden Reed.

Miles spent on horseback over almost imperceptible routes through the desert didn't mellow the Egyptian's stubborn resistance to Jed's leadership. After a hard day of riding, they'd reached the oasis and Ali wanted nothing more than to turn over the ransom and head back. Jed, however, had other notions.

"By the life of the Prophet, American, you are *magnun*, crazy! Risking our lives for a woman we did not know was insane, but we had no choice once you opened your mouth to Reed. This new scheme of yours, however, makes no sense. No matter how you threaten me, I will not agree. Your foolishness will not cost me my life," muttered Ali as they lay in the sand, watching the small camp in the oasis for signs of movement.

Well removed from the most frequented trails across the desert, this small haven of shade and water had seen no arrivals since they'd begun their vigil in late afternoon. Clearly the kidnappers had known what they were doing when they chose it. Indeed, from what Jed could discern, they hadn't even set a guard, though that didn't mean a trap wasn't laid within the oasis.

"Reed said we were to work together," complained Ali. It was not that he wanted to venture into the camp himself, but he could not justify Jed's acting alone, nor could he trust the dangerous gleam lighting his companion's eyes.

"Reed is an unqualified jackass," answered Jed, hard put to respect even those of legitimate authority. While there was the smallest chance of success, he could not let it pass. "Look at it this way, Sharouk, if it is a trap and we go in together, who will be left to report what happened to Hayden Reed?"

"But if they think you are alone—"

"They may be careless and give me the chance to save the girl *and* the money—"

"No! You swore you were not going to try that," protested Ali, jumping up and pulling his knife. "I will cut you myself before the others have a chance if you are so foolhardy as to risk our lives so you can be a hero—"

"All right, all right. No heroics, but I *am* going in alone to deliver the money."

"Why you? I am perfectly capable of doing as Reed ordered, handing over the English pounds while you sit here with the flies buzzing in your ear and the fleas biting at your—"

"I give the orders, damn it! Don't you know the only reason Reed sent you was to prevent me from taking off with the cash? Regardless of your fine opinion of yourself, you're nothing but a glorified watchdog."

"And you would trust such a lowly dog to guard your back? How do you know I won't put a knife in it instead?" challenged the Egyptian. Had he known what his brass coffee set would cost him, he would have long ago forgone its price.

"You're too blasted concerned with your good name and your shop to do anything so disreputable, which is what got you into this fix in the first place. Besides, if you ever thought to cross me, I would sense it and you'd never live long enough to make your plans a reality. Stop your complaining and listen," ordered the American. "If you hear trouble, come in fast, ready to toss that knife."

"If I don't hear trouble, you mean. Death in the desert is swift and silent," warned Ali grudgingly.

Nodding at the advice, Jed slung the money pouch over his shoulder and moved stealthily through the darkness, determined to see what he could before he himself was seen.

A thousand yards from where Ali waited, a single man sat by a small campfire, smoking and drinking from a jug. The low tent behind him had a lantern shining within, so doubtless there was at least one more kidnapper around. The only question remaining was whether or not Victoria Shaw was at the oasis, as well. In all likelihood, they were holding her elsewhere, but Jed couldn't afford to risk the young woman's life on a miscalculation. In truth, he was surprised at the concern he felt for this female he'd never set eyes on, but given her attachment to Hayden Reed, she surely deserved his sympathy, if not his condolences.

He had to admit that as Ali suspected, he would like nothing better than to return the money and Reed's fiancée unharmed, just for the satisfaction of making the Englishman apologize.

Hesitating in the inky shadows, Jed weighed his options. If he did rush the camp, he might take them by surprise, but that would count for nothing should he be greatly outnumbered. Then, too, he had promised Sharouk not to give in to heroics, no matter how tempting it might be. Instead, he would learn what he could before he surrendered the ransom. But, if he stood here much longer, nothing would ever happen. The American secreted the money bag beneath his shirt and stood up.

"*Salam habib.* Greetings, friend, could you spare a smoke?" he called, strolling casually into the light of the campfire. "I find myself fresh out of my brand."

The Arab was on his feet at once, calling for help even as Jed raised his hands in the air and gave a short chuckle.

"Stepped into a viper's nest, have I, then? Well, let me assure you, this American doesn't intend any harm," he drawled, deciding he would learn more feigning ignorance of Arabic than speaking it. "You got somebody around who knows English?"

"*Amerikani,* are you?" asked a voice from the open tent where a second man stood watching, a rifle ready as he moved forward to confront the stranger. "Far from home, wouldn't you say?"

"I can't deny it, but then you haven't met my missus," Jed lied jokingly, noting the modern weapon was expertly handled by the Arab, despite his unsophisticated appearance. "The farther I am from that woman, the better I like it. I don't suppose you have a more accommodating female around here? I'd pay well."

For a moment the Arab's eyes narrowed as he considered whether the dusty, unkempt male before him might be the Shaws' messenger. Then he shook his head at the improbability of it. No lone man would be so bold as to blithely step into his enemies' camp. No, this was only some eccentric American who would be dead before he left the desert.

"I'm afraid not, but if you want to share a drink or two, I've some *zabeeb* you might enjoy," he offered, motioning the other to relax his guard. "Hammud's the name."

"Jed Kincaid. My horse turned up lame a few miles out and I had no choice but to shoot her. Any chance you could spare one? I fear it's a long way to the nearest village."

"There again I'll have to disappoint you, American. Once we have concluded our business, we head to Khartoum. We only have horses for ourselves," explained the Sudanese, pouring liberal tots of the native liquor.

"Khartoum? What's down there?" Jed pressed, playing with his drink as he watched the others empty their cups in short order. "Other than miles and miles of savannah, I mean?"

"He wants to know why we go to Khartoum," the leader translated for his cohort.

"High prices for blond English women," snickered the guard in Arabic. "Zobeir pays well."

"Yes, and he's shrewd, too. While we keep the ransom for our efforts, he'll sell the girl and line his pockets," reminded Hammud, his caution gone as he refilled their glasses.

"It's just too bad we couldn't have enjoyed the merchandise before the bill was paid," complained his associate. "But our job was to be here while Farouk and the kidnappers took the girl to Khartoum."

"We trade there," said Hammud, reverting to English. Dealing in white slavery was a serious matter and he belatedly remembered he must take all possible precautions not to be caught. Still, if the American had understood what they'd said, he would have reacted. "What's your business in the desert?"

"I'm looking for Victoria Shaw," Jed answered calmly, grabbing the rifle from where it rested against the tent and turning it on the unresisting kidnappers.

"That's unfortunate," announced another man from behind him. "She's not here, and you are about to be very sorry you are."

Even as Jed wheeled around and fired, a knife whizzed through the still night air, moonlight glinting off its silver blade as it aimed straight for Jed's heart. Hearing the two Sudanese chuckle as it embedded itself in his chest, Jed turned to direct a bullet at one of them as their compatriot fell in his tracks, victim of the first shot.

Pulling the knife from where its point had landed smack in the depths of that tightly packed wad of British notes resting against his chest, Jed threw it at the last man, now brandishing a scimitar. The American's aim, as always, was true.

"Kincaid, you need help?" called Ali, stepping out of the darkness.

"See if that one is still alive, will you?" suggested the American casually in Arabic. "Maybe he'll tell us where in Khartoum we can find Vicky Shaw."

"He's dead. Khartoum? Kincaid, you promised—" protested the shopkeeper. Surveying the two other bodies, he supposed he shouldn't have been surprised, but if they went to Khartoum, when would he see Fatima again? "You swore you wouldn't do this!"

"I guess I got carried away," chuckled Jed, upending the fallen bottle of *zabeeb*. "Want a drink?"

Shaking his weary head at the American's nonchalance, Ali accepted the bottle and raised it to his lips. He was not experienced with alcohol, but somehow he felt in this instance, Allah would understand. Traveling with Jed Kincaid would drive any man to drink. Besides, if his fate consigned him to be this infidel's companion, maybe he had better learn his ways. The Egyptian sighed, surprised at the sudden burst of warmth in his gut. In the meantime, he would pray that the road on which he journeyed with the American would not be quite so fiery.

Though Victoria Shaw had also invoked the heavens, she was perturbed that her prayers had not as yet been answered. At the moment, in the gentle light of morning, she wore her impatience for all to see as she paced the boundaries of the women's quarters at the home of Zobeir, the slave trader, under the man's watchful eye.

He was concerned by the behavior of the Englishwoman so recently delivered to him. Despite her desperate circumstances, condescension toward her new masters marked her as a woman of spirit. Although her imperious attitude had prompted him to keep her from the slave pens where she could start an insurrection, the rotund Zobeir had yet to decide whether or not to beat the pretty female into submission. After all, her proud, uncowed demeanor could very well raise her asking price, he mused, aware that there were many who would pay an exorbitant amount for the chance to tame so wild a creature.

Still, Zobeir concluded, witnessing the blonde issue a haughty denial to the servant who had brought her fresh garments to replace her own attire, she had to be gentled somewhat. No man would part with gold for a shrew, no matter how exquisite her looks.

Watching the woman continue her graceful caged walking to and fro, Zobeir wished he could afford the luxury of humbling her himself. But with a sigh, the slaver put such thoughts aside. One did not get rich by giving in to temptation. To steal Victoria Shaw's virginity or to mar her delicate flesh with whips would only lower her price along with her pride. No, she would be disciplined, to be sure, but in more subtle ways.

Signaling to the serving girl who still stood holding the sheer harem garments, Zobeir approached his newest acquisition.

"Perhaps you failed to understand that after bathing you were to don these," he said, fingering the indecently transparent pantaloons. "Put them on now."

"I most certainly will not!" Victoria proclaimed, her frosty tones an indication that she considered the man her inferior.

"Yes, you will, or you will regret it," Zobeir stated with a dangerous softness.

"I hardly think that likely," Victoria scoffed.

"Ah, but you underestimate the power I hold over your destiny," Zobeir replied, his cheeks growing rounder in the wake of his odious smile. "Do as I say and you will be sold to a kind master. There are those with whom you would not fare well."

"I will not be sold at all," Victoria said emphatically, though these last few days her belief in that statement had started to waver. "The Europeans living in Khartoum will not allow such an atrocity to be visited upon one of their own."

"And have you seen any of them since your arrival?" Zobeir asked with a chuckle. "With auctions of slaves as private as they are, no one will ever be aware you have been in Khartoum."

"I have already told you that I am a British citizen and the daughter of a wealthy man," Victoria announced, tilting her chin defiantly. "I am worth more in ransom than any price you could ever hope to fetch for me in the slave market. If that is not enough to sway you, perhaps the idea of my fiancé's terminating your vile life will change your mind."

"Do not try my patience, English flower, or I will see you transplanted into a garden not fit for dogs, rather than into one containing blossoms as delicate as yourself," the slave trader threatened. He had no inclination to explain to the girl that she had been marked for death by the powerful figure who had charged him and his men with her abduction. It was only the result of his own greed and the fact that the one to whom he answered was miles away that he had dared to defy his orders and keep her alive at all. However tempting returning her to her father for reward was, Zobeir knew it was an option that he did not have—not if he wanted to live.

"See here, I have already traveled endlessly bound in the bottom of a *falucca*, only to find myself carted into your despicable city under a pile of blankets. I survived that. Your talk doesn't frighten me."

"But my description of the sort of master to whom you could be sold will make an impression. Do you know how a man can treat a woman when he wishes to be cruel? Do you realize how he can tear into her body so that he rips at her very soul? If you do not fear pain, perhaps the idea of indignities will move you to do as I bid." When the Englishwoman did not react, Zobeir decided to offer her details.

"I can sell you to a man so slothful that he will not waste his time arousing you, not even so that you may bring him pleasure. There are those who have the female they have selected for the night held down by eunuchs while the other women of the harem inflame the chosen one until she is ready for her master. Should you think the women would refuse to do such a thing, realize that there are those in every large harem so starved for physical joy that they would find such a duty a treat. They would relish bringing their victim to the brink of ecstasy so that their master had merely to enter her with no more finesse than a rutting ram in order to find his own satisfaction. Do you think you would like to belong to such a man? Does the idea of other women kissing and caressing your most private parts excite you?"

"How dare you talk to me of such things?" Victoria whispered fiercely, face pale but her voice still drenched with contempt.

"Ah, it is not the talking you will come to fear," Zobeir said, his fingers stroking his straggly beard. "Do as I ordered and change your attire."

"You will find that Englishwomen have more backbone than you suspected. I am not frightened by your disgusting threats."

"Put on this clothing or I will beat you now!" the slave merchant thundered, his patience at an end.

"You wouldn't," Victoria retorted with a contemptuous laugh. "Lay one filthy finger on me and your life is over."

"Your bravado is almost commendable. Still, if fear doesn't move you, I will have to persuade you to submission by other means. Clothe yourself in those garments now or I will beat this woman." With that, he reached out to grab the serving girl by the hair and pulled her to him, striking her repeatedly about the face and head.

Victoria couldn't decide which sound she detested the most, the slap of fist upon flesh or the girl's piteous cries. Unable to think of an option that would end the sobbing woman's torment, Victoria Shaw reluctantly agreed to do as she was told.

"All right. Give me the clothing! Just stop hitting her!"

"I thought you would see logic eventually," the slaver said smugly, casting the other woman aside. "And realize that the only reason I did not forcibly dress you myself is that I do not want any marks on your fair skin when you mount the block."

"Do you promise to leave that girl alone if I do as you ask?" Victoria inquired in a calmer voice than Zobeir had expected.

"I swear before Allah that if you but wear the things I have given you, I will not touch the slave again . . . at least not in anger," the man said with a wicked laugh.

"Leave, then," Victoria directed, reverting to her usual position of authority despite her circumstances. But even as she held out her hands to receive the diaphanous garments, she vowed that this would not be the first step toward surrender.

If only Hayden would arrive, she thought, her eyes boring into Zobeir's retreating back. Surely her fiancé's failure to materialize was the result of inordinate caution, caution prompted by his great love for her and his reluctance to act too precipitously. But didn't he realize that if he didn't rescue her soon, she might experience injury, anyway?

True, she was English and would do her best not to let down the side, she mused, the skin of her thigh cringing at the cool caress of the indecent pantaloons as she stepped into them.

Still, how much could any British subject be expected to endure? Victoria wondered, garbing herself in the scant jeweled jacket that barely covered her breasts.

The sound of Zobeir's return echoed in the hall a few brief moments later. Present danger was what she had to concentrate upon now, the young socialite reminded herself as she stood awaiting the slave peddler's entrance.

"Disobedient slave!" came his outraged cry when he beheld her. "Do you still think to defy me?"

"I have kept my part of the bargain," Victoria said smugly.

"You are a liar, like all your race," Zobeir bellowed, hard put not to throttle this troublemaker. It was only his vision of the profit she could bring that stopped him.

"English honor is revered the world round," Victoria replied coolly. "I am as honorable as any of my countrymen." With that she lifted the hem of her skirt to reveal the harem garb beneath her own clothing. "You told me to put these things on. I have done as you asked, and I expect you to keep your promise."

"Do you think to outwit me?" Zobeir asked in rage. He should have had his men kill the girl as he had been ordered to do. "Time in the slave pen will do you good. And if you are not truly humbled by tomorrow, I will come up with something that will amuse me more than you have angered me at this moment. Perhaps you are not the virgin I suppose you to be. A physician's certificate attesting to your purity might be in order."

"If you or anyone else comes near me, I will kill him and then myself," Victoria stated with deadly coldness.

"Take the woman out," Zobeir ordered in exasperation. "Place her in the pens!"

Though Victoria held her head high as she walked away, her heart cried out, *Oh, Hayden! Where are you?*

Chapter Four

The great walls of Khartoum loomed ahead. Their dusty surface, awash with the light of morning, projected a foreboding aura that unsettled Ali Sharouk's stomach and his throbbing head.

Last night he had thought to ease his plight by partaking of some more *zabeeb* at El Naharal, a village situated between Khartoum and the quarries to the north, where Jed Kincaid had freely spent a great deal of the ransom money for supplies in pursuit of his wild and improbable rescue scheme.

Though alcohol and Ali had not been acquainted before his encounter with the American, the shopkeeper had embraced it quite willingly yesterday evening, attempting to blot out the presence of the irritating foreigner to whom fate had bound him. Surely Allah would not withhold his forgiveness for such a small transgression, Ali had told himself, especially when the Almighty considered the reason for his humble servant's uncharacteristic fall from grace. But this morning found Ali less than sharp, and that was a thing that worried him greatly.

"This is not going to work," he muttered in exasperation. Nevertheless, he plodded along beside Jed as he had for the past few hours, ever since the horses and provisions the American had purchased had been left concealed within a narrow niche in the cliffs to the north.

"Quit your complaining," Jed replied absently, his sharp green eyes already assessing Khartoum's walls and the *faluccas* bobbing in the Blue Nile's currents before the city's main gate.

Looking at his fellow traveler, Ali could almost see Jed Kincaid's silent calculations taking place, his rejection or acceptance of the various options he discerned. The cold, perilous gleam in Kincaid's eyes made Ali shudder. Surely only a madman could be capable of such intense, single-minded concentration.

To conceal his uneasiness, the tall Egyptian shifted the saddlebag containing explosives that Kincaid had procured from a Frenchman running the quarry below Kerrari. The wisdom of transporting such materials was something else Ali had questioned, but the American was obviously comfortable with danger.

Yet for all Jed Kincaid's preparations, Ali considered the plan so insane that he wondered how anyone with an ounce of intelligence could think it might succeed. It was the product of either a fool's thinking or that of a man so bold and arrogant, he could not conceive of failing. Looking at Jed Kincaid, his stubborn jaw set in determination as he continued to scan the city walls, Ali knew into which category his companion fell.

"You know what to do once we pass into the city, don't you, Ali?" the American drawled, his attention drawn to the swift currents of the Blue Nile as it flowed westward to join the White and form the Great Nile River.

"You've only explained it half a dozen times. I do comprehend your language, barbaric a tongue as it may be."

"No need to get testy," Jed rejoined, his mouth curved carelessly into a dangerous smile. "At least you'll be entering Khartoum as a free man. You're not the one posing as a captive and going into the slave pens."

"This whole thing is preposterous. You're simple guessing that's where the woman is being held. I ought to really sell you for dragging me into this madness and be done with you," Ali threatened.

Jed stopped abruptly and whirled around to face the merchant, roughly grabbing the neckline of Ali's *gallabiya* and pulling the Egyptian so close to him that their faces were only inches apart. "Don't even think about it, you desert-hatched son of a bitch. Should anything go wrong in there, I'll track you down and leave your dismembered body for the jackals. Is that understood? Do you think your Fatima would enjoy being a widow?"

"You can't hold me responsible when this business ends in disaster," Ali replied, calmly removing Jed's hands. "If it wasn't for your damned impulsiveness, the money would have been delivered and we would be on our way back to Cairo."

"Tell me you'd pay for a delivery of brass at that miserable little shop of yours without getting the goods. Go ahead, convince me of that. It's no different with Victoria Shaw."

"By Allah, look at you!" Ali exclaimed. "You're enjoying every moment of this! If the Shaw woman had not been abducted, you'd be in the middle of something else right now, just as hazardous as this is."

"Be quiet, Ali," Jed growled in warning.

"It's true! You are as drunk on impending danger as I was on last night's liquor. It's in your blood, something you crave. You're so obsessed by it, Kincaid, you don't even understand the audacity of what you're doing—or what you've already done."

"What I don't understand is why a big fellow like you is hesitant about changing things and making them the way he wants them to be," Jed stated, his voice as sincere as it was critical.

"Of course you don't. There's not a shred of civilization about you," Ali replied with a snort. "Unlike me, you are a man with nothing to lose."

"I've had just about enough of your jabbering," Jed snapped, turning back to face Khartoum, the city now showing signs of the day's business getting underway. "I swear, when we get back, I'm going to kill Reed for tying me to you."

"*If* we get back. As for being tied, that was *your* idea, not mine."

"And that's why I'm certain this plan will work," Jed answered with a grim smile as he glanced down at the rope imprisoning his wrists.

"You'll need more than confidence to escape once you're placed in the slave pens," Ali fumed, an anxious frown furrowing his forehead as he wondered how he could ever return home without the woman, Kincaid or the ransom money.

"That's where I have to rely on you, God help me," Jed said with a sorry shake of his dark head. "But it can't be avoided. Once we see the lay of the land, I'll decide where to place the explosives, and if you can keep me in the shadows for a few moments, it will be easy for me to get that job done. From what we've heard, Khartoum is building up an arsenal and constructing a powder magazine outside the city on Tuti Island rather than in the city proper. But I'm sure there'll be something else we can send to smithereens and cause a ruckus. When I give the signal, you set off the fireworks. By the time we're through, it will look like the Fourth of July in there."

"July? Your month of July is a few weeks away, isn't it?" Ali asked, drawing his eyebrows together and regarding Jed curiously.

"Never mind," Jed intoned, his deep voice rife with disgust. "All you have to know is that you light the fuses when you hear the signal." With that, the rugged American whistled a few jaunty bars of "Yankee Doodle." "Think you can remember that tune?"

"Who could forget such a disharmonious melody," Ali responded dryly. "Still, it's not too late to return to Cairo."

"What do you reckon Reed will do if we show up without the woman and with a big chunk of the money gone? You have no choice, Ali. Now, come along," ordered Jed as he began to lead the way.

"No," said the merchant, his voice adamant.

"No?" repeated Jed in his most menacing fashion.

"No," Ali reiterated. "If we are to have even a prayer of this insanity succeeding, I will do the leading and you will follow like a respectful slave. I shall hold the rifle, and, like a beast of burden, you will carry the sack containing the explosives. Should you enter Khartoum with your usual swagger and foul temper, you'll be cast in irons the moment you enter the pens. And in all likelihood, I'll be chained to the wall right beside you. You must appear to be submissive, resigned to your fate, perhaps even a bit timid or fearful. And above all, you must remember I will be the one giving the orders. Is that clear?"

"All right," Jed yielded, irked that the Egyptian's demeaning suggestions had merit. "But I'm warning you, don't overplay your role."

"I think this might be the only part of this ill-advised adventure that I enjoy," Ali said. He grabbed the halter around Jed's neck and gave it a tug. "Come, slave."

"Watch it, you bastard," Jed growled. Nonetheless, he affected a hopeless shuffle and followed in Ali's wake. "Just remember, you're going to have to live with me on the journey back to Cairo."

* * *

She had come this far without giving in to tears, Victoria reminded herself as Zobeir's men hurried her through the seemingly endless maze of corridors after preparations had been made to transfer her to the pens. No matter how desperate she felt, how hopeless it seemed, she would not surrender to emotion. Hadn't she outmaneuvered Zobeir, the wealthiest slave merchant in Khartoum? The memory of his anger-mottled face cheered her immediately.

Indeed, since he had sent five guards to serve as her escort after making her wait hours alone in a closetlike cell, he no longer considered her helpless. Forcing him to take such precautions had to be a victory of sorts, Victoria assured her flagging spirits.

His men surrounded her, the one at her side grasping her elbow so firmly it was a wonder she had not lost circulation in her arm. The situation was intolerable for a British citizen.

"You are holding me too tightly," Victoria announced curtly, stopping suddenly. While the men were still startled, she twisted her upper body forcefully to the left. Wrenching her arm free from its human vise, she glared at the one responsible for her discomfort, her blue eyes challenging his implacable black ones.

"Your manners are sadly lacking," she chided. "I realize you answer to Zobeir, but aren't you man enough to defend a helpless female from abuse rather than perpetrate such behavior?"

Fury flashed across the face of the guard and the feisty blonde found herself on her knees, her long hair wrapped tightly around the man's hand as the pain of his tugging it caused unbidden tears. Even as she squeezed her eyes shut and swallowed to ease the agony, Victoria knew she was defeated.

"A man is *always* master, though he may in turn answer to another," replied her tormentor while the others chuckled. An abrupt jerk of the hand forced Victoria to look up into his cruel smile. "Have I convinced you to walk or shall I drag you? It is the same to me."

"Zobeir will—" she began to threaten weakly until his fingers twitched, viciously tightening his hold on her blond tresses.

"He won't object since your skin won't show any ill effects. Indeed, I shall make it a point to inform your buyer of this particular form of discipline," promised Zobeir's man. Then, using her hair, he yanked her roughly to her feet. "Now will you walk?"

"Yes." There was no need to say more, nor any ability to do so. Stung now by the painful reality of her situation, Victoria regretted her pointless defiance. There would come a time when he was less vigilant, she promised herself, refusing to despair.

With a satisfied grunt, the Sudanese released her curls, took her elbow and addressed his cohorts, his words causing loud guffaws. Then they were moving once more through the still-deserted halls of Zobeir's grand home.

With each step across the lush carpets, Victoria questioned her presence in this world of masculine brutality and power. It was more than a week since she had been kidnapped, nine days if she calculated correctly. Why hadn't Hayden or her father found her? Cameron Shaw had always said, "Money buys power—or at least the semblance of it." Surely if her father contacted the khedive, the political leader would interfere on her behalf.

Could it be possible that no one knew she was in Khartoum? For a long moment this thought stunned her, almost as badly as the harsh sunlight that blinded her as they left the sheltered rooms.

Outside, the guards moved closer, herding her at a quick pace through the dusty streets. A few heavily veiled women averted their eyes as they passed, while a large group of men leered openly and began to follow her, shouting in Arabic. Two particularly persistent fellows tried to push past Zobeir's men to reach her, but they were easily repelled by her human shield. The slave trader had not exaggerated when he said many men would want her. But would Hayden continue to desire her, if he ever found her?

All too quickly, they stopped before a guarded enclosure, its eight-foot-high walls topped with spikes embedded in the sandstone. Heavy wooden gates provided the only interruption in the rough-textured expanse, at the top of which stood a sentry's post.

"Zobeir wants her in the pens until tomorrow's auction," announced the man beside her. "We will take her through."

"There is no need—"

"Zobeir knows you have sampled his wares in the past and he wants her untouched," refuted the slave trader's deputy.

Not understanding the sharply spoken exchange, Victoria dared hope for a moment that she was being turned away. Instead, the high gate opened and they were motioned inside.

As she moved, the young Englishwoman looked about and was startled to see men on every side of her: short, tall, dark-toned, light-skinned, bearded, clean-shaven, clothed in every possible garb. Some were asleep, but more were standing about, carefully watching her progress across the compound.

"Zobeir said the women's pen," she reminded her keeper. She was nervous because of the hungry leers on dozens of faces, most of them destined for slavery themselves.

"They are sheltered behind the men's quarters to offer extra security from anyone who would interfere," the man explained gruffly. "The guards and these slaves are between the women and the street in case of trouble."

"Has anyone ever tried to free Zobeir's women?" Victoria asked, a tiny glimmer of hope sparking to life.

"To be certain, no one has succeeded, though once in a while there's been a halfhearted attempt by the Europeans to interrupt an auction. But all that happened was a temporary postponement or relocation of the sale."

Dropping her eyes to the ground, Victoria tried not to acknowledge her fear as the guards led her forward. The lounging men awaiting their own purchase by others continued to watch her every move, devouring her pale flesh with their ravenous eyes, despite her escorts' cursing and shoving them out of the way.

In front of the interior gate, she stood silently, searching for some chink in the security, determined to find a means of escape. If she could rally the other women, perhaps they could break and run when they were led to the market.... They couldn't all be docile when it came to being sold into slavery.

"A word of advice, do as you are told or you will know pain," said the leader of Zobeir's contingent as he released her arm. "If you listen to your master, you may find your life not too unbearable, though I expect you've many more lessons to learn before that happens."

Then, with his hand at the small of her back, he pushed her through the gate and signaled that it be shut.

The area was much the same as the men's compound. Women of various shades, though none as light as Victoria, paced uneasily, apparently too nervous to stay still.

Victoria was the first white woman any of them had ever seen, and some of them crowded around her, reaching out to stroke her skin, only to pull back in fear when they saw her blue eyes.

"It is all right. I am a woman like you," she assured them, holding out her hand to display its color. If she could convince these women that they had something in common, there might be a chance. "I am here against my will, just as you are, but I am not ready to be sold. What about you?"

But the women had withdrawn from her, eyeing the pale witch with suspicion and giving no indication of whether they had understood. Once more she was alone to contemplate her future.

In the short while they had been inside the city, he and Ali had learned a lot, Jed realized with satisfaction. The hardest part had been restraining himself from beating the hell out of his spurious captor to put a stop to that sand rat's lordly manner.

If the damned Egyptian didn't watch his step, Jed just might consider leaving Ali Sharouk behind when things started heating up and it came time to flee the city. But even as the temptation crossed his mind, Jed knew he would never do such a thing. Unaccustomed as he was to working with a partner, he and Ali were in this together, and Jed Kincaid was, if nothing else, an honorable man—at least of sorts.

A snap of the halter around his neck caused a resentful Jed to hasten his steps and struggle to keep his demeanor docile as he followed Ali along a dark, narrow alley.

Their path ran along the outer wall for a short distance, past a minor gate, Jed noted, surreptitiously raising his eyes to take in every detail while he planned their escape route and alternate ones, as well. Then the narrow street turned in upon itself, and shifted direction once more.

The slave block was located at the center of this maze full of twisting turns and forbidding passageways so that it was hidden from prying eyes. Slavery might be an accepted way of life in Khartoum, yet it appeared the local citizenry was smart enough not to want to offend the sensibilities of visiting Europeans, especially when one of those foreigners was occasionally placed on the block. From what he had heard about

Khartoum, its foreign residents ignored the trading in human
flesh that took place here, pretending it existed only in the realm
of rumor. Nonetheless, they kept their women close at hand,
knowing they would be lost forever if they disappeared into the
serpentine streets of the city.

Jed's thoughts ended abruptly as the alleyway left the darkness behind and spilled out into the strong, oppressive heat of
a sunlit marketplace. Realizing danger surrounded them, the
American felt a rush of excitement course through his blood.
Ali *had* been right. Jed Kincaid needed adventure like this as
surely as he needed air.

Anxious to set things into motion, Jed nonetheless patiently
allowed Ali to lead him around the perimeter of the bazaar, the
Egyptian stopping often to talk to Khartoum's inhabitants in
Arabic. Within a short time, Jed had discerned the layout of the
pens, chosen the partially concealed spots in which to plant the
explosives, and stealthily accomplished the task while Ali stood
in front of him, presenting a shield to anyone who would be
curious enough to observe them.

Still, they had yet to uncover the slave merchant mentioned
by the kidnappers at the oasis. And without locating him, Jed
couldn't be certain Victoria Shaw was anywhere near Khartoum's infamous marketplace.

"Time's growing short, Ali. Find Zobeir," Jed commanded
with whispered authority. The Egyptian's only response was to
pull Jed behind him as he approached an ancient water seller.

This was hardly the time to get thirsty, Jed thought in disbelief when the old man, his back bent under the weight of the
large, long-spouted cask he carried, leaned forward to pour Ali
a cup of the precious liquid.

"I will have some more, grandfather, along with information," Ali said, pressing a coin into the gnarled hand. "I need
advice on how to sell this worthless slave. Can you direct me to
a knowledgeable man, a slaver who knows what needs to be
done in order to get a decent price for such poor merchandise?"

"The most celebrated of all is Zobeir. There he is, the fat one
sitting in the midst of the others. It is he who can best advise
you. And for such a pretty man as this, he might offer to purchase the slave himself. It would save you the auctioneer's fee."

Pretty man! a ruffled Jed balked in quiet indignation. He
wasn't at all sure he liked the water seller's words as Ali thanked

the elder and then crossed the compound, keeping the American tightly in tow.

"*Es-salam 'aleikum*," Ali called in greeting, nearing the men and dragging Jed none too gently.

The Egyptian hunkered down next to the others. With the rifle the ransom money had brought cradled in his hands and the glowering look he sent in Jed's direction, Ali Sharouk seemed more like a formidable desert dweller than a harmless city shopkeeper. The journey from Cairo had hardened him, and Jed found no fault with Ali's appearance while they waited for the slave merchants to acknowledge their presence.

"*U 'aleikum es-salam warahmet Allah wabarakatu*," one of the men finally replied, uttering the usual response to Ali's greeting. He eyed the unknown pair suspiciously all the same.

"Can you tell me if there is to be an auction soon? I wish to earn some gold and at the same time shed this burden," Ali stated with a jerk of his head in Jed's direction.

"You are Egyptian, aren't you?" the rotund figure identified as Zobeir asked shrewdly.

"Yes. My family roams the southern lands near Berenika," a nonchalant Ali replied.

"And you came here to sell a slave?" inquired a third slaver, assessing the man tethered at the end of the rope.

"It is said that such a task is easier to accomplish and much more rewarding in Khartoum than in Egypt," the newcomer said, his expression daring the others to contradict him, "especially when the slave is white."

"Still, for a man living in a land ruled by Europeans rather than the khedive, who possesses a title and little else, selling a Caucasian is an audacious undertaking," Zobeir stated quietly.

"Not as bold as the crime this jackal has committed," Ali asserted, his face set in hard lines as he forced Jed to his knees and struck him harshly.

Son of a bitch! I owe you one, Jed thought savagely, resenting the need to cower under Ali's blow.

"And that crime was?" Zobeir inquired politely.

"He approached my wife," Ali announced through clenched teeth, telling the tale Jed had concocted. "I vowed before Allah that this heap of camel dung would pay for his transgression. Death is too easy for him. I would rather he know misery for years to come. Besides, I like the idea of filling my purse at his expense. Now, is there to be an auction or must I seek a buyer on my own?''

"There will be a private auction tomorrow. But I doubt you will get much for him. He looks rather submissive for so large and well muscled a man," Zobeir said, his glittering eyes raking Jed's huddled form speculatively.

"He has learned to be," Ali stated grimly. "Still, he is strong and can do much work."

"His back is well scarred, then?" asked Zobeir. His voice was dispassionate, but he continued to scrutinize Jed's broad shoulders and slender hips with an intensity that made the American uneasy.

"Not at all," Ali assured, knowing a lie would be uncovered. "I am wise enough to know that someone might want to buy him for reasons other than his capacity for labor. There are many ways to discipline a man, and this slave is practically flawless."

A stunned Jed listened to the exchange, straining to remain silent as Ali deviated from the script he had worked out for him.

"I might be interested in buying this slave for myself," Zobeir said, salacious interest fleeting across his face for an instant. "And I will give you a fair price, too."

"Let us see what offers I receive tomorrow," Ali replied smoothly, causing Jed to breathe a furtive sigh of relief.

"But what can you hope to get for him? You know he has no spirit," the obese slave merchant argued.

"True, yet it could be that someone might want a man of size and meek temperament to stand guard over a harem."

Jed's eyes, hidden as he rested his head on his arms in an attempt to look dejected, popped open. What the hell was Ali doing? If his improvising didn't stop, there would be an explosion in the marketplace that needed no match.

"It might be so, but wouldn't alterations have to be made?" Zobeir asked with a wicked chuckle and a glance at Jed's crotch.

"From what I have seen they would be very minor alterations," Ali replied with a smirk, ignoring the look of disappointment that crossed Zobeir's pudgy face.

That carrion-eating bastard was going to be dead when they got out of here, Jed raged inwardly, calling on all of his inner resources not to wrap his fingers around Ali's lying throat.

"I see," Zobeir said, stroking his beard thoughtfully, wondering if the Egyptian was telling the truth or merely bragging about his own endowment. "In that case, why don't you take him into the pens and put him with the others to be sold tomorrow? Perhaps later I will inspect him and either make an offer or else advise you as to what you can expect to get for him. Tell the guards Zobeir sent you, and get a receipt for your merchandise."

But we have to find out if the girl is in there first, otherwise we're only creating more problems, Jed thought frantically. He swore Ali had the brains of a beetle. The Egyptian rose and yanked him roughly to his feet.

"Selling a Caucasian will bring no difficulty?" Ali asked as though reading the American's mind.

"None at all," Zobeir replied, raising a glass-lined cup to his lips and sipping at his heavily sweetened coffee.

"Still, I have reservations. I would hate to see this dog rescued. Perhaps I should seek a private sale," Ali muttered.

You idiot, Jed wanted to scream. What are you trying to do, get him to make another offer so he can take me home to his bed?

"As you will. But I can tell you there is another European in there, a woman I, myself, am putting up for bid," Zobeir stated with a shrug of his rounded shoulders.

"Is that so?" Ali inquired, his interest all too apparent to Jed's way of thinking.

"Yes, and a lovely thing, too," Zobeir replied, not bothering to mention her inherent disobedience and shrewish disposition.

"Then possibly we could trade. Your slave for mine. My wife could use a maid, and so could I. As for yourself, this man might be to your liking," Ali said suggestively.

Sweet God in heaven! What are you, some Nile-spawned numskull? a disbelieving Jed fumed. He was ready to reach for the knife hidden in his boot and slit Zobeir's throat if the bastard so much as touched him, and, at the moment, he'd enjoy opening Ali's veins, as well.

"That's not possible. The one I sell is too rich a prize for a man who wanders the desert. She's destined for some wealthy sheik's bed," Zobeir responded pompously, his thoughts on the woman he had been ordered to kill.

"Ah, at least there was no harm in my asking," Ali responded good-naturedly as he turned to lead Jed across the square to the slave pen, their retreat followed closely by Zobeir's lusting eyes.

"That went well enough," Ali said in a low voice.

"Well? You damned jackass," Jed hissed. "What did you think you were doing back there? I'm going to wring your neck."

"Quiet, slave," Ali ordered, relishing the angry fire that sprang into Jed's eyes at the command. Perhaps there was some pleasure to be had in dangerous adventuring, after all.

Jed didn't see things in quite that light, however, as he stood in the shadows of the tall walls surrounding the slave pens. His ire continued to grow when Ali delivered his orders to the overseer in imperious tones. To Jed's way of thinking, such posturing was becoming all too easy and familiar for the formerly reticent shopkeeper, and he vowed that as soon as they left Khartoum, Ali was one hombre who would be reminded quickly and effectively just who the leader of this operation actually was.

In the meantime, there was little Jed could do about it other than try to brush his anger aside and concentrate on the matter at hand. Calculating the strength of the forbidding sandstone walls enclosing the captives bound for slavery, he was satisfied as to the amount and placement of the explosives he had planted.

Things were under control if Ali could but accomplish the simple task that had been set him. Yet, as the overseer took Jed's halter and led him through the slated wooden gates into the dreary interior of the holding area, Jed Kincaid felt uneasy, despite the fact that he didn't expect to be here for very long. The sight of the towering walls and the restless milling about of men, some of them with eyes full of hatred and others wearing an expression bereft of hope, caused the fine hairs on the back of his neck to rise ominously.

It was only his natural abhorrence of confinement that made him feel as he did, Jed reminded himself—that and his perception of what it would feel like to be actually destined for the slave block the next morning. Ignoring the vivid workings of his imagination, Jed affected a dejected shuffle behind the overseer. The wandering adventurer knew that his accelerated heartbeat and the rushing of his blood gave him a decided edge.

Everyone else confined in the pens would be momentarily stunned when the unexpected occurred. He would be ready. His hardened body would be prepared to spring into rapid action like the great cats that roamed this region.

When the overseer finally released his grip on the rope around the American's neck and pushed him tumbling forward, Jed remained crouched, a seemingly defeated captive. Though the sight of a white man was not totally uncommon, a few curious eyes lit upon the Caucasian in their midst. But no one saw Jed extract the blade concealed in his boot top and begin his furtive shredding of the heavy rope binding his wrists. His slumping shoulders and curled body simply marked him as one more cowed bit of humanity unable to adjust to the miserable fate that had befallen him.

Chapter Five

Perhaps her mistake had been trying to speak to all the women at once, Victoria considered. If she could prevail on one or two at a time, they might be more receptive to her urgings. She studied the more reserved females huddled by the far wall, their posture clearly revealing their anxiety. Cowed by their situation, they might be ready to consider any alternative, no matter how rash. Victoria straightened her spine, rose to her feet and began to move about the enclosure, her hesitant steps and frequent changes of direction mirroring the actions of many of the captives.

Nearing a mocha-skinned girl no more than fourteen, Victoria lingered to share a few whispered words of encouragement.

"You are helpless only if you believe it so," she said, uttering the words softly, first in English and then French. A brief flicker of hope crossed the child's face, and though she made no verbal response, her dark eyes studied Victoria carefully.

More confident, Victoria approached the next woman, speaking her message quietly and then continuing her erratic path about the pen to her next target. She was pleased a few women she'd addressed were standing a bit taller and watching her closely as she rested for a while before beginning yet another circuit of the area.

She had just started her fourth ramble when a guard came up, waving his arms and berating her, clearly agitated by her behavior.

"No talk, English! Walk or sit, but no talking together," he ordered, scattering the women with his shouts.

"But most women talk when they are frightened. I do no harm."

"Talk with me," suggested the Sudanese, his fingers stroking her pale cheek. "I would soothe your nerves."

"Isn't your duty to protect the merchandise, not abuse it?" she demanded, slapping his hand away.

"Hunger and thirst will soften your mood before long," warned the guard harshly. "I could make it easier for you."

"The white woman is right," challenged a voice from behind Victoria. "Go back to your post, dog. She does not need help from the likes of you."

"Before Allah, I wish to see you proud wenches when your master's whips have tamed you. Your cries will be far different then," snorted the sentry, turning away in annoyance.

"Thank you," murmured Victoria to the large woman who had spoken up on her behalf. She was surprised to see her defender was not one of those to whom she had whispered earlier.

"Do not thank me. Tell me what we can do to be free of here," the stranger urged as others pressed in close upon them. "If you think it possible, maybe there is hope of escape."

"Of course there is hope," assured Victoria, daring to believe it for the first time since entering the pens. "My fiancé and half the British Army are on their way to the city this very minute. If we can only..."

Jed had reduced his bonds to a single strand of hemp that could be easily broken when he sensed a disturbance. Fearing that some watchful sentinel had seen him, he cautiously lifted his dark head. But there was no one glaring at him, nor could he discern any reason for the threatening curses that had been uttered. None of his guards appeared to think anything was amiss.

It was then that he heard a forceful but feminine voice coming from the other side of the wall that separated male from female slaves. The speaker was giving vent to frustrated anger, and Jed lifted an eyebrow in silent approval of the fiery woman who maintained enough spirit to revolt under such trying circumstances. His approbation quickly deteriorated to condemnation, however, when he realized the loud protest was being lodged in fluent English. These strident, haranguing tones, inciting others to riot, had to belong to Hayden Reed's fiancée. By Zobeir's account, she was the only white female currently imprisoned here.

Damnation, his fireworks hadn't started yet, but this carping, insistent female had begun an explosion all her own.

If good old Vicky didn't quiet down soon, she'd likely find herself chained to a post somewhere. Not that she didn't deserve it for calling attention to herself just when he wanted her to be ignored, but such a punishment would make the escape he had planned all the more difficult.

Turning to watch three guards walk the perimeter of the walls, Jed hoped that Victoria Shaw would be more docile during the flight he had plotted across the desert. Their ride would be hot enough without some nagging woman making things more heated. But *he* shouldn't have to worry, Jed assured himself. Victoria Shaw's temperament was no doubt something he could handle. In his experience, women had always been only too happy to do his bidding.

Sidling over to the barrier between the two slave pens, Jed saw that he was in luck. Apparently it was chow time. Four more men had entered the area, one carrying sacks of fruit and the flat bread indigenous to the region, and another laboring under a large skin of water. The final two acted as additional guards.

Immediately the inmates began to move to the spot where the food and drink was being distributed, while the sentries on the walls turned both their attention and their rifles in that direction. Not one of them thought anything of the new man standing aloof in the shadows. In time, he would know thirst and hunger, even if misery dulled his appetite for the moment.

As the voices of the captives rose in plaintive pleas for sustenance, Jed prayed that Ali would be able to hear his signal above the din. The distraction made this moment seem the best time to move. Suddenly the first seven notes of a shrill rendition of "Yankee Doodle" rent the air. The guards shifted their weapons in Jed's direction, and he pretended to tremble so pitifully that the Sudanese decided they must have been mistaken. One so cowardly would not cause a disturbance in the pens. The noise must have come from the market square on the other side of the wall. Thinking no more of it, they turned back to watch over the others clamoring for food and drink.

Jed remained expectantly prepared, the muscles of his arms tensed to pull apart the final strand of the rope hampering his hands. Surely, any second now, the fuses would burn down and the explosions would start, and he could scale the wall into the women's pen, grab Victoria Shaw and get the hell out of Khartoum.

However, there were no detonations. Seconds all too silent dragged by with agonizing slowness. The tendons of Jed's body began to protest their rigid readiness. Still, life in Khartoum went on with no interruptions.

"Damn you, Ali!" Jed muttered in a low, feral growl. "Is lighting a match beyond you? I swear, you'll be sorry for making me wait like this."

But for all Jed's fuming, nothing happened, no booming blasts, no shattering sandstone—nothing. Could the Egyptian have been caught, Jed worried, or perhaps be too yellow to go through with their scheme now that the moment had arrived? He had no idea. All he knew was that if things didn't start happening soon, he was going to have to take matters into his own hands.

Working alone at this point would greatly diminish his chances for success, yet Jed supposed he would have no choice, even if he didn't particularly like the odds. He'd like it less if he were still incarcerated when Zobeir arrived to inspect Ali's *merchandise.*

Determining the position of the guards, Jed debated as to whether he should attack one of them, grab the man's rifle and shoot his way out, or wait for Zobeir, put a knife to the slaver's throat and use him as a human shield to effect an escape. Either option was going to make it well-nigh impossible to get out of the pens with Victoria Shaw, but Jed was adamant. He was not going to leave her behind, though he might be tempted to do so if the woman didn't shut her damn mouth, which still erupted every few minutes.

The sinewy American had just about made up his mind which plan he would follow when an ear-shattering noise rocked the compound, accompanied by the cracking and crumbling of a portion of the sandstone.

"It took you long enough," he grumbled as the humanity inside the pens reacted to the unnatural occurrence.

The initial response of both riflemen and slaves had been cries of fear, but when those bound for servitude realized a doorway to freedom had appeared, there arose a joyous roar.

Chaos prevailed as frantic captives climbed over one another, the guards trying to stop their bid for liberty. Rifle shots rang out. Deadly sounds echoed off the high stone enclosure to mingle with the shouts of terror coming from the marketplace outside. Frightened livestock protested the uproar loudly as terrorized citizens ran, trying to escape danger. All the while, pitiful wails poured forth from the women still trapped in the females' pen. But the entire cacophony was drowned out by the deep rumble of a second blast on the other side of the market, and the frenzied commotion escalated to a new level.

Men still attempting to shove their way out of the pens sought shelter from the shower of debris caused by a rapidly following third explosion. In the midst of it all, Jed broke the rope confining his hands and casually sauntered over to the gate separating him from the women. Made of stout wood and securely locked, the barrier resisted his efforts to force it open.

With a shrug of his shoulders and a careless smile that proclaimed he hadn't really expected it to be that simple, Jed slipped the halter from around his neck and fashioned a short lariat. With reckless grace, he lassoed the spike atop the gate post, and easily scaled the wall.

When he reached the top, he momentarily sat astride the sandstone barrier until his keen eyes found the woman he was seeking, the small blonde in European dress huddled with the others.

Bellowing an order in Arabic and English for them to vacate the far corner of the pen before Ali lit the next fuse, he dropped inside and rushed to her side. Wrapping the woman in his arms, he threw himself on top of her, mindless of her protests. They both fell to the ground where he shielded her when the next explosion blew a hole in the facade that imprisoned the women.

"You must be Vicky," he said with a devilish grin as he loosened his hold on the struggling form beneath him, and smiled into the face of a wildcat.

"It's Victoria." She grunted as she worked herself out from under the hard masculine body that had trapped her while her companions streamed out into the marketplace. She struggled for composure. When she found it, she coolly assessed the disheveled, unshaven stranger. Not liking the primitive air of the man returning her inspection so boldly, she added in her most cultured, condescending tones, "However, I suggest *you* call me Miss Shaw."

Thoughts of how well suited the haughty *Miss Shaw* and Hayden Reed were ran through Jed's mind as he pulled himself and the ungrateful woman upright.

"Listen, honey," he drawled dangerously as he grabbed Victoria's hand. "I don't care if it's *Queen* Victoria. We're getting out of here now."

"But I can't leave," Victoria stated in annoyance, pulling her fingers free from the large masculine ones that had captured them.

"You what?" Jed roared, his green eyes flashing in disbelief.

"Well, it's simply impossible, of course," Victoria told him in her most reasonable voice, instinctively taking a step backward from the glowering stranger.

"And just why is that?" Jed demanded. He closed the gap between them and brought his fierce face down close to hers.

"Surely you've heard the cannon fire," Victoria asserted with as much dignity as she could muster under the man's baleful stare. "The British army and my fiancé have come to rescue me. They're attacking Khartoum right now. If I step out into the confusion, how will they ever find me? I'll wait for Hayden right here, thank you. I'm not about to go running off with the likes of you."

"Now, I'm unsure of how to break this to you," Jed countered, his mocking voice making it plain that he was ready to throw her over his shoulder in order to leave. "But it's me or nobody, lady. Hayden's still in his plush office in Cairo."

"You mean he sent *you?*" Victoria asked, aghast, her eyes branding him ruffian as they once more traveled over his rugged, unsavory appearance.

"No, he didn't send me," Jed mimicked, his voice colored by extreme exasperation. Catching himself, the American reverted to his natural husky tones and continued with forced civility. "He didn't even have the courage to do that. I came on my own. Now, if you ever want to see that pompous ass again, Vicky, I suggest you move your sweet little posterior so we can get the devil out of here."

Ali's detonation of the final blast drowned out a shocked Victoria Shaw's acerbic retort. She had no opportunity to repeat herself, however, as Jed's patience with her was at an end.

"Run," he ordered, grabbing the woman and pulling her toward the broken wall that promised them both a chance at freedom.

"Damn you, woman! I said *run,* not dawdle about watching everyone else escape. At this rate, we'll both be damned to life as slaves, if they don't shoot us first," Jed raged over his shoulder as the guards fired into the women's pen.

Without waiting for her to protest again, he shoved her in front of him, shielding her as they scrambled over the rubble of the wall. Their pace, however, was maddeningly slow as those ahead found it difficult to navigate the mounds of irregular stone blocking their way. Trapped in the smoke-laden air, unable to push forward, Jed found the next few minutes nerve-racking until finally they stood together in the shadows of the slave mart, catching their breath amid the turmoil.

Pandemonium was the order of the hour. Many of the escaping slaves had upended the tables along the perimeter of the square while the shopkeepers bellowed and tried to douse the small fires threatening their livelihood. Busily grabbing what goods they could carry off to start their new lives, fleeing captives shouted obscenities at those who would stop them and shoved their way to freedom. Then another ominous rumble sounded, the ground seemed to vibrate and a dark powdery haze drifted quickly over the slave quarter, providing temporary obscurity.

"This way, woman. Quickly, now, hurry," Jed urged his companion forward as a blue *gallabiya* caught his eye and he swept it up in passing. The guards would be searching especially hard for the two European prisoners who would stand out readily in inner Khartoum. He and Victoria would be far safer if he could disguise her.

With a sudden jerk on her elbow, Jed pulled her into a narrow twist of the alley and whispered urgently, "Here, put this on."

"Make up your mind. Put this on—or go quickly? Which is it?" cried Victoria angrily. Her eyes smarted from the soot in the air, her feet hurt from the stones that pierced her dainty slippers, and she *still* feared for her life. But, most of all, her heart ached with the possibility, however unlikely, that Hayden had placed her safety in the hands of this uncouth hooligan. How could her fiancé claim to love her and permit this scoundrel to come after her? "I am not moving another inch until you explain yourself."

"Your hair and pale face will serve as a beacon for anyone searching for us," he argued impatiently. By all the saints above, he was trying to save the woman's hide, why was she squawking? "In this outfit, there is a chance you might be overlooked."

"And you?"

"I'm brown enough from the sun to pass at a glance, and if they look closer than that, the game will be over, anyway." Refusing to await her cooperation, he bunched up the flowing garment and dropped it over her head, thankfully muffling her complaints for the moment. "It's rather long, but it'll hide your skirts and those trim ankles I noticed earlier."

"As if you haven't better things to worry about," muttered the blonde. "Never mind, give me your belt."

"What?"

"If you expect me to move without tripping over my feet every few inches, I have to secure this somehow."

Shouts sounded behind them in the alley, and rather than pursue their debate, Jed removed the leather strap and tied it about her waist, hiking the shapeless gown up and pulling the hood over her hair. An instant later he had grabbed her hand and they were running toward the city gates.

Dodging around the rubble in their path, he led Victoria forward, confident their route was the right one, if a little longer than he had remembered. It seemed to him they should have been at the gates by now, then he discarded the notion. It was just nerves that made him question himself.

Another roar sounded behind them somewhere as Jed pulled her along, but soon the voices of pursuit dropped away. Then, when Victoria doubted her ability to run another step, the gates were before them, and at last they were outside the city of Khartoum.

"Now what?" she gasped, leaning against the trunk of a mustard tree to catch her breath. "Where are the British troops?"

"What?" Jed couldn't believe his ears. She continued to expect the army to rescue her.

"I'll admit you got me out of the slave pens, and even out of the city, not that I couldn't have escaped myself—"

"You do have an inflated opinion of yourself, Vicky, don't you," said the American, chuckling, impressed by her stamina. Most of the women he knew would have been weeping copiously, but her tongue was as venomous as ever. Did nothing shake her?

"I told you the name is Victoria, although you have yet to introduce *yourself*. For all I know you could be stealing me from Zobeir so your master can claim the fortune I would bring."

"I am a man who serves no master but myself, unlike your pencil-pushing Hayden Reed."

"He has a very responsible position, I'll have you know. In fact, Hayden expects to receive a title in the near future," bragged Victoria. Why it mattered, she didn't know, but she could not tolerate this impudent male's criticism of her fiancé. Hayden had a sound future ahead of him. Given his manner, this blowhard would undoubtedly end up in a jail cell, despite his physical charms, if he continued his explosive bent.

"A title to coincide with your marriage?" guessed Jed with a smirk. "Then I suppose Hayden will have it all. Too bad none of it can make him a man, willing to risk his life for the woman he loves."

"That's not true."

"Vicky, I was with your dear Hayden when he received the kidnapper's demands. First he protested that he couldn't raise the ransom. Then, when he learned your mother had pledged the sum, his excuse was that he couldn't be spared from his office—"

"But you don't understand, Hayden is an important diplomat. He couldn't risk—" Even as the words escaped her lips, Victoria realized that, in her heart, she didn't really believe them. *She* should have been first in Hayden's mind, not the money or his career. She should have been worth risking his *own* life, not that of some man for hire. Damn Hayden! Now she owed her life to this uncouth cad so ill-mannered he had yet to tell her his name. Well, damn him, too, she would not inquire what it was.

"I never asked you to save me. If you prefer to abandon me, go right ahead. I am certain I can get back to Cairo on my own."

"As much as I would like to do just that, it isn't in the cards. Hayden, for whatever his reasons, wants you back, and I will deliver you," grumbled Jed, moving toward the Nile. "I must admit, though, having met you, I don't understand why he would want you at all. It can't be a love match—"

"And what would you know about love? With your lack of manners no woman could ever be attracted to you," retorted Victoria. However, the words she spoke were not entirely true, she had to admit to herself as the stranger took her arm and urged her forward, ignoring her insults. Whether it was the danger of their situation or the uncommon comfort of masculine competence, she couldn't decide, but for all his faults, her rescuer's touch was definitely reassuring. That did not mean, however, she need speak to him!

Jed was so preoccupied with hurrying his charge through the ornate gardens surrounding the city that he took no notice of her sudden reticence. Thus far, things had proceeded well enough. All that was left was to rendezvous with the Egyptian, steal a *falucca* and sail off to freedom. Suddenly there beyond the monkey bread trees was the Nile. This would be the riskiest part of the trip. Jed pulled Victoria under the canopy of the obliging leaves.

"Shh!" he warned, covering her mouth with his large hand as she started to balk. "Once we've set sail, you can harangue me all you want, but now I need you quiet and cooperative or we'll be back in those slave pens faster than you can cry *Hayden Reed.*"

For one brief, irrational moment, Victoria longed to do nothing other than bite down hard on his oppressive hand and bring her knee up with equal force into his groin. Who was *he* to order her about in such an infuriating manner? Hayden had never treated her so rudely. Then logic interfered and she realized that the arrogant male with her was the only one on whom she could rely, however uneasily. Leashing her anger, the weary blonde gave a quick nod of her head and he obligingly released her.

"Short of sleeping with you, I will do whatever you say to escape from here and eventually from you," Victoria continued, her eyes sparkling angrily.

"Believe me, lady, the feeling is mutual, but until then you will have to watch my back while I cover yours. Understood?"

"I already said yes. What more do you want of me?"

Under other circumstances there might have been other responses, but now Jed merely gritted his teeth at her impertinence and scanned the almost deserted area in front of the river gates to the city. Spotting Ali, he felt a sudden surge of confidence as well as relief that the Cairene had escaped, too. His plan would succeed, despite their quarry's lack of faith in him.

"See the tall Egyptian over there by the right gateway? That is Ali Sharouk, the other half of your rescue party," Jed explained.

"I would not have thought you needed help," she retorted, "or rather that you would admit you did."

"He was not my idea, but since Ali was responsible for setting off those explosions that freed you, I wouldn't question his presence or his efficiency," rebuked Jed. "He and I will liberate a *falucca* while you wait here."

"I will come with you now."

"A woman down at the water will rouse attention we don't want—"

"There doesn't seem to be anyone here, and besides, in this getup, who would even know I'm a woman?" she protested.

"Don't underestimate your charms, Vicky," Jed advised dryly. "No Sudanese I've seen has a chest like yours, let alone the curvaceous wiggle in your walk."

"You are disgusting to notice that at a time like this—"

"I never claimed to be a gentleman, honey." Noting that Ali had left the gates and was headed for the open area where the *faluccas* were beached, Jed abandoned the argument.

"Follow me in three minutes," he ordered as he started off, trusting she was clever enough to obey despite her complaints.

Left alone, Victoria stole a furtive glance around, pleased there was no one in the area to take an interest in her. Perhaps the explosions had drawn whoever might ordinarily linger along the river into the city to see what had occurred. Feeling a bit more reassured, Victoria started after her rescuers just as the *muezzin* sounded the call for midday prayers.

Seeing Ali begin to make the obligatory gesture of devotion, she was surprised when Jed did not follow suit. Wouldn't he alert everyone to his foreign origins and criminal intentions? As she watched his movements, Victoria saw him stealthily approach the lone watchman prostrate in prayer.

Minutes later, the guard was still on the ground, but now unconscious and gagged as Ali and Jed lifted a *falucca*'s sail from the sand and righted the craft. They slid the boat far enough into the water to maintain its balance, still held in place by the anchor that rested ashore.

"Here, Vicky, hurry," called her savior while Ali moved away and began slicing through the canvas sheeting of the other nearby *faluccas*. "It won't be long before the call to prayer is over."

"But the boat is in the water and there's no dock—"

"Lift your skirts and wade out to the bow. You'll only get wet to your calves," he coaxed, fighting the temptation to drag her into the boat by her hair. "Come on, now. We haven't much time."

"Isn't there another way?"

Then, from up above, near the gates, shots rang out. Victoria dove into the *falucca* as though propelled by some of Ali's charges. Jed couldn't help but chuckle as he ducked his own head to hack at the anchor ropes holding the craft near to the shore.

"Halt, you there! Leave my boat alone or I'll have the soldier kill you with the next round," threatened the angry voice.

Raising his head just enough to look over the side, Jed felt a sudden tightening in his gut. He and Victoria were not the ones being threatened with extinction; Ali was. A well-fed merchant stood on the upper path near the river gates, a soldier beside him with his rifle trained on the Egyptian huddled behind a *falucca* fifty yards away down the beach.

"Ali, make a run for it," urged Jed in English, confident the Sudanese wouldn't understand. The *falucca* was all set, and if he could angle it around, it might block the soldier's view—

Crracck!

Ali had followed his advice too late, damn it! The Egyptian was facedown in the sand, thirty yards from the boat, and the Sudanese was already scrambling down the path toward him. For a moment Jed hesitated, weighing his responsibilities. The river was straining at the *falucca*, ready to start Victoria on her homebound journey, and she *was* his primary concern. Once he released the anchoring rope, they would be off with the current in minutes, safely away from here. Still . . .

"Here, take hold of this line and don't let go," he barked at her, leaping overboard.

Before she could argue, he was splashing through the water as the soldier raised his rifle to take aim at this new mark. Heart in her mouth, Victoria watched as her supposed protector dodged left and right then left again, running bent over to afford as small a target as possible. Reaching Ali's unmoving body, he knelt briefly beside him while bullets spotted the sand around them.

"Damn that man!" she complained as the drag of the boat against the current increased. Her hands were raw from the effort to keep the *falucca* where it was, and she wasn't certain she was doing all she could to protect herself. What if they began shooting at her?

While it was undoubtedly true she would be in jeopardy traveling alone on the Nile, would it be any more dangerous than lingering here? The temptation to release the rope grew stronger as her palms smarted all the more. It was not that she begrudged the Egyptian help, but what was taking so long? Any minute and she'd lose her grip on the hemp even if she wanted to hold on to it.

Lifting her head slightly, Victoria looked toward the city, panicking at the people crowding to watch the excitement. The shooting soldier was nowhere to be seen. Might he be sneaking up on her even now? Before she decided to abandon the line, there was a heavy thump forward and she turned anxiously, only to see Ali's body dumped aboard and Jed pulling himself in after it.

"Let go of the rope and hand me the long pole," he ordered, swinging the sail about. "Here, hold the canvas while I get us farther out into the current."

Although she resented his lordly manner, she obeyed without complaint, permitting herself but a brief glance at the angry mob growing on the beach.

"Won't they follow us?"

"Not if Ali did his job properly," he answered curtly, propelling the *falucca* far enough from the beach that the occasional rifle shot was no longer a threat. "I'll take the sail. Stow the pole and check on Ali. The bullet will have to stay in until we get ashore again, but see if the bleeding has stopped. Otherwise, find something to staunch the blood."

Would this nightmare never end? wondered Victoria, making her way hesitantly to Ali's side. As much as she hated the sight of blood, she couldn't refuse to care for the man. The back of his shirt was already sticky with crimson, but there didn't seem to be any more oozing. Quickly she rinsed her hand and dripped water on his forehead, but he didn't waken.

Sighing at the unfairness of it all, the blonde looked back at the other man, the one who had been in the pens with her. As unmannered as he was, he had gone back for his partner. Could he be as bad as she had presumed him to be? She still didn't know his name or his story. It was time for some answers, she decided abruptly, abandoning Ali to his continued unconsciousness.

"Look, your friend has passed out cold."

"Passed out? Why?"

"How should I know? Maybe from shock or loss of blood or the way you so *tenderly* tossed him on board like a sack of potatoes."

"Tenderly or not, I saved his life, lady, just like I saved yours!"

"So you keep reminding me, but who in heaven's name, or should that be hell's name, are you?"

"Just a man who had a choice of rotting in jail or coming to rescue you," Jed snapped. "I made the wrong choice."

"I think I did, too. I should have stayed in Khartoum."

"Seeing that you are engaged to Reed, I understand your second thoughts—"

"It's not Hayden who's the problem. It's you! You're totally insufferable, ordering me about like—"

"Sorry if the service doesn't suit you, but Jed Kincaid wasn't raised to be any lady's maid."

"Service? What would you know about service? It is quite evident that you weren't reared in a civilized home."

"To my way of thinking, Kentucky is a hell of a lot more civilized than Egypt. We don't steal women and sell them to the highest bidder."

"You're from America?" realized Victoria, shaking her head in sudden comprehension. "Well, that explains everything."

With that, she made her way back to Ali, clearly preferring his company.

The sudden red-hot flare of his temper was familiar to Jed, but not the timing of its appearance. Ordinarily on a job, he prided himself in his ability to overlook irritants, concentrating on the task at hand and blocking out all else. Victoria Shaw, however, had become a burr under his saddle in less time than anyone but his youngest brother, Rory, could manage. It was all Jed could do to focus his attention on the *falucca*.

His life, as well as Ali's, depended on his disregarding that irksome female, Jed told himself, sending a hateful glare in her direction. He must adhere to their plan, even though Ali was unable to assist him. For the moment, his own need to set Victoria Shaw down a notch or two would have to wait. Still, the pleasure that would eventually provide him would indeed be sweet, Jed promised himself, glancing over to where she sat. Very sweet, indeed.

Chapter Six

An American! After hours of sailing, Victoria raged silently in the stern of the *falucca,* recalling stories of tobacco-chewing, gunslinging cowboys from across the Atlantic, men who stopped at nothing in their desperate pursuit of pleasure and adventure. Is that what he imagined her to be, not that she would willingly give him pleasure!

Of course, knowing his nationality, she wasn't at all shocked that he had dared to thwart Zobeir's guards and steal her from the pens. Everyone knew that crude Americans had no common sense, no self-discipline, and no concern whatsoever for propriety.

Risking a glance over her shoulder at the renegade, Victoria shuddered. Even in profile, half obscured by the sail and the lengthening shadows of twilight, the man appeared menacing. His unshaven face and sun-burnished skin, grimy with gunpowder, proclaimed him a barbarous individual, no better than a criminal. Yet, unbelievably, Hayden had entrusted her well-being to him . . . unless Kincaid was lying and he wasn't taking her back to Cairo.

After all, how would she know the difference? There were no landmarks she would recognize, no consulates to offer protection or advice, no one on whom she could rely, and she certainly didn't know the first thing about surviving alone. Lord help her! Until she could revive the Egyptian, Kincaid was her only ally.

Determined to see to Ali's welfare, Victoria stood up abruptly, eliciting unwelcome attention from her theoretical savior.

"For pity's sake," Jed scolded. "Can't you sit still?"

"I—I only wanted to bathe your friend's forehead, or can' you spare a thought for him?"

"I wouldn't have dodged bullets with Ali on my back if I didn't plan to return him safely to his wife. However, right now I prefer him unconscious."

"How can you be that callous? Unless you have evil intentions toward me?"

"I am not that desperate, lady. My name isn't Hayden."

"Then why do you wish your friend ill?" she demanded, too distraught to respond to Jed's insult.

"Ali has a slug in his back. He's better off dead to the world until I can remove it and give him something for the pain."

"And when will that be?" Victoria had not wanted to ask. She had had no intention of acknowledging the fact that Kincaid gave the orders, but the words had escaped her lips. Was it possible that on some level she believed he knew what he was doing and would protect her? No! No sane person would trust an arrogant animal like him.

"A bit farther downriver we'll go ashore. Ali and I cached supplies and hid horses a mile or two inland."

"A mile or two inland? But how will we get to them?"

"By using the two good legs God gave you," snorted Jed. "Now, hold your tongue so I can concentrate on getting my bearings. The darker it gets, the more treacherous the river can be, and I don't want to fall afoul of Zobeir's men because I was listening to you."

"Are you saying that I am a distraction?"

Jed considered slowly, weighing his words and throwing caution to the winds. Perhaps his frankness would obtain the temporary respite he needed and, at the same time, let him exorcize the unwelcome, devilish urges building within.

"Lady, those eyes alone would have made Odysseus abandon all thoughts of home and Penelope, but when you factor in that trim little rump of yours, those mile-long legs and your sweet—"

"Stop drooling, Kincaid. I'm not on the auction block in the slave market."

"Only because of yours truly, honey, so I'll salivate as much as I want to. I've earned it!"

"Perhaps, but I don't have to stay here and listen." She swiveled back to Ali so quickly that she missed Jed's quiet laugh.

Once more he had gotten his way, he realized thankfully, but now much longer would his luck hold? He had already negotiated the treacherous joining of the White and Blue Niles safely, leaving the grassy plains of the savannah behind. Now, however, he needed to time their actions perfectly to make Zobeir's men believe they had continued downriver. Then, too, he had to worry about getting Ali and Vicky to shore safely.

"Hey, Vicky, can you swim?"

"It has never been a favorite pastime of mine, but I can stay afloat if need be. Why? Have we sprung a leak?"

"Not yet, but soon," Jed answered calmly, intending to tell her no more until absolutely necessary. It was enough for him to know that he would not have to get both her and Ali to shore alone.

Annoyed by his laconic response, the blonde resolved not to question the American further since he probably wanted her to do so. Settling down beside the Egyptian, Victoria was careful not to jar him. With deft fingers, she checked his forehead for fever, relieved that he was still relatively cool. Perhaps he *was* better off unaware of their circumstances. She certainly wasn't thrilled to know their plight, fleeing north through the deepening shadows with God-knew-who after them.

Zobeir the slave merchant sighed heartily as he wallowed amid the pile of cushions beside the bathing pool of his home. Eyes closed, he tried to concentrate on the pleasure of having his temples bathed with water made fragrant by rose petals. But as light and soothing as the touch of the handsome young slave was meant to be, even this indulgence brought Zobeir little solace. The day had seen him suffer tremendously, and his rapacious soul was filled with wrathful anguish.

He could have made a fortune had that troublesome European female been placed on the block and sold to the highest bidder. As it was, not only had she escaped, but so had many others he had intended to sell. His purse was considerably lighter than he had expected it to be by day's end. But far worse was the fact that his reputation as an astute trader in human flesh had crumbled along with the walls of the slave pens. Since all of Khartoum had concluded it was the white woman he had placed in the enclosure who had brought so much chaos and destruction upon their city, it was he whom they held responsible. There were not many who would want to conduct business with him anytime soon.

A groan escaped the trader's lips despite the gentle ministrations of the young man attending him. This had been the worst day of his life. His only consolation was that it could not become worse.

But it would appear his trials were not yet at an end, Zobeir decided with a frown as the worthless idiot seeing to him suddenly ceased any attempt to bring his master consolation.

Raising his hand to slap the young slave, Zobeir opened his eyes to find his target, and saw the visitor who had entered the area on silent feet. The man was swathed in black and loomed over him like some avenging angel. Zobeir, himself frightened by the stranger's presence, could not fault his ignorant servant for freezing at the sight of so intimidating a figure.

With a swiftness that seemed incongruous in light of his obesity, the slaver climbed to his feet and bowed in obeisance to his visitor. Zobeir had no doubt as to the man's affiliation even if his identity was unknown.

"A thousand welcomes, worthy master," Zobeir murmured as he prayed a connection had not been made between the white woman who had been rescued from the bazaar and the rich banker's daughter who had been marked for death by the man this mysterious messenger represented. "And Allah's blessings on him whom you serve."

"May Allah hear your prayer and grant it," the dark figure responded, his voice slightly muffled by the obsidian cloth winding down from the crown of his head to the base of his neck and trailing over his shoulder so that only his equally black eyes were visible.

"Is there another service you desire, master?" Zobeir asked nervously, his squat body twitching from anxiety. "If there is, I dare not believe my good fortune, unworthy as I am, in being asked again to help the one who will rid our land of nonbelievers."

"No, Zobeir. The Chosen One has no more to ask of you," the visitor said, his voice as flat as the disklike bread being baked in the slave trader's ovens at that moment.

"Then—then why am I so hon-honored with your presence?" the portly figure stammered. He rued the moment he had decided to disobey the directive of the Chosen One. He should have simply had the European girl slaughtered as he had been ordered to do, but then, he had not understood why he had been commanded to kill the daughter of a rich man. It had eaten at his very being. What a fool he had been, he silently berated himself as he stood fixed in place by the harsh stare of the man who regarded him so coldly.

"I have come to issue payment for what you have already done," the robed figure stated.

"Payment?" Zobeir asked hopefully, his small eyes beginning to glitter in spite of the fear that had gripped him only seconds before. Allah be praised, perhaps he was yet safe.

"Payment," the shrouded man repeated, his fingers moving back to rest on the purse dangling beneath the dagger. "Though I am certain such a devoted servant as yourself desires no reward, it is only just that you receive what you deserve."

"That is most generous, mighty master. I have suffered grave losses this day, or else I would insist that any money due me be distributed among the poor," Zobeir lied, extending his hands to receive the purse. "But as it is, I must see to it that my men are compensated for their service to the Mahdi."

"Your men have been taken care of," the visitor assured Zobeir. "And now it is your turn."

With that, his hands released the strings of the purse and flew to his dagger, which was unsheathed before Zobeir could comprehend what was happening.

"And now, receive payment in full for your disobedience, treacherous wretch," the ominous figure intoned, his voice still void of emotion as he lifted the weapon high into the air and brought it down with a vicious celerity, plunging it into Zobeir's chest. Efficiently, he withdrew his blade. Then, while a staggering Zobeir tried unsuccessfully to staunch the gush of blood, the visitor turned his back on the dying traitor as the whimpering slave fled from the room.

Miles away, Victoria slowly considered the horrors that had brought her to be on the Nile in the company of two strangers, both out of their minds, the Egyptian because of his wound and the American, she feared, by the very nature of his personality. Kincaid had said they were to leave the river and go inland, but why? Couldn't they stay on the water all the way to Cairo?

Perhaps he had meant they would go ashore temporarily to reclaim the food and supplies he had hidden, she mused. That might be the scenario he planned, but hadn't he mentioned horses?

Frowning at her increasing certainty that Kincaid intended to return to Cairo across the desert, Victoria marshaled her arguments to challenge his plans. Suddenly, however, she looked up and unexpectedly found him beside her.

"Unlace your slippers, take them off and tuck them in your pockets," he instructed, removing his boots and stuffing them inside his shirt. "They will slow you down in the water."

"What? You said we were going ashore—"

"We are. But the shore is over there and we're here."

"So? Sail the boat into shore."

"If I risk taking us any closer, the *falucca* might run aground and ruin the suggestion that we're still traveling downriver, a ruse we desperately need to outwit our pursuers."

"Is that really necessary?"

"It is if you want to reach Cairo alive," pronounced Jed. "Unless you want to sit on board and wait for Zobeir's men to catch up with you, it's time to take your swim." When Victoria made no reply, he knelt beside Ali. "Once you're in the water, I'll slide Ali over the side. Just hold on to him until I join you and then I'll take him to shore."

"Wait a minute. I haven't agreed to this—"

"You don't have a choice! If you want to return to Reed, I'm your only available guide, and I have no intention of following you to Khartoum again."

"I—aren't there crocodiles?"

"None that have a bite anywhere near as lethal as yours," he snapped, impatient to be moving. Every minute they stayed on the Nile increased the possibility they'd be overtaken.

Glancing in her direction, Jed felt a sudden jolt of pity. She looked so nervous and frightfully small in the *gallabiya,* he almost relented, recalling all she had been through of late. Would it be that dangerous to chance completing their return to Cairo on the river? he reflected before reality readjusted his thinking. Years of calculating the best odds of survival and living by them reasserted themselves and his heart hardened.

"This is not an evening at a debutante's ball designed for your entertainment, lady. Either jump in or I will take great pleasure in tossing you overboard!"

"You wouldn't dare!"

He did.

Kincaid would pay for his cruelty, Victoria swore silently as she plummeted into the Nile. Gasping, she unwittingly swallowed some water as she went under, kicking frantically to bring herself back up. Finally she reached the surface...only to find that Kincaid hadn't stirred. She could have drowned while he watched!

"Ready?" he asked softly, lowering the Egyptian's feet into the water even before she replied.

"You don't leave me any alternative," Victoria observed, trying to grasp Ali with one arm and the side of the boat with the other. "The current is dragging him away from me."

"Hold him tighter against your body, then. Use both hands. I have to adjust the sail before I come in."

"If you even think about abandoning the two of us here—"

"I wouldn't. Ali deserves better."

Oh! Never had she hated anyone before, realized Victoria suddenly, the heat of her fury warming her to the core. Hatred violated the Christian principles to which her parents had bound their lives and hers, but that man—*that* man deserved to be hated. On second thought, hatred was too mild. Loathing or abhorrence fit him better.

Then he was treading water beside her and Ali was no longer her burden, but one they shared.

"Come on. Shore is straight ahead. I'll manage Ali. You conserve your energy so you can call me names when your feet touch dry land," suggested the American, a hint of a chuckle in his voice.

With that, he struck out for the bank, trusting she would follow. Already the *falucca,* caught by the current, was some fifty feet away from them and she was alone. Damn the man! It seemed he could anticipate her reactions to him.

Before she expected it, her feet struck bottom, and she quickly rose to find the water level barely to her waist. There was no one about, and she lost no time wading the rest of the way to the grassy bank where Kincaid waited with the Egyptian.

"If you're going to complain, do it quickly, because we have to press on in a few minutes. Out here, moonlight reveals too much for anyone looking for us," he cautioned.

Instead of replying, Victoria bent down, took hold of the sodden hem of her *gallabiya*, pulled it up over her head and threw the watery mass at him. Unfortunately, the weight of the water made it land with a loud splat two feet in front of her target.

"You made me take off my shoes so I could swim, but you never gave a thought to that ton of heavy material dragging me down. *That* would have been the practical thing to remove!"

"You're undoubtedly right, but I never thought of it," Jed said innocently. "Now that you mention it, however, wouldn't you be more comfortable taking off your skirt and blouse, as well? They must be just as wet."

"You would just love that, wouldn't you, Kincaid? The chance to ogle another man's half-naked fiancée? Well, dismiss the notion at once. I'll wring out the skirt and it will be fine."

"For heaven's sake, Vicky—"

"Vic-toria!"

"Even if you take off that layer, you're probably wearing a chemise, if not a corset. Judging from the undergarments I've removed from women, it's not as if I would see a whole lot of skin—"

"No!" cried the blonde anxiously as she recalled what *was* under her skirt and blouse, the practically transparent harem garb she had donned at Zobeir's insistence. Realizing from Kincaid's expression that her reaction had been too excessive given his comments, she took a calming breath, lifted her chin high and assumed her iciest tones. "You are wasting time with your boyish fantasies, Kincaid, so shouldn't we move on?"

Shrugging his shoulders at missing what might have been a delightful sight, Jed moved forward a few steps, bent down and picked up the *gallabiya*. Quickly he wrung it out.

"We can't leave it here, on the chance Zobeir's men might find it," he explained, hoisting Ali over his shoulders as a shepherd would carry a sheep. "Since you are ready, let's go. We're heading for those cliffs, probably about an hour's walk."

And then he moved off, his lengthy stride leaving Victoria hard-pressed to keep up with him. Soon she abandoned the effort, content to keep his unkempt figure in sight as her tender feet protested their mistreatment by the coarse sand over which they trod.

He had said it was only a mile or two, she reminded herself. After all, Kincaid was carrying the Egyptian, twelve or more stone, and not objecting. She could certainly be responsible for herself. She had no other choice as he had so rudely pointed out. Then suddenly Kincaid disappeared into the cliffs and she forgot her aching legs and ran to catch up with him.

There, between two slabs of granite, was an opening a few feet across, wide enough for men and horses to slip through easily. They had arrived, she realized thankfully.

She saw immediately that the American was making the Egyptian comfortable. But before she could sink down to the ground and relax, Kincaid's voice barked authoritatively.

"You can rest after we've seen to Ali. Take the wood over there and start a small fire. The cliffs should hide its light, and I'll need some boiling water to cleanse my knife and his wound. Well, what are you waiting for?"

"I can't start a fire, Kincaid, even a small one. I don't know how. Besides, I thought you were the expert at everything."

"I was going to check the horses and unpack some of the supplies so we can eat," explained Jed, his voice tight with annoyance as he started to slam the wood together in an irregular pile. Why did everything become more complicated with her around? "All right, you can see if the animals have enough water. They're farther back, and the water buckets are behind the rocks."

"I—I don't particularly like horses. They make me nervous."

"How did I not know that?" quizzed the American, running his hands through his hair and shaking his head in exasperation. She *would* have to be a prima donna, he frowned. "Very well, then, Miss Shaw, I'll see to the horses after I light the fire and before I extract Ali's bullet. Do you suppose *you* could manage to open the large sack over there and find the bandages? Bring one of the sleeping rolls over here for Ali."

Still she hesitated, looking at him questioningly.

"What now?"

"You don't think there are scorpions in the bags, do you?"

"For pity's sake, woman, if you are not going to make yourself useful, you should have stayed in that damned slave pen! I didn't rescue you to be your blasted nursemaid!"

Storming away from her, Jed moved rapidly to where the horses were hobbled. They sensed his anger and whinnied anxiously, backing away from his approach. In an instant, he had slowed his pace and softened his movements, speaking to them gently, stroking their necks, reassuring them. They still had water, but he added fresh to their temporary drinking trough and reflected that he could be kind to a dumb beast but upbraid a frightened woman. The idea filled him with remorse.

But, damn, Victoria Shaw got under his skin in ways he hadn't expected. She was so prim and proper, she acted as though he had crawled out from under some nearby rock. Did she even know the sensuality she possessed? There was a beckoning aura about her that could make a man forget all that was honorable. Incredibly, her woman's body cried out to be touched and his yearned to oblige her. Unless he maintained a distance from her, he feared it would be difficult to fight the unreasoning attraction she was beginning to hold for him.

"Kincaid!"

Until she opened her mouth, he amended, figuring that, with her propensity for doing that, he should be safe enough during their sojourn in the desert.

"Here, Vicky, I'm coming—"

It was a snake that had her panicked this time, a small non-poisonous snake, no more than a foot long, but it had her pressed to the granite walls as if she could melt into the rock and escape.

Biting back a laugh, he approached the offending creature, quickly stomped on its head and flung it into the fire.

"Did you find the bandages?" he asked, squatting down to hold his knife over the flames. "Or did that monster deter your search?"

"I, yes," she answered when she could find enough moisture in her mouth to permit a reply. "Here are the bandages and a bottle of liquor you might want."

"Good idea, honey." Before she could object, Kincaid took the bottle from her hand, opened it and began drinking. "Want some?"

"I meant for it to cleanse Ali's wound."

"Oh, I'll share, but a few drops will keep my hand steady," Jed assured her, perversely pleased by her disapproving look. "Be a good girl and find a candle. You'll hold it while I operate."

"I am not good when it comes to blood," warned Victoria, extricating a candle from the nearest saddlebag.

"Then don't look while I'm cutting," he instructed. "Now, hold his head while I pour some alcohol down his throat."

"Isn't he Muslim?"

"Yes, but he told me Allah understands that in emergencies a man sometimes needs extra courage," Jed explained, recalling the number of nights Ali had announced there *were* emergencies. Fatima might not recognize the man he was bringing back to her, a man who had been tested and found himself stronger than he had ever dreamed.

A soft cough recalled Jed from his contemplation of Ali's future and he lowered the bottle, waiting for Victoria's rebuke. Surprisingly it did not come.

"Are you ready?" she asked instead, holding out a pan of steaming water and the white cloth that would serve as bandages.

"As much as I'll ever be, sugar. This is one part of adventuring I would gladly avoid," he confessed. He wet Ali's *gallabiya* and lifted it gently from the wound. Then, with a quick jerk of his hands, he tore the cloth, exposing the reddened area. "Here, sit behind him and support his body."

Carefully the American sponged away the dried blood and ran his fingers along the fleshy area behind the shoulder where the bullet probably was lodged. Remembering the many men he had seen cut open over the years, Jed closed his eyes a moment and cleared his mind of everything but Ali and his welfare. Hesitating but an instant, he motioned Victoria to hold the candle closer and swiftly lanced the skin, praying Ali would not die at his hands.

It took longer than he'd hoped, and a few times Jed thought he might lose Victoria, if not Ali, too, but finally the bullet was out and he stitched the Egyptian closed. He made a few quick tucks in the muscles he'd had to invade. Then came uneven but effective stitches on the outer flesh and he sat back on his heels, totally spent. Moving his hand toward his eyes to wipe away the sweat clouding them, he was startled to feel Victoria's hand stay his.

"You are full of blood," she said softly. "Use this to sponge your face and your hands."

She had the light touch of an angel, Jed noticed when she placed the material in his outstretched palm. Involuntarily, his lips turned up as he appreciated her thoughtful gesture of concern. Perhaps she wasn't quite as spoiled as he had suspected.

"Now, what was it you said about something to eat?"

"What?"

"Ali is as comfortable as you can make him for the time being and I'm hungry. Aren't you?"

"I don't suppose you know how to cook or make coffee?" Jed inquired without any real hope.

"Of course not. At home, we have servants for that."

"In that case, you'll have to make do with the dried meat and flat bread in the largest saddlebag. It'll hold us until we can reach an oasis on the caravan route."

"You don't plan to move Ali, do you?"

"We have to be on our way, Vicky—"

"Vic-toria!"

"I don't think there's any doubt that Zobeir's men will be looking for you, and we're still too close to the Nile to be safe."

"But I'm exhausted," the blonde protested.

"Would you rather be exhausted or back on the slave block?" he challenged cruelly. "Believe me, I would love to sleep for ten or twelve hours, especially with you next to me," he added in an attempt to get her to leave him alone.

"Kincaid!"

"Don't worry. I'll forego that particular pleasure for tonight. Here, eat this and then rest a while."

It was useless to argue, Victoria realized, and he *had* brought them this far safely. As unlikely at it seemed, maybe Kincaid did know what he was doing. Without further discussion, she ate the meager meal he apportioned and stretched out, anticipating a swift sleep, despite the cold night air.

Yet, as weary as her aching body was, Victoria was too overwrought to relax. Unbidden memories of Jed's arrogance warred with irrational mental images of him as a hero. Probably because of her utter exhaustion, his firmly muscled chest lingered in her mind as broad and impenetrable as a knight's armor, reminding her that Kincaid had risked his own life first to rescue her and then Ali. Her logical nature dismissed these foolish fantasies, yet the high-pitched emotions that had controlled the day would not stop churning about. Jed's undeniable presence haunted her. Only the realization that *he* and possibly Zobeir's men would hear her stilled her urge to scream aloud.

Finally, after much tossing and turning, Victoria rolled over on her back, folded her arms beneath her head and admitted to herself that any attempt to find sleep was doomed. She would abandon all thoughts of it and concentrate instead on her life-to-be with Hayden.

Hayden! He was truly her hero, the man to whom she had pledged her troth. She had last seen him for luncheon the day she had been abducted and he had been ever so attentive. As usual, he had been singled out by many of the other diners at Shepheard's Hotel. He was a man who was noticed, a dependable man with a good future ahead of him.

However, even attempting to distract herself with visions of Hayden, so dapper and gentlemanly, Victoria couldn't help but contrast his polished demeanor with that of the roguish American. Never would Hayden be caught needing a shave, let alone unwashed and barefoot. His clothing was always immaculately tailored to skim his shoulders, presenting the perfect image of a solid, responsible government employee.

Kincaid, the Englishwoman realized with a start, didn't need to worry about his image. That was the difference between the two of them. The American had no pretensions. He looked exactly like what he was, an independent, amoral renegade, perhaps as dangerous to her as Zobeir, but in a different way. Kincaid beleaguered her privately, in the depths of her heart.

Whereas Hayden, though he cared for her deeply, waited in Cairo, Kincaid didn't hesitate to act, even crushing a snake under his bare heel. As much as she should have been repelled by the idea, Victoria found herself wondering how he would behave if aroused.

Once again, her roving mind turned traitor as she imagined being caught up in Kincaid's fierce embrace and crushed against his broad chest. Though her slender fingers would protest, pushing him back, his head would lower itself to hers, his hand lifting her chin ever so gently. Then, too quickly for her to object, his rough lips would possess hers, arrogantly taking her response as his due. She would struggle futilely against his hard manhood, outraged at the intimacy of his claim on her, while her body began to yield. At the vision she had conjured, Victoria's heart began to beat faster and her breathing to grow more shallow. He was so very manly in a brutish sort of way—

"Stop dreaming about me, darlin'. It's time to get up."

The callused hand touching her shoulder had the blonde on her feet at once. His taunting words were more offensive than his touch, especially since they were true.

"What? I was not—"

"Don't bother to deny it, Vicky. No woman who's met me can avoid it, or so they've all claimed," Jed teased, sure that the proper Miss Shaw would consider any dream that featured him a nightmare.

"Then they all lied, Kincaid," Victoria spat. "Or perhaps they dreamed of killing you, slowly and painfully as I'd like to do."

"Could be, I suppose, but I hope they planned to do it with kindness," he drawled insolently. "Never mind. Pack up the gear while I get Ali ready to travel."

"I am not your slave, Kincaid."

"Linger around here much longer and you could be Zobeir's," the American warned, moving off to where the horses waited.

Victoria stared after him. From the heat exploding in her cheeks, she must be blushing, damn it all! What was wrong with her?

She had heard tales of women taking sudden leave of their senses after horrendous shocks. Perhaps recent events had shaken her more than she realized. It had to be the effect of her abduction combined with Zobeir's threats that made her react that way, she decided, relieved at finding an explanation for her mind's peculiar aberrations. Thank God she wasn't actually attracted to the man!

"You haven't packed a single thing!" raged his voice behind her. "It's going to be a hard-enough trek through the desert with a helpless man, let alone a helpless woman. Either get used to the idea of pulling your own weight, Vicky, or we'll never reach Cairo alive—and I, for one, have no wish to become carrion for the vultures."

"The name is *Vic-toria* and I would appreciate it if you stopped shouting, Kincaid. You were the one who insisted I come with you, so if I don't move fast enough, do the chores yourself."

"Not on your life, lady. From here on out, the food and the sleeping bags are your responsibility, along with your own mount. I'll handle Ali, the rest of the horses and the water.

That way, when you slack off, we'll only be hungry and cold—''

How dare he assume she was incompetent? Victoria fumed.

"And when *you* fail?" she demanded.

"Then we die," he answered calmly, determined to spare her from any illusion of what lay ahead. Too often he had seen travelers in the desert weaken at the first unexpected disaster, and he couldn't let that happen to her, even if she hated him for his attitude.

Turning her back on him, Victoria bent down and folded her bed roll, securing it with a band of leather he tossed her. Without acknowledging him, she repeated the process with the blankets he had barely used and then gathered the dried meat and bread. Only when she had packed everything into the various saddlebags did she dump them all in a large pile at his feet and glare at him, surprised at the ready grin softening his face.

"When you put your mind to it, you move mighty prettily," he offered. "But I'm not carrying this load across the sands myself. Help me distribute it among the horses."

"I told you last night. Horses don't like me."

"They're not alone," Jed muttered softly. Aloud, he said, "They don't have to like you. They just have to carry you."

"What about Ali? He can't ride."

"I made a travois before you got up, and I just settled him in it. Ali will sleep while the horse pulls him," Jed explained, seeing her puzzled look. "It works fine in Kentucky, so I imagine it will do the job here."

"Oh, an American invention?"

"So was the scheme that got you free of Zobeir—"

"I didn't mean anything—"

"You never do. Here, this roan mare is yours, and so is this," he said, plopping a soft felt hat on her head. Muslin draped the crown of the practical, if unfashionable, bonnet, spilling down in the back across her neck and shoulders.

"You don't expect me to actually wear this monstrosity—"

"It doesn't matter to me. If you get sunstroke, I won't have to listen to you," he retorted, donning a hat of his own.

"And to think, I found Zobeir's taste in clothing bizarre," she complained, adjusting the crumpled hat. "I despise you, Kincaid."

"I don't care, just step into my hands and I'll boost you up."

"But the horse doesn't have a sidesaddle—"

"The quarry foreman didn't have any available. Unless you want to walk, hop up."

"My skirt will never allow me to ride that way."

"I told you last night, take it off!"

"You must be joking. I could never do that."

"Lady, you should have realized by now, when it comes to you, I don't find much to laugh about," snorted Jed. Before she realized his purpose, he grabbed the hem of her skirt with both hands and tore upward along the side seam.

A low whistle escaped his lips when he saw her odd undergarments.

"How dare you?"

"Holy Hannah, Vicky. If I had known what sights were open to view under that skirt, I would have—"

"Damn you! I knew you couldn't be trusted. First you humiliate me and then you insist on talking about it! Have you absolutely no shame?"

Her voice quavered as though she was about to cry, but for the life of him, Jed couldn't understand what had set her off so.

"From where I stand, honey, I don't see a damned thing to be ashamed of."

"Quiet, you American ape! Do you think I want to hear your perverted ramblings? Zobeir was bad enough, but you—"

"Did he touch you?"

"No, he forced me to wear this ridiculous costume."

"You could take it off," suggested Jed, knowing she would misunderstand even as the words escaped his lips. "I mean—"

"Oh, you would like that, wouldn't you? Then you could see my totally naked leg through the slit you tore."

"I was only trying to make it easier for you to ride."

"Never mind any more of your lies, Kincaid. Help me on this damned animal and let's get started. The sooner I'm back in Cairo, the sooner I can forget that people like you and Zobeir exist."

He had traveled hundreds of miles to rescue her, suffered the embarrassment of being thought Ali's slave, jeopardized his life for hers, and the ungrateful bitch grouped him with the most villainous slave merchant in Khartoum? Hell, maybe Reed had known what he was doing when he had ordered the ransom paid without taking any risks. The longer Kincaid was acquainted with Victoria Shaw, the more he regretted the impetuous chivalry that had led him to the Sudan. Unfortunately, it was too late for hindsight now. He had no choice but to get her safely back home, but he'd do it as quickly as he could, Jed vowed, as quickly was humanly possible.

Though the sun was barely over the Mokattan Hills, which bordered Cairo to the east, Hayden Reed had been up for hours. He had shaved and breakfasted alone to avoid the stares of his colleagues. These days, only the daily appearance of Grace Shaw was more of an ordeal than a meal in the consulate dining room. By now everyone knew of his fiancée's abduction and no one was reluctant to voice criticism of his handling of it, whether or not he was within earshot.

"It is well over a week since I gave you the ransom money, Mr. Reed," Grace Shaw had reminded him last night...as if he might forget. "All these days and nights with no word of my daughter or the money. Can you be certain it even reached the kidnappers?"

"I sent the best men I had available, Mrs. Shaw. Kincaid is an expert. There is none better, I assure you."

"And the shopkeeper? What superior skills does he possess, sir?" Victoria's mother had demanded. "If you loved Victoria as much as you claim, *you* would have delivered the money."

"Have no doubt whatsoever that Victoria is every bit as precious to me as she is to you, Mrs. Shaw, but my job here makes personal involvement in the situation extremely difficult. Your daughter would understand my doing my duty to England." Damn Kincaid! If the American wasn't already dead, it would be his pleasure to see to the task, Reed promised himself. There was no excuse for the man's continued silence, none at all, especially when it put him in such an untenable position. "Believe me, ma'am, I am doing everything possible to find out what happened."

"But you did not go out to that oasis in the first place, did you, Hayden Reed? For that I blame you."

Grace Shaw's words had repeated themselves throughout the long night, all the more irksome because Hayden could not deny their truth. It had been his decision not to go to the oasis, but the risk that journey presented had been too great for someone like him. How could he be certain Victoria's disappearance was the kidnapping of a wealthy man's daughter

rather than a warning directed at him, a lure to get him alone
and vulnerable? After all, he had become entangled with many
political factions over the past months. The question remained, what could he do to rectify the situation?

He had already dispatched a couple of men to the oasis south
of the Wadi Halfa to try to find some trace of Victoria, the
American or the Egyptian, Sharouk. But he had nothing con-
crete to tell the Shaws. Indeed, if he weren't extremely careful
in his dealings with them, they might break off the engagement even if Victoria was returned unharmed. And that would
be a tragedy, frowned Hayden, brushing a bit of lint off his
cuff. He did hope she was all right.

Chapter Seven

Victoria vowed through gritted teeth that she had never been so miserable in her life. Her lips were parched, her once-pampered skin was taut and burning, and her saddle-sore posterior felt as though someone had blistered it with a strap. Yet still, that madman who had snatched her from the slave pens pressed on, despite the scorching sun overhead. Those words he had spoken so glibly before dawn, that leaving prior to sunrise would save them from traveling during the hottest part of the day, were clearly as worthless as the American himself.

Here it was, a few hours past noon, and Jed Kincaid continued to force them onward, an exhausted, ill-treated woman, and a wounded Egyptian. Not that the Egyptian was in any condition to complain, Victoria noted, glancing at Ali lashed to the strange contrivance Kincaid had fashioned. No, despite occasionally fluttering his eyelids, Ali appeared to be blissfully unaware of discomfort while his horse, with its unwieldy burden, followed Jed's across the sands. Growing more angry and resentful with each step their steeds took, she almost wished she were in his place.

Why, the cliffs that had seen the origin of their journey had now completely disappeared, lost somewhere to the southeast in the shimmering heat that had conquered the cooler air of dawn. Surely they had traveled far enough for one day.

However, a glance at Jed Kincaid's rigid back gave no hint of either fatigue or an inclination to make camp. The man was a complete and utter beast, Victoria decided, her temper blazing and fiery like the ruthless sun overhead. Though he might be accustomed to such deplorable conditions, the lout did nothing to see to her comfort or ease her hardship.

Of course, it wasn't as if she were dealing with a gentleman, Victoria reminded herself. No, the primitive Jed Kincaid was certainly not a man of refinement and breeding. His tearing her skirt along with everything else he had done told her that. Yet, his easy movements when they were preparing to leave their hiding place in the cliffs marked him with a certain natural grace, and inexplicably Victoria began to consider how he would fare on a dance floor. The idea conjured up an image of broad shoulders encased in expensive, well-tailored, masculine cloth, and golden skin contrasting richly with a snowy white shirtfront. The picture created in her mind was so realistic that a shiver ran along her body, the sensation thankfully shaking some sense into her.

Jed Kincaid in formal wear? It was too ridiculous and absurd to be imagined. Even if the barbarian stood still long enough to be fitted for such attire, he couldn't possibly possess the manners needed to carry him through an evening of dancing and civilized conversation. Whatever could have put such a vision into her head, Victoria wondered, thoroughly angry at herself.

Flustered by her odd musings, she became determined to stop and rest before she lost her wits entirely. She told herself she would not be deterred by the fierce scowl that would likely appear on Kincaid's face when she made her demand. She had had enough of this mad flight, and she was going to terminate it immediately.

"Kincaid," she called, the dryness of her throat causing her voice to sound like a feeble croak, completely robbing it of any note of authority she wished to convey.

"What is it *now*, Vicky?" Jed asked, swinging around easily in his saddle.

"I'm tired. We'll make camp here," she announced, silently cursing the squawks that disguised her usual well-cultured tones.

"I don't think so," Jed replied, turning around to face front once more, dismissing Victoria's presence and her dictates.

"But I insist," the petite blonde persisted, riding faster, despite her raw bottom, in order to come abreast of him.

"You can insist on anything you want, lady, but your whims don't change the facts. We'll set up camp when we come to an appropriate place and not before."

"I'm afraid you don't understand, Kincaid. I refuse to go any farther," Victoria assured him, the icy quality of her demeanor immune to the sun's blazing rays. "As for an appropriate site, one patch of sand is as good as another I should think."

"The thing is, you shouldn't think, Vicky. You don't know the desert. I do. I'm the one who'll decide when it's time to call it a day. Whether you like it or not, I'm your salvation."

"What a reprehensible thought."

"It might be, but get used to the idea," Jed said, his stubble-covered jaws clamping together tightly, irrevocable proof of the American's stubbornness. With that, he kicked his horse slightly and left Hayden Reed's harping bride-to-be a few paces behind.

"You can't simply dismiss me like that," Victoria insisted, urging her horse to once more ride alongside Jed Kincaid.

"I just did," Jed growled, not bothering to look in Victoria's direction. Damnation but the woman was a handful. You'd think he was trying to torture her instead of save her.

"Well, I won't have it," came Victoria's raspy yet outraged reply.

"There's not much you can do about the situation," Jed stated, a smug smirk transforming his irritated countenance into the radiant expression of a man well pleased with himself.

"There certainly is! I'm going to dismount here. And when I do, you will be forced to do the same. After all, you can't just ride off and leave me behind."

"Can't I?" Jed asked softly, turning his head to fix his companion with a stare communicating a rage so tightly held in check that Victoria shuddered to think what this dangerous male would be like should he lose control. "You do what you want, but as for me, I'm going on. Maybe with any luck, you can catch up with Ali and me sometime tomorrow. That is, if the jackals don't spend the night feasting on your undoubtedly tender flesh."

"But it can't make that much of a difference if we stop now rather than later," Victoria pleaded, taken aback by Jed's response. "Surely you don't pretend to know exactly where we are. And besides, before we set out, you told me we wouldn't be traveling during the most unbearable part of the day. Doesn't your word mean anything to you?"

"Vicky, where I come from, a man's word means more than you'll ever know. And what we say, we say plainly without a lot of diplomatic balderdash, but I hadn't figured on Ali's travois slowing us down so damn much," Jed retorted wearily, suddenly tired of this Englishwoman's relentless haranguing. Hell's fire, he was used to complacent women who eagerly did whatever he directed them to do. But this little English rose was so hot-tempered that even one of his infamous glares couldn't cause her to shrink back into silence. Didn't the woman have any sense at all?

"If that's true, then keep your promise."

"I don't remember actually promising you anything other than to get you back safely to that powder puff you intend to marry," Jed replied, his lips compressing into a thin line. "And if you really loved him, you wouldn't mind putting up with a little inconvenience in order to fly to his side as quickly as possible."

"How dare you!"

"You'll learn quickly enough that I dare just about anything, Vicky," Jed said, sliding his gaze up and down her still-exposed leg and lingering on her knee.

"If you even think of touching me, I'll slaughter you myself," Victoria hissed, pulling hard on her reins, "and I assure you, I would take great pleasure in doing so."

"Vicky, get back on the horse," Jed commanded with a calmness he didn't feel as he watched her slide from the saddle, inadvertently uncovering another few inches of leg before her feet found the sand.

"I think I'd prefer to take my chances with jackals of the four-legged variety," she said scornfully, then unlashed an animal skin filled with water and held it up to her lips.

"I said for you to mount up," Jed bellowed, watching her grimace as the unsavory taste of the water pierced her annoyance and lingered on her palate.

"For the love of Allah, can't you two stop bickering and give a dying man some peace?" came a weakened voice from the travois.

In spite of his fury with Victoria, Jed's face broke into a wide grin. He jumped to the ground and walked to Ali's side. The sudden and complete transformation in the rugged American's manner gave Victoria pause as she watched him interact once more with the man who had aided in her rescue. Could this solicitous man be the same one who had been so mean-spirited only a moment ago?

"You're not dying," Jed said gruffly, taking the water skin from Victoria and pouring some into his hand before moving aside the flaps of Ali's *kaffiyeh* to bathe his face gently. "But I can't promise Fatima won't be out looking for a new husband, anyway, by the time I get you back."

"Not Fatima," Ali whispered.

"How can you be so sure?" Jed chuckled, glad to see the shopkeeper regain not only consciousness, but his contrary nature, as well.

"Some women are predictable," Ali murmured with a painful shrug of his shoulders.

"And some aren't," Jed replied tersely, shooting Victoria a black and disgruntled look. "But maybe you're right. Maybe your Fatima will be waiting for you."

"If I don't find myself knocking at the gates of Paradise. I doubt you make a good physician," Ali said sarcastically.

"I dug the bullet out and stitched you up, didn't I? And after I risked my neck to save yours, you wouldn't dare die," Jed replied. "But I promise you this, you son of a bitch, once you're on your feet, I'm going to knock you down again for almost costing all of us our lives back there."

"It was my heroics that saved us," Ali asserted faintly. The effort to speak was starting to take its toll.

"We'll talk about it later. Right now, we had better move out. We're traveling parallel to a caravan route, and another hour, two at the most, in the saddle will see us bedded down at a small oasis. How would you like to spend the night amid greenery with all the water you can drink?"

"I would like that very much, but not if it means I have to endure more of your fighting with the Englishwoman."

"Vicky won't give me any more arguments," Jed stated, raising his head and staring searchingly at the woman in question.

"Why didn't you tell me you were trying to reach an oasis?" Victoria asked.

"I didn't have an opportunity. You were so busy giving me orders and telling me what we were going to do that you didn't want to hear anything I had to say."

"I can't agree with that."

"Of course not. That would be asking too much," Jed grumbled. "Come on, woman, saddle up."

"If I go with you, we must make a pact," Victoria bargained. "Don't ever hide anything from me about this journey again. Do I have your precious word on that?"

"You do, if you promise in return that you'll listen to what I have to say and accept it," Jed replied, striding over to Victoria and looking down into her upturned face.

"I'll listen," Victoria said. She was startled when Jed's large hands found her waist and she felt herself lifted aloft and seated once more astride her horse.

"Good," Jed said, the satisfaction of the conquering male imprinted on his rugged features.

"I'll listen, and *then* I'll have my say," Victoria muttered. She bit her lip to smother her laughter as Jed's head snapped around in her direction and his mouth puckered angrily.

"One more thing, Vicky," Jed said casually when he was finally able to trust his voice to speak without any traces of the temper this woman brought so effortlessly to the surface.

"What is it?" a cautious Victoria inquired.

"Don't drink any more of the horses' water. You never know when we'll need it for our mounts. Besides," Jed said, cutting off Victoria's protests, "what you drank can't have tasted very good after being sloshed around in those half-cured skins. The stuff I have reserved for us is much better."

At the sight of Victoria's anger-stained cheeks, Jed raised his hat in a lighthearted salute and flicked the reins against his horse's neck, leaving a seething Miss Shaw to follow in his wake.

She hated him, she hated him, she truly and utterly hated him! Victoria thought as she rode along behind the insufferable Jed Kincaid. And after seemingly endless hours in the saddle, she would have no qualms about telling Kincaid just how she felt. That is, if it were not for her reluctance to open her mouth and chance its being filled with the sand sent falling toward her by both the travois and the horse's hooves as Jed led the way up a steep incline.

One to two hours, indeed! They must have journeyed at least three, though it would not have surprised Victoria to learn it had been five hours since Kincaid had dangled the promise of refreshing water and grassy banks before her. His deep, masculine tones, drenched in self-assurance, had inspired confidence. But what a dolt she had been to believe him!

However, trusting him in even the most trivial of matters was a mistake she would not make again. Traveling alongside a caravan route, he had said! Imagine thinking that Kincaid knew what he was doing ... and more important, where he was going. Why, the man would no doubt have difficulty navigating the streets of Cairo, never mind the desert, where one undulating ridge of sand looked exactly like another. Jed Kincaid was as lost as she was and just too stubborn to admit it, Victoria decided.

Impatient to confront him with her incisive knowledge, Victoria kicked at the sides of her steed halfheartedly, having little hope the exhausted animal would respond to her urging. To her delight, however, the horse raised its head, its nostrils flaring slightly as it quickened its pace to reach the top of the dune where Kincaid waited with uncharacteristic gallantry.

Pulling up beside him, Victoria focused on the man who had tortured her for the last several hours by denying her any rest.

"All right, Kincaid," she said accusingly, her voice so raspy it sounded as if it belonged to a stranger, "where is—"

"Where's what?" Jed drawled when Victoria's little mare suddenly reared and began to stamp impatiently, its neophyte rider fighting to control it. "The oasis?"

With a laugh, he nodded to the small pool of water and patch of greenery below them. "I told you we'd be camping here for the night."

"It was mere luck that you happened upon such a place," Victoria grumbled in an unladylike fashion, struggling to keep her mount from rushing down the incline to drink. Though she, herself, wanted nothing so much as to do the same thing, she would roast in hell, a location that could be no hotter than this desert, before she allowed Jed Kincaid to see how desperately she relished the idea of cold water trickling down her dry throat.

"Luck, hell!" Jed all but spat out the words.

"I don't appreciate your language," she snapped, ignoring the unacceptable phrases that had been running through her own mind.

"And evidently you don't appreciate my skill in leading you to this oasis, either."

"Your so-called skill has nothing to do with it," Victoria stated calmly. "This is simply God's answer to my prayers these last few horrible hours."

"Listen, lady," Jed announced with deadly impatience, "you'd better understand once and for all that I'm the answer to your prayers—at least until I get you back to Cairo."

"If that's so, then God does, indeed, work in mysterious ways," Victoria retorted. "However, I am not going to waste time arguing with you now. There'll be plenty of opportunity for that later." She ran the tip of a pink tongue over dry lips while she eyed the beckoning water below. "At the moment, I plan on refreshing myself after that brutal ride you forced me to endure."

"In all likelihood, that *brutal* ride saved your life," Jed replied, keeping pace with the mare as they descended from the ridge. Hell's fire, he had expected praise, not more carping, for bringing them to the oasis, and he was damn well going to get what he deserved. "A little gratitude might be in order."

"Gratitude?" Victoria asked in genuine surprise. "When we could have stayed aboard that boat and suffered none of to-day's hardships?"

"I told you before, our pursuers might have overtaken *that boat*," Jed pronounced in the superior tones of a man who had plenty of experience with escaping from dangerous situations. "That's why I sent the *falucca* downriver—to keep them busy chasing it until the damn thing ran aground somewhere. By then, they'd have no idea of where we disembarked."

"I believe thrown overboard is the correct phrasing, at least in my case," Victoria interjected dryly.

"Call it what you will," came the gruff reply. "It enabled us to lose the good citizens of Khartoum and bought us time for our flight through the desert. If it had just been Ali and me, I would have chanced outrunning them and stayed on the river. But I couldn't count on fighting off a slew of avenging Su-danese while protecting you at the same time."

"You mean there's something that might be beyond your capabilities?" Victoria asked with a sweetness that sent Jed's blood to boiling. "Oh, dear, to think I've been deluded all this time. I'm shattered."

"Listen here, Vicky, I don't like being stuck with you any more than you like being saddled with me. I was on my way to something really important before I got sidetracked into coming after you."

"Important? What was it?" she cooed. "Drinking yourself into oblivion or crawling into some unfortunate woman's bed?"

"Never you mind what it was!" Jed growled, stung by the accuracy of Victoria Shaw's guess. Suddenly what had seemed like a perfectly fine idea during his last evening in Cairo had been made to sound sordid and common by her cultured voice. Well, he'd had enough of this blue-blooded filly prancing around with her nose in the air, and he had no compunctions in telling her so.

"For God's sake," he started, once more surprised at her ability to ruffle him. "Here I am arguing with you when I'm more parched than I ever remember being. If there's one thing I've learned today, it's that you're the most exasperating, distracting female I've ever had the misfortune to meet."

"Distracting! I kept my thoughts to myself for quite some time this afternoon," Victoria protested indignantly as the impatient horses finally reached the perimeter of the oasis. Sliding gratefully from her saddle, she afforded Jed an unobstructed view of her gauze-encased thighs, and the word *distracting* took on a meaning quite different from the one he had originally intended.

Feeling as though a mule had kicked him forcefully enough to knock the wind out of him, Jed swallowed hard. Vicky had the longest, shapeliest legs!

Then Jed shook his head as if to clear it, and dismounted, telling himself sternly that his arousal had nothing to do with Victoria Shaw's charms. It was only the result of having been without a woman for a long time, of having his quest for a female so abruptly interrupted during his last night in Cairo.

But feeling as anxious as some young buck who had never lain with a woman and was chomping at the bit to do so was almost beyond his comprehension. He hadn't realized he was that desperate.

Oh, he might have teased her and made her blush, Jed admitted, but he certainly hadn't meant anything by it. Had he? No, he quickly decided, trying to keep his wariness of this blonde bit of femininity in check. After all, as prim and proper as she was, she probably had no idea of what it was to be a woman. In fact, judging by her tastes in fiancés, he was sure of it. And, besides, virgins were not to his taste. He liked his women unrestrained and a little bit wild.

"Here, Kincaid," Victoria said, unaware of the direction the American's thoughts had taken as she casually handed him her horse's reins and began walking toward the water with a light step.

"Whoa! One minute, *Queen* Victoria," Jed commanded, coming around to block her path and look down on her with a threatening glare. While he blamed his anger on her attitude, he suspected that it was fueled, too, by the unsettling impact she had on him. Yet, affect his manhood as she might, she gave no indication that she saw him as a man at all. It fact, it appeared she considered him as nothing more than an irritating though necessary servant.

"What is it?" Victoria asked haughtily, so put out at having her intentions thwarted that she missed the fiery glint in Jed's eyes.

"What do you call your butler?" he asked so softly that his lips hardly appeared to move, a sign that Jed Kincaid was choked with anger.

"What!" Victoria exclaimed, quite obviously taken aback. She began to consider the possibility that the American had been out in the sun so long that he had gone quite mad. A Jed Kincaid more insane than the one who had climbed over the walls of the slave pen to find her, who had nearly killed the two of them with the explosives he had ordered set off? On top of everything else she would have to handle that, as well? It was too much.

"I asked what you called your butler," Jed repeated, coming ominously closer so that Victoria was forced to look up at him. Yet no matter how ferocious his features, it was a view more preferable than staring straight at his muscular chest, its fine mat of hair peeping out over the deep, open neckline of his shirt.

"Hawkins," she replied, wondering what Kincaid was up to.

"Why?" he demanded. His face came closer to hers.

"Obviously because that's his name."

"Why not Mr. Hawkins?" Jed pressed. His breath was hot upon her cheeks as he continued to hold her captive with his incensed stare.

"Don't be foolish," Victoria said with impatience. "One simply doesn't address one's butler as Mr., or any other household servant for that matter. Now, do remove yourself from my path, Kincaid, and tend to the horses while I get a drink."

"There you go again, Vicky. Listen to yourself—calling me Kincaid as though I'm your damnable butler, as though I'm a servant. Let's set things straight once and for all. Out here, you are superior to no one, least of all me. From now on, you'll call me Mr. Kincaid, or Jed if you prefer. But more important, you'll do your share of the work, the way I told you back at the cliffs, and you'll stop expecting me to wait on you. Do I make myself clear?" he asked, catching her jaw in his long, strong fingers and forcing Victoria's gaze to remain with his own.

"Quite," she said curtly. "But I'm afraid it will have to be Jed. Mr. is a title reserved for a gentleman. It wouldn't do in your case."

"Suit yourself," the American said with an indolent grin, releasing his hold on her and finding immense satisfaction in the scowl that twisted her pretty little mouth. "Jed will be just fine. Unsaddle the mare and then water the horses. They can have what's left in the skins we're carrying, that is, unless you don't mind them lapping from that pool over there before we do."

"Can't I have a drink first?" she insisted.

"Out in the desert, it's wiser to take care of your animals before seeing to your own needs," Jed pronounced. "These horses might mean the difference between life and death. As it is, it's going to be tough on them when there's no oasis to be had. Pamper them while you can."

"But—"

"If I'm going to teach you to survive out here, I'm going to do it right. I want you to know how to handle yourself if anything should happen to me before we get back."

"The only danger you face is my killing you," Victoria declared, standing her ground defiantly.

"Stop your complaining and get to it, Vicky, before I think of something else for you to do, something you might find a pleasure instead of a chore."

"You truly are a beast, Kincaid," Victoria muttered with disdain, apprehensively eying the docile mare, now snorting and skittish in anticipation of being watered.

"It's *Jed*, remember?" he asked, taking a threatening step in her direction. Victoria scurried to do as he had commanded.

The self-satisfied laughter that followed her retreat rankled the blonde, and she called out defiantly over her shoulder, "And while I'm laboring, just what will you be doing, your lordship?"

"Me? I'll be seeing to Ali, unsaddling my stallion and setting up camp," he answered, discovering just how much he enjoyed the sight Victoria made as she bent over to peer under the mare's belly in search of the buckle on the saddle's cinch. No matter how exasperating she was when she opened her mouth, he concluded in spite of himself, Vicky did have the most nicely rounded derriere!

Curious at the unnatural silence behind her, Victoria glanced back sharply over her shoulder and caught Jed staring. She stood up abruptly, her sun-reddened cheeks turning a deeper crimson.

"You really are no gentleman. Hayden would certainly never dream of behaving so poorly," she informed him.

"Yeah, and he didn't dream of coming after you, either," Jed said with an easy shrug of his broad shoulders as he unhitched the travois and gently lowered the Cairene to the ground.

"You bastard!" Victoria muttered, finally undoing the cinch and staggering under the weight of the mare's saddle.

"Tsk, tsk! It was supposed to be Mr. Kincaid or Jed. Bastard was never an option," Jed replied. He hunkered down at the edge of the water to fill a canteen for Ali. "Really, Vicky, such language is very unladylike. I'm surprised at you."

"If I'm in your company much longer I'm apt to forget everything I've ever learned about being a lady," Victoria shot back, furious with herself for allowing this man to push her into losing her temper and to ignore her upbringing.

"That could prove mighty interesting," Jed said with a wicked grin. He handed the canteen to Ali, who had recovered sufficiently to hold it for himself. "Start behaving wantonly and I've an idea that as hot as today has been, tomorrow could be hotter still."

"You are impossible—so crudely salacious," Victoria fumed. "Hayden would never say anything so suggestive."

"No?" Jed asked offhandedly, helping Ali to take a few feeble steps to the shade of a date palm so that he could rest in relative coolness. "Then why did you ever agree to marry him?"

A strangled, frustrated scream was the only reply as the mare, its mouth still buried in the water skin, snorted, sending a spray of malodorous water all over Victoria. Suddenly Jed Kincaid found himself laughing outright, his spirits soaring for the first time since they had escaped Khartoum.

Chapter Eight

A while later, after rubbing down the stallion as well as Ali's horse, Jed turned his attention to dressing the Egyptian's wound. Pleased to discover it was not as bad as he had at first thought, Jed nevertheless determined that Ali should restrict his movement. Such a plan, however, needed Ali's agreement, and Jed found himself hard-pressed to keep the Cairene from trying to rise.

Running a hand through his dark brown hair in frustration, Jed had almost settled upon allowing Ali to overdo, convinced it would force Ali to accept his weakened state, when Victoria joined them.

"Now, don't go poking at him, Vicky. I'm trying to get the varmint settled down, and I don't need you stirring things up again," Jed stated, his deep tones making it quite evident he expected to be obeyed.

"Allah bless you for your kindness," Ali interjected with a shy smile before Victoria could form a reply to Jed's gruff order. Exhausted, the Egyptian had no desire for these two foreigners to start rowing all over again. "Hard as it may be to believe, Jed Kincaid has spoken the truth. There is no need for you to see to me."

"Quiet, you. Any more insults and you'll be sporting two bullet holes," Jed said to Ali, but a suppressed smile was evidence that the American was glad to see the other man feeling like his usual quarrelsome self. The handsome planes of Jed's face hardened, however, when he turned to address Victoria.

"As for you, if you still have some energy left, you can make yourself useful. Gather as much of this as you can find so I can

get a fire going," he said, kicking at a clump of some uniden-
ifiable, well-dried substance with the hard toe of his boot.

"And if I don't?"

"Then you'll have no campfire to keep the jackals at bay,"
Jed replied with a casual smile. "Surely even a desert green-
horn like you realizes those critters will want to creep down to
the water tonight and drink their fill."

"It's just too bad you're one jackal the flames won't keep
away," Victoria grumbled, bending down to scoop up the odd-
looking fuel. "What is this, anyway, some sort of fossilized
peat or silt?"

Jed's eyes widened a fraction when he realized that the fas-
tidious Englishwoman truly didn't know what she had in her
possession. No wonder she hadn't given him more of an argument.

"No, sugar, where are you going to get anything like that in
the middle of the desert?" he asked, a wide grin showing off his
even white teeth and a devilish gleam lighting his eyes. Observing Ali cringing at what was to come only added to his enjoyment of the moment. "What you're holding is something
conveniently left behind by the caravans that have bedded down
here. It's camel dung."

"What!" Victoria shrieked, looking down in horrified disbelief at the crumbling mass in her hands.

"In order to survive in the desert, a body has to utilize
whatever the Good Lord provides."

"And he has just provided me with an inspiration for a new
way to put this to use," Victoria muttered. She drew back her
hand and flung its contents in Jed's direction. But he simply
ducked and Victoria's ammunition went sailing harmlessly past
him.

"You insufferable bastard," she hissed.

"We've already had this conversation, if I recall correctly,
and I'd swear we settled on your calling me Jed," he said,
amusement crinkling the corners of his eyes.

"How dare you deceive me that way? Hayden will see that
you pay for this," Victoria threatened, her fists clenched and
her mouth tightly pursed.

"Hayden? Make me pay?" Jed echoed with a chuckle. "I
didn't realize you were given to jesting, Vicky."

In light of Jed's quiet laughter, the words she had uttered
began to sound false and hollow even to her own ears when

Victoria tried to conjure up a picture of Hayden besting Jed
Kincaid. But what was she thinking of to feel such a stab of
disappointment? Hayden was a fine man, a wonderful one with
superior qualities that became more apparent than ever when
compared with this brash American.

"I'm not of a mind to provide you with entertainment, or to
bolster your already high opinion of yourself," Victoria stated
with every bit of dignity she could muster. "At least in Khartoum, when Zobeir was trying to humiliate me, he made certain I was aware of it. But you couldn't find enough decency
within your black soul to do even that. After your despicable
little joke, I feel more in need of a bath than ever. If you and
Ali would take yourselves off to the other side of that small
dune, I shall bathe now."

"Not before I've had my fill to drink," Jed said, indignant
that despite the circumstances, Victoria Shaw managed to
sound like some absolute monarch. "Besides, Ali is in no condition to be moved anywhere. If you weren't so selfish, you'd
realize that."

"You're right," Victoria stated contritely, taking Jed by
surprise so that he narrowed his eyes and studied her.

"But it is no problem," Ali insisted. Touched by the sincerity Jed Kincaid refused to recognize, and troubled by the disappointment he saw registered on Victoria's soft features, the
wounded man slowly raised himself until he was sitting upright.

"Don't be an imbecile, Ali," Jed protested irritably. "You're
not going anywhere. If Vicky wants a bath so badly, I'll go wait
behind the dune. You can just turn around. She'll be able to
splash to her heart's content.

"Of course . . ." Victoria began, not entirely happy with the
situation but unwilling to abandon the fantasy of submerging
herself in the beckoning waters of the oasis.

"No, it would be unthinkable," Ali said with finality, using
the tree trunk to help pull himself to unsteady feet. "It is no
inconvenience to move a few yards. In fact, after being lashed
to that contraption all day, I have need of a little exercise."

"You have need of an asylum," Jed proclaimed in disgust.

"Either you will assist me, Kincaid, or I will make my way
there myself," Ali announced obstinately.

"You're a damned fool pampering this woman," Jed uttered in exasperation after fetching the canteens and filling them.

Stalking to the other man's side and slipping his shoulder under Ali's arm, Jed put a hand at his waist to steady the Egyptian's uneven steps.

"But what else is a man to do with a beautiful woman?" Ali asked, stiffly turning toward the mound a short distance away.

"I can think of something to do with this one," Jed grumbled. "Too bad there are no switches to be had."

Guilty as she was to have disturbed Ali, Victoria nevertheless breathed a sigh of relief when the duo disappeared behind the sand. Promising herself that she would make this up to the wounded Egyptian by being particularly considerate during the rest of their journey, she peered cautiously at the crest of the dune and then glanced all around. Satisfied that she was alone, Victoria began to slip out of her clothing, feeling delightfully sinful.

First she doffed the bedraggled blouse and skirt she had been wearing when she had been abducted, the skirt that brute Kincaid had slit open to her thigh. Then her hands moved to the scandalous garments Zobeir had forced upon her. Impatient to be rid of the last vestiges of Khartoum, Victoria stepped out of the diaphanous pantaloons, and her face wrinkled in distaste when she cast aside the short, bejeweled bodice.

Shivering at her nakedness in spite of the still-oppressive heat, Victoria scampered to the water's edge. Without further ado, she gingerly entered the pool.

Though not exceedingly cool, the water felt so initially to her sun-baked skin. Having it lap around her nipples evoked mysterious sensations of forbidden pleasure, and shame mingled with inexplicable longing. She blamed her odd frame of mind on her nudity beneath the open sky and washed the dust and grime of the desert from her body, startled at how sensitive parts of it had suddenly become.

Remembering Jed's departing words, she made a face. Switch indeed! she thought, submerging herself beneath the liquid's surface in order to clean her hair. Why, her bottom was so raw from those endless hours in the saddle she wouldn't be able to feel the sting of a switch, anyway. So Mr. Jed Kincaid could just keep his barbaric threats to himself. She certainly wasn't afraid of him.

Such a realization did not dismiss thoughts of the arrogant American, however. Instead, it summoned forth unwelcome images of a face so compellingly handsome that not even the stubble adorning his unshaven cheeks could detract from it. Still, pleasing as Victoria found the attractive lines of his strong jaw and straight nose, it had been Jed's eyes that both fascinated and frightened her from the start.

They were dangerous eyes, belonging to a man who answered to no one other than himself, a man so self-assured that he possessed no doubts but that his commands would be obeyed. Victoria had seen those eyes narrow in anger and glint in amusement. But no matter what his mood, there had always been a wild spark lurking in their depths that hinted at a masculine essence so strong, Victoria was drawn to it even as she was horrified by it.

It was there, too, in the easy gait of Jed's proud stride, and the carriage of his broad-shouldered, muscular frame. In fact, it was in every ounce of his being, and the realization made Victoria shudder. She had never before encountered anyone like Jed Kincaid. No wonder she didn't know how to deal with him.

He'd met her type plenty of times before, Jed fumed, lying on his back, his dark head cradled by his strong, interlocked fingers as he waited for *Queen* Victoria to finally finish her ablutions.

Yes, women as haughty and selfish as Vicky were a dime a dozen in "polite society," and he knew exactly how to handle them. Of course, there weren't many who were quite as pretty as the woman sharing the trail with him, Jed admitted reluctantly. She was a fetching little thing. Those big blue eyes of hers and all that blond hair could drive a man to do strange things if he weren't careful. And that figure, Lord have mercy! That tight little seat and those high, firm breasts of hers just cried out to be caressed.

Jed squeezed his eyes shut, hoping to erase the unbidden images of Vicky's fiery beauty. But no matter how much effort he made, he only succeeded in bringing forth new, more erotic visions of Vicky gloriously naked, frolicking uninhibitedly in the waters of the oasis. Damnation, but the woman bedeviled him. He would have groaned aloud if Ali had not been resting at his side.

Then, a wicked grin spread slowly across his deeply tanned face. He was certain to be bothered by her for a great while unless he satisfied his curiosity and got Vicky out of his system once and for all. Surely the reality of her unclad curves could never compare to the lushness with which his woman-starved appetites endowed her in his mind's eye.

One quick look and this present, unbearable affliction would disappear. After all, he was bound to be disappointed. None of the many women of his acquaintance had ever possessed the feminine allure that his feverish brain assigned to Vicky.

Impulsively, he rolled onto his taut stomach and was about to begin inching his way to the top of the dune, answering a summons he couldn't control, when a dark hand shot out to restrain him.

"Don't, Jed," Ali admonished. "Leave the woman in peace."

"Oh, so Vicky has a protector now, does she?" Jed drawled with a placidity he didn't feel. Why did Ali care, unless the Egyptian, married though he was, felt drawn to Vicky, too? "There's no way you can stop me, you know."

"She belongs to another man," Ali reminded him, ignoring Jed's challenge.

"It might be that's something we should *both* remember," Jed answered. He almost winced at the illogical tenor of his reply, and the harshness of his tone. Ali had been mostly unconscious since they had rescued Miss Shaw. Yet, idiotic as it was, Jed felt a stab of envy at the few friendly words the Egyptian and Vicky had shared. Why couldn't she talk to him that way?

"I do not forget," Ali replied, affronted by Jed's unfounded insinuations. "Nor do I forget my Fatima. But you, Jed, cannot really mean to spy on the woman while she is bathing. Such an act is contemptible."

"Vicky doesn't reckon I'm much of a gentleman, anyway, so what difference does it make?"

"Doesn't your own sense of honor tell you such spying is unworthy of you?"

"I reckon you might be right," Jed said with a frustrated sigh. "No matter how much I try to deny what my mama taught me about being a gentleman, some of the lessons stuck. I can't be sneaky in taking advantage of that woman over yonder."

"I knew you would agree," Ali said, satisfaction evident in his hawklike features. It was an expression that quickly faded, however, with Jed's next words.

"Hey, Vicky, I'm coming over the top of the dune," the American bellowed suddenly, giving Ali a triumphant look.

"Jed Kincaid, how dare you?" Victoria squawked in protest, scrunching down in the water so that the tops of her breasts were hidden, though barely. As she watched Jed's determined tread bring him closer, Victoria's slender arms immediately flew across her chest to cover her nipples, grown traitorously erect. More surprising was that when Jed reached her, the set of his mouth and the predatory expression in his eyes made a part of her yearn to unveil herself to him, to rise from the water, sleek and wet, languidly exhibiting herself for his hungry perusal.

But what insanity was this? she asked herself in sharp rebuke. She was to be married shortly to Hayden Reed, one of the most refined men who had ever lived. Angry at herself for her body's reaction to Jed's sudden appearance, she turned her wrath on him.

"What are you doing, you despicable cur? Get back behind that incline where you belong," she ordered imperiously.

"You don't own the desert, Vicky. The way I see it, I belong anyplace I want to be," Jed replied, his eyes casually piercing the surface of the water and dancing over what he could see of Victoria's creamy breasts. "Actually, I'm here to do you a favor."

"Don't flatter yourself," Victoria intoned crisply. Her haughty, disinterested demeanor gave lie to the little thrills that mysteriously prickled along the surface of her skin at the possibilities Jed's mocking words invoked.

"You misjudge me, Vicky," Jed said, his voice a shade huskier than normal as the petite blonde's nakedness began to drive him to madness he was finding hard to contain. Slowly, he turned to his saddlebag. Extracting a *gallabiya* from the supplies obtained from the foreman of the quarries, he returned to the water's edge.

"What I was thinking is that you might want a change of clothing," he said, dropping the garment beside the pool. "That is, unless you had something else in mind."

In order to maintain his self-control in the face of her appealing blush, his sharp gaze moved reluctantly from Victoria to the harem outfit she had discarded on the bank. Drawn to it like iron filings to a magnet, Jed picked up the ornate bodice that still bore her scent. Allowing his fingers to run slowly across the rich fabric, he spoke with a hoarseness he hoped Victoria didn't notice. "To tell you the truth, though, Vicky, I surely wouldn't mind if you wanted to slip this on again."

"I can't believe what a scoundrel you are," Victoria said after a moment's silence, almost mesmerized by the manner in which Jed's long, sure fingers had stroked the jeweled vest. "Hayden would never take advantage of a lady like this."

"From what I've seen of Hayden, he wouldn't know what to do with a woman if she lay down naked beside him. But that's your problem, not mine," Jed replied coolly. He'd been enjoying this little set-to until that damnable Englishman's name had come up.

His irreverence vanished, Jed was becoming exceedingly serious as his eyes settled once more on Victoria Shaw. To his discomfort, she appeared to be every bit as delectable as he had imagined. It was a monumental waste of such loveliness to be destined for a man of Reed's ilk, a notion that ate at Jed until he remembered Victoria's argumentative nature and sharp tongue. She would undoubtedly run the man ragged. For some reason, the thought brightened Jed's outlook considerably.

"Don't be too much longer," he said with a wry smile, "or I may decide to join you." With that, he turned on his heel and left.

The moment Jed's straight, muscular form began to disappear over the crest of the sand, Victoria scrambled to the bank and grabbed the *gallabiya* he had left her. She wanted to take no chances on being in the water should he take it into his thick skull to turn around and come back. While he had been standing on the bank, she had felt trapped, completely at his mercy. Although something told her Jed Kincaid would never force her to lie with him, his being so near while she hadn't a stitch on had proved a singularly disturbing experience, one she didn't dare repeat.

Frantically grabbing at the hem of the *gallabiya,* she didn't see Jed grimace and give in to temptation, glancing back over his shoulder before completely vanishing from view. Nor did she hear his sharply indrawn breath as his captive gaze slid slowly over her feminine curves.

"Kincaid!" Ali reproved.

"I told her I was coming, didn't I?" Jed asked after releasing his breath in a rush. "Besides, she was in the water. There wasn't much to see."

"Until you turned around, I warrant," Ali replied, his voice rife with condemnation. "What about your mother's struggle to turn you into a gentleman?"

"I guess her lessons didn't stick much, after all," Jed commented wryly. Still reeling from the vision of Victoria after she emerged from the pool, all wet and sleek, her ivory skin glistening, he was in no mood for a lecture. He hadn't liked the way his throat had constricted at the sight of her, and he tried to dismiss the manner in which his blood had begun to sing in his veins. Nor did he want to acknowledge what an error it had been to think that Victoria Shaw's lush little body would not live up to his expectations.

It would appear that instead of extinguishing his smoldering masculine urges, glimpsing Vicky had started his fires going, and thoughts of her belonging to Hayden Reed no longer seemed a matter for levity. In fact, the flames licking at his self-control made him long to find a physical outlet of any sort for the emotional frustration he felt.

"I've finished, if you'd like to return to camp," he heard Victoria say as she came around the side of the sandy embankment.

Though she pretended to be calm and acted as if his outrageous conduct was nothing more than she expected, Jed swore it was not just sunburn that tinged her delicate cheekbones when her eyes chanced to meet his.

"Have a nice bath?" he asked, wanting her to remember, as he did, the physical tension that had hung in the air between them at the waters of the oasis. Offhand as he tried to sound, Jed found his voice was still tight in his throat at the memory of seeing Vicky under the desert's sun as natural as the day she had been born.

"Yes, no thanks to you," Victoria replied scathingly. "Every time I think that you can behave no worse than you already have, you manage to prove me wrong. Not that I didn't appreciate him before, but having met you, I thank God for allowing me to have ever found a man as fine as Hayden."

"Hayden, Hayden, Hayden!" Jed exploded, storming to Victoria's side and towering over her, his eyes sparking flame. The force of his emotions startled even him. But once begun, his outburst had to run its course. "If I have to hear that jack-ass's name one more time, Vicky, I swear you'll be sorry."

"Oh, really? And just what do you intend to do?" Victoria inquired disdainfully, knowing with a woman's instinct that as wild as Jed Kincaid might be, he would never physically hurt her.

"I'm warning you, woman, keep it up and you'll find out. I won't be responsible for my actions," Jed promised ominously.

"I refuse to be threatened by you, Jed Kincaid," Victoria scoffed. "Why, Hayden would never treat a lady so. Hayden—"

"That's it!" Jed growled. With the ferocity of a springing wolf, he pulled Victoria to his chest so roughly that she began to doubt her assessment of him. Frightened, she wondered just where this snarling male's rage would take her, when quite unexpectedly, his mouth descended upon hers, hard and demanding.

Not only had he touched her, he had done so unwashed and unshaven. The sheer masculine force of him took Victoria by surprise. He was fierce and primitive in the way his mouth laid claim to hers. It was most ungentlemanly. It was totally... wonderful. In Jed Kincaid's embrace, Victoria forgot the desert, Ali and even Hayden. But most amazing of all was the manner in which she forgot herself, submitting to Jed's punishing kiss and then relishing it, exalting in it, shamelessly abandoning herself to the continued pressure of his mouth.

She could not deny that the streak of brutish masculinity she had claimed to find repulsive now had her enslaved to the will of the reckless American she had once considered her inferior. What a perfect idiot she had been, Victoria conceded as a delicious sensation began to engulf her. Jed Kincaid, unpolished as he appeared, was superior to any man she had ever known.

Pressing her soft, feminine form against his hardened, masculine one, she moaned softly, impatient to see what would occur next. But of all the things she had anticipated, she never imagined being abruptly released. Suddenly, Victoria found herself standing alone, while the man who had set her senses aquiver stepped back, angrily muttering words she couldn't decipher.

Feeling more vulnerable than she ever had, even during those despairing hours in the slave pens, Victoria wanted to pluck at

Jed's sleeve, to beg him to tell her what she had done wrong. Apparently he hadn't found much to enjoy in the response she had given him. For the first time since he had come swaggering into her life, Victoria found herself without a sharp-tongued comment. Lowering her eyes to erase the sight of Jed's glowering, she turned and walked back to camp, staring blindly out over the waves of sand.

Jed watched Victoria go. Unconsciously, he wiped the back of his hand across his mouth, his stance rigid. He hadn't liked that kiss—not one bit. It certainly wasn't what he had expected.

Victoria Shaw was no ice queen. Her skin had been hot and moist, the response she had left lingering on his lips seared his mouth still. She had quivered beneath his touch, sending sparks of hungry sensation coursing through his own body.

"You should not have done that," Ali commented reprovingly from where he rested in the desert's deepening purple shadows.

"You're damn right I shouldn't have," Jed concurred. But his reasons for agreeing with the Egyptian had nothing to do with morality and everything to do with the fire burning in his loins, a conflagration that threatened to devour him and any shreds of common sense and decency he had left.

What had driven him to give in to impulse and take Victoria Shaw in his arms? The lines of her perfect body emerging from the water of the oasis sprang readily to mind, until he hurriedly banished them, once more blaming his weakness, though with less conviction than before, on not having had a woman in quite some time.

It *couldn't* have been that he was susceptible to Victoria Shaw, he argued silently with that part of him that demanded he take her in his arms again. He had been able to walk away from her bathing site without touching her, after all.

No, he had merely thought to silence her, to show her once and for all who the trail boss was, to demonstrate that fine manners and manicured hands had nothing to do with a man's worth. But without even trying, she had taught him something, as well. He had learned no matter what reason it was that had driven him to kiss her, Vicky was a beautiful, desirable woman. And with that admission came an unwelcome realization. He wanted her. He wanted her badly.

Snorting in self-derision and silently swearing that he was nothing if not loco, Jed left Ali where he was and walked the short distance to the campsite. Stalking over to his saddlebag, he extracted a fresh *gallabiya*. Perhaps the cool waters of the oasis would extinguish the fire that still burned in his blood, singeing his heart each time it beat.

"You'll want to go sit with Ali," Jed all but snarled, fixing Victoria with an intense stare that made them both uneasy.

"I'm content here," she mumbled, hardly daring to move.

Damn it, did she have to look at him with eyes as velvety as a doe's? He never had gotten over his aversion to training his rifle on a doe, hunting them only when no other food was available. Well, it was an undeniable fact that he was starving now, though in quite a different fashion, and Victoria was the only quarry around. He had to send her scampering on her way before his ravenous appetite got the better of him.

"You might be happy sitting there now, but how will you feel while I get ready for my swim?" Jed asked, shedding his already opened shirt and moving his hands to the buttons of his trousers.

"Oh!" Victoria exclaimed, her eyes widening with understanding. Scrambling to her feet, she darted past Jed, a deep crimson staining her already sun-reddened skin.

Jed would have laughed aloud at Vicky's haste if her departure hadn't made him feel more miserable. He groaned, removed his remaining clothing and plunged into the small pool as if it were the only thing in the world that could grant him salvation.

But refreshing as the water was, it brought him no relief from his burning arousal. Was this what hell was like? Jed wondered abjectly when his traitorous imagination conjured up visions of what it would be like to share this pool with Vicky.

In desperation, he resorted to sternly reminding himself of what it was he detested about women like the decorous Miss Shaw. How could one kiss have caused him to forget, even for a moment, that Vicky was spoiled, pampered and demanding?

Suits and ties, fancy parties and fancier manners, these were the things a woman like Victoria would expect. There would have to be commitment, stability and some mundane job with a chance of advancement. Once all of these things crowded into a man's life, there was no room for impulsiveness and adventure. Jed scrubbed his skin so briskly it began to sting. Hadn't he learned that lesson after his mother had remarried and she had introduced him, along with his brothers, into polite society? He had walked away from that sort of life before. He wasn't going to embrace it now. It was a foolish man who placed his head in a noose he had already escaped.

Still, with the right man and the right loving, Vicky might not be such a shrew, he mused, until he caught himself and inwardly cringed. He had to be plumb crazy for such an idea to pop into his head. Victoria Shaw and Hayden Reed deserved each other and that was that. As for him, commitment wasn't a word in his vocabulary. He was a free man, with no obligations beyond the irregular missives he sent to his mother in San Francisco.

Horrified by the direction in which his thoughts had turned, Jed climbed out of the pool and stood on the sandbank. He was undeniably tense as the water clinging to him rapidly evaporated in the dry desert air. It was as if he were preparing to escape, to make a desperate bid for freedom by outrunning the nameless demon ready to pounce on him the moment he let down his guard.

There were no two ways about it. Jed grimaced, pulling on his *gallabiya*. Vicky might have the face of an angel, but she was one dangerous female.

Unconsciously crooking his forefinger, Jed ran it around the inside of the *gallabiya*'s neckline, as if he could feel the noose tightening. Vigilance, he swore, that would be his byword until he could turn the disconcerting Englishwoman over to Reed.

Still, now that the moment had come to bring the others back into camp, Jed Kincaid discovered himself hesitating. For the first time in memory, he was at a loss as to how to handle a woman. Part of him yearned for Vicky's company, but that side of him ruled by self-preservation balked at being anywhere in her vicinity.

Baffled, Jed worked his long fingers distractedly through his thick damp hair while he paced back and forth. It was unlike him to be unsure how to proceed in any situation, and it signaled a lack of self-confidence not at all to his liking.

Suddenly, his masculine pride began to stir. In spite of the way Vicky had affected him, and no matter how perilous her blue eyes and ripe curves made her, no female was going to cause him to hightail it. Surely he was man enough to face that little bit of femininity waiting behind the nearby mound of sand.

With a purposeful step, Jed made his way to the others. But his intentions almost crumbled when he rounded the dune.

There sat Vicky, more quietly vulnerable than he had ever known her to be. All at once, Jed felt a guilty flush wash over him at being the reason for her distress. He wanted to go to her and apologize, to enfold her in his arms and tenderly kiss away the furrows marring her brow. In short, a surprised Jed had a fierce urge to protect and comfort her.

At least, that was what he wanted to do until he recognized that there would be no need. It was apparent that a sympathetic Ali had already taken it upon himself to tend to that. And from what Jed could see, the Egyptian's kindness had created a blossoming closeness between the two.

Moving closer, the American wondered irritably just what words Ali had used to forge such a bond. The haughty English heiress and the Egyptian shopkeeper made an unlikely pair. Yet there were plenty of women who could find the tall, sharp-featured Ali attractive, Jed realized with an unnerving start, and being wounded always guaranteed rousing a woman's natural sympathy.

Well, damnation, that had better be all Ali had aroused, Jed swore silently, coming to stand before the two, his feet planted wide in a challenging stance.

"Time to head back to camp," he barked.

"That would be for the best," Ali agreed, his face showing the strain of exertion. "We have all endured too much this day," he added with a pointed look of reproof in Jed's direction.

Ignoring him, Jed helped the merchant to his feet, reminding himself that gentleness was called for rather than the rough, emotion-releasing movements he wanted to employ.

Slipping Ali's arm around his neck, he was ready to proceed, when he was shocked to see Vicky trying to lend aid with her slight frame on the other side. Immediately Jed's teeth ground together. It would seem he had returned none too soon.

"No, Miss Victoria," Ali protested with a small smile. "I will not allow my weakness to sap you of your strength."

"But, Ali, surely I can help," she argued softly.

"No," he insisted. "Allow me to do this for myself with Kincaid's assistance."

Do it for *himself* with *assistance?* Jed wanted to bellow.
Didn't the man know that if he wasn't supported he'd topple
over at their feet? Was this some ploy Ali was using as an opportunity to impress Vicky? The muscles along Jed's jaw
clenched visibly. Or had the bastard finally remembered he had
a wife back in Cairo?

The journey back to the campsite proved a lengthy and la-
borious one despite the short distance involved. With each inch
Ali edged forward, it became apparent that he grew weaker, so
that a solicitous Victoria began to fuss over him more and
more.

By the time they arrived, Ali's swarthy complexion had
grown white. Jed, on the other hand, could feel the red stain of
anger creeping up his corded neck and across his face, brought
on by Vicky's unwavering concern over the injured man.

Depositing the Egyptian on his bedroll, Jed thought to diminish his own tension through labor, the only release available to him. Turning away from the others, he began to gather
fuel for the fire, hoping the task would give him some soli-
tude. But from the corner of his eye, he saw Vicky approaching.

"Don't bother to dirty your hands. I'll take care of this. You
can go sit with *Ali,*" he stated, sarcasm tinging his words in
spite of his efforts to project a calm, nonchalant exterior.

Victoria regarded him curiously. When she cocked her head
to one side, Jed swore she was about to argue with him. But
instead, she merely nodded in quiet assent and did as he bid.

Jed marked this as the first time she had ever done what he
had told her without causing a commotion. To his mind, she
was all too eager to return to the side of the handsome man who
had shown her a little kindness. With a snort of disgust, Jed got
on with his work.

An hour later, Victoria smelled the tempting odor of food
that began to waft through the oasis as a result of Jed's toils.
It startled her how hungry she was, having thought herself too
exhausted and upset to eat. But the aroma of whatever dish Jed
was preparing brought her appetite to life, so that she waited
impatiently for the American to signal that the meal was ready.

Surreptitiously she had watched Jed complete one task after
another, and been quite taken by his effortless competence. But
his dominance and its toll upon her had lingered in her mind,
as well, no matter how she had sought to obliterate them.

She had attempted to focus on Ali as Jed had ordered, but her mind returned again and again to his last curt directive. There had been some odd, hidden meaning beneath his words, she was certain of it, but whatever it was, it had been beyond her.

Still, she had done as he had commanded and had been particularly conscientious about her duties, too, bathing Ali's forehead, making him comfortable, fetching him a canteen. Yet whenever she had worked up the courage to look in Jed's direction, she inevitably received a black scowl in return. Each glare had prompted her to be more attentive to the Egyptian, but her increased endeavors had earned her more foul looks instead of the approval she sought.

Not that she resented nursing Ali. He had been good to her. Besides, keeping herself occupied would prevent her thoughts from returning to the devastating kiss Jed had planted so firmly on her much too willing mouth, the kiss that haunted her still.

Stealing another glance at Jed as he moved through the camp, Victoria knew that it was best to keep away from him. Certainly it was better than having to deal with the sense of disloyalty to Hayden that had begun to eat at her conscience whenever Jed was around. And so she turned her attention to Ali once more, blocking out all else until finally the Egyptian drifted off to sleep. Then Victoria leaned back against a small date palm and closed her eyes rather than allow them to hungrily roam the landscape for one more peek at Jed Kincaid.

Her self-imposed isolation was short-lived, however. Though Victoria couldn't see him, she sensed Jed standing before her, obstructing the remaining rays of the sun. Fluttering her eyelids open, Victoria felt her breath all but catch in her throat at the sight of him. Some time within the last half hour, he had evidently returned to the small pool of the oasis in order to shave.

Bereft of the stubble that had covered his cheeks, Jed was more appealing than ever. The lips that had given her such pleasure were now more defined. And the clean lines of his cheekbones and jaw endowed him with a compelling masculine beauty. As he stood there in his *gallabiya* looming over her, he had the look of some magnificent desert prince, the sort to abduct young women, not return them to their fiancés.

"Here," he said gruffly, hunkering down and pressing a cup into her hands instead of the dinner she expected.

"Oh, you've brewed tea," she exclaimed in delight, feeling flustered by his commanding presence and baffled by his charity. "It's a bit cool, but I'm sure it will taste delicious."

"You're not supposed to drink it, Vicky."

"Why ever not?" she asked, blinking her eyes in confusion.

"Because I said so," he responded. He produced a square of cloth and dropped it into the cup. Then his sure fingers wrung out the excess liquid, and he used the material to bathe part of her face, his touch more gentle than Victoria would have imagined.

"Use this on any skin that was exposed to the sun, including that leg you had peeping out from the slit in your skirt," he said, his voice husky. "It will take out the sting."

Before Victoria could respond, Jed got hastily to his feet and departed, leaving her to complete the task he had started.

Chapter Nine

By the time Jed stretched his long, muscular frame upon his bedroll later that night, he was in a much better state of mind than he had been all day. It wasn't going to be impossible to ignore Vicky, after all, he asserted, a satisfied grin seizing his mouth, and the taste of *zabeeb* lingering on his palate.

Of course, it would have been a whole sight easier if he had behaved himself to begin with. It had been outright foolish to go to the pool when she was bathing, and danged reckless to kiss her. But still, he had managed to survive the day without succumbing altogether, and for that he was thankful.

Oh, there might have been a few instances when he had been tempted to surrender. Despite his best intentions, he had not been able to resist touching her when he had brought her the remedy for sunburn. Yet, when he had caught himself becoming faintly aroused by what he was doing, he had been strong enough to walk away, no matter how much he had wanted to stay.

Dinner, too, had been a dangerous situation. Sitting there watching her pick at her food and glance up at him nervously had nearly prompted him to assure her that she had nothing to fear from him. But he had managed to hold his tongue and the meal had proceeded, a strained affair at best. As a result, the tension that had hung in the air became a wedge driving Vicky and him further apart, in spite of Ali's attempts to initiate conversation.

Afterward, when the cookware had been washed and stored away, it had been easy enough to keep himself distracted. There were chores to be seen to before their departure prior to dawn. And when Vicky had timidly come forward asking how she could help, he had assigned her jobs that would take her well away from him.

While it hadn't escaped his notice that Vicky had engaged in easy conversation with Ali, the pair sharing a laugh or two, he had happily been able to disregard it by concentrating on cleaning his pistol and the rifle usually slung from his saddle. He was to be commended for his restraint, Jed thought, even as he pushed the image of Victoria's fair head bent toward Ali's dark one from his mind.

Now, however, everyone had finally settled in for the night, Vicky's bedroll tactfully moved to the other side of the campfire. Consciously keeping his eyes on the stars overhead, Jed offered himself hearty if silent congratulations for replacing lust with caution.

He'd make a push to reach Cairo as quickly as Ali's injury would allow. Surely, if tonight was any indication, he'd have little trouble keeping Vicky at arm's length until then.

Contented, he shifted to his side so that it would be the sight of the desert that greeted him, and not Vicky, should he open his eyes. He was just drifting off to sleep, when soft movement in the middle of the camp sent adrenaline speeding through his body. Jed's senses came rapidly alert and his muscles tensed. Yet only silence followed. He had found himself in peril too many times in the past, however, to ignore the warning signal his sixth sense had sent him.

Casually rolling over, as though in sleep, Jed turned to the campfire, his fingers tightening on the pistol he kept beside him. Slowly, he opened one eye, his body prepared to react.

The sight he encountered shook him. Here he was poised to kill and the only figure visible in the dim glow of the campfire was Vicky Shaw.

What the blazes was the woman up to now? he wondered cantankerously until he saw her slight form shift to pull her blanket closer against the chill of the desert night. He swore he could even hear her teeth chatter as he lay watching her.

Tarnation! What had he just been telling himself about keeping the woman at a distance? It would appear his self-congratulations had been premature. Propping himself up on one elbow, he heaved a mighty sigh, silently cussing what he was about to do. But now that he had witnessed Vicky's distress, Jed found it impossible to turn his back on her.

"Come here," he called begrudgingly. He raised a corner of his blanket and indicated an empty spot atop his bedroll.

It took Victoria a moment to adjust her eyes to the darkness beyond the campfire. But when their focus was complete, she understood why he had summoned her.

Trying to sort out her conflicting feelings, Victoria hesitated. Was Jed Kincaid offering her only the warmth of his body, or did he want her near for other reasons? It certainly had not taken much effort for him to elicit a response when he had kissed her. Could he be expecting such enthusiasm tonight, as well?

"The offer's not open all night," he said, seeing her waver. "I need my sleep."

All at once Victoria knew there was nothing lewd or suggestive in the invitation. It was a simple act of generosity. She moved to join him with a grateful nod of her head and crawled beneath the blanket he held aside for her.

"It's hard to fathom how a place so hot in the day can turn so cold at night," she whispered. Not waiting for a reply, she fitted herself to Jed's hard, masculine length, not so much snuggling as huddling against him. Far from the disturbing sensations she had expected in being so intimately close to Jed Kincaid, Victoria discerned only his warmth as it slowly spread to her, that and a delicious feeling of security. Before she knew it, she had fallen contentedly to sleep.

Aware of the slow, even breathing of the woman next to him, Jed craned his head to look at her face, so peaceful now in slumber. Dang it all! he thought miserably, a deep frown creasing his face. It was going to be a damned difficult feat to keep Vicky at arm's length when she was curled up right alongside him.

"All right, Vicky, time to move out," Jed ordered, shaking her awake in the pale gray light that presaged dawn.

It was evident that Jed had been up for a while. Most things were packed away and the horses were saddled, including her own. Victoria felt touched by his consideration until the swaggering American began to bully her and impersonally bark orders.

"Wash up if you want to, there'll be no oasis for us to stop at tonight. Shake out the bedding and roll it up, then water the horses," Jed commanded. "After that, you'll find coffee near the embers of the campfire, and there's some dried fruit and bread, as well. I'll be busy with Ali. The fool thinks he can sit his horse today."

Stalking away, Jed shook his head and muttered, his words quite audible in the stillness of the sandy wilderness. "As if I need him falling off and injuring his ugly hide again. How the hell does he expect me to drag him and some damned, pampered woman across the desert if that happens?"

As she splashed water over her face, Victoria found it hard to believe that the man who had kept her so mercifully warm last night could be so callously cold today. In the darkness he had shared the heat of his body, but with the dawn, it appeared he was willing to give her nothing. There was no attempt at friendship or even civility. Yet she couldn't blame him for his abruptness when she considered the responsibility he shouldered. Their lives depended upon Jed. For the first time Victoria felt as though she were a burden to him. The idea made her feel guilty, prompting her to do her share of the work and more. She put aside the mystery that was Jed Kincaid, knowing she had to concentrate on survival. After she returned to Cairo and he was gone, there would be plenty of time to think about Jed. But somehow such a realization seemed suddenly very sad rather than the comfort it was meant to be.

Appreciating the fullness of the *gallabiya* she wore and the freedom it gave her as she set about the tasks assigned her, Victoria envisioned no difficulty in wearing it for the remainder of the day.

Packing her clothing away, Victoria looked indecisively at the hideous and indecent slave outfit Zobeir had forced upon her. She might not want a reminder of her time in Khartoum, but she dared not leave behind any trace of their having been at the oasis. Quickly she buried the offensive garments beneath the sand, hoping to bury along with them all memories of her encounter with Zobeir.

Victoria had just finished her chores and had barely raised the coffee to her lips when she saw Jed helping Ali onto his mount, berating the Egyptian all the while.

"I said you could ride only if you agreed to *this*," Jed insisted, fishing a thick rawhide strip from his own saddlebag.

"I will not be tied to my horse," Ali objected.

"If you're not quiet, I'll end up gagging you, as well."

"Why? Because I warned you to stay away from the woman?" Ali asked in a lowered voice that did very little to keep Victoria from hearing what he had to say. "I saw her sleeping beside you when I woke last night. She belongs to another man, Kincaid."

"And just what were you doing looking to see where she was?" Jed wanted to know, obstinately refusing to defend himself.

"I would protect Miss Victoria with my life," Ali proclaimed in a fierce whisper. "It matters not to me from whom."

"Is that so?" Jed inquired, his voice casual but his eyes flashing dangerously. "Seems to me that's a mighty great length to go for a woman you just met."

"You've known her hardly longer than I," Ali asserted, "and see how possessively you behave. I remind you once more, the woman is Reed's."

"He's welcome to her," Jed said with a grunt, moving Ali's hands out of the way and deftly winding the leather thong around the Egyptian's waist, then tying it to the saddle horn. "There. That ought to keep you perched up there for a spell."

"Such precautions are not necessary," Ali repeated, clumsily trying to undo the knot Jed had fastened.

"It is unless you want to be strapped to the travois again," Jed pronounced with a glower. "Now, leave that damn binding alone or I'll tie your hands to the saddle horn.

"Time to mount up, Vicky," the American called before Ali could begin voicing his objections again. Swinging himself up effortlessly into his saddle, Jed glanced over his shoulder to make certain Victoria did as she was instructed, then led the way from the oasis without another word, his tall, *gallabiya*-clad form appearing as though it were fashioned for a life in the desert.

For the rest of the morning, Jed remained taciturn. On occasion he looked in Ali's direction to see how the shopkeeper fared as the morning heated up with brutal intensity. But he assiduously made sure his eyes never fell on Vicky. Having her beside him last night had taken its toll. The soft feminine feel and scent of her still lingered in his mind so that he had faced today with new resolve to have as little as possible to do with her.

After a few hours of pushing the horses as much as he dared, Jed glanced up to find the woman he was trying to forget pulling abreast of him, demanding his attention.

"I need some water," she announced. She eyed him nervously even as the rasping of her voice supported the truth of her words.

Tarnation, Jed thought, his frustration escalating. Vicky was looking at him as if she expected him to jump all over her simply because she was thirsty. Not that he wouldn't like to pounce on her like some big cat on its prey, he admitted ruefully, but didn't she know by now that he would never hurt a little bit of a thing like her, no matter how he might sometimes roar?

Oh, he'd been willing enough to tease her and bait her when he had wanted to see her riled up. Now, however, everything had changed. If he didn't leave her alone, he'd chance a repeat of the urgent kiss he had given her yesterday. And if that occurred, he knew there was no telling where it might lead.

But for all his fine, monkish vows, Jed was well aware that the night still loomed ahead of him, when there would be no fuel to be found and thus no fire. Without that, they would be colder than they had been previously, and he knew what that portended. He almost groaned aloud at the prospect.

His face dark and brooding, Jed wordlessly handed Victoria a canteen as Ali rode up beside them. At least the Egyptian looked none the worse for his hours in the saddle, Jed noted. With a sidelong glance at Victoria, the envious American only wished this journey could prove as innocuous for him.

The rest of the morning proceeded without incident, the trio halting shortly after noon for a few hours' respite. Setting up a small canopy with the travois poles and a blanket, Jed noticed Victoria watering the horses and then setting out bread and dried apricots for a light luncheon. It was remarkable how a woman who had probably done nothing so physical as dress her own hair had suddenly become adept in the ways of the desert, Jed mused, until he realized that if he wanted to rest, all thoughts of Vicky would have to be banished. And sleep during this hottest part of the day would be essential, he knew, in light of the restlessness nighttime would bring.

His efforts had little result, however. Jed found himself far from refreshed when they set out again late in the afternoon, journeying until the purple haze of twilight began to color the desert's golden sands. Choosing a small indentation between two larger drifts, Jed signaled the others to stop. Again Victoria helped without being told, which caused Jed to wonder if she wanted as little contact with him as he did with her. Maybe he didn't have to worry about her seeking him out once the sun had completely disappeared.

After a simple dinner, Jed retrieved his precious supply of *zabeeb* and tried to pass it around, hoping Vicky would find the warmth it imparted preferable to last night's source of heat. But, with a shake of her blond head, she declined to try it.

So much for that, Jed thought miserably. He grabbed the bottle from Ali and brought it to his mouth, taking a long, deep swallow to fortify himself against what the darkness would force him to endure.

Yet when it was time to crawl beneath the blankets, Vicky went her own way, and Jed began to pray he might still be spared. Ali's soft snores soon rent the quiet of the night, and Jed reckoned that if the Egyptian was that exhausted, Vicky was probably more so. It could be that she had fallen into a sleep so deep the cold was no longer a problem for her. But just when Jed began to relax, he raised his eyes to find Vicky, blanket in hand, standing silently before him.

"Oh, all right, come on," he grumbled, holding his cover aside.

"I tried, Jed," she whispered in apology as she lay down.

"Just shut up and go to sleep," he muttered, his voice indicating just how ornery he felt while he draped both their blankets over them.

To his surprise, Vicky soon complied, the slow rhythmic rise and fall of her chest attesting to her fatigue.

If that doesn't just beat all, Jed thought as he fought to get comfortable. Here she was sleeping like some angel, when her presence was the demon that damned him to restlessness.

The next day followed the pattern of the one before until it was time to avoid the most brutal rays of the desert sun. The group had stopped and Victoria was busy with her mare when suddenly Jed appeared from nowhere, his hand shooting out to thrust her behind him.

Hot and cross, Victoria was about to demand what she had done to deserve such treatment when Ali drew her attention to approaching strangers, four men leading a small string of camels.

Though Jed remained outwardly calm and blasé, Victoria noticed he took the precaution of moving his hand to the pistol stuck into the waistband of his trousers.

"Bedouins?" Victoria asked, taking comfort for the first time during daylight in Jed's nearness. The ominous strength he projected would surely be enough to dissuade anyone from trying to do them harm.

"No, these are village boys, I reckon," Jed said in response, his voice low. "From the look of them, I'd say they are dervishes, probably *Sammaniyeh*, a fairly new sect, and some of them can be downright fanatical. They've very little love for outsiders, folks like you and me. So no matter what happens, Vicky, you damn well better stay quietly in the background. And if I tell you to do something, I want you to jump. Do you understand me?"

"Yes, Jed," she responded submissively. Her willingness to cooperate made him feel better, as did the rifle Ali had retrieved. Its stock rested in the sand, the barrel lying along the Egyptian's leg with deceptive casualness. While his injury would make shooting damn nigh impossible, the dervishes wouldn't know that, Jed thought with grim satisfaction as he watched them draw closer.

"Naharak said," the smallest of the men called in greeting. Thy day be happy.

"Naharak said wemubarak," Jed replied. He was all polite charm, but his fingers remained clutched around the pistol's handle, even though the travelers remained on their camels.

"What brings you out in the middle of the desert?" one of the men asked in his native tongue.

Having no idea of what was being said, Victoria felt an uneasy chill creep up her spine, despite Jed's brash smile and the sure, unwavering quality of his voice as he answered, the strange-sounding words rippling forth from his mouth with apparent ease.

"Why, I'm just scouting out a route for a new caravan master," Jed replied languidly, his fluency in their language impressing the Arabs as much as the firearms he and Ali possessed. But their notice was soon drawn elsewhere. Once their eyes lit on Victoria, they stared like a bunch of hungry buzzards, so that Jed had to fight to ignore the itch of the pistol butt beneath his palm.

For her part, encountering such unsavory characters in the middle of the desert, under any circumstances, would have filled Victoria with apprehension. But with the memory of her recent abduction, terror threatened to run rampant when she attracted the strangers' attention. It was only Jed's presence that allowed her to hope everything would be all right.

"You are off the main route," the leader of the group commented, his eyes impudently caressing Victoria. "Could it be you are lost?"

"No. Let's just say my boss doesn't want his merchandise disappearing somewhere along the more traveled paths crisscrossing the desert. He desires a private route, if you know what I mean."

"A slaver?" the leader asked. His eyes glittered with possibility as he rode closer to openly inspect Victoria.

"The merchandise he wishes to transport is of a more explosive sort," Jed replied with an enigmatic shrug of his shoulders meant to turn the dervishes' thoughts away from Victoria.

"Ah, guns! Yes?" the youngest of the group burst out. "I have heard of such trafficking taking place."

"Mostly he deals in ammunition," Jed informed him. "That's a mighty big powder magazine they've built down in Khartoum. He knows they'll need something to fill it with."

"According to the new prophet, the guns and powder housed there will be much needed, and very soon."

"That's what I've been told," Jed replied, grateful for all poker had taught him about bluffing. "Now I'm sure you boys don't want to detain me too long. The sooner I've finished my job, the sooner your prophet will get what he wants."

"But I see no rifles or ammunition," a more skeptical member of the quartet challenged.

"I told you, I'm just scouting the route," Jed said quietly, his attitude daring the dervishes to call him a liar.

"And the woman?" asked the man to whom the others answered. His silk-laden voice was salacious, though his words were not.

"She's *mine*," Jed stated flatly. To emphasize that point, he pulled Victoria forward and threw his arm over her shoulder, casually allowing his hand to fall near her breast, so that it brushed against her in a most possessive manner.

"As you say," the disappointed stranger murmured, put off by the fierce look of ownership the American wore.

"But perhaps you would consider a swap for the horses," Jed offered. "They're worth more than the woman, anyway."

"True, yet that would leave you without transport," another of the dervishes said quietly as he considered the possibility of killing the two men and taking both the woman and the horses.

"Not when you trade me three of those camels," Jed informed him, calmly withdrawing his pistol and cocking its hammer, pretending to study the mechanism.

Though not a verbal warning, Jed's actions told the strangers they had best beware. Ali's fierce glower made it plainer still.

"Three horses for a like number of camels?" the leader of the Arabs asked, his lip curled into a mocking smile. "You are not much of a trader."

"Oh, I know the horses are more valuable," Jed said with a cavalier nod of his head. "But at the moment, I find the camels would better suit my purposes. We have a lot of desert to cross before we return to Cairo."

"You work with the Mahdi's contact in Cairo?" the youngest and least cautious of the men asked in surprise before the admonishing glares of his fellows caused him to fall abashedly silent.

"All you have to know about me is that I trade horses for camels. I assume we have a deal," Jed stated, his eyes sliding meaningfully along the barrel of his gun.

"So be it," the chief dervish pronounced. "It is done."

"Good," Jed replied as a slow, lazy grin made his white teeth glisten. "Ali, make certain our saddlebags, bedrolls and provisions don't disappear."

When Ali moved away from their small group, a curious Victoria began to turn in the direction he had taken. But the additional pressure of Jed's arm across her shoulders kept her docilely in place.

"Smile, sugar," she heard Jed hiss when she started at seeing her mare and the other horses suddenly being led forward. The look in his eyes told her she dare not make a fuss, but damn the man, couldn't he give her some indication of what was happening? He knew she didn't understand Arabic.

"I'll take those, too," Jed announced when two of the dervishes began to remove the saddles, richly adorned with velvet and silver, from the riderless camels.

"Our bargain mentioned nothing about that!" the leader protested, his already-wizened face twisting in determination.

"That could be, but they don't really belong to you," Jed drawled. "Three riderless camels rigged out like that suggests to me that you have either lost three comrades, or more likely, that you set upon the original owners and killed them. That's no concern of mine," the American continued, holding up a hand to signal the dervishes to silence when they all began to talk at once. "But I'm a fair man. I didn't say anything about the water skins the horses will need in order to get to the next oasis, either. The water skins for the saddles...and the bridles."

Though Victoria had no idea what Jed had said to set the Arabs muttering discontentedly, she nevertheless breathed a sigh of relief when she saw the leader nod in assent. She couldn't wait until the strangers departed so that she could find out what had taken place, *and* move out from beneath Jed's impudent hand!

"You are shrewder than I thought," the leader said at last.

"Meaner and faster, too," Jed added with studied nonchalance as he twirled his pistol with lightning speed once around his finger as though it were a six-shooter.

"You will have what you desire," the other man replied tersely. Then he ordered the camels brought forward ready to ride.

"That's always been my aim," Jed said with a chortle that died away when his gaze came to rest once more on the woman he held beside him. She was one thing he wanted. But damn it all, she was also the one thing he couldn't have.

Jed's abruptly ended laughter meant nothing to Victoria, who watched as three sets of reins were exchanged for three others. Horror held her enthralled every bit as much as the relentless restraint of Jed's arm when she began to suspect what had just taken place. He wasn't really going to ask her to ride such a beast, was he?

Soon it became all too apparent that was exactly what Jed intended. She silently swore that once the dervishes left, he'd learn he had acquired not only the camels, but a hellcat as well.

"Khattar khairak," Jed called as the Arabs left. May your goods be increased.

Turning to regard him with a stony countenance, the leader offered no polite reply. Instead, he and his men began to move swiftly across the burnished sands.

The instant the strangers were well under way, Victoria twisted out from beneath Jed's hold, batting away the hand that had thrilled as much as annoyed her, keeping her where he had wanted her.

"Why did you give away our horses?" she demanded furiously, choosing to deal with that topic first so he would have no inkling as to the devastating impact of his accidental caresses.

"I traded them, not gave them away. And you're lucky that's all I bartered," Jed growled, wanting to irk the blond virago by telling her how much he had been tempted to rid himself of her, as well. But the lie stuck in his throat, unable to pass his lips.

"And what is that supposed to mean?" Victoria asked, placing herself in front of Jed when he tried to sidestep her.

"Nothing, Miss Victoria," Ali interjected, attempting to forestall more trouble. "There was no insult intended. In fact, to keep you safe, Jed told the dervishes you were his woman."

"Did you have to do that?" Victoria asked, her cheeks aglow with anger too long denied. And did she have to wish it were so? she thought in self-rebuke.

"I did if you wanted to stay with us rather than ride off with them," Jed retorted. Didn't the woman have any idea of the sacrifice he had just made, letting her get close to him, pretending she was truly his to protect, all this when he wanted nothing so much as to forget her very existence? "You can thank me later," he commented acidly.

"The only thing I'll thank you for is to keep your hands off me in the future," Victoria answered.

But her indignation made no impression on Jed, who calmly placed his hands around her waist. Picking her up, he carried her over to one of the camels, ignoring her flailing hands and kicking feet.

"I surely would love to finish this friendly conversation, Vicky," he said, his voice edged with grimness, "but it will have to wait. Right now I want to get us the hell out of here before those fellows decide to double back. Ali, help me get our stuff stowed on those critters pronto.''

"Pronto," the Egyptian echoed with determination, never having heard the word before but knowing just what it meant.

"Urkud!" Jed sternly issued his command to the smallest of the beasts. The camel quickly lay down as it had been ordered.

"Hold on tightly, Vicky," Jed suggested with amusement, dumping Victoria unceremoniously onto the saddle.

"Kam," he shouted, and the beast obediently began to rise. In an ungainly motion, it unfolded its forelegs first, so that Victoria screeched unashamedly when she pitched backward, afraid she would tumble over the animal's hindquarters to the ground. But before she could do so, the camel gained its back feet, as well, and the apprehensive Englishwoman found herself sitting altogether too high above the ground to suit her tastes.

First a horse, then a camel. Who knew what the wild American would expect her to ride next? Victoria fumed, until an unbidden answer arose half formed in her mind, causing her to blush furiously and lapse into uncharacteristic silence.

Taking the saddlebags from Ali, Jed did not question his good fortune when Vicky suddenly fell quiet. He was too intent on slinging the supplies across the neck of the camel he had chosen as his.

"Rah!" he called, settling himself. Go. And the travelers set out under the sun's punishing rays without further delay.

Jed drove the little band later than usual that night, wanting to put as great a distance as possible between them and the dervishes. It was not that he really expected the Arabs to be so foolish as to try anything; still, his natural instincts cautioned him to err on the side of safety.

Besides, there was another, more disturbing, reason that made him wish to keep Vicky and Ali in their saddles well past the hour when darkness had fallen.

The simple truth of the matter was the longer they rode, the less time he would have to spend with Vicky cradled alongside him. Such intimacy had been painful before, smelling the womanly scent of her, listening to her occasional breathy little moans as she slept. And all the while, lying awake with her body pressed against his, he had wondered what it would be like to trace the curve of her neck with his lips, or what sort of provocative sounds she would make if she were lying beneath him, the recipient of those male urgings that were driving him to distraction.

Tonight, however, he knew that the sweet torment he had experienced the last two nights would bring him to the brink of madness, and he couldn't be certain he was man enough to resist sliding over the edge into rapturous lunacy.

It would be so easy to surrender, following their afternoon encounter with the dervishes, he thought with a snort of self-derision. He'd played his part too well, the possessive male willing to maim or kill in order to protect his woman. He had been chagrined to realize that when the Arabs had departed, his feelings had not. They were still running away with him like a driverless stagecoach, careening wildly as he left the path of common sense he had always prided himself on traveling.

But the reins of self-control had slipped beyond his reach for the moment, and he knew he would find it impossible to slow things down and set himself on the right course once again.

He began to understand why he had so often provoked Vicky into arguing. Squabbling was a more acceptable release for the tension her nearness created within him than the one his too-vivid imagination engendered. And because of the emotions he had tasted that day watching the dervishes crave the woman in his care, he was having great difficulty coping with his feelings at present.

And so, in spite of his selfishness, Jed planned to keep Vicky and Ali plodding across the sand, transformed into fine silver dust by the glow of the moonlight, until he was so exhausted Vicky would be no temptation for him when they camped for the night.

On and on they went, the stars dimly lighting their way and the jackals, invisible in the darkness of the night, crossing their path, just as visions of Vicky stole across Jed's mind until he found it hard to concentrate on the things that should be claiming his attention—their survival, for one.

Eventually, however, Jed began to feel his capacity to think become clouded and the rigidity of his body melt into softness with the weariness rapidly stealing over him.

It was safe to stop now, he reflected with relief, finally calling a halt to their swaying ride aboard the bartered dromedaries.

"Urkud," he called to his beast, easily handling its descent as it fell upon its front knees before lowering its hindquarters.

Riding camels was no problem for him. Vicky, however, would need his assistance, he thought, his dark eyebrows drawing together in annoyance.

For a moment, he resented being so totally responsible for her, until he felt himself flush at his uncharitable attitude. He had always seen it as his duty to lend a helping hand to folks in need. When he considered the strangers he had assisted, how could he ever countenance turning away from Vicky when he might make this taxing journey less difficult for her? He couldn't, and well he knew it.

His mouth set in a grim line, he walked to stand in front of Victoria's camel, while she sat pale and fatigued above him, the dark smudges under her eyes evident even in the moonlight.

The sight of her made him feel guilty for keeping her riding solely to ease his own unsettlement. But he hastily brushed that aside. He already suffered from too many emotions where Victoria Shaw was concerned, and he was not about to tolerate another one.

"All right, Vicky, when the camel begins to go down, I want you to stand up in your stirrups and lean back so far that you think you're about to fall on that little tail of yours. That's the only thing that will keep you from toppling over this fool varmint's neck. Think you can do that?"

"I can do anything that's required in order to dismount from this vile creature," she replied through lips compressed so tightly Jed was surprised she could speak at all.

With the camel's unrelenting swaying as they had traversed the moonlit landscape, Victoria had come to understand exactly why the beasts were called the ships of the desert. She was even now experiencing a sensation akin to mal de mer, and she had the awful feeling she would disgrace herself by being sick if she didn't dismount immediately. Who would have ever supposed a few days ago that she would be longing desperately to sit upon the little mare that had carried her into the desert?

"Good girl," Jed said with grudging admiration. Despite her pampered upbringing, the woman had pluck; he couldn't take that away from her.

Wielding the stick used by camel drivers, Jed barked the order that would bring the animal to its knees. Aside from the widening whites of Vicky's eyes, she gave no indication of how frightened she was, though she did scramble off the beast with alacrity.

As the obdurate dromedary took it into its head to rise again, Victoria delighted in having the sand once more beneath her feet. If she hadn't been tired, she would have smiled softly in amusement. The mare, the uneven surface of the desert, even Jed himself, things she had generally detested at the outset of this journey, were suddenly sources of familiar comfort. Dear Lord, but she had changed. She answered Jed's gaze with one of her own. Regarding him in silence, she thought of Hayden, and realized that no matter how much she was transformed, it would never be enough.

Heaving a sigh that might have been exhaustion, might have been regret, Victoria remembered that there was work to be done.

"How am I supposed to unsaddle this demon?" she asked, gingerly stepping closer to the camel who was eyeing her with the same sort of suspicion apparent on her own face.

"You're not," Jed stated. "If you tried to pick up that saddle, you'd only get hurt . . . or else be plain ineffectual. Tend to the bedrolls and scrounge up something for us to eat. I'll see to the animals tonight. Ali can help me if he's fit."

Just then, Victoria's camel decided to allow its usual nasty disposition to surface. It began to bray in a loud, raucous voice, scolding these two humans to hurry in its care. To emphasize its impatience, it spit, missing Victoria by a fraction of an inch.

"Abominable creature," she muttered as she unlashed the bedding from Jed's mount, a beast that was slightly better behaved.

Jed chuckled. For an instant, he had thought Victoria was going to spit back square in the camel's eye. Good God, but she was a fiery woman, he thought, becoming engrossed in the gentle sway of her hips as she walked away to relay his orders to Ali. Even in her rumpled *gallabiya,* so large it was virtually shapeless, and with that ridiculous felt hat perched on her head, Jed found Vicky Shaw to be incredibly sexy. With a whoosh of breath meant to expel her from his thoughts and release the tension building within him, Jed turned to the camel, surprised at how difficult he found it to concentrate on even this simple task.

Once again he had been caught off guard. No matter how many times he had vowed to ignore the woman, where Vicky was concerned, promises were worthless as fool's gold. All nice and shiny on the surface, they had no value whatsoever. He was filled with self-disgust at his inability to remain distant when it came to her.

Exhausted as he was, and caught up in the incongruity of his attraction to Miss Victoria Shaw, Jed Kincaid grew careless. He didn't hear the soft whinnying of a horse in the surrounding blackness. Worse yet, he was completely unprepared for the bloodcurdling yell suddenly severing the tranquillity of the night, accompanied by the blur of marauding horsemen and the glint of moonlight on brandished swords. Before he knew what was happening, a group of brigands, three of whom were mounted on steeds all too familiar, came swooping into the camp.

"Son of a bitch!" Jed exclaimed as he raced toward Victoria, pulling the pistol from his waistband. What the hell was the matter with him, not to have seen this coming instead of mooning around like some useless, lovesick calf? He wasn't a man if he couldn't keep the woman he guarded safe from harm.

Defeat was not something that sat right with Jed Kincaid. He would save Victoria or he'd damn well die trying. About to issue a war cry himself, Yankee-style, the challenging yell dissolved before it truly formed when he saw one of the dervishes riding down hard on Victoria. Though Ali was already engaged in combat with another brigand, he sought to protect her body with his. Yet Jed feared she would be trampled. In an instant, he knew terror of the type he had not experienced since he was a young, tree-climbing boy, when the darkness of the night had hidden all that was familiar. But now, it was forfeiting the unknown, each new and unexplored facet of Vicky that he had yet to uncover, that filled him with dread.

Run, Vicky, he wanted to scream. *Run into the blackness, the safety of the night. I'll find you when this is over.* But he had caught the broadside of a large, curved blade, losing both his breath and gun in the process. After that, he had no wind left for anything but survival. And he had to survive, he told himself, his heart beating in his chest as fast as a steam locomotive, or else Vicky would be lost forever.

Still struggling to get to her side as Ali did his best to fight off the dervish swinging down to capture her, Jed managed to avoid the deadly slashing of two horsemen by staying between them at close range. Feinting right and then left, he rolled under nervous hooves at one point, all in his struggle to reach Vicky.

Yet the two dervishes would not relinquish him. The sharp edge of a sword almost caught him, but Jed's natural dexterity saved him, and he was left with only a scratch running below his cheekbone. Had he not dodged when he had, his head would have been severed from his body, and the awareness of what had almost occurred gave him new vitality as he swore not to fail Vicky again.

Somehow, he was able to retrieve the knife kept in the top of his boot. With a fierce strength born of desperation, he grabbed at the hemline of one of his attackers and, with a mighty wrench, unseated him, bringing the bastard to the ground.

His knife quickly found its mark, but he had barely rolled aside when the second attacker rushed him again. Narrowly escaping the descending blade, Jed turned, the hard planes of his face a deadly mask filled with fury. Grabbing the dead man's weapon and leaping onto the horse left riderless, he engaged the assailant in battle, frantic to dispatch the enemy and hasten to the other side of the camp before it was too late.

Hacking wildly, he advanced, his countenance that of a madman, forcing his foe to retreat against his violent onslaught. Soon understanding that he would be no match for a man who fought so recklessly, the intruder took flight, leaving Jed free to hurriedly cover the ground between him and Vicky.

But as he turned his horse in her direction, he saw her being lifted up onto the leader's saddle. The dervish sneered at her fruitless attempts to kick and scratch while Ali was busy fighting for his life with yet another of the raiders.

"Vicky!" Jed yelled loudly. Her name was torn from his throat in a roar of anguished fear and pain so rife with emotion that if either of them had truly listened, they would have heard in that one word all of the things Jed felt but had never admitted, even to himself.

However, there was no time to consider anything. There was barely time for action. Without a care for his own safety when the leader raised a rifle and aimed in his direction, Jed charged. Instinctively, he threw his arms around his mount's neck and slipped from the saddle, riding suspended above the ground along the side of the horse like some warring Indian brave.

Cursing that his target had eluded him, the dervish turned his attention to Victoria and escape. But before he could do so, Jed was beside him, leaping upward from his horse to the stallion. He landed on the rump of the skittish beast, where the dervish and his rifle no longer posed a threat. Mercilessly, Jed crooked a powerful forearm around the villain's throat and squeezed.

His supply of air effectively stopped, the Arab's hands flew to his neck to fight off Jed's muscular arm, while Victoria jumped from the saddle. Ignoring the rearing and pawing of the nervous horse, she was only concerned for Jed's safety. Her anxiety grew when she saw the dervish pull a knife just as the two men fell to the ground, engaged in a life-and-death struggle.

She had no reason to worry. Summoning every reserve of brute force he possessed, Jed tightened his arm around the abductor's neck and a snapping of bone signaled the fight was over.

As Jed rose to his feet, his lungs gulping for air, the two dervishes who had survived made ready to flee. While the one retreated from Ali, the other grabbed the reins of the riderless horses. Then they galloped swiftly into the night leaving the bodies of their fallen comrades behind.

Barely conscious of Ali picking up a rifle and somehow managing to discharge shots in the wake of the attackers' departure, Jed paid them little heed. His only concern at the moment was that Victoria had not been harmed.

Holding out a protective hand, he helped her rise from the spot where she had remained on her knees in the sand. When his fingers closed around hers, he became aware of her trembling and castigated himself for having allowed the raid to ever take place.

"Are you all right?" he asked. His voice was husky as his eyes swiftly moved in assessment over her slight form.

"Yes," she replied, her vulnerability obvious. But she paid no heed to her own needs as she tenderly wiped the blood from his face. "You're a brave man, Jed. Thank you for saving me."

At her words, a steely look descended like a curtain across Jed's eyes, turning their clear emerald green to a smoky hue. Saving her? It was *his* fault she was nearly kidnapped. Why didn't she understand that? Jed asked himself, rejecting any rights he had to accept this woman's thanks.

But Vicky didn't seem to comprehend his blame in the matter. Instead, she stood on tiptoe, her hand against his cheek, coaxing his head down so that she could place her lips against his as a sign of her gratitude.

Feeling unworthy as he did, Jed could not bear Vicky's touch, let alone her kiss. He drew back from her, ignoring the look of hurt confusion in her eyes, and busied himself with replacing the saddle he had only recently removed. The pain that had sliced through his heart when he thought she would be stolen had told Jed that he could never kiss this woman again. It was too dangerous. Nor could he ever be lax with her safety. From now on, he would take every precaution available, no matter how needless it appeared to be.

"What are you doing?" Ali demanded indignantly.

"What does it look like?" Jed retorted, his voice laced with anger. "I'm getting ready to take us the hell out of here before those boys come back with some of their friends."

"I agree we should remove ourselves from this place," Ali continued. "But must it be so soon, before Miss Victoria has had an opportunity to properly recover from her fright?"

"I don't want to gamble on another bushwhacking," Jed said with a calmness that belied his still-racing heart. "If that happened, there's every possibility there would be no chance for Vicky to recover—properly or otherwise. We're leaving here now."

"Miss Victoria?" Ali questioned gently.

"It's fine, Ali," she said, patting his hand and finding comfort in the human contact Jed had denied her. "Don't worry about me. I'm sure I'm too unsettled now to sleep or even rest, anyway."

Grunting his approval, Jed helped Victoria mount up, and then proceeded to lead them on through the starlit night.

Taking the time to look over her shoulder as her camel followed Jed's, Victoria's keen gaze took in the remnants of the destruction they were leaving strewn across the sands. She found her heart hardened when her eyes came to rest on the corpses of the two dervishes. Had Jed not been so skilled, it might have been his body and Ali's she was leaving behind.

Turning to face front once more, she regarded Jed with a shy, sideward glance. To Victoria, his proud, chiseled profile silhouetted in the moonlight was surely one of the most beautiful sights she had ever seen. The stubble that dotted his chin was no longer repulsive to her, but merely an indication of his extreme manliness. And though he could be domineering, reckless and crude, lacking in all of the social graces she had been raised to value, Victoria Shaw had come to recognize that Jed Kincaid was quite a man in his own right. He appeared to follow some code of his own, one that was more demanding in some respects than the one society adhered to.

This night he had unselfishly risked his life for hers. The manner in which he had fought to save her might have made her think she was important to him, except for the fact that when it was all over, when she had needed to feel his masculine strength surrounding her protectively and she had attempted to show her gratitude, he had most definitely pushed her away. She didn't understand him at all, or her own reaction to him, but then there were miles of desert yet ahead.

Chapter Ten

Despite the late hour, Hayden's office door opened without prelude and, just as quickly, slammed shut behind the unexpected intruder. About to issue a sharp reprimand to the underling who would dare behave so, Hayden looked up from the papers littering his desk. His angry words, however, caught in his throat.

"Reed—"

"I am very sorry, sir. I was planning on coming to you as soon as I assimilated these reports—"

"Neither Mrs. Shaw nor I could wait for you to build up your courage," said Cameron Shaw coldly. A large man, Shaw gave evidence to his age only in his thinning gray hair. And, at this moment, Victoria's father was confident that his righteous fury would allow him to trounce this pompous paper pusher thirty years his junior without raising a sweat.

Finally concluding his business in Constantinople, he had returned to Cairo only today to find Victoria missing.

His wife and daughter might consider Reed quite the matrimonial catch, but it took all of Cameron's patience not to blame him for this entire situation. After all, what the hell had he done for the past twelve days other than blither about?

"Well, what have you learned concerning my Victoria?"

Recognizing the territorial challenge, Hayden deflected it easily, rising and circling the desk to confront his visitor.

"*My* fiancée was not at the oasis when my men arrived. In fact, there was no evidence to suggest Victoria was ever present. My journeying there would have been pointless, and, as I repeatedly explained to Mrs. Shaw, with my position I would have embroiled England in an international situation had I done so."

"Did you ever hear the word *resign?* If my daughter doesn't come home soon, it would stand you in good stead to learn it. And what about the money my wife gave you? What of the vagabonds to whom you entrusted it? Can you account for them or have they vanished along with my daughter?"

"Why don't we sit down and have a drink while we talk, sir?" suggested the English diplomat. Though he and Victoria's father were of similar heights, standing during any interview made him feel threatened, reminding him of being summoned to the headmaster's office for a dressing down as a lad.

"I want answers, not gin and sympathy," snapped Victoria's father. "Stop dithering and tell me the worst."

"Of course, Mr. Shaw. Actually, there is no worst. I mean, it is true that Victoria has not been found, but we believe that she has been taken to Khartoum—"

"Khartoum? The white slaver's paradise?" Cameron's voice echoed his horror as he sank into a chair. His daughter in such a place? Why then was this idiot standing here so calmly?

"The city does have that reputation, but, remember, the man on the trail of the kidnappers is Jed Kincaid, the same chap who squelched a tribal war. He is quite resourceful in tight situations and eminently qualified for survival in the desert," assured Hayden, praying his sources were valid. "Believe me, I would never have relied on anyone else to rescue my fiancée."

"Then you knew of Kincaid's qualifications before you sent him, did you? My wife did not mention that," admitted Shaw, daring to hope a little.

"Well, frankly, sir, Kincaid's reputation as an adventuring scoundrel is not one I would discuss with a lady like Mrs. Shaw," sidestepped the government employee.

"So then, what is Kincaid doing now?"

"I believe he has pursued Victoria—"

"Don't you know for a fact?"

"I must remind you that once the kidnappers left Egypt for the Sudan, this was no longer a matter for British involvement. Though Egyptian influence extends farther south, ours does not. Besides, Mohammed Rauf Pasha, the governor general of the Sudan, is totally ineffectual in monitoring Khartoum. He would be of no help. I have, however, done what I could. Calling on favors past due, I sent a few men after Kincaid to explore the site at which he was to deliver the ransom. They found three natives dead and a message from the American, mentioning Khartoum.'' Unfortunately, reflected Hayden, taking a sip of water, Kincaid's words had not been enough to make him confident of Victoria's safety.

"So, then, your men continued south to meet up with Kincaid and lend him a hand?" prompted Cameron Shaw.

"No, sir, they returned here to brief me."

"Damn! That's valuable time wasted when they could have been there already."

"I violated governmental regulations just sending them that far, Mr. Shaw. Their instructions were merely to observe and report back to me. To tell the truth, I expected Victoria to be safely home by the time those men returned to Cairo, but—"

"Send them now. By river they could be there in—"

"It would do no good. Khartoum may be under the nominal jurisdiction of the khedive, but the man is powerless," protested Hayden.

"I shall contact Tewfik myself—"

"To issue Tewfik a challenge like saving Victoria when he stands no possibility of succeeding could topple his government altogether, Mr. Shaw." When he did not reply, Hayden dared to continue. "Kincaid, if my men read the evidence accurately, killed three men without assistance. That makes him a pretty impressive weapon."

"Just because he's an expert at defending himself doesn't mean he can rescue Victoria. He has to find her, for pity's sake."

"I suspect he already has," said Hayden.

"And if you are wrong?"

"We shall know shortly. I warrant Kincaid will be returning with Victoria sometime in the next week."

"Fleeing from Khartoum, there can't be many routes back to Cairo. Surely you can send men out to find them as they cross the border into Egypt, should they be lucky enough to get that far."

"If they are on the run, Kincaid will make certain his party is not found until he wishes it to be. No, we have only to be patient and Victoria will be in our arms in a matter of days."

"You told my wife that nearly two weeks ago. I hope your expectations are more reliable this time." Without extending his hand, Shaw started for the door, then turned and spoke, his voice deadly still.

"So help me, Reed, if you are wrong about this—or about Kincaid's reliability—I will personally have your head on a silver platter, not to mention your career. Make no mistake. My daughter is more precious to me than my own life, though I doubt a court would convict a father of avenging his daughter's mistreatment."

"And when she *is* returned safely as I am certain she will be?" challenged Hayden.

"As a man of honor, I shall apologize for doubting you and welcome you into my family," acceded Shaw.

Then Victoria's father was gone from the room and Hayden settled shakily into his chair, resting his head in his hands. Please God, he prayed, let Kincaid know what he's doing, for Victoria's sake, and my own.

Victoria was hot, thirsty and tired, not that any of those states was unfamiliar after the last few days. Indeed, she could not imagine a scenario more taxing than the one she was living.

In her weakest moments, wondering if they would ever reach civilization again, the blonde found herself doubting that life as a slave could be any worse. True, Kincaid did not crack a whip or throw her down in the sand to ravage her body, but since their encounter with the dervishes, their fragile truce had disintegrated so that Jed barely spoke to her anymore. All he was interested in now was returning her to her home as quickly as possible.

There he sat, appearing even taller than usual the way he perched ramrod straight atop his beast of burden, as calm as if he were riding his green hills of Kentucky on a thoroughbred. Victoria had to admire Jed's determination, though she prayed daily for him to falter in his enthusiasm just a little. After all, she and Ali were not the experienced desert travelers he was, and his drive was killing them.

At the moment, for some unknown reason, the American had halted his camel and sat staring off to the west. Surprised that anything could distract Jed from his pursuit of the next oasis, Victoria shaded her eyes and looked in the same direction. However, she saw nothing unusual other than a very faint

cloud far off in the distance. That was surely a reason to re-
joice, not worry. If it didn't signal an oasis, it might provide
some shade from the brutal sun.

"Jed, is something wrong?" A deep worry line creased his
normally smooth brow and the sight of it startled her. Rarely
had she seen the American perturbed, even amid the chaos of
Khartoum.

"I think that's a storm bearing down on us. It could be quite
dangerous out here in the open if we're not prepared. Ali, we'll
stop and take no chances—"

"A storm? Even I know it doesn't rain in the desert this time
of year," scoffed Victoria as Jed urged his camel to its knees.

"Not rain, Vicky, a sandstorm, and, believe me, wind-
propelled grains of sand flaying every inch of your skin until
you can't see or breathe is not an experience you'll relish.
Hopefully I'm wrong, though we had better be ready just in
case."

"It seems distant," she protested, twisting about to look at
the dust cloud. To her surprise, it was much larger than it had
been minutes ago. "Oh, I think you're right. It's growing."

"There's no time to waste. Fetch the blankets while Ali and
I try to position these beasts to provide us with a wind screen of
sorts," Jed instructed, forcing her camel to kneel and helping
her down. Victoria immediately set about doing as he requested. "Ali, if we set them head to rump, in a triangle, they
should shield us from the worst of the sand."

"I have heard of such shelters," agreed the Egyptian. He
alighted awkwardly, his shoulder still stiff, then struggled to
turn his camel as Jed indicated. "I have never been in a sandstorm, but, Allah preserve us, it is one more experience I will
have to share with Fatima when I reach home."

"What protects the animals?" asked Victoria.

"Don't worry about the camels. They are bred to handle the
hazards of the desert," advised the Egyptian, sympathetic as
ever to her compassion, though Jed snorted.

"With their shaggy hides and protective eyelids, the camels
are far better off than we are. Judging from how quickly the sky
is darkening," he cautioned, "our lives are the ones in peril."

"It can't be as bad as you make it sound."

"You'll see soon enough. For now, crouch down on the
ground and flatten yourself against the camel in as small a ball
as you can. Wrap the blanket tightly around your body. If the

wind grabs even a corner, it will whip it away and you'll be exposed to sand so coarse that it can scar."

Watching the fear grow in her eyes, Jed regretted his harsh warning, but he couldn't chance her being careless, not when his own distraction had nearly cost her life earlier. Gently he pulled the hood of her *gallabiya* up over the soft hat crowning her hair and tucked a few errant curls inside, his fingers lingering on her smooth cheek. "I didn't mean to upset you, but the desert is a hostile enough environment. In a storm, I can't afford to take any chances where you are concerned, Vicky."

Struggling to answer his unexpected kindness with a small smile, Victoria marveled that this was the ogre who had bullied her on the trail, only to shut her out completely when she had tried to thank him for saving her life. Yet he had allowed her to continue to sleep beside him each night, stealing his body's warmth. The desert sun may have toughened her, but it had softened him, she reflected, bewildered that a man who could treat her so coolly would be so conscientious about her welfare. Then, before she could voice her thoughts, Ali sounded the alarm.

"Jed, you can barely see the sun. Get ready, Victoria."

Obediently, she dropped to the sand and rolled herself in the tightly woven cloth, crawling over to where the camels lay.

"Vicky, keep your eyes closed and cover your face. No matter what, don't let go of that blanket. I'm right beside you."

Then she could hear nothing but a deep throbbing that slowly escalated to a howl. She squeezed her eyes shut as Jed had instructed, but still she sensed the sudden darkness, the terrible heaviness of the air. It was a thousand times worse than the tension before a thunderstorm when she wanted to scream for relief, but here it was the wind screaming and she unmoving and silent.

The fierce gale tugged at her covering, pulling it one way and then the other, teasing its corners, tempting every strand, unseen fingers trying to snatch the prize from her weary grasp. All at once, she felt the first vicious sting of the sand. Penetrating the blanket, it peppered her face like bits of railway grit, sneaking in through a private parlor car's window. This assault, however, was more constant and came from all directions.

"Oh," she cried, shifting position to try to shield more of her body from nature's onslaught. Unhappily, that futile attempt was all the storm needed. Suddenly the blanket was gone, whipped away to dance on the wind. "Ali, help me. Jed—"

"Damnation!"

She had called for Ali first, Jed realized even as he reacted, leaving his own safety behind to care for her. Hurriedly, he kicked free of his own cocoon, abandoning it to the storm. Unable to see for the flying sand, he moved by instinct to where Vicky lay, exposed to the elements. In an instant, he was over her, sheltering her body with his, consoling her with gentle words.

"I'm here, Vicky, I'll protect you. It's all right, Ali," he yelled, hoping his voice would reach the Egyptian before the gusts garbled its message. "You stay where you are."

Spitting out the unwelcome grains of sand, Jed buried his face in the hood of Victoria's *gallabiya*.

"Stay still, Vicky, we'll ride it out together," he urged, his voice muffled by cloth, wind and sand.

Yet, even in the midst of the horrific storm, Jed received recompense for sheltering Victoria's body with his. His face buried against her neck, he became aware of her scent. It was like the sweetest flower, uniquely, specially her, so that the rugged American judged his efforts trifling when compared to his reward.

But the stimulation of one sense suddenly unleashed others, and, just as every night in camp, it unsettled him to be so near her and helpless to claim her favors. Already his body was becoming uncomfortable with this proximity and he prayed not to embarrass himself. Despite his desperation, he could not avoid contact with her, so soft and yielding amid the furor of the hard-driven sand. He groaned against her graceful neck. If this wasn't a prelude to hell, to be so tempted and unable to respond, he couldn't imagine a worse one.

"Are you all right, Jed?" He was so rigid, Victoria found his presence more physically disturbing than comforting.

"I'm fine," he muttered. "Hush until the storm passes."

Well, she would have to take his word for it, she supposed, but *she* was *not* fine. It wasn't that Jed was heavy or that she couldn't support his weight, but rather that her body had softened and grown warmer at his touch. She had been tense and hot when she had waited for the storm to start, but now she felt as if her flesh was being scalded wherever Jed's body touched hers. Her nerves were screaming for release—and the only method that came to mind to effect satisfaction was to turn over and kiss the man above her. That notion, of course, was totally absurd considering the storm, and besides, she was engaged to Hayden.

Her current physical uneasiness was probably nothing more than extreme discomfort, Victoria assured herself, irritated at the dampness between her legs. It *had* to be the storm. She was, after all, facedown in sand, trapped beneath a six-foot male who must weigh at least thirteen stone, her *gallabiya* twisted awkwardly about her waist. Wouldn't any woman feel unnerved with the wind roaring, the waves of sand assaulting her and the length of a masculine body pressed against her?

No, responded her heart, only a woman who recognized the desirability of the male above her would forget to wish for an immediate end to the storm. One fearing for her life would not be concerned with thoughts of a kiss.

Suddenly, with a whimper, Victoria recognized the truth. She had lost all fear of Nature's fury, completely distracted by her body's craving for Jed Kincaid. He was more lethal than she had ever suspected. Without effort, he had laid careless siege to her heart and conquered it. The only question that remained was what she would do now that she understood the situation. Tears began to form at the absurdity of her predicament, but Victoria blinked them away, refusing to give in to her whirling emotions. So wrapped up was she in her inner debate, in fact, that she failed to realize Jed was about to rise until he spoke.

"Vicky, it's all right. You can get up now. The storm has passed," he announced, reaching out a hand to help her to her feet. "Hey, there's no need to look so somber, we're safe."

"Jed's quick thinking saved us again, Miss Victoria. He is a man among men," praised the Egyptian. "Do not worry. He will deliver you safely home to your Hayden Reed. Never doubt that!"

There was absolutely no reason that Ali's reassurances should have released her tears so unexpectedly. She never cried. Never! But she did then—without inhibition.

"Ali, we'll rest awhile yet. Would you fetch the canteens? Vicky, take a drink, maybe splash a little water on your face," suggested Jed. Uncertain how to handle her weeping, he walked away, leaving Ali to deal with her. On the one hand, Jed wanted nothing more than to take her into his arms and ease her pain.

On the other, he had promised himself not to take advantage. If he embraced her, he couldn't be responsible for what happened next.

Victoria Shaw had been through hell, but until now tears had never been her reaction to any of it. What was it Ali had said that upset her so? Jed wondered as he busied himself checking the camels.

The merchant had done nothing more than assure her she would be delivered safely to her beloved Hayden. Could she be having doubts about Reed? If so, it was about time she wised up. There were a million men who deserved a woman like Vicky more than Reed did. Still, it was strange for her to burst into tears when the man's name was mentioned. Just as peculiar was his own sudden cheerfulness. Usually he was completely undone when a woman began to cry.

"Kincaid, I am ready to go on," Victoria called, anxious to flee the site of her self-discovery. Perhaps as she got closer to Cairo, her love for Hayden would resurface and the magnetism Kincaid exerted would lessen. At least, she could hope it would be so. "Can't we start?"

"Have you forgotten my name is Jed?" he reminded softly, pleased she had regained control so quickly. There would be time enough to consider the sandstorm and its consequences later.

"I'm sorry about my emotional outburst, *Jed,* but I fear the storm frightened me more than I expected. I've never witnessed anything of the kind," the young woman explained. She came up next to him and placed her small hand on his arm in a gesture of reconciliation. "And I do want to thank you for saving me . . . again."

Her voice was so tremulous, her eyes so wide and trusting, it was all Jed could do not to sweep Victoria into his arms and assure her that Jedediah Kincaid would always keep her safe. For the briefest of seconds, his overheated brain considered such an action, but Reed was expecting his fiancée. He would return her untouched, Jed vowed silently, as difficult as that was rapidly becoming.

"I—ah, you're welcome, Vicky," he said, searching for words to break the mood springing up between them. "Actually, you provided a pleasant cushion, much softer and more yielding than the sand. In fact, you can cushion me again tonight . . . and we can create our own storm."

"Oh! I should have known better than to expect anything but rudeness from you. You will never change." She turned on her heel and marched to where the camels lay. As she grabbed her beast's halter, Ali approached and took it gently from her hand.

"Climb on first, Victoria, and then I will get him up," the Egyptian suggested. "It will be easier for me than you."

"I don't know. I think she does pretty well rousing males," muttered Jed. "Besides, your shoulder isn't fully healed."

"I am fine, Jed."

"But *I* am in charge," said the American, overriding him.

At Ali's glum nod, Jed replaced him in front of Victoria's camel and got the beast upright. After repeating the effort for Ali, he then mounted the lead camel and forced it to stand, as well. Then, once more they were plodding in single file across the seemingly endless sand, each rider caught in his or her own thoughts.

There was no sign that the storm had ever touched this part of the desert, mused Victoria. Though some might be closer to civilization than others, one rolling sand dune seemed much the same as another to her, unlike men, whose outward appearance varied greatly and didn't necessarily predict the inner man at all.

Jed Kincaid was rough and ragged in looks and manner, yet in treating Ali's wound he had been as gentle as a mother with a newborn. Reared in the backwoods of Kentucky, he was as ferocious as a bear and twice as nasty when crossed, but he possessed strength and passion enough for twenty men. Hayden, as poised and polished as he was after nearly six years in service to the Crown, could never possess Jed's exuberant zest for life. But would such a mercurial soul as Jed Kincaid ever settle down long enough to be loved?

Loved? Where had that notion come from? *She* certainly did not love the man! True, her body recognized him as a male and reacted to him in unsettling ways, but impulses caused by physical cravings were not signs of love. They were but eccentricities of the moment. Or lust, she thought, surprised that her appetites would advertise their needs when Hayden was so far away. Still, with all she had been through lately, she supposed it only natural that the rigors of propriety would collapse, though she would never have expected a man like Jed to topple them. Regardless of her irrational urges, Victoria assured herself, she had absolutely no intention of letting Kincaid touch her again. It was too unhinging an occurrence. She had to start building a wall between them. Just one careless spark and the tinderbox of her heart would explode into flames, flames she feared she'd never control.

Four days more, Jed calculated, five if they were unfortunate enough to encounter another storm or catastrophe. He should be able to keep his hands off her that long. Then, in Cairo, there would be no stopping him in his pursuit of pleasure. Ali might relish the constancy of his Fatima, but Jed Kincaid would celebrate his return to civilization with a different woman every night. No, every few hours his first night, he amended with a grin, already envisioning the choices he would make. First there would be a small-breasted blonde....

"Jed, is it not time to stop for a while?" intruded Ali's voice. "It is well past noon and I'm feeling the sun."

"All right," the American agreed, signaling Victoria. Usually it was she who besieged him for the midday break, but perhaps the sandstorm had tired Ali more than he had let on. "We will not reach the next oasis until tomorrow evening, so be frugal with the water. We already used a good portion of the day's ration after the sandstorm."

"We were filthy and thirsty," explained Victoria. "How else were we to get the sand out of our mouths and eyes without water?"

"I was not criticizing, Vicky, merely cautioning," clarified Jed. Forcing her camel to kneel, he helped her down, relishing the feel of her small-waisted figure between his hands, even as he cursed the increased heat flowing through his veins. He had but to touch the woman and he became aroused.

"I could have managed by myself," she asserted, slipping from his grasp before disturbing sensations began to overtake her yet again. Determined not to let Jed dominate her thoughts as he had of late, she gathered the bag of foodstuffs and the blankets and moved off without another word.

Quickly Victoria took the travois poles from Ali, set up their canopy and spread a blanket beneath it. By the time Jed had settled the animals, she had their meager meal apportioned and was conversing with Ali in the man-made shade.

"You have talked about your shop and your family, but tell me more about Fatima. Clearly you love her very much."

"More than a blind beggar loves the sound of each coin that falls into his cup. Fatima's love gives me life."

"Oh, come now, Ali," scoffed Jed. "Fatima's father's money gives you life—or a livelihood. You might be fond of her, but without that ready cash behind her, you cannot tell me that Fatima would be so appealing." Jed, still smarting from the unfulfilled urges that had arisen during the sandstorm, didn't want to hear or think about love. If he desired anything at all, it was evidence that love didn't really exist.

"Ah, but I can," argued Ali. "My dearest treasure is my beloved wife—and she still would be were her father penniless."

"But it's mighty convenient you don't have to worry about that, isn't it?" pushed an aggravated Jed.

"Insult my integrity once more, American, and I will make you eat your words," threatened the Cairene, jumping to his feet, his fists raised. "I have already said that I wed Fatima for love not money, and by Allah, it is so. Indeed, her father will not pay her promised dowry until she is happily wed for two years, an anniversary shortly approaching. With this unexpected journey from my business and her side, however, a journey that is your fault, Kincaid, I cannot be certain my bride will tell her father that she *is* happy. Perhaps I shall return home to an empty house."

"Ali, I would never let that happen," assured Victoria. "I will explain everything to Fatima. She will understand."

"If Allah wills it," conceded the Egyptian, settling back on the blanket. "I would not let her go without a fight."

"If you hadn't fought back in Cairo, we wouldn't be here."

"And Victoria would belong to Zobeir or who knows who. No, it is good that we saved her from such a fate, and I will tell Fatima so."

"Fatima is lucky to have such a fine husband as you," said Victoria, touched by his gentle words.

"Oh, he's a saint, to be sure," muttered Jed, his pride stung. It did not help that it was his own ill temper that made Ali appear the better man. "And I am just the poor devil who led Ali to Khartoum, who set the explosives so Ali could ignite them, who ran along the beach to rescue Ali, who dragged Ali to safety—"

"Stop being such a child, Jed, and let us get some sleep," admonished Victoria, turning away from him. "Undoubtedly you will be haunting us to move on all too soon."

"Undoubtedly," echoed Jed, doubly irritated because she had read his mood for the tantrum that it was. The desert sun had never affected him like this before, he thought, gulping a mouthful of *zabeeb*. At least the Egyptian liquor would soothe his humor. How long had he figured? Four or five days?

The thought of flinging forty-five hundred pounds of the ransom money—and Victoria—in Reed's face made Jed grin from ear to ear as he drifted off to sleep. That was one pleasure no one was going to cheat him out of.

"I'm sorry, Victoria, but my canteens are nearly empty as well," apologized Ali later that night when they'd stopped to make camp. "I can offer you only a sip or two."

"It will be enough, Ali, thank you. I kept tasting the sand all afternoon and drank more than I should have."

"Splashing it on your face when you thought I wasn't looking wasted a good bit, too," criticized Jed.

"My skin felt as though it was cracking open from the heat."

"Whatever, it's too late to fret about it. Have some *zabeeb* and leave Ali's water for tomorrow."

"I don't drink alcohol—"

"Neither did Ali until he teamed up with me."

She hesitated, debating the issue with herself. She was thirsty and the liquor *was* a beverage.

"Well, Vicky?" Jed offered her the half-full bottle.

For a moment she just looked at it and then she nodded, accepted the liquor and tilted her head back to take a drink.

"Just take a small sip," cautioned Jed, having second thoughts about introducing the feisty female to a stimulant she really didn't need.

"Are you rationing this, too? Well, Kincaid, you're too late," retorted the woman, too annoyed to use his given name. And she had thought she might be attracted to him? To show him exactly what his advice meant to her, Victoria drank deeply, totally unprepared for the sudden inferno coursing its way down her throat to her stomach. Were she able, she would have spit out the burning venom, but she was much too busy coughing and wiping the tears from her eyes.

"Have you noticed she never listens the first time I say anything?" asked Jed in disgust as he rescued the precious bottle from the sand, wet where she had flung it. "See here, she's wasted nearly a third of what was left."

"Damn you, Kincaid. You did that on purpose, knowing I would defy your orders. I could kill you." Her arms extended, Victoria ran at the American, knocking him off-balance and landing atop him. Venting the frustration that had been growing for days, she angrily began to pummel his chest. "That is for making fun of Hayden and for making me swim in the Nile and—"

"Victoria, let Jed up. He is not at fault. You drank—"

"Ali, stay out of this. Someone has to teach him a lesson."

"I can handle her, Ali," said Jed, winking. "Leave us be."

"Do not hurt her," cautioned the Egyptian while she continued to batter Jed's chest and head with her fists.

"Hurt her?" Jed laughed.

"Don't even think of that happening," yelled Victoria.

Then, before she could anticipate his movement, Jed rolled over, imprisoning her beneath him, his weight trapping her hands between them.

"You bastard, let me up right now."

"Oh, uncomfortable, are you?"

"You—you miserable excuse for a man—"

"Careful now, Vicky. Don't say anything you might regret," he drawled. "Your weapon of choice may have been your fists, but mine is my lips and you'll find they can be quite punishing."

Even as the tiny shiver of anticipation quavered in her throat, his hands reached up to her hair and wrapped themselves in its length. Then, gently, he pulled her head up until her mouth met his. Rather than punishing, however, his evocative lips were artfully teasing. They caressed hers lengthily before dancing softly over the contours of her face, brushing feather-soft kisses on her temples and eyelids. When at last his lips returned to hers to nibble delicately, they traced the contours of her mouth in an unhurried exploration. Without warning, his tongue began to lick at the remains of the *zabeeb* on her chin.

Victoria moaned. She found herself responding willingly, pressuring his mouth as he crushed hers, sensing a deepening warmth throughout her body as it released her desires, welcoming the act of loving. Then, just as she was delighting in Jed's embrace, he ended it, rising abruptly to his feet.

"Jed?" she asked in surprise.

"Go to sleep now," he said gruffly, striding away before he lost the will to do so. "Punishment is over."

Punishment? He called kissing her punishment? How dare he be such a fool? She wanted to scream at him in furious frustration, but her pride wouldn't permit it. Then, from deep in the confines of her heart, arose the question. If this heady experience was Jed's idea of discipline, how much more wonderful would it be if he loved her as a reward?

"Kincaid," challenged Ali, moving into the American's path. "That was absolutely despicable. You are a man without shame."

"I walked away from the woman, didn't I?"

"Not finishing what you ought never have started is no badge of honor. Your mother would be appalled by your conduct."

"It wouldn't be the first time and assuredly not the last." Jed gave a harsh laugh. "If you feel the need to protect Vicky's honor, however, you sleep beside her tonight to keep her warm. I'm going for a walk."

"Now?"

"Unless you have a cold stream available, it's the only acceptable alternative," muttered Jed as he strode off into the darkness. "Four more blasted days..."

Ali watched him go without further comment, shaking his head at the foolishness of this pair. Clearly they were attracted to each other, but, just as clearly, he was too stubborn and she was too principled to explore that attraction or even admit it existed. Looking up at the vast array of stars overhead, the Egyptian wondered at the mystery of it.

Chapter Eleven

Tempers the next morning were short since neither Victoria nor Ali had slept well, and Jed, preferring to avoid Vicky's proximity, had never retired at all. After nearly a week on the trail, however, each knew his chores and went about them by rote, clearing signs of the camp and repacking the dwindling supplies. Two hours before dawn, they were traveling again, having exchanged barely a dozen words since rising.

If they rode until noon and then again from five until midnight or so, that would be fourteen hours in the saddle, calculated Jed silently, a lengthy day, but worth the price if they could complete the trip to the Egyptian border in three days rather than the four or five he had estimated earlier. It was becoming too dangerous to linger in the desert with Hayden's fiancée.

Behind him, he heard her speaking with Ali, but, still furious with himself for having taking advantage of Victoria, he couldn't be bothered listening. She was too damned desirable by far, but that was no excuse. At twenty-eight, he wasn't a callow youth, unable to control his urges. Ali had spoken the truth last night. His behavior had been despicable, Jed thought, removing his hat to run a restless hand through his dark hair. During his long sleepless night, he had concluded the only way he could possibly atone for his behavior was to return Victoria to Hayden as swiftly as he was able, avoiding contact with her whenever he could.

Hours later, looking over his shoulder at her, still fetching after days in the desert heat, Jed could not help but admire the woman's stamina. Despite her coddled existence in Cairo, she had blossomed in the desert, meeting each challenge admirably, though usually not silently. In other circumstances... But no, it was out of the question, he admonished himself, startled that his heart was so reluctant to abandon what his mind knew was but a fantasy. They were two completely different people, from two different worlds, and neither was familiar with the notion of compromise. A relationship between them could never succeed, he decided, trying to discard any idea of it once and for all.

"*Rah,*" he bellowed suddenly, urging his camel into a faster pace. Based on the bearings he took at dawn, the oasis should be over the next ridge of sand dunes. They could have a midday break there and press on by late afternoon. "Let's find water."

The expected watering hole was not over the next ridge, however, but two more distant ones. By now, even the usually stoic camels were anxious to slake their thirst, and as they spotted the telltale dwarf palms, Victoria's animal raced furiously down the incline toward the oasis, snorting loudly. She struggled to temper his frenzied run, but he was out of control. Flying past Jed's camel, he galloped straight into the pool itself and began to lap vigorously at the brownish fluid.

"Vicky, pull his nose out of there, right now," instructed Jed sharply, holding his own animal back from the water's edge.

"Have you ever tried to make half a ton of muscle do what it doesn't want to?" she replied. After a few minutes of unsuccessful yanking on his bridle and kicking at his flanks, Victoria shook her own head and gave up. "You know what, Jed? I'm so thirsty I don't care if he did get here first. I'm going to enjoy a long drink, too. In fact, I think I'll follow his example and cool off and drink at the same time. Why don't you come join me?"

"No, Vicky, wait—"

Dropping from her saddle with a gleeful wave in Jed's direction, she landed rump first in the water, laughing in delight. While her camel snorted its annoyance and moved away from her, she splashed about in total joy, finally feeling comfortable for the first time in days.

"Considering the sun's heat, this feels like heaven," she called, ducking her head beneath the muddy surface. As she came up sputtering and wiping the moisture from her eyes, Jed was there beside her, thigh deep in the pond as anger clouds warred behind his eyes.

"Out!" he ordered.

"What is wrong with you? Can't you ever relax and let go of that stern demeanor? Or are you looking for an excuse to 'punish' me again?"

Without further prelude Jed lifted her out of the water and tossed her over his shoulder. Holding her in place with one arm, he grabbed the camel's lead with the other and headed for the sand.

"Kincaid, put me down at once," she demanded, pounding on his back. It was to no avail though as he strode purposefully on, while Ali watched from where he held his and Jed's animals back from the pool.

"I suspect the water is bad, and I don't want to take a chance of your being sick from drinking something poisoned," he explained, releasing Victoria. She slid down gently to stand, dripping on the hot sand. "We'll fill a few waterbags and use them later, if your camel doesn't show any ill effects."

"Poisoned? That is absurd. How could it be poisoned?"

"One trade caravan might have wanted to eliminate another, or perhaps a dead animal contaminated it, but we will not drink here."

"I think you are being ridiculous—"

"No, Victoria, Jed is right," said Ali. "The grass is dead and the date palms are shriveled. Think how green the other oasis was and tell me you don't see a difference."

"That doesn't mean poison—"

"Perhaps not, but as we came down the sands, I saw two half-rotten carcasses. Animals wouldn't have died so close to water if it were potable."

"Can't we at least wade in it to cool off?" She knew she sounded like a petulant child, but the water had felt so splendid, it was difficult to believe it was tainted.

"Absolutely not," answered Jed, eying her wet form regretfully as he struggled to keep himself in check. Were he not so committed to doing his duty, he might enjoy the temptations of the desert. "I'm sorry you exposed yourself to the water at all, but hopefully you won't suffer for it. As for your young camel, time will reveal soon enough whether he'll live to grow old. We may yet be lucky."

* * *

Toward evening, however, it was clear that good fortune was not with them. Victoria's camel had been slowing down, unable to keep the pace Jed set, but gamely trekking across the sand nonetheless. Then, all at once, it began to shudder and dropped to its knees. Shouting a warning, Victoria jumped from its back just before the animal rolled to its side, bellowing its pain.

"Jed, what can we do?" she appealed helplessly as the large body shook violently, spasming out of control.

"End his suffering," he answered, dismounting and grabbing his rifle.

"But, Jed—"

"To leave the beast in agony would be inhuman," offered Ali sympathetically. "Come, walk a ways, Victoria, you need not watch."

Turning aside did not make it any easier. The sound of the shots echoed over the open sand and Victoria knew all too well what they signified. Had she been able to control the animal, he would still be alive. And if Jed had not been able to control her, she realized suddenly with a shiver, her death might well have followed the camel's. Once more, the American had been her protector. When she looked back, Jed was untying the camel's saddlebags and blankets.

"We'll put the extra load on your animal, Ali, and I will take Victoria to ride with me," he said.

"What about the waterbags we filled?" questioned the Egyptian.

"Empty them in the sand and then bury them. We cannot risk using them and carrying their contamination to other wells."

"Jed—" Victoria began.

He was still unburdening the carcass, but he turned at the sound of her voice, anxiety fleeting across his rugged face.

"Are you all right, Vicky? No symptoms, I hope."

"I am fine, except for being embarrassed for doubting you," she admitted softly. He straightened from his task and she stood, unflinching, studying his searching eyes. "You have been right about everything since you rescued me and I've struggled against you every inch of the way. It may not mean much, but I am sorry, Jed. And I do appreciate your saving my life, yet again."

"Who's keeping score?" interrupted the sun-burnished male with a laugh. He found this side of Victoria soft and enchanting and not as easy to dismiss.

"I am," Victoria persisted, determined to let Jed know exactly how she felt. There had been enough hidden between them and she was tired of the subterfuge. "I know you see me as a spoiled debutante and perhaps I was, but I am trying to change."

"And doing an admirable job of it," Jed conceded, reaching down to brush a lock of hair out of her eyes despite his intent to keep his hand off. Worse yet, his fingers lingered on the soft curve of her cheek until he could finally force them to leave.

"It is still quite a distance to the next oasis, however, and even farther to Cairo. Help me carry this stuff to Ali's camel," he ordered gruffly. He hoped the authoritative sound of his words would help *him* restore their relationship to what it had been before he touched her.

Watching Jed maneuver the added baggage onto the camel's back, Victoria was again aware of the gentleness of those strong hands. He was a rare combination of strength and compassion as he helped Ali. Hayden would have stood back complaining while he waited for a servant to complete the chores. But then Hayden was a gentleman, and Jed was just a man, a man with no fear of offending society with his behavior or opinions. A man who would scandalize her parents and Cairo society, warned her conscience.

"Victoria?"

It was Jed, standing before her and using her full name. Why?

"I'll help you mount. You shouldn't be too uncomfortable."

"You called me *Victoria*."

"Isn't that what you prefer?" he asked, his hard green eyes dancing up at her as she settled herself in his saddle.

He was offering her a choice, she realized, noting the tentative smile gracing his lips, as if uncertain it would be appreciated.

"Victoria will do, unless you wish to address me as *Queen* Victoria," she admitted, her laughter bubbling over as she recalled her decidedly imperial attitude in their first days together.

"Nah, you're too skinny to tote that title," he retorted with a grin. In an instant, he was seated behind her on the camel and was urging the animal to its feet. *"Rah!"*

It was hard to keep her eyes open when she was so comfortable, Victoria noticed later that afternoon. While she had been responsible for her own camel, she had to be alert, but it was so pleasant to lie back against Jed's broad chest she didn't care about anything else. Besides, it was still so damnably hot she felt as though she was on fire. Certainly she was completely drained of energy.

"Jed, is there any water left at all, even a few drops? I'm parched so, I don't think I can go on much farther—"

Jed looked down at his companion, disturbed to see that her face was flushed and her skin clammy. Could she have absorbed the poison from the bad water after all and be starting to show the symptoms? Or was she suffering sunstroke or dehydration? In either case there was little he could do until they reached the next oasis, and even with the strenuous pace he had been setting, that would not be for another three or four hours, at least.

"There might be a tiny bit," he said, halting the camel and reaching back to one of the saddlebags. Carefully he put a cloth over the top and upended the container. A few droplets fell on the piece of fabric and he handed it to Victoria. "Suck on that for a while. It should ease the discomfort somewhat. I'm sorry, but it's the best I can do."

It was enough, decided Victoria. Jed *was* protecting her, and that was all that mattered now.

They had seen the campfire at the oasis from the distance before they had doubled back to make camp, and Ali was leery about Jed's plan. They had counted four figures huddled about the flames, but that didn't mean there weren't more.

"Maybe we should just wait until tomorrow morning after they have left," suggested Ali.

"And if they're traveling in this direction, they'll find us before that happens. We can't take that chance. Don't you think that they'll be tempted to take Vicky, just like the others?" disputed Jed, his brow creased with worry. He didn't like the way she continued to sleep so soundly even though he and Ali had set up the camp around her. Her body was warm to the touch, but he consoled himself that it could be the effects of the journey as easily as an illness. "I'll go in on foot and fetch the water under the cover of darkness tonight. Then before dawn, we can circle farther west and avoid them altogether."

"Suppose they catch you filling the water bags?" protested Ali.

"I'll tell them I got lost in the sandstorm and my camel collapsed."

"I would be more believable traveling alone in the desert."

"Ali, you're not strong enough to walk as far as their camp unaided, let alone return here carrying water. No, I'll go. You keep my rifle in case of trouble and look after Vicky." Kneeling beside the sleeping woman, Jed stroked her cheek and once again felt her forehead. "She doesn't seem any warmer than before. When I return, we'll bathe her head."

"And if you don't return?"

"Another day should see you across the Egyptian border, and if need be, you can return to the river for the rest of the trip."

"If you are determined to do this, may Allah walk before you."

"May he abide with you, as well."

His destination was perhaps two miles away, but Jed preferred to be extra cautious in his approach. With a bit of luck, he should be able to sneak into the oasis, obtain the necessary water and escape without notice. Staying close to the ground, he concentrated on stealth rather than speed.

Thankful there was no moon to reveal his silhouette against the sand, the man who found himself so at home in the desert reached his objective in under an hour. The darkness of the sky lent him a tenuous sense of security, yet at the same time it made him all too aware of his smallness amid the workings of the universe. Were he to disappear on this outing, he realized, it would only be Ali and perhaps Vicky who would notice, a sobering thought guaranteed to insure his care.

Jed inched his way slowly around the perimeter of the oasis to survey the goings-on within the campsite before attempting to fetch the needed water. To his surprise, he noted eight horses hobbled near the water hole and felt a momentary twinge of uncertainty. As experienced as he was, even he might be bested by odds of eight to one. Yet the camp the travelers had established wasn't large enough to accommodate that many men, and he and Ali had only spotted four from afar.

Two fellows still sat by the fire and a small tent nearby could possibly hold three others, but no more than that. There were no additional sleeping rolls laid out and he had seen no one stationed as a guard, although two large canvas-shrouded mounds rested near the horses. Perhaps the party was but a group of traders transporting goods south through the desert to Khartoum. If so, it would have made more sense for them to take their merchandise up the Nile, unless they, like he, feared discovery. Maybe these were some of the smugglers that the dervishes had mentioned.

Intent on getting closer to those near the fire so he could hear what the men were saying, Jed stretched his lanky frame on the ground once more and slithered through the still-warm sand. Perhaps they would reveal their purpose and ease his concern about meeting up with them in the morning.

One of the two was whittling, a sharp-bladed knife in hand. A rifle rested not far from where the other sat cross-legged on the sand.

Like those who had attacked them a few days before, these men were dervishes, though more ascetic than the others. Their robes bore no embroidery and their black turbans were dark against the inky sky, with no gem to secure them or signal their station in life.

"Do you suppose that fool Englishman will dare challenge the Mahdi's word again?" asked one of the men idly. "Even though Cairo is far away from the Mahdi, he should have realized our leader has lengthy arms."

"I was surprised the infidel had the nerve to attempt it even once, but since the count of the rifles was accurate this time, Hamid, I would say the villain learned his lesson quickly," said the other, slicing a long narrow strip off the wood in his hands. "Though, should he need another reminder, I could happily do some human carving, perhaps his—"

"I doubt such will be necessary, Jamal, not when he added three extra boxes of gunpowder—as a gift, he said, to make up for his unfortunate error on the last shipment."

"Humph," snorted his companion. "That one *gives* away nothing. Somewhere else he will overcharge the accounts, anxious for a profit rather than salvation, but that is not our province. As long as we deliver what he sells, our job is complete and the Mahdi's rise to power is that much closer. Long live the Mahdi!''

''For now, long sleep his servants! We leave before dawn, so snatch a few hours of rest,'' instructed Hamid. Rising to his feet, he tossed his cup aside and turned toward the tent. ''If you sleep out here, the horses will alert you to any jackals that come calling, the four-legged or two-legged variety.''

''Most caravans use the larger oasis south of here. This one rarely sees travelers,'' agreed Jamal. ''It will be safe enough.''

Safe enough unless he could somehow explode that gunpowder, considered Jed, his mind already hard at work. If only he had some fuses . . . No, what was he thinking? Such a plan would be foolhardy when his main concern was Victoria Shaw's well-being. But old habits died hard, and if he had been responsible only for himself, things would have been different. As it was, he could not chance the dervishes finding his trail and taking the Englishwoman.

Englishwoman, he mused. The Sudanese had mentioned an *Englishman* as their supplier! Someone, supposedly loyal to the Crown, was evidently supplying the Mahdi's supporters with arms and enough ammunition to encourage a revolution in the Sudan.

Now, not only would Reed have to be thankful for Vicky's safe return, but for the opportunity to impress his superiors with this information Jed would deliver about the Mahdi's subterfuge.

Convinced he had learned all he could, Jed slipped back through the darkness to where he had left the two water bags. Carefully removing the stoppers, he took one container in each hand and approached the pool of fresh water, thankful he didn't have to fear contamination here.

A quick look reassured the American that Jamal was still occupied with his carving. Yet Jed would have to either crawl to the water with the man too near for comfort or fill the bags on the other side of the desert spring, closer to the horses. Not willing to gamble on eight animals' silence, Jed slithered to the water's edge. Gradually he lowered the first bag into the pool, trying to minimize the gurgling.

In the utter blackness, it was difficult to tell how full the bag was, so Jed was forced to hoist it out of the water. He froze at the sucking sound the pool made, but there was no outcry. Gently, he grasped the leather pouch and squeezed its neck. When no water spilled forth, he lowered it once more and waited for it to reach its capacity. The task was not only time-consuming, but nerve-racking. How long could he expect to go unnoticed, he worried, turning his head to look at Jamal.

Finally he finished with the first skin. Swiveling about, he laid it on the bank. He only had to worry about one more and then he could head back to Victoria. Already Jed's anxiety about her welfare had replaced his earlier excitement over learning of the peculiar connection between the amassing of weapons in Khartoum and the English in Cairo. Suddenly a horrible thought occurred to him. Would Vicky still be alive when he returned?

He was a fool to worry needlessly, he berated himself, irritated at the unfamiliar emotions plaguing him. Until he met Victoria Shaw, Jed Kincaid had been a man who did his job without distractions, concentrating on nothing but the completion of his task. Now she had him considering tragedies for which there was no basis, and he scowled at such nonsense. Annoyed, he plunged the second water bag below the surface of the pond, realizing too late how forceful his thrust had been.

"Who goes there?" demanded Jamal. The dervish jumped to his feet and looked about in confusion. He hadn't identified the source of the sound yet, but he grabbed his rifle for reassurance. "I heard you moving. Come up to the fire now."

Jed swallowed hard and pressed his body against the sloping sand. With all his being he hoped Jamal wouldn't venture down to the water's edge. If he did, the American would have no option but to kill him.

"I said, come out. There is no reason to hide."

Again Jed played possum, praying for a miracle—or a less than vigilant guard.

"Show yourself. I know you are there," ordered the dervish.

"Can a man have no privacy to answer nature's call?" demanded an unexpected voice from behind the tent.

"What? Who is there?"

Jamal sounded relieved, Jed reflected, though the dervish could not have been any more pleased than he was.

"I drank too much coffee," muttered Hamid, coming forward. "I didn't expect to have to justify myself."

"But the noise was nearer the pool—"

"You heard a stream and assumed it came from the pool," snorted Jed's savior. "Would the horses be quiet if an intruder were about?"

"I suppose not," agreed Jamal reluctantly.

"Get some rest then and stop looking for trouble where there is none."

Then only Jamal was before the tent, looking rueful at having embarrassed his superior. For a rash second, Jed wanted to cheer. Any further noise he made would be dismissed by the guard as his imagination, certainly not worth risking Hamid's fury. Soon enough he could be on his way back to Victoria . . . and Ali.

And so it was. The remaining bag was quickly taken care of and the long trek back to camp did not seem not half so arduous as he expected. Though once Jed Kincaid would have been disgruntled to have passed up the opportunity of engaging the dervishes in a brawl, tonight he felt triumphant simply to be returning to camp with two bags full of water. It was strange the effect a woman could have on a man.

"Well, how is she?" Jed demanded, striding up to where Ali sat next to Victoria.

"Restless, but somewhat cooler when last I checked," the Egyptian replied. "Did you have any trouble?"

"No, though I learned a few interesting things, but they can wait until we're back on the trail." Sinking down beside Victoria, Jed shifted her body so her head rested in his lap. "Pour some water into a cup and add the last of the honey. Then wet a cloth and bring it here."

Ali was quick to obey. Without further instructions, he began to sponge Victoria's forehead as Jed raised the cup to her parched lips, allowing the liquid to just tease them.

The change was gradual, but slowly her eyes fluttered open.

"Don't try to move yet," ordered a voice from behind. "Open your mouth and take a small sip."

Victoria realized it was Jed speaking. He was holding her gently and dripping golden nectar down her dry throat as though it were the most natural act in the world.

"Take your time, Victoria," urged Ali. "You were without water a long while, but Jed has brought us plenty now."

"Brought us?" she whispered. "Didn't we reach the oasis?"

"Shh," urged the man who held her. "There were strangers up ahead so I thought it better to slip in and bring the water back here. Ali is making more of it than it was."

"Thank you," she said softly. Her blue eyes fixed themselves on his, and she tried to express her gratitude with a small smile, trusting he understood her enough to grasp her intent.

Her answer was a gentle caress as Jed bent low over her and touched his lips tenderly to her forehead. Though this was not the action of a man bent on staying away from an attractive woman, coming close to losing Vicky had made maintaining his distance unimportant.

"I know you have a lot to say," he assured her, "but for the moment, concentrate on regaining your strength. We'll have to be traveling all too soon. I want to be long away from here before the dervishes head this way."

"More dervishes?" squawked Ali. Hadn't they had enough grief from the last group? "Let us break camp now."

"Not for a few hours," decreed Jed, shifting his position so he could lie beside his charge and cushion her. "Vicky needs her rest and I've had none."

Snuggling against her protector with a tender smile, Victoria was pleased they had made another truce. In spite of his rough edges, Jed Kincaid was quite a man to know, and with his coolness of late, she had missed him. Now, however, though she could not say how she knew, Victoria instinctively sensed that the gap between them had closed. Oddly enough, that realization was every bit as invigorating as the water Jed had risked his life to fetch for her.

The sky was still a deep gray when they broke camp later, leaving no evidence of their brief stay. As a recovered Victoria knelt to finish tying her bedroll, Jed approached her and, taking her hand, raised her to her feet.

"I know you're exhausted, but if we press on—"

Victoria interrupted his explanation by leaning forward and placing her fingers gently across his lips.

"Considering what Ali has been telling me about your efforts last night, you must be even more drained than I," she said softly. "If you're ready to continue our trip, then so am I."

What had happened to the willful female who had fought im so furiously in the early days of their journey? Under his ery eyes she had evolved into a woman, a gentle, caring voman who thought of others before herself. A woman he was leased to know, Jed thought, *real* pleased.

He kissed her slender fingers where they lay, instinctively opening his mouth and sending his tongue to lick slowly. Then, ealizing the error of his impulsive action, he stepped huriedly backward, ending the contact between them.

"I'm sorry, Victoria," he muttered, awaiting her anger. Having surrendered so mindlessly to temptation, Jed did not need to hear Victoria's objections to his improper behavior. He would be living with the effects of it all day if his body's reaction was any sign. "I shouldn't have done that and I promise ou it won't happen again."

Uncertain whether she was more startled by Jed's intimate gesture or his apology for it, Victoria hesitated before speaking, her blue eyes searching his rugged face for some clue to his feelings. While Jed had just breached society's code, she knew only that his touch had excited her—and *that* was her sin as much as Jed's. Engaged to Hayden, she should not be welcoming another man's caress and regretting its conclusion, yet she had done both.

"There is no need to apologize, Jed. No harm was done," he said aloud, praying that were truly the case. She did not want to spend the remainder of the day reliving the fascinating little shiver that had quickened her pulse and made her wish for more.

Forcing herself to treat the episode lightly, Victoria laughed softly and smiled at the man before her.

"No other gentleman has ever kissed my hand in such a manner before."

"I'm out of practice. Shall I try it again, just to make sure I do it properly?" offered Jed, a weight lifting from his shoulders at her teasing. Had she truly called *him* a gentleman?

"What is keeping the two of you?" called Ali, already astride his camel. "I thought you were in a hurry, Jed."

At his words, Jed bent over, grabbed Victoria's bedroll and tossed it up to the Egyptian. As much as Jed regretted the interruption, Victoria would be riding with him all day. There would be plenty of time to explore their newfound rapport.

"By the time you stow that bundle, we'll be a half mile ahead of you," he yelled. "Time to ride, Vicky—ah, sorry, *Victoria*."

"Vicky is fine," she acknowledged, accepting his assistance. Settling herself in the saddle, she smoothed the skirt of her *gallabiya* and bestowed a happy glance on the American below her. Since they had made peace with each other, she found that his nickname did not grate on her as it once had. In fact, *Vicky* sounded somehow more appropriate coming from him.

"Whatever you say, Vicky," he agreed, conscious of the privilege she had allowed him. Hurriedly, he pulled himself up behind her on the camel, wrapped his arm about her waist and tugged at the camel's bit. "*Kam*, you mangy creature. *Rah!*"

The day was passing surprisingly quickly, Victoria found, when Jed signaled the midday halt. They had ridden until past noon, detouring away from the dervish camp, and then headed northeast toward the Nile. Yet the hours had flown by. Trusting Jed to manage the camel, she had persuaded him to talk about his brothers and his family, growing up in the wilds of Kentucky, as well as later when he came to adulthood.

"You mean Jed Kincaid has actually been seen in evening clothes?" she teased as she set out the dried meats and fruit for their midday meal. "I don't believe it."

"My favorite night wear is nothing at all," he said with a wicked grin, lowering himself to sit beside her on the sand. "But if I have to leave the house, casual trousers and a cotton shirt."

"But that would not suffice in the hallowed presence of society matrons," objected Victoria.

"Out of deference to my mother and Mr. Bradshaw, I did occasionally don formal attire," admitted Jed, a grimace crossing his features. "However, I would not venture out onto the dance floor for anyone. Even if I was wearing a monkey suit, I wasn't about to act like a trained chimp. That was where I drew the line, no dancing!"

"Oh, come now, Jed. You ride gracefully—"

"That's because the horse does the stepping—"

What better excuse to be back in Jed's arms than teaching him to waltz, Victoria thought as inspiration overtook her.

"We're not in the public eye here, and the floor has no limits. Ali, would you keep time for us? One, two, three, one, two, three . . ."

"But of course, Victoria," the Egyptian agreed, not believing she would succeed. Kincaid dance? It would be a rare sight to behold, another miracle to share with Fatima. "One, two, three, and one, two—"

"Ali, shut up, we don't need your counting."

"That's fine, Ali. Continue," she instructed, dismissing her partner's reluctance. "Come on, Jed, it will be fun."

"Don't be ridiculous, Vicky. I have no feel for the rhythm of real music, let alone Ali's substitute. And you and I aren't the same height so it'll be awkward. The sand will get in our way," argued Jed, busily listing objections, foolish as they might be. "Besides, we really don't have the time. We should be traveling so we can reach the Nile and get a *falucca* tonight."

"We just stopped a few minutes ago, Jed, and we usually rest at least three hours at noon," she responded, "so don't use time as an excuse. I mean, I can understand if you are afraid—"

"Afraid?" he snorted. "That's hardly the case."

"One, two, three, and one, two, three . . ."

"Yes, you are. You think Ali and I might laugh at you. But if we should, remember dancing is meant to be an amusement."

"I can think of an amusement that would be much more entertaining," muttered Jed.

"Oh, don't be so stodgy. We have been riding for days and my legs are stiff. A waltz would let me work out the knots," claimed the blonde, stretching her shapely legs out in front of her. Slowly rising to her feet, she tossed her head, sending her hat flying so her sun-bleached curls danced in the sunshine as she pretended to pout. "Of course, if you really don't care about my welfare . . ."

But her feminine wiles bore no fruit as Jed remained seated.

"Come here and show me how we don't fit together," she challenged, grabbing his hand and urging him to his feet. Reluctantly, Jed allowed her to do so.

"One, two, three, and one, two . . ." intoned Ali.

"See, this isn't so bad," she said triumphantly.

"In case you haven't noticed, we're standing still."

Deciding more aggressive action was needed, Victoria took Jed's hand and placed it on her waist, confident he wouldn't object.

"Hmm, this part feels good," he murmured.

"It all will, I promise. Now, turn toward me and take my left hand in your right."

"Without gloves—or a chaperone?" he asked with a devilish gleam in his eyes.

"I'm sure it's no more unseemly than the two of us riding one camel," she replied, determined to have her way. On horseback or simply walking, Jed displayed a supple grace that had to translate well to dancing, and she was not about to give up without proving it. In fact, she suspected the American was probably a better dancer than Hayden, who always held himself too firmly in control to move easily on the dance floor.

"Let your body relax, Jed, and move one foot, then the other," she urged, maneuvering him to follow her directions. "One, two, three, and one, two, three..."

"A song might offer better inspiration, Ali," criticized Jed. He had thus far avoided stepping on Victoria's feet, but there was no guarantee that it wouldn't happen any minute. Indeed, he would have quit the exercise altogether, only she felt so wonderful in his arms.

"Egyptian music is not for waltzing, Jed," replied the Cairene, "though I doubt any music would help your wooden stance there. One, two, three, and one..."

"Ali is right, Jed. Feel the tempo," Victoria encouraged. Hugging Jed closer, she tried to help him absorb the rhythm by humming in his ear as Ali continued to count. "Let your body respond to what mine is doing."

If only she hadn't suggested that, thought Jed, fighting the urge to ravish her as she swayed against him, torturing every fiber of his self-control.

"Vicky, let's forget the whole thing."

"Nonsense, you're improving already," she said, trying to give him confidence. "Just surrender to your body's natural instincts."

"Oh, honey, I'd love to," Jed moaned, knowing he should stop the lesson, but unable to deny himself the pleasure of feeling her curves move against him in the most tantalizing manner. She felt as though she were born to be in his arms, an extension of himself. But how much longer could he stand this sweet agony?

Then, just as Jed was about to give up and admit defeat, he understood what she meant. He could tell from her body's subtle shift where she was going next, and he moved that way, pleased to hear her laughter tinkle up at him.

"One, two, three, and one, two, three . . ."

And all at once, with Vicky in his arms, Jed understood what Keats had meant about unheard melodies being sweeter. He whirled her around the sand as though the London Orchestra was providing the music, the same music that sang in his heart. When she laughed, he echoed the sound as it rippled across the dun-colored sand, imbuing the lethal desert with unexpected joy.

"Those women in San Francisco didn't know what they were missing, or they would never have allowed you to stay off the dance floor," Victoria praised breathlessly. So taken was she with the firm muscles in Jed's shoulders and the rock-hard planes of his chest that she hated the idea of stepping away from her partner. Yet even the most magical of parties must end, she decided reluctantly. "Ali, thank you, but that's enough."

"One, two, three." Jed took up the call, increasing the tempo as he swung Victoria in a wide circle. Without warning, he lifted her up against him, hugged her tightly and set her down again, bowing deeply from the waist. "Thank you for a most unexpected pleasure."

"It was mine, Jed," answered Victoria as she gazed shyly up at him. He needed a shave again and his wardrobe might not be de rigueur, but Jed Kincaid was a prince of a man. However, she remembered with a start, unfortunately, Hayden Reed had a prior claim on her heart, a claim she could not, in good conscience, ignore any longer.

"I could use a nice cool drink," said Jed as he reached for one of the water bags. "Vicky?"

"Thank you, there's something I must attend to first," she declared softly, needing a reason to get away from Jed and still her racing heart. "If you two will excuse me . . ."

"I fear you will have to settle for a *long* drink rather than a cool one," corrected Ali. "Nothing is cool in this heat. By the end of your performance, you looked as though you almost knew what you were doing."

"Thanks for your less than generous compliment," replied Jed. "Dancing was not my idea."

"Nor was it a good one," scolded the Egyptian quietly as Victoria moved off. "The woman belongs to another man. You have no right to tempt her as you have been doing."

"*Me* tempt *her?* Damn it, Ali, are you going blind? She leaned against me all morning, she laughed and smiled, and then she put my arms around her, and you say I am at fault?"

"I said nothing of fault, that is your conscience speaking," quibbled Ali. "It remains a fact, however, that you encourage her to be near you, even sleeping beside her, all the while knowing she is young and inexperienced—"

"So you accuse me of preying on an innocent?"

"Not yet, but I imagine it is inevitable given the passions that run between the two of you."

"You've been in the sun too long, shopkeeper! Put your *kaffiyeh* back on your head and perhaps this insane talk will pass. There is no passion between us," he declared, only half-truthfully. There *could* be passion on his part, it was possible, even probable, but thus far he had kept the flames at bay.

"Do not take me for a fool. You know well that the fire burning in her eyes from anger will glow twice as hot when she is in the throes of loving. My Fatima is much like her—"

"But Victoria doesn't love me!" Here at least was a truth Jed could defend honestly. "She loves that pompous ass Reed."

"Then do not distract her from that love. It is not fair to her or to you to taste fruits that are not rightfully yours to harvest," warned Ali. "In fact, it might be better were Victoria to ride with me—"

"I hardly think your wife would approve of that arrangement," Jed hedged, running his fingers through his hair. Moments in the saddle with Vicky's derriere rubbing suggestively between his thighs were too pleasurable to forgo. Many was the time he thanked heaven for the concealment of his *gallabiya*. He was living on a tightrope stretched taut between desire and conscience, but he was not about to abandon the challenge. "No, I am certain the lovely Fatima would much prefer that Victoria remain my charge."

"Fatima?" echoed Victoria as she rejoined the men. "Have you met her, Jed?"

"Not yet, but Ali was saying how much you are alike."

"Really? Do we share the same features?"

"No, not alike in looks, though she is small like you. In spirit, however, you are much the same. You both have strong preferences and large hearts, and you allow nothing to interfere with either, though, at times, that is not the wisest of paths. Often it is safer to overrule one's heart rather than tempt disaster."

Raising her eyebrows at Ali's solemn tone, Victoria looked at him closely. Was he trying to warn her about something? It certainly sounded like it, but what? Riding with Jed? Dancing in the desert? Before she could question him, he continued.

"I miss my Fatima very much. She is the breath I need to live, and without her, my days are dark and dreary, even under the midday sun," the Cairene admitted with a rueful smile. "Still, I am certain I am not alone in such feelings. It must be much the same as you feel toward your Mr. Reed—"

Jed snorted in disbelief at Ali's obvious ploy to discourage Vicky's attention. Why was the bastard making such an issue of it now? In three days they would be back in Cairo. What could happen between now and then?

"Mr. Reed? Oh, Hayden... yes, I suppose it is the same," demurred Victoria, looking up at the sky, down at the ground, anywhere but at Jed. "Of course, I cannot wait to see him again."

"By not coming after you himself, Hayden is the one responsible for your still being apart," interjected Jed. Enough of this nonsense about Reed, let Victoria realize just what a coward the man was. "Had he been brave enough to come with me—"

"Brave or not, he is Victoria's choice," reminded Ali.

"No, he didn't come to Khartoum, he sent you," argued Victoria, overriding the Egyptian's words to defend the fiancé she betrayed each time she looked at Jed Kincaid. "And he was right to employ you. Haven't you done your utmost to get me back to his arms? In fact, I'm surprised we are not traveling even now instead of listening to you pontificate."

As soon as the words were out of her mouth, she regretted them, but the falsity of Ali's belief that she was longing for Hayden with every breath made her lash out. How could she explain to Jed that she felt guilty for responding to him and forgetting Hayden in his presence? Watching the angry flush deepen the American's sun-burnished face, however, Victoria knew she had to attempt an apology, if not an explanation.

"Jed, I'm sorry—"

"Don't be. You were right, I forgot that I was only the hired hand. Ali, we'll ride shortly, so stow the supplies."

"Of course, Jed."

At once the Egyptian was on his feet gathering the blankets and food, but Victoria gave him no thought. She had wounded Jed's pride and she could not let the matter end there.

"Jed Kincaid, I want you to stop and listen to me a minute. I'll be disappointed if you don't do so."

"Most people have to live with disappointment every day of their lives, Vicky. It's time you got used to it," he advised, moving toward his camel to attach the water bag to its saddle.

"Damn it, Jed, what I said was wrong—"

"But thinking it wasn't?" he challenged without turning around. "Soft words are handy shields to hide behind when things go amiss."

"I don't want to have to watch my words around you. I want to be myself—"

Determined to confront Jed, Victoria came up behind him, trapping him between the camel and herself so he could not avoid looking at her. When he finally finished his chores and spun around, his face hard, she held up a hand as if to halt his flight.

For a moment it looked as though he meant to strike it aside and pass her, but instead he swallowed and fixed his eyes on the horizon, saying nothing. Obstinate as the man was, Victoria knew that if she were to get a reaction, she had to be blunt.

"Listen, you pigheaded, stubborn Yankee, I had no right to speak to you like that and I apologize. I only said what I did because I *don't* think about Hayden every single waking moment…and when Ali talked of his love for Fatima, I felt guilty and ashamed. But I shouldn't have taken my feelings out on you. I am sorry, Jed."

"And just what do you spend your time thinking about?" asked Jed quietly. He lowered his glance to study the young woman before him, piercing her defenses, reading her soul.

Swallowing her pride, Victoria proudly met his gaze, albeit reluctantly. She would rather have avoided the issue, but she could not help but be honest with him.

"All that's happened lately—and you, a good part of the time, anyway," she confessed in a small voice.

"Me?" Jed didn't know why her admission startled him. He spent hours contemplating her, but that a woman like Victoria might have similar disturbing thoughts confounded him.

"Yes, Jed Kincaid, you," the young woman admitted with unexpected vehemence, "though not deliberately. Now, can we drop the subject?"

"Not before I tell you that you're a large part of my daily thoughts, as well," bargained the American, pushing back his hat. Realizing what Vicky's confession had cost her, he knew he needed to balance her honest exposure of her heart with his own.

"Oh," murmured Victoria, taking a step backward as though afraid to confront this newfound familiarity.

"Are you ready to ride with me, then?" Jed asked, catching one of Ali's disapproving looks. Ironically he had tried to dissuade them from giving in to the attraction between them, and instead he had brought them to a new level of awareness of each other. "I think Ali is waiting."

"All right," Victoria agreed, permitting him to help her astride the camel. "But perhaps we should talk about something less personal this afternoon, like politics or religion."

"Or maybe we should resolve our simmering curiosity and discuss our lives in detail since childhood," he responded, as he joined her in the saddle. "I have visions of you dressed in a starched white pinafore, your hair in long golden curls, and you have blueberry stains all over your face and hands—but not a blue drop on that snowy dress. *Kam!*"

At the camel's abrupt rise to his feet, Victoria was thrown back against Jed's chest, yet she couldn't help but giggle at the endearing image he suggested.

"No, I never was partial to blueberries, though I did sneak into the gardens regularly to steal the strawberries. The poor gardener was always blaming the rabbits."

At the sound of Jed's chuckle, Ali shook his head sadly and turned his camel to follow them. He had tried to ease their fate, but it would seem the unlikely pair was determined to embrace their destiny willingly, two vibrant souls building slowly to a climax. He only hoped that neither of them would regret the inevitable explosion.

Chapter Twelve

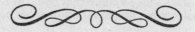

As the sun slipped lower on the horizon, signs of vegetation began to appear in what, miles back, had been only barren desert. When they finally reached the bluffs that overlooked the Nile, the trio's spirits soared. There they paused to admire not only the rapidly flowing river, but the small village situated below them. After days of enduring the treacherous hazards of the cruel desert, seeing so much water and civilization filled them with triumph.

As Ali gave praise to Allah, Jed impulsively shared his exaltation with Victoria by lowering his face alongside hers and placing a resounding kiss on her cheek.

"We've done it!" he crowed, tightening his arms around her in a good-natured hug. "The worst is behind us."

But when she glanced back at him, the expression that flitted through her eyes as a result of his exuberance almost made Jed forget that bringing them out of the desert had been an accomplishment. Instead of celebrating their survival, he only knew he was filled with vague longings for things left undone.

"Where are we?" asked Victoria, as much to break the tension as to satisfy her curiosity. She should have been thrilled to be so close to home, but she was reluctant to see this journey end.

"We passed the Egyptian border some time ago," Jed replied, concentrating on his answer rather than the fact that Victoria wouldn't be near much longer. "I didn't want to come in out of the desert at Assuan itself. Too many caravans headed for Khartoum originate there. If I turned my head for an instant, you could be on your way back south before I knew it. It's better to head a bit farther north and bypass the place altogether. That little village below us is Gharb Assuan. We'll camp a few miles downriver.''

"And then what?" Victoria murmured. Her eyes were rife with questions she didn't even know she was asking.

"One of us will double back to Assuan and trade the camels for a *falucca* so we can sail the rest of the way. It will be quicker and more comfortable," Jed said, his voice huskier than normal.

"But will camping there be safe?" Memories of her kidnappers bundling her into the bottom of their boat came flooding back, and Victoria shivered. Obeying the habit established during the nights on the trail, she unconsciously moved closer to Jed for warmth.

"I think so," he said honestly, unaware of how naturally he accepted Victoria's action. "Zobeir's men wouldn't expect us to come out of the western desert. And if they're still looking for us, it will be in Assuan. My instincts are good. Trust me."

"I do," Victoria admitted softly, turning her head to look up into the adventurer's eyes. At her words, they sparkled with pleasure.

"That's my girl," he said with an approving wink.

Victoria almost winced at his words. She wasn't Jed's girl, she was Hayden's fiancée. To distract herself before she gave way to emotions better kept hidden, Victoria directed Jed's attention to Gharb Assuan once more.

"Won't we be going into the village at all? It's bound to have things we consider luxuries after life in the desert."

"No, there's nothing there except possible trouble," Jed pronounced, removing his hat to wipe his brow with the back of his golden, muscular forearm. "I'm afraid a white woman would stir up a lot of interest, and we don't know who would hear about it. Much as I hate to deny you anything, I'd feel safer not to chance it."

"There's no doubt Victoria would make every man in the village turn out, and those that saw her would talk about her loveliness to a hundred others who did not," agreed Ali. "But exactly how far north do you propose we travel before we set up camp?"

"There is a small inlet a few miles north of the village. Not too many people pass there. You and she can wait while I hightail it back to Assuan proper and make the trade. Then I'll bring the *falucca* downriver to you."

"Someone else might happen along to abduct her," objected Ali. "A woman as beautiful as she with a rich father is tempting to a poor man. Do you actually think I would be able to protect her as well as you could?"

"I don't know you'd be all that bad at it," Jed said, suddenly loath to be alone with Victoria. For some reason, she appeared terribly vulnerable to him at the moment, and thus riper for loving than he had ever seen her. Though he honestly wanted to keep his vow, his male instincts were stirring, and he felt himself weakening in his resolve not to touch her. "I'm sure you'd do fine."

"Those men who grabbed me from my parents' estate still haunt my dreams, Jed. I'd feel safer with you." Victoria said quietly, wanting no one but the American to safeguard her. The expression on her delicate face was a heartfelt entreaty Jed could not ignore, but Ali, hastening to soothe the girl's fear, did not notice what passed between them.

"Don't let those demons distress you," advised the Egyptian.

"Ali is right. We will do as he suggested and let him engineer the trade," Jed reassured her.

"Fine. I will even fetch Victoria some soothing oil for her skin," volunteered the shopkeeper.

"And perhaps some fresh meat," requested Jed. "I will give you money in case the camels don't bring enough and you have to buy—"

"Buy nothing, it will be part of the barter," snorted the experienced man of commerce. "Fatima has a cousin who knows the *Bisharin*, the traders living in the old cemetery. He will help me find a fair merchant. Besides, these are fine camels and expensive saddles. They will bring good value."

"Quickly, Ali. Don't waste hours haggling," cautioned Jed. He was familiar with the formality of serious trading which required shared cups of strong coffee, exchanged histories of families and multiple offers and counteroffers.

"I will try to do as you ask, American, but some things go against the blood," admitted Ali as they rode north.

Victoria said nothing. The knowledge that her ordeal was nearly over made her feel incredibly weary and extremely sad.

* * *

An hour later, Ali had barely disappeared from sight when Jed decided he had to shake Victoria from her unusual reticence. Since the conversation on the bluffs, the blonde had completely withdrawn from him, retreating into her own thoughts and leaving no chink in her armor for him to penetrate. Once or twice he suspected she had been weeping, though he had seen no trace of tears. Jed was determined to do whatever was necessary to end her melancholy. Her unnatural desolation aroused his protective instincts and caused him to forget the promise he had made to himself to be completely circumspect in Ali's absence.

Abandoning the pile of saddlebags, he came to where Victoria sat on the grassy bank, her stiff posture echoing her discomfort.

"Do you want to bathe first or shall I?" he asked casually.

"Bathe? In the river?"

"Why not? It's been three days since we were at an oasis. The Nile isn't sacred. For centuries, people have drunk from it, washed in it and done a lot worse, I'm certain."

"But it's so public. Anyone could see—"

"No one will see anything if we stay near the inlet. Besides, it's near dusk and growing darker."

"*We?*"

"Come on, Vicky, before we get back to civilization, let yourself do something wild for once in your life. I know you want to break loose, I've seen it in your eyes. And with the type of world you live in, you might never get another chance."

"But—"

"Hell, I'm not talking about anything *really* wicked, just slightly naughty and a lot of fun. Throw caution to the wind, doff your clothes and come swimming with me," Jed invited in a devilish tone, his face a combination of mischievous imp and fallen angel. The suggestion was made as much to cheer Vicky as to fulfill the provocative fantasies he had had of frolicking with her in the water since the first oasis. The way Jed saw it, not only would such an activity pull Vicky out of her doldrums, it would reward him for all the nights he had lain quiet, behaving like a celibate with her curled up teasingly beside him.

"Do you mean without wearing a stitch?" she asked in a shocked whisper, appalled yet fascinated by the idea.

"Yeah," he drawled, his eyes alight with wicked invitation.

"No, it's out of the question. You go ahead. I'll sponge off later."

"As you prefer." Reaching down to grab the hem of his *gallabiya,* Jed quickly drew it up over his head and tossed it to the ground. He'd be damned if he'd return Vicky to Hayden without tempting her as she had tempted him since leaving Khartoum.

"Jed!" she cried, averting her eyes even as his magnificence impressed itself on her memory. Though Jed Kincaid was the first man she had ever seen unclothed, she knew immediately he was not the norm. The way his hips tapered toward the junction of his legs called to her so that she'd never forget the sight, though, of course, a proper lady would.

"How else do you want me to bathe?" Jed grinned, impudently striding past her toward the river. "It's all right. You can look now."

Victoria did, only to witness the slow descent of his muscled legs into the water, followed by those sinewy thighs of his. It was a relief when the Nile finally covered the firm planes of his posterior so she could draw a breath. For a brief irrational moment, she felt the urge to join him and run her fingers over his buttocks, testing the apparent solidity of his flesh, but she shook her head and the impulse fled.

"That wasn't very gentlemanly."

"What wasn't?" Pretending ignorance, Jed turned lazily toward the shore and glanced at Victoria, pleased at the reddish tinge that heightened the sun's color in her cheeks.

"Telling me to look when you weren't in the water yet. I mean, I saw—well, never mind."

"Hell, Vicky, I don't mind in the least if you look. I have nothing to be ashamed of, nor as I recall from my observations at the oasis, do you."

"No wonder you didn't fare well in society. Jed Kincaid, you are completely, totally outrageous." Strange as it was, even while she chided him, Victoria couldn't help but enjoy her view of Jed's chest, its dark mat of ringlets half covered by the water. She had leaned against that broad expanse for hours. How could the rest of him, that part below the water, be any less appealing?

"Honey, the river feels wonderful. Why not come in and we can continue our discussion out here? If you like, I'll turn my back—"

Enter the water where temptation stood, naked and exposed? The young Englishwoman shook her head at the very thought of it.

"I couldn't—it wouldn't be proper."

"Who would be hurt by our bathing together? No one." She looked suddenly uncertain and Jed pursued his cause. "Some societies live their lives totally unclothed, just for the joy of it."

Should she listen to him or was his the voice of the devil?

"Vicky, what's common in one culture is taboo in another, but that doesn't make one people right and the other wrong. Ali's Fatima observes purdah. Are you a sinner for showing your face?"

"If I do as you suggest, I'd be showing a lot more than my face—"

"And there's nothing wrong with a single inch of any of it, I swear," he said, his tone urgent. "Give in to the temptation. In this case, it's innocent enough, after all. Clothes—or the lack of them—don't make a man what he is, or a woman, for that matter."

"No," she agreed slowly, her eyes searching his intently for any sign that he might be trying to seduce her. She found none.

"Think about it. I'm going to swim out a ways."

Ducking his head and shoulders down into the water, the American stretched his muscles and struck off upriver, enjoying the physical release the Nile provided. Vicky was too exciting a woman to be hog-tied by convention and he was resolute that she know that. He suspected, however, she would take a bit more convincing before she understood the lesson.

Looking back toward the river bank he'd just left, Jed was startled not to see Vicky sitting there. Quickly he swung around and headed for shore. Could someone have conceivably grabbed her in the few minutes he had been swimming?

Anxiously, he scanned the shoreline as he neared it, puzzled at the pile of cloth near his own abandoned *gallabiya*. Then suddenly he understood and breathed a deep sigh of relief. Slowing his pace, Jed came closer to the bank and relaxed. She was there, in the water near the shore, her entire body submerged in the Nile, her blond hair streaming on the surface, a golden circle of radiance about her head.

"I'm glad you reconsidered," he said, trying to keep his voice casual despite his body's awareness of her naked proximity. "Isn't the water refreshing?"

"It's splendid," she agreed. "If only I had some soap, I could wash my hair."

"I have a bit I used for shaving. I'll get it for you," he offered, moving rapidly to the bank and leaving the water before she could protest. If nothing else, he would teach Victoria not to be ashamed of her own body... or of looking at his.

She started to open her mouth to object, but didn't. Rather than fret about the situation, she thought, eyeing his tightly planed cheeks as he bent to get the soap from the saddlebags, she should enjoy the view. It was certainly a rare one, she marveled, thrilled by the grace with which he moved.

When Jed turned back to the Nile, her eyes widened at the bounty of the man before her as her body began to tingle with excitement. For a moment she felt faint, but a deep breath eased the panic before it seized hold. Realizing from his grin that he had caught her staring, Victoria blushed and quickly looked away.

"I'm sorry," she whispered.

"Vicky, in spite of what your governess may have taught you, there is nothing wrong with ogling a member of the opposite sex," teased Jed. Seeing that she was still embarrassed to face him, Jed tried again to reassure her. "In truth, your staring is a compliment and your avoiding me an insult."

Reentering the water, he waded toward her.

"See, lightning won't strike."

"I almost feel as though it did," Vicky confessed shyly. She glanced down at her nipples just below the surface of the water. "Like the last instant before a wonderful surprise when you know that as much as you want it, you may not truly deserve it," she admitted, keeping her eyes trained on Jed's face and chest.

He couldn't help but smile at her innocence. To his amazement, though blessed with a spectacular body, Vicky was totally unfamiliar with its urgings.

"Well, I don't know if this qualifies as a wonderful surprise, but, if you like, I'll wash your hair and you won't have to worry about anyone seeing anything."

"Anyone except you," she said with a smile. Not that she would mind, she realized in surprise. Jed's glances were warm and loving, not lewd as Zobeir's and his guards' had been. Oddly, the American's intense scrutiny made her feel prized, not violated.

"Except me," he agreed readily. "Unless you want me to go ashore and leave you alone—"

"No, you saw me naked at the oasis. What do I have to hide?"

Less than he did, Jed reflected, circling behind her and swallowing deeply at the sight of the luscious curves of her buttocks visible through the water. His fingers itched to grasp them and lift her toward him, and he was hard-pressed to ignore such an overwhelming urge. Still, the water was an inhibitor, Jed told himself, and he was man enough to maintain control.

"Just relax," he advised Vicky, wishing he could heed his own words. With the easy practice of a man used to creating shaving lather, he worked the fat-based soap slowly.

Then he reached forward and took her head gently in his hands, allowing it to loll back in the water. Permitting his fingers to travel slowly across her temples, he began massaging the silky strands at their roots, pleased by her low murmur of contentment as he increased the tempo and rhythm of his movement. Enjoying her trust, Jed strove to be at once gentle yet impersonal, but it was nearly impossible to ignore the implications of his action. When the satiny tendrils claimed him as their own, wrapping themselves around his wrists, he shivered at the thought of being possessed so totally under other circumstances.

He took his time, lathering and then urging the suds from her curls, watching her posture soften as his fingers traced ever-enlarging circles on her scalp, soothing her as she opened herself to his repeated caresses.

A deep sigh of satisfaction escaped Vicky's lips and Jed grinned in self-derision. He was miserable, his body throbbing with need, and *she* was moaning with pleasure.

Then, too soon, he was through. Her hair floated soft and soap-free on the surface of the Nile, and he had no reason to continue, and every reason to stop.

"There you are, all done. I hope the service pleased you," he said, unable to hide the raspy quality of his voice.

"It did indeed," she answered a trifle breathlessly, turning to face the man whose hands had been so evocative. "But now, it's your turn, or perhaps I should say, *my* turn."

"What?" He had never expected her to repay the favor, if that was what she meant. How could he withstand such temptation?

"You washed my hair, but since yours isn't as long, perhaps I will wash your chest, as well." Vicky's heart-shaped mouth curved into a smile as Jed hesitated. "Aren't you the one who told me I had nothing to be ashamed of? You don't, either. I've seen it all."

"No woman since my mother has bathed me," confessed Jed, somewhat startled at that realization. Of all the females he'd known, none had ever demonstrated Victoria's giving nature.

"Then I think it's about time one did." She giggled as she took the soap and began to rub it against his chest. Newly introduced to this game of physical flirtation, she decided she had waited too long to learn about it. Perhaps a lady didn't indulge in such behavior, but then how many ladies spent time in the desert with a wild, wonderful American?

As her soft palms rotated across his chest, teasing the small hairs and sending shivers up his spine, Jed struggled to remain motionless. Every muscle in his body craved release, and he found even breathing a chore, so tense was he from the battle not to reach out and gather her toward him. Instead, he held his arms out to the sides to avoid touching her as Victoria's alluring breasts floated so visibly before him.

"I never realized men's nipples were as sensitive as women's," she reflected, circling and caressing those tender nubs of sensation. Unaware of the agony she was generating, Victoria reveled in the feel of Jed's flesh beneath her dancing fingers. Unlike Ali, whom she had tended when he was unconscious and hurt, Jed was very much alert and responsive to her smallest motion.

It was enough, he decided finally, beginning to step away from her. No, it was *too* much. Jed was no longer able to resist her artless seduction. The water and the slight evening breezes fluttering over the river could no longer tame the heat that had built in his loins. He was male and she was female and they were together. That was all he knew.

Almost before he was conscious of his decision to claim her, Victoria was in his arms, the soap forgotten as he bent his head to hers, kissing her with a ferocity that startled even him. It had been too long since he'd had a woman, his mind reasoned, but then he was beyond thought, rejoicing in her ardent response. Their lips were joined as though life depended on this union, as though they had never existed separately.

For days Jed had envisioned Victoria's reaction to his loving gestures and she didn't disappoint him. She was clearly as enthralled by him as he was by her. Standing with her, naked in the Nile at twilight, he sent his hands trailing down her spine and back up again, urging her to fit her body closer to his, relishing the feel of her sleekness against his coarser skin.

It was like the sandstorm that had sprung up out of nowhere, thought Victoria dizzily, parting her lips to welcome Jed's anxious, demanding assault. As his tongue sought hers and began to parry, its tip licking one minute and dueling the next, the young woman understood the drive that powered Jed's excitement and fed on it herself, answering his needs while satisfying her own.

She could barely breathe, her heart was pounding as though it might explode, and she was quivering, but there was a certainty that this was right. Jed would never harm her, not when he made her feel so unbelievably cherished.

Gradually, as the evening winds blew along his bare back, Jed reluctantly came to his senses, chilled by his irresponsibility and the magnitude of what he had precipitated. What had begun as a game exploded into flames as desire took over. But Victoria, however responsive to his attention, was not his to dally with.

As she leaned against him, his arms draped over her shoulders, hers around his waist, he steeled himself against what must be done. Jed drew a deep breath and moved out of her embrace, desperately regretting each step away from the paradise she offered.

"Vicky," he murmured, his voice hoarse with unspent passion. "It's time to stop and get dressed."

"Now? Why?"

"I think we have to consider all of this carefully," he ventured. He was uncertain how to explain his reluctance to continue what undoubtedly could lead to a level of sensual release he had often imagined, but never foreseen as a reality. "It was wonderful to kiss you, but..."

"But I belong to Hayden," she acknowledged, reading his mind. Unable to deny the truth of the matter, her conscience would not allow her to ignore that commitment no matter how special Jed had made her feel.

"Yes, you do, but it's not only that. Loving you is a privilege I don't deserve."

"How can you say that? Of course you do."

"No, what you feel is merely gratitude for my saving you from Zobeir and the brigands—"

"And the snake and the sandstorm," Victoria added, trying to keep her tone light. She knew he was not rejecting her but offering her the choice to halt their impulsive foray into passion or to continue. Unfortunately, at this moment, that was not a decision she could make rationally. Her body was overwrought with sensations, trembling yet with the excitement of his touch, quivering with the pleasure of his kisses.

"Those, too," Jed acknowledged with a half smile, his agate eyes smoky with emotion, "and I couldn't accept anything from you because you think you owe me or because you are too thrilled by the newness of passion to think clearly—"

"Thank you, Jed," she said quietly, standing up on tiptoe to kiss him gently, her hand caressing his unshaven cheek. She knew instinctively it could not be easy for a man like him to deny himself, but, for her, he had. "It seems you are a gentleman, despite your wishes to the contrary."

Then Victoria turned from him and waded to shore, each step a deliberate denial. Reaching the bank, she opened a saddlebag and rummaged about, finally pulling out her own clothing, the blouse and skirt in which Jed had first seen her.

"Since we are returning to civilization, this might be more appropriate to wear," she called. "Besides, it's clean."

"I suppose so," Jed answered without enthusiasm. Did that choice of clothes mean she wanted Hayden? Was it that formal world she craved, then, rather than the one of sensual pleasure he had offered her? Suddenly he needed to escape the overwhelming temptation of her. They had seen no one in hours. Surely she would be safe alone. Safer than with him just now. "I'm going to swim upriver a ways. Do you mind?"

"I wouldn't deny you anything," Vicky replied, a soft smile telegraphing her unspoken offer. She stood proudly on the grassy bank, unashamed and beautiful.

Instead of going to her, he turned southward to fight the current and expend the passionate energy he had denied himself. He had done what was right. He knew he was right. But still, Jed wished the Nile was cooler.

By the time Jed returned to the camp, twilight had turned to darkness and stars were scattered across the heavens. The sight of the *falucca* and the small fire drew him into the shore, that and the luscious smell of roasting lamb.

"Dinner is ready, Jed. Fresh meat, just as I promised," Ali called when he saw the American emerge from the water. "You will have to do something about your lack of attire before you join us, however. Victoria, don't look around."

How could she *not* look, the young woman wondered, her eyes surreptitiously feasting on the male standing in the shadows. As he retrieved his trousers from the saddlebag and drew them on, she memorized the corded muscles in his legs and the firmness of his buttocks. When Jed's worn cotton shirt obscured his strong back and broad shoulders, Victoria sighed for the loss.

"Come, sit here, Jed," she invited, patting a place on the grass beside her. "You've taken care of the two of us for days. Tonight we'll return the favor. There's roasted lamb, fresh bread, even onions. And Ali managed to find a flute as part of the trade."

Powerless to resist Vicky's entreaty, Jed settled himself beside her, astounded at Ali's success.

"Tarnation, Ali, what did you tell them? That the camels laid golden eggs rather than—"

"There is a lady with us, Jed," scolded the Egyptian. "I told no lies."

"No, you merely robbed those poor beggars blind. Instead of Zobeir and the brigands chasing us, we'll have the *Bisharin.*"

"I'm sure Ali simply used his own experience in haggling to wear the sellers down," interjected Victoria. "Tell us about it, Ali. I'll listen even if Jed doesn't."

"Fatima's cousin led me to a trader who needed extra beasts immediately for an unexpectedly rich caravan. But when he learned the camels came from Jed Kincaid, the American who had redeemed Sheik Abdul Nabar's amulet, any price I asked would not have been too much. It was Jed's reputation, not my skill, that determined our good fortune," said Ali. "However, out of respect for his name, I was fair."

"I can see that." Jed chuckled. Taking note of the numerous supplies that lay by the fire, he spotted not only foodstuffs, but native liquor and a few bolts of fabric. "We're only two days from Cairo. I don't think we'll eat all of this—or wear that purple silk."

"No, that is a gift for Fatima to assuage her pain during my absence," explained the Cairene with a sudden grin.

"Won't your very presence do that?" asked Jed, his gaze fixed on Vicky. As she handed him a plate, her skirt fell open, exposing a slender length of shapely leg, and he swallowed deeply at the hot flash of desire that overtook him. What would it be like to go home every night to the same woman? Never having made a habit of commitment, the very idea of such stability seemed foreign though not necessarily repulsive to Jed, especially if the woman were as appealing as Vicky Shaw.

"One prays for such graces," Ali agreed. "But eat, and we will celebrate with music and *zabeeb*."

"This tasty meal is celebration enough. What more could a man desire?" Jed drawled, his eyes devouring Victoria as thoroughly as his mouth did justice to the lamb. The air had turned cool, so the smell of the fire, the aroma of the lamb and the savory taste of the simple fare made him nearly content. Yet, there sat Vicky, just beyond his reach.

"The meat is quite flavorful. It's the conclusion to a wonderful evening," Victoria said softly. Catching Jed licking his lips suggestively as he studied her in a most possessive manner, she blushed even as she continued. "All in all, I am quite satisfied with the day's events, though, at the moment, I couldn't indulge myself in anything more."

"Men generally have more demanding appetites than do women," said the man who had kissed her so artfully that afternoon. "Right, Ali?"

"That is true. Do you want more lamb?"

"That's not what I meant," Jed said with a reproving frown.

"Oh," Ali muttered, his skin taking on a darker hue. "While it is true Fatima's hunger is often satisfied more quickly than mine, she is most willing to wait for me to take my fill."

"You're a lucky man." Shifting his position slightly, Jed placed his arm lightly on Vicky's shoulders and drew her toward him so she rested against his chest.

"I saw you shiver," he said solicitously. "This should help, or you could indulge in some of Ali's booty of *zabeeb*."

"No, thank you." She shuddered, recalling the foul taste of the strong liquor. "You and the fire will keep me warm enough."

"Glad to oblige," Jed replied, reaching out his hand toward her exposed leg. That thigh had beckoned him since he sat down. He trusted the darkness and the Egyptian's interest in his newly obtained flute would hide his indiscretion.

"Jed! Stop that," Vicky scolded softly as she felt him stroke her leg. Truth be told, she was too comfortable leaning against him to stir, but she realized she should make some objection to his familiarity. "It's bad enough you tore the skirt. Don't abuse it."

"Hush, Vicky, Ali is playing. Don't talk now," Jed advised, wishing Ali would continue to be oblivious. Slowly, gently, he allowed his fingers to trace a meandering path up and down her outer thigh in rhythm with the soft melody Ali played. Lazily, as Jed closed his eyes to reclaim the images of Vicky's dripping body when she exited the Nile, his roving hand circled her satiny flesh.

"Behave yourself," she warned in a whisper, darting him a reproving glance, "or I'll never bathe with you again."

"Now, that is a punishment I surely don't deserve," protested Jed. Nonetheless, he removed his hand and placed it over Vicky's, his heart soaring.

"Ali is surprisingly competent on that thing," he murmured a while later as the Egyptian continued to call forth native sounds from the flute.

When Vicky made no reply, Jed looked down into her face and was oddly disturbed to find her asleep in his arms.

"Why are you playing lullabies, Ali? You've put Vicky to sleep," he complained, only half in jest.

"And if you keep fussing so, you will awaken her," cautioned Ali. Putting down the flute, he rose to stretch his stiffened muscles and smiled at the sleeping woman. "Let the poor girl rest, for heaven's sake. The journey surely has not been easy on her."

"And if she sleeps in my arms this way, the night won't be easy on me."

"Then shift her off of you to the ground. The grass is soft enough and I managed to get an extra blanket—"

"What didn't you get?" muttered Jed beneath his breath. "Just toss me a bedroll and I'll see to her."

She had trusted him enough to literally fall asleep atop him. He could not misuse that trust and abandon her to the ground. Besides, Vicky had become a nighttime habit, he admitted to himself, her soft presence as comforting in her proximity as it was disquieting.

Never had he spent so many consecutive nights sleeping chastely beside a beautiful woman, Jed realized in amusement, unable to decide how he felt—at peace or in torment. He only knew that suddenly he regretted Cairo was but two days' north of them and he vowed to treasure every remaining hour of their journey.

Chapter Thirteen

Yet despite his best intentions, Jed found the following day to be more grueling than any they had spent in the desert. Where before he had been fully occupied, on board the *falucca* there was little that needed his intense supervision. Too often he found himself staring at Vicky, his mind hard at work teasing his resolve with seductive memories.

Ali had insisted on controlling the sail, and since the early rays of dawn had cut across the sky, he had delighted in taking them speedily past the small farms and settlements on the banks of the river in their northward journey. While Jed might have lowered the canvas for a bit and let them flow with the steady current, the Cairene persisted in turning the sail to catch each gust of wind and hurry them farther forward.

When Jed had suggested lingering ashore after their midday meal, the others had looked at him aghast.

"Jed, my Fatima is doubtlessly fraught with worry, fearing that I may never return to her," Ali had protested. "Would you lengthen her torment so you might enjoy a nap on the bank?"

Finally the American had reluctantly conceded, returning to the *falucca* and ruing each blast of wind that drove them closer to Cairo. He sat apart from them, unable to shake his dark mood and unwilling to subject Victoria and Ali to it.

His emerald eyes studied Vicky, noting the way she tossed her head periodically, freeing her curls to fly in the air. At one point, she attempted to secure them up under the soft hat he had provided, but their satiny texture prohibited their confinement and soon the golden tendrils slipped from bondage to lie against her back again, and the hat was abandoned.

New freckles caressed her pert nose and cheeks, and the paler blond of her hair caught his attention, too, as she unwittingly engraved her image on his unprotected soul. The sun had kissed Vicky as he had, but where she bore visible traces of nature's embrace, she carried no sign of his. Jed knew that was for the best, yet as he watched her amuse herself, he couldn't help but regret the inevitable loss of her. Without his conscious assent, she had become an integral part of his life.

"A piaster for your thoughts, Jed," she suddenly intruded, settling herself beside him. "Or should I venture a pound? From the frown on your face, I imagine they're pretty weighty ones."

"Not really." Chasing away his doubts, he grinned and reached out to run his finger across her cheek. "I was thinking how incredible it is that the sun can kill hardy men and beasts but for you, it merely adds greater beauty, a slight dusting of freckles—"

"Freckles? Oh, no, not really." Victoria sighed, her hand brushing his when she made as if to wipe away the offensive spots. "Mother's adamant about my avoiding the sun for just that reason."

"I imagine she'll forgive you this time." Jed chuckled. "Personally, I find them quite an attractive feature."

"You don't find them unappealing?" She was surprised, but then, Jed's opinions often caught her unaware.

"You already know I'm a maverick, why should one more unconventional view startle you?" he asked, dispatching his fingers to once more gently stroke the sun's sprinklings.

"*Maverick?* I don't believe I know the word," she said with a smile, relishing his touch. As his fingers softly caressed her skin, his thumb anchored itself beneath her chin and quickened her pulse, the effect as enchanting as always when he touched her lately.

"A *maverick* is a calf who isn't branded and goes its own way until a rancher corrals it and ends its independence with a hot iron applied to its rump," Jed explained. "But people like my stepfather use the word to describe rebels like me who don't follow society's rules—unless we're caught and branded."

"I don't believe there's any chance of that happening to you, Jed," called Ali, observing the interplay between them. "You never sit still long enough for anyone to claim you."

"True, I never have been one for staying put," acknowledged the American, dropping his hand from Vicky's face.
"But maybe there was never a reason to do so."

"Does that mean you won't be staying in Cairo?" she asked,
moistening her lips and opening her eyes wide in dismay. "I'd
be sorry to lose contact with you." What made her *say* such a
thing—even if it was true? Lately, in Jed's presence, she
couldn't control her errant thoughts and they escaped her lips
as words.

"I'll be around for a day or two," he said, rising to his feet
to avoid her questioning look. "Then it's off to another job."
The sun was warm this afternoon as always, but Vicky's innocent distress had raised his temperature until he felt like a vol-
cano about to explode. Of course, he should have known better
than to have touched her. Playing with fire, that's what he was
doing, and he was afraid Vicky's burn would be long in heal-
ing.

"Let me take the sail, Ali," he demanded abruptly. "I don't
want you straining that shoulder any longer."

"I'm fine," protested the Egyptian. Sparks had been flying
between Jed and Victoria all day, and while he wasn't certain
who was striking the flint, he preferred to stay out of range.
"You took charge in the desert, let me guide us on the river."

"I *said* I'll work the sail," repeated Jed. Damn it, if he didn't
escape Vicky's woeful glance, he might do something even
more irresponsible.

"All right, all right," agreed Ali, startled to see the desperation in Jed's face. The man was trying to escape Vicky's attentions, he realized in amazement. Perhaps Jed *was* honorable
where she was concerned. "I expect you'll be stopping soon for
the night, though."

"Soon," muttered Jed. *The night*—the last night before they
reached Cairo. As much as he wished it would never arrive, he
also hoped it would pass so quickly that he would have no time
for further temptation. As it was, watching Vicky, he found
himself dreaming of what he might have done had he been the
one to abduct her from Cairo. Irrational thoughts of taking her
back into the desert danced through his mind until he cursed the
active imagination that haunted him.

Sitting alone in the bow of the *falucca,* dressed in her high-
necked, long-sleeved blouse and skirt, Vicky looked every inch

an unapproachable lady. Had she always appeared so private, there would have been no issue to resolve.

But yesterday afternoon, naked in the river, she had been all woman and very willing to be his . . . though he had chivalrously declined the opportunity. As he watched Vicky take an orange from one of the bags containing Ali's booty, Jed took a deep breath and tried to look away, praying that he might be as strong tonight.

Across the boat, Vicky's slender fingers tugged at the orange peel. A curved nail drew itself over the uneven skin. Then, her tongue peeking from between her lips as she concentrated, she began to tease the rind protecting the fruit. With a gleeful smile of anticipation, she licked her lips and separated a piece of orange from the whole, bringing it to her mouth. Her pink tongue darted out to lick at the sweet juice leaking from the small sliver as her eyes closed in sensual delight.

Startled to discover he was holding his breath as he observed the suggestive tableau, Jed swallowed heavily and compelled his eyes once again to flee the provocative sight. Vicky was a siren, able to mesmerize a man with her incredible charms, he realized. Where the women of mythology had attracted men to inevitable doom with their glorious songs, Vicky called him forth with her natural but untutored passion for life.

On the journey from the slave pens she had changed—but so had he, from the expert concerned only with his job to a man tempted all too readily by personal involvement. . . .

Perhaps he should wait a bit before stopping for the night and concentrate his attention instead on the herons near the shore rather than on the lovely swan in the *falucca,* Jed considered. The less time they had ashore together, the safer she would be. And so would he.

She was hot, Victoria concluded a while later, lifting her curls up off her neck. She was hotter than she ever remembered being, yet it was not just the late afternoon sun that had overheated her, but a fire growing within. Each time she looked at Jed, she burned a little more. He had kissed her, he had caressed her, he had begun to love her last evening, and then he had offered her the choice. Today she had begun to believe that she had chosen wrongly.

Every lingering glance of those hard green eyes filled her with excitement, making her recall the smokiness of their depths when he had lowered his mouth to hers, the huskiness of his voice when he had freed her. Once more she marveled at the man who had risked everything to save her but sought nothing in return. He *was* a maverick, a renegade who would never be caged by convention, but that was all right, her heart whispered. The world needed Jed Kincaids more urgently than it needed Hayden Reeds—and tonight, so did she.

Before she could think about her obligations to Hayden and change her mind, Victoria stood up and moved toward Jed. All thoughts of her past as well as her future dissolved in the reality of the present moment. She discarded decorum and society's expectations, embracing the impetuous streak Jed had seen in her. Deliberately, she exposed the full length of her leg as she stood before him awaiting his attention.

"I think it's time," she murmured softly.

"Time?" Jed muttered hoarsely. Unable to look away from her, he was finding it difficult to concentrate on her words.

"Jed, I want to be ashore," she said. Intentionally, she leaned forward to run her hand down his shoulder to where his rolled-up sleeve exposed his well-muscled forearm. Her fingers idly traced a path among the small hairs that curled against his skin as she moistened her lips.

His eyes flew up to her face and Jed knew he had no hope of refusing what she offered him. Last night she had been unsure. This evening, clearly she was not.

Grabbing her hand, he lifted it to his lips and slowly kissed its palm, tantalized by the sweet orange fragrance clinging to her. If the shivers wending their way down his spine were any indication, after Ali was asleep tonight, they would share untold joys of loving.

"Ali, wake up, the left bank looks like a good spot to spend the night," Jed called loudly, rousing the Egyptian from his torpor in the bow. "I'll need a hand with the sail. We could all use a good night's sleep," he added. His eyes were trained on Vicky and full of roguish promise as he relinquished his hold on her.

The evening meal was disappointing, Jed noticed an hour later. Amused that the same menu that had been so pleasing twenty-four hours ago left him unimpressed tonight, he forced himself to eat nonetheless. Of course, his plans for after dinner might be affecting his appetite, he supposed.

Lifting his eyes from his plate, he watched Vicky moving the roast lamb about her plate as though she too had other hungers more pressing. But then she speared a piece of meat and brought it daintily to her mouth and his breath quickened. Once more Jed felt the excitement her mouth open beneath his had generated last evening. Running a shaking hand through his dark hair, he prayed that after the hours Ali had spent at the sail, he was particularly weary. Perhaps he could set an example, Jed thought, yawning loudly and making a show of stretching his arms.

"Sorry, I don't know what's come over me. I am just plumb exhausted tonight," he ventured.

"After more than two weeks of perilous adventures, your body is finally admitting its human limitations. The rest of us have been thoroughly spent for days," said Ali.

"Ali is right," agreed Victoria, rising to her feet and gathering their plates. "It is time we *all* went to sleep."

Soon each of the travelers was abed, one waiting for sleep and the other two for something quite different.

When next Vicky opened her eyes, the night was quiet. Ali was snoring gently and Jed was kneeling beside her.

"The fire is out," she murmured softly, rising to accept his unspoken invitation. He was all she had thought about the entire day. For her, nothing else existed but this man and this place. There was no future and no past—only now and Jed Kincaid.

"We won't need it once we're away from camp." With a practiced stealth that came from avoiding the curiosity of a slew of brothers, Jed grabbed two blankets and led the way past the sleeping Egyptian. She followed gladly, her pulse quickening with each step she took as she willingly answered the seductive call beckoning her woman's soul.

Moving quietly across the grass near the shore, Victoria was struck by the untouched beauty of the night. The sky was an inky black, stretching from one horizon to the other, a perfect foil for the heavenly lights that spoke of infinite glory and majesty. Each star was set apart by the darkness surrounding it, a sparkling diamond resting on a bed of rich ebony velvet, while in the west the crescent moon seemed carved from alabaster, its ivory sheen pure and milky.

Then Jed stopped and spread the blankets on the ground, rising quickly to take her in his arms. When he came to her, she found the heat of his body at once soothing and provocative, reminding her of what was to come.

She was so small, her blond head barely met his chin. All day he had longed to clutch her fiercely to him and drive her mad with ecstasy, but now that she was in reach, he found he wanted to go slowly and make their night together last forever. Looking down into her expectant face, he smiled and bent to kiss her.

As his lips covered hers, Victoria felt a surge of excitement, recalling their feverish embraces of the night before. His touch this time was gentle though, each tender caress of his lips a reassurance of his patience. His kisses danced across her face, alighting briefly like a hummingbird atop the freckles scattered across her cheeks, tasting and teasing. His firm mouth traced its own meandering path in no hurry, tantalizing her eyes, her chin, even the tip of her nose, before returning once more to pleasure her impatient lips. Paying her loving tribute, his worship was thorough and unselfish. Where once Jed would have thought to dominate, now his only instinct was to satisfy.

When Vicky would have parted her lips to welcome him, however, he chose instead to lick the corner of her rosebud mouth, his rough tongue inflaming her with brief strokes of unbridled fire. Then he claimed her lower lip and nibbled lightly at it.

Shivers of wordless sensation echoed through her, coursing sudden heat from her feet to her head. Unprepared, Victoria gasped aloud at the pleasure he evoked so effortlessly.

"Jed," she moaned softly, her small hands clinging to him for support as her body yielded control to his touch.

"Right here," he murmured against her ear. The warmth of his breath sent waves of delight spilling over her. By the time she recovered her sense of balance, he was assailing her senses again.

"Je-Jed." Vicky had trouble forming his name, so intense were the sensations crowding her. She felt as though she were drowning in a sea of ever-increasing fire, and while she didn't want it to end, neither could she go on without a brief respite. "I—I need to catch my breath."

At once Jed was repentant for his urgency even as he rejoiced in her inexperience. Of course, he should have anticipated Vicky's unfamiliarity with her body's responses.

"I'm sorry," he apologized quietly, his fingers stroking her neck while he held her close. "I shouldn't have hurried you."

"No, no. You've done nothing to apologize for," Vicky answered, her words coming in small panting phrases. Hesitantly she drew back from his embrace so she could see his face. "I just didn't expect to be so overwhelmed."

Jed's eyes were dark and unreadable in the starlight, but his warm smile told her that her words had pleased him.

"If you trust me, I promise to take you to the stars and back tonight," he said softly.

"Of course I trust you, but *I* spent the evening imagining that we'd bathe together first," she reminded him with a seductive smile.

Reaching down, she undid the clasp at her waist and dropped her skirt, stepping out of it and tossing it onto the waiting blankets as Jed watched.

If Vicky wanted to direct part of their journey of discovery by returning to the river, as much as it might try his self-control, Jed decided that he couldn't deny her. He could, however, assist.

As she lifted her hand to unfasten the buttons of her high-necked blouse, Jed's hands stayed hers.

"May I?" he asked, his voice hoarse as his body telegraphed its surging need, a need he would have to keep in check.

At her ready nod, Jed swallowed deeply and brought tremulous fingers up to meet the challenge. Awkward as a schoolboy, he struggled with the first fastening while Victoria watched in amusement until finally, after excruciating minutes, the stubborn button fell to the ground. Suddenly the sweet hollow at the base of her throat was visible, its rapid pulse demanding Jed's immediate attention.

Slanting his head to kiss the small patch of quivering flesh, the American found his hands surprisingly able to complete the rest of their task unsupervised. Quickly he undid the last closure, but as he parted the fabric, unveiling the beauty of her high, firm breasts, Jed's breath caught in his throat.

"You're magnificent," he praised, drawing the blouse off her shoulders and dropping it to the ground. Impertinent nipples, half erect in the night air, called to him, and he could not refuse to reward their allure.

Then he was kneeling before her, one arm wrapped around her waist to lend her support as he raised his head and feasted his eyes on her breasts, all thoughts of the river forgotten. He reached out, carefully caressing the small pink nubs with rhythmic strokes until Vicky writhed at the sparks his touch set off. When his lips opened and he leaned forward, his tongue laving one nipple while his fingers continued to fondle the other, she could not contain the tantalizing shivers riddling her body, making her yearn for she knew not what. Curling her fingers in Jed's hair, she wordlessly appealed to the heavens for release.

When he heard her moan and felt her tremble in his grasp, Jed belatedly recalled his intention to introduce her *slowly* to loving and he cursed himself. Her pleasure and her acceptance of it should have been his primary concern, and yet he had selfishly taken when he should have been giving. At once he ceased his delicate ministrations and held her tight, his head pressed against her chest, newly appreciating the warm, musky smell of her. Running his hand down her well-formed back until she quieted, he felt her relax in his arms as her breathing slowly eased.

"Jed," he heard her whisper a few minutes later. "I can't speak for you, but I think I reached the stars."

"You're only halfway. Come down here, sugar, and we'll get there together." In an instant, she was kneeling on the blanket beside him, caught once again in his feverish embrace, this time meeting and answering each thrust of his tongue with her own demands. Somewhere deep within, her lust had been set aflame, its unleashed power threatening to vanquish all else, and Victoria knew she must yield to its demands.

She craved the feel of Jed's naked flesh against her own, and anxiously undid the buttons of his shirt, yanking it free of his trousers and trying to push it off his shoulders as they kissed.

When her rustling about disturbed Jed sufficiently, he reluctantly released her and shrugged out of the garment, but before he could pull her close again, Victoria reached for the buttons of his trousers.

"Wait," she protested, her hands lowering to the task.

"No, let me," he ordered hoarsely. Jed stood, removed his pants, and rejoined her, reclaiming her lips as his due.

"What about our swim?" she murmured against his splendid assault.

"Later."

In no mood to argue, Victoria splayed her fingers across the broad expanse of his chest. Teasing the fine dark hair that formed a triangular path downward, she circled his nipples with the flat of her palms, massaging him softly as she trailed her touch lower and lower with each rotation she made.

Just as her hand slipped near enough to touch him, however, he caught it and drew it to his mouth, desperate to distract her before the cost of the game became too dear. While he wanted to avoid setting limits on her exploration, Vicky was not yet ready to accept him.

Gently Jed took one of her slender fingers between his lips, sucking it briefly, nipping it with his teeth and encircling it with his tongue before surrendering it and moving on to the next.

She watched him, too tremulous to do more than observe, her skin flushed, her blue eyes heavy with passion, the roar of her blood pulsing too quickly to allow for rational thought.

Then they were lying side by side and he shifted his attention once more to her breasts. Loving them devotedly with his mouth, he dispatched his large hands to rove the wondrous contours of her body, fondling every inch of her sensitive skin, learning her as no one ever had, sending off brilliant flares of excitement that penetrated her very core.

When his teasing fingers reached the juncture of her thighs, Vicky stiffened briefly, but as he caressed the soft inner flesh of her leg, concentrating his favors there, she trembled with untold fire and realized she could deny Jed Kincaid nothing. Even as she trembled, he made her feel as though she were aflame.

When he brushed against her feminine essence, Victoria knew she was losing her mind from the fierce shudder he precipitated. But then as Jed coaxed his fingers within her, igniting her soul, she knew this frenetic madness was only the beginning.

Tremors took control of her, growing with each stroke, and she found herself arching upward to meet his touch, wanting the moment to last forever.

"Je-ed? What should I do?"

Her voice was strained, he noted, every syllable as much a signal of her readiness as the sweet, wet feel of her.

"Be patient a little longer," he urged, positioning himself between her thighs.

"Hurry. I can see the stars, Jed, but I have to reach them with you," she cried, nearly weeping for the sudden emptiness within.

Covering her mouth with his own, Jed hesitated only briefly before thrusting past nature's curtain into Vicky's moist warmth. Once he assured her all pain was past, she began to stir beneath him, eager to satisfy her body's demands.

Though Jed, concerned for her inexperience, struggled to ease her pace, Victoria was determined to climb to the heights fast and furiously. Unwilling to be left behind, he acquiesced, escalating his rhythm to match hers. Together they rode the wild waves of summative desire, the tempo of their loving building rapidly to a crescendo of frenzied delight.

Victoria's heart was pounding madly, her whole body was aquiver, and still she knew the pinnacle was yet to be reached. Urgently she pushed on and suddenly she heard Jed gasping for air, his voice imprinting her name upon the heavens. Then all creation split asunder for her as well, as jagged bolts of white-hot lightning splintered her soul into a thousand fragments, each spinning mindlessly out of control, carrying her far beyond the stars, into the very center of the universe.

Long moments later as she found herself slowly drifting back to earth, Victoria opened her eyes, almost expecting to see the face of an angel before her.

Instead Jed tenderly smiled down at her, his flushed face mirroring the joy that she felt.

"Thank you," she murmured, lifting her hand to caress his unshaven cheek, "for my tour of the stars. I doubt anything in this world could ever compare to it."

"Then, honey, you don't know Jed Kincaid very well," he retorted. "If it's comparison you want—"

"You mean . . . do it again, now?"

"Unless you want to take that bath you mentioned?" Jed drawled, shifting as if to rise.

"Later."

Her reply was brief, but the kiss with which she accompanied it left Jed no doubt what was on the lady's mind. And, for once, relishing the role of gentleman, he gladly obliged her wishes.

Chapter Fourteen

It was barely dawn when Jed awoke to the symphony provided by the wildlife living on the banks of the Nile. Luxuriating in the lushness of the cool grass against his back and sight of the pink-and-gold sky announcing the imminent arrival of the sun, he listened to the squawk and chatter of ducks, ibises and herons, and the lazy humming of countless insects.

He felt pretty indolent himself this morning—indolent and satisfied. A contented smile tugged at his lips while the memories of the passion he and Vicky had fashioned in the darkness welled up inside him. They were the sort of memories that could last a man a lifetime, but they wouldn't have to, he thought, his mouth broadening into a grin.

Inclining his tousled head, he studied the beautiful feminine face at rest atop his bare chest. In sleep Vicky's fiery beauty was softened and her delicate features more fragile. The heavy lashes that swept gracefully along her shuttered eyes became a source of momentary interest for him until he allowed his gaze to roam to her full, pouting lips. Yet, yielding as she appeared in repose, she couldn't hide the slightly stubborn line in which her chin was set, and the discovery made Jed want to chuckle in delight. It was an urge he resisted to spare her from disturbance.

Instead, Jed ran a forefinger along a shining curl with a reverence that was quickly transformed to possessiveness. Vicky was his now, every bit as much as he was hers. Her sweet, hungry response to him had told him that more clearly than words ever could. At the thought, a new wave of well-being surged through him, leaving him feeling more domesticated than a man of his temperament had any right to be.

The handsome American crinkled his brow in amazement. Despite the fact that he had been leery and had bucked like a bronco, Miss Victoria Shaw had gentled him. She had placed her mark upon him as surely as if she had heated a branding iron and literally applied it to his hide. His days of being a maverick were over.

He laughed at the incongruity of it all, watching his woman stir slightly in her sleep, her lips parting and a breathy little moan escaping them in the most provocative manner. Regarding her with tenderness, Jed knew that words like bachelorhood and freedom held little meaning any longer. Their importance had been irrevocably diminished, brushed away by the gentle touch of his lover's lips beneath his own.

And though he might have thought he had glimpsed it before, high in the Rockies in springtime or during sunset along Mykonos's shore, he knew now he hadn't truly discovered paradise until last night beside the Nile, wrapped in the arms of the woman he loved.

Loved! Jed wanted to whoop his joy out loud. He didn't know how it had happened, but last night he and Vicky had uncovered the secret that eluded so many who searched for it. Under the panoply of stars playing overhead, the passion they shared had been alchemized into something rarer and more refined than physical need.

What was Ali going to say, and Mama Abigail, and...Vicky's parents? A shadow crossed his face for a fleeting instant at the idea, until his jaw clamped down in determination. If they didn't like it, if they preferred a man such as Hayden for a son-in-law, he wouldn't allow them a say at all.

Any way he considered it, they had no cause to be riled about the way things had turned out no matter what dreams they may have harbored for their daughter. Certainly he hadn't set out to woo Vicky. If anything, he had intended to keep away from her and her high-society life.

Still, he could put up with a tad of it for Vicky's sake, he supposed with an indulgent sigh, just as she would no doubt yield to a little adventuring for his. As for the Shaws, they would come around eventually, he concluded with his usual confidence.

"Jed?" Victoria murmured suddenly, her sapphire eyes flittering slowly open.

"Who else would it be?" he asked. Bending to place a kiss on the tip of her nose, he smugly noted she wore the look of a woman who had been well loved. "Good morning."

"Good morning," Victoria echoed faintly. She burrowed her head back into his shoulder in an effort to prolong such a luscious moment. She didn't want to consider anything other than the fact that she was in Jed's arms, naked, beneath the open sky, relishing the feel of this man, the scent, taste and sound of him. She thrilled to the vibrations of his chest against her cheek as he spoke to her, his strong voice made all the more appealing by the gentleness that had crept into it, the same tenderness that had tempered the raw masculine power she had seen unleased within him under the starlight.

"Has anyone ever told you that you make the most marvelous pillow?" she asked, filled with contentment. "No, never mind, don't answer that," she amended. "I don't really want to know."

"All you have to know is that no one else will ever have the chance to tell me again," he returned, his tones husky and his breath coming hot and soft against her neck as he permitted his hand the luxury of stroking her silken skin.

"What do you mean?" Victoria asked, bewildered.

"Just that you'll never have to worry about me straying, sugar. From what I saw last night, I think I'm going to like staying home just fine."

"Pardon?" she asked, her heart constricting when his words dissipated the drowsy haze that had so comfortably enveloped her. His smile radiated through her like sudden sunshine on a rainy day. But like the sun's strongest rays, it harshly illuminated the flaws in their flight of fantasy, flaws that had been too well hidden in the night's velvety blackness.

"You're not exceptionally sharp in the morning, are you, sleepyhead?" Jed said with a chuckle that began to die away when he saw Victoria's eyes widen. If he didn't know better, he could have sworn he had heard a small gasp, as well.

"Aw, forgive me, darlin', I'm doing this all wrong," he said with endearing sheepishness. "Here I am talking about the type of husband I'll be, and I haven't formalized things by asking you yet. I just figured that after last night there'd be no need for words. But if you're insisting on a proper proposal, I'll be glad to oblige. Vicky, I love you. Will you become my wife?"

Victoria's thoughts ran wildly as she looked at him. Last night, she had known when she had accompanied Jed out of camp how such an excursion would end, yet she had gone, anyway, needing to answer the urgent call that had spoken to her. Burning with desire, she had been a creature crazed. Driven by a mad obsession, she had acted impulsively if instinctively. She had responded to the man's magnetism, the masculinity that had haunted her all throughout their journey into the desert, the primitive essence that had drawn her to him and made her want him even when she had hated him most.

And when she had finally capitulated, he had not disappointed her. He had been everything she had thought would be forever beyond her reach, the sort of male not allowed to dwell within the narrow confines of her staid world. He had, in short, been Jed.

She had answered his virile summons with no care for anyone or anything, but in the eyes of the world, she had been Hayden's fiancée last night. And regardless of the joy Jed had given her, Victoria discovered in the first rays of morning that, in her mind, God help her, she still was.

Yet, here was Jed giving her the opportunity to partake of all he was, all he could give, for an entire lifetime. Completely unprepared for his offer, she was overwhelmed. But from the anticipatory gleam lighting his dark green eyes, Victoria knew that Jed both expected and needed her answer immediately. What she required, however, was time to think.

As incoherent, half-formed thoughts whirled around in her head, Victoria yearned to be as wild and impulsive as the man who held her in his arms. But such behavior was not a part of her nature.

Certainly Jed knew her by now. He should see they would never suit. She belonged in his world no more than he belonged in hers. In fact, she would be a terrible wife for him, and eventually he would only come to hate her. She couldn't bear the thought.

Though she had always been spoiled, and had everything she wanted, for the first time in her young life, Victoria Shaw was faced with denial. And the most ironic thing about it was that it would be entirely self-imposed.

"Well, Vicky, I'm waiting for your answer," Jed reminded her with warm amusement. Women tended to complicate the simplest matters. All she had to do was say yes.

Victoria steeled herself to give him a response. "No," sh
finally whispered, wishing she could say otherwise.

"No!" he repeated in surprise, sitting up so abruptly tha
Victoria found herself flat on the ground. But before she coul
recover, he had leaned over, bringing his face next to hers. "I
this is meant to be humorous, Vicky, I'm not laughing. Wha
do you mean, 'no'?"

"It's not a very complex word," Victoria muttered, turnin
her head to the side so she didn't have to witness the hur
clouding Jed's eyes, reducing their usual brilliance to a dul
gleam.

"Now, listen to me, Vicky," Jed insisted, jumping to his fee
and pulling Victoria with him, refusing to relinquish his grip o
her. "I don't know what this danged foolishness is, woman
I'm not a man who makes commitments easily, but when
do..." His words trailed off as he released one of her hands s
that he could run his own through his thick dark hair in frus
tration. "Why the hell won't you be my wife?" he bellowed.

"You forget I'm engaged to marry Hayden," Victoria re
plied. The earnest supplication in Jed's eyes almost undid he
resolve, until she recalled what an affliction she had been to hir
since they had fled Khartoum. On several occasions she ha
almost cost him his life. How long would it be before he real
ized she was a burden he didn't wish to bear? Why couldn't h
understand that her pampered upbringing hadn't prepared he
to be the wife he needed, and that she loved him too much t
give way to her selfish urgings by binding him to her?

"Oh, is that all?" Jed murmured in relief. "You can't reall
want to go through with that after the night we spent. Hayde
isn't the first man to be jilted, Vicky. I know you don't want t
hurt him, but all you have to do is let him down easily." Yet a
Jed uttered the words, he had a strong sense of foreboding hi
instructions would come to pertain to him and not Hayde
Reed.

"I *want* to marry Hayden," Vicky persisted, confirmin
Jed's instinctive dread. Her words caused him to set her fre
altogether.

"You're lying!" Jed said, his prior vulnerability hidden in a
instant as his face became thunderous. "I was there last night
remember? I heard the way you called my name, just as I fel
you tremble beneath my touch. And I distinctly heard yo
moan without shame as I peeled away each stultifying layer o

civilization encrusting your passionate core. Passion would never be that way with Reed, and you know it.''

"Exactly," she answered in clipped, emotionless tones while she retrieved her clothing. Hastily, she pulled the garments over the curves Jed wanted to claim as his own forever, hoping the material, along with her words, would erect a barrier between them. "Hayden is a gentleman who knows how to treat a lady."

"And I'm a man who knows how to make you feel like a woman," Jed growled, his voice deep and dangerous. He wanted nothing so much as to enfold this stubborn female in his arms and prove his point, falling with her upon the grass, its crushed blades evidence of the fulfillment they had already shared. But though he cursed himself for a coward, he found he couldn't force her, and the birds he had thought so melodic when his own heart had been singing mocked him for his failings.

"But I was *born* a lady. I'm going to marry Hayden and he's going to receive a title. I was bred for such an existence and nothing else," Vicky responded quietly, her heart wrenching painfully within her when she placed a conciliatory hand upon Jed's shoulder only to have him shrug it off.

"And breeding always tells, doesn't it?" he muttered. Here he had believed he had penetrated Vicky's natural restraint—no *damn* it, he *knew* he had. Could it be fear that was making her skittish? Was all this because she was afraid to abandon her life for his? But before he could explore such a possibility, she spoke again.

"Certainly you can see that you and I don't belong together," she lied. The pain of telling such an untruth deepened when Jed stalked away from her and roughly shoved his legs into his trousers.

"The only thing I can see is that you have a mighty big problem looming ahead of you," Jed said coldly, his face stony and impassive. "How do you think Hayden will react when he discovers his future bride is no longer a virgin? Will your gentleman still want you after you inform him that you have lain with me?"

"I'll never disclose that it was you," Victoria said, her face paling. "Hayden can think it was one of my abductors who ravished me, and I won't tell him any differently."

"So you figure he'll find it easier dealing with an Arab taking your maidenhead rather than a barbaric American mercenary?" Jed asked, his quiet voice nevertheless bursting with rage.

"It will be better if he doesn't suspect the truth."

"And what makes you think I won't tell him?" he demanded.

"Because," Victoria whispered with sincerity, "for all the damage we have done to each other, Jed, I know you would never willingly hurt me."

With that, she raised herself up, reached over the barrier he had constructed by folding his muscular arms across his bare chest, and planted a kiss on his cheek. Then she turned and ran back to camp before the images of their shared rapture and the torment lurking in Jed's expression caused her to change her mind.

"Damn you, Vicky!" he muttered, ruefully admitting that Victoria had spoken some truth. He wouldn't do anything to cause her harm—but he wasn't about to let her go, either. He called out, his deep voice fierce and threatening, "Run off if you like, Vicky, but how far do you think you can go? You'll have to stop when you reach the river. And I swear on all that's holy, this discussion isn't over yet."

Jed finished dressing and did his best to tamp down his smoldering temper. Then, with an outer calmness that quarreled with his inner fury, he returned to the spot where they had beached the *falucca*.

To his consternation, however, Ali had already loaded the river craft and pulled it into the Nile, where it bobbed erratically, like some animate water creature straining to escape.

Victoria sat in the prow, graceful and regal. For Jed, such impatience to depart appeared another indication that the woman he loved was all too eager to return to the arms of another man. The notion filled him with fresh rage, and he roared like a wounded lion as he paced the shore.

"I'm not going anywhere, Vicky, until we get this matter settled to my satisfaction. Ali, get that damned boat back here."

"Prepare to sail, Ali," Victoria countermanded, her quiet reserve more effective than Jed's bellowing. "If you want to come with us, Jed, I suggest you do so now."

Ali looked from one to the other. Though he had warned against such a relationship, the Egyptian had known upon awakening this morning that Jed and Victoria had abandoned im in order to find each other. But something had obviously gone wrong.

Assuming their newly conceived relationship was doomed before it had ever really begun, Ali was startled to spy Victoria's sidelong glance at the American as she pretended to assiduously ignore him. Jed, in turn, continued to vigorously insist upon her notice. To Ali's eyes, it was obvious that the seductive dance begun in the heat of the desert had yet to be concluded.

"Ali! We're partners. Get that damnable hunk of wood back here. Vicky and I have something to talk about," Jed called again, his tone promising dire consequences if his wishes were thwarted.

"Tell him we're leaving," Victoria entreated, seeing the Egyptian's indecision. "Remind him that I'm anxious to return home to the life and fiancé waiting for me there."

His loyalties divided, Ali looked from Jed to Victoria once more. He considered it a great pity that the Jed Kincaid who had brought them safely through the relentless hazards of a lethal desert could not follow the simple path of his own heart. Or for that matter, that Victoria, so well educated in the demands of society, knew nothing about the behavior of a man in love. But they were both blind as beggars as their argument continued.

"I told you, Vicky," Jed called, not bothering to wait for Ali to convey Victoria's message before he replied, "I'm not going anywhere until you change your mind. And there's nothing you can do about it short of abandoning me here."

"If you force my hand, that's exactly what I'll do," Victoria countered. She feared if she did as he bid, her already weak resolve would evaporate. Terrorized that her surrender would ultimately mean his sacrifice, she held fast. "Ali, set the sail."

"What!" Jed thundered. "After I escorted you all of the way back from Khartoum, you're willing to desert me!" He wanted to throttle her, he wanted to bend her to his will, but most of all, he wanted desperately for Vicky to return to him of her own accord.

"We're leaving now, Jed," Ali finally interjected when it appeared that the two had reached a stalemate. From what he could observe, this was not an issue that would be settled quickly. Close as they were to Cairo, he was unwilling to squander more time. He had been away from Fatima overlong as it was. If Jed and the woman had anything to say to each other, they could do it aboard the *falucca*, not on the banks of the Nile. "Join us or stay as you will. We are getting under way directly."

"Go ahead, Brutus, but I'm staying here," Jed repeated, his obdurate features set in stone. He stood, golden arms folded across his well-muscled chest, waiting for the others to relent.

"That's your choice, Jed," Victoria shouted loudly but calmly, unwilling for his sake as well as hers to be forced into enduring any more of the deadly assault he waged upon her heart. "I know a man of your skills will have no trouble getting himself to Cairo."

It wasn't until the *falucca* began to drift farther from the riverbank that Jed perceived Victoria was quite serious.

"Wait!" he called, swallowing his pride yet managing to sound imperious all the same. "After keeping you alive this long, Vicky, I can't entrust your safety to a damn fool like Ali. Once I undertake a job, I see it through to its conclusion. I'll take responsibility for returning you to your precious Hayden in one piece."

"Too bad you didn't think of that last night," Ali muttered, his words lost in the wind beginning to fill the boat's sail.

"Bring the boat back to shore so I can board," Jed dictated.

Suddenly Victoria felt herself once again in a quandary. Of course she couldn't actually leave the man to whom she owed her life standing alone on the sandbank. But neither could she bear for Jed to begin his arguments anew under the misguided notion that he could override her objections. Maneuvering the *falucca* into position as he directed would only be construed through his distinctly distorted male perspective, as some sort of victory. And she couldn't permit Jed the slightest glimmer of hope that if he could persuade her to steer the boat into shallow water, he could persuade her to be his wife, as well.

Placing her fingertips alongside her throbbing temples, Victoria considered her dilemma, conscious of the two men regarding her with blistering intensity. Watching the ripples of the Nile flow by, she had an inspiration.

"There's plenty of room aboard, Jed," she called, "but if you want to come with Ali and me, you'll have to come to us."

"What am I supposed to do, swim?" he asked incredulously.

"Why not?" she called with forced gaiety. "I seem to recall ou telling me how much you like frolicking in the water." rom Jed's scowling reaction, Victoria sensed she had been uccessful. Forced to swim out to the *falucca*, he would un-oubtedly be in such a temper that he would shut her out and eep to himself once he arrived. At least that was the pattern he ad followed on their journey across the desert whenever she ad done anything to particularly annoy him. As she watched ed lunge into the great river and begin his powerful strokes, utting through the surface of the water with apparent ease, ictoria prayed that such would be the case now, as well.

From the moment he had pulled himself into the boat, drip-ing and infuriated, Jed had maintained a stony silence. He sat part from the others in the stern of the *falucca*, an ominous resence seeking to hide his rent heart and injured pride be-ind the fierce glowering he aimed at Vicky and, occasionally, li.

Only the term *utter betrayal* could aptly describe the griev-us wrong Vicky had done him, at least to Jed's way of think-ng. Rejection was something new to him, and he was at a loss s to how to deal with it. It was ironic, he thought bitterly, that e had spent most of his adult life eluding the grasp of wily fe-ales who saw him as a perspective spouse, only to be spurned y the one woman who had made him think of marriage.

His steely eyes riveted to Victoria's profile, Jed swore to onceal the raw gash of grief that ran through him.

Alone with his thoughts, he eventually turned to watch the ertile land fronting Egypt's great river slip by as Ali skillfully teered the *falucca* closer and closer to Cairo. But the troubled merican didn't really see the whitewashed houses with their omed pigeon coops and outdoor ovens. He didn't notice the xen set to turning the irrigation wheels, coaxing the river's aters into shallow ditches meant to reclaim arid land. Nor did e observe the *fellaheen* at work and at play alongside the Nile's anks.

Instead, Jed saw only Victoria's face as it floated through his vretched memories, stubbornly courageous in the pens of Khartoum, blushing in response to one of his more colorful emarks, alive with anger when they had battled along the trail, nd most vivid of all, the face she had worn last night, lips ripe and eyes alive with blue flame, when she had joined him in sweet ecstasy.

Such a countenance was nothing like the icy facade she was displaying during this last leg of their journey, allowing it to slip only when she conversed with Ali. In so vile a mood, Jed attempted to dismiss the light, idle patter that passed between the woman he had idolized and the man he had considered his friend. But his irate frustration grew each time he observed their camaraderie and felt himself the outsider.

He also noted with aggravation that they had journeyed since dawn, and in his companions' haste to reach Cairo, they had stopped for neither the midday nor evening meal, preferring to nibble at their food while sailing. At the rate at which they traveled, they would reach their destination just after nightfall, when they could rush to the homes they were so anxious to see again. Well, he'd find someplace to go, too, Jed assured himself, someplace where he could forget blue-eyed women who said one thing with their caresses and something entirely different with words.

But it was no use. He found he couldn't delude himself. *Khere ohe,* or Cairo, was approaching much too rapidly to suit him. The great city might be known as the diamond on the handle of the Nile Delta's fan, yet for Jed Kincaid, it was not a destination rich with promise. Instead, it was a place that would tender him nothing other than an end to his impossible dreams.

And still the *falucca* pressed forward. On his left, he saw the village of Esh Shobak, and situated on the right was Et Teben. Soon they would pass the crumbled foundations of fabled Memphis, and after that, Giza, its ancient pyramids visible against the desert wilderness awash with impending sunset. Then, skirting the islands in the middle of the Nile River, Cairo would finally rise up on the eastern bank of the river, the Mokattan Hills providing a dramatic backdrop behind it.

As the debris of centuries sprawled before him along the shores of the majestic Nile, its very presence seeming to grasp at ages long gone, Jed silently cursed the fact that time was something that could not be recaptured. If it were possible, he would travel back in time but a dozen hours and extract Vicky's promise to become his wife while they had been in the throes of loving and she had been unable to deny him anything.

But as it was, his life was no different than the shattered ruins strewn along the bank. Jed felt that like them, he would never again be whole. Soon Vicky would disembark, and then she would be lost to him forever.

At the notion, Jed began to wage a mighty struggle with his ego, wanting to confront her once more and contest her decision before it was too late. Yet he was unable to make the first move until he heard her silken voice advising Ali about the location of her father's estate, a few miles north of the city. Then he felt his courage surface, buoyed up by his rising sense of desperation. Unfolding his well-muscled body, Jed stood and turned toward Victoria, his purposeful step echoing along the *falucca*'s keel.

Forcing herself to concentrate on the ripples of the Nile as they fragmented the sunset into a thousand gleaming jewels, Victoria was too timid to allow her thoughts free rein. She knew with certainty that, unchecked, every single idea would center around the fiery, virile man who all day had sat rigid with pride such a short distance away, and yet, forever beyond her reach.

For hours on end, she had tried to keep her guilt at bay for the treatment to which she had subjected Jed when they had departed the landing site north of Gharb Assuan. But he was the sort of man to assume acquiescence in one area meant surrender in all. While it had been cruel to make him swim out to the *falucca*, it would have been entirely heartless to have allowed his expectations for their future to renew themselves by giving in on even that issue. The penitent blonde held on to the thought, but it didn't make her feel any better, nor did the sudden sound of Jed's approach, leather boots on sun-dried wood.

"Vicky, we have to talk," Jed said. The soft persistence in his voice made Victoria's heart ache. Whatever hell she had inadvertently created for him, for both of them if truth be told, it was apparent Jed stubbornly refused to abandon all hope.

"There's nothing to discuss," she stated, refusing to turn her head until the gentle pressure of his fingers along her jaw forced her.

"Have the decency to look me in the face when you lie to me," he commanded firmly. "We both left a lot unsaid. Maybe in my eagerness, I rushed you, demanding a response you weren't ready to give—"

"I'll never be ready to give you what you want," Victoria hastily retorted, as an eavesdropping Ali listened intently and misinterpreted her meaning.

"Never is a long time, Vicky," Jed commented. He allowed his forefinger to trace the curve of her cheek lightly before falling across her lips and moving down to her chin.

"Your demand didn't bother me. In fact, it was a relief to get things out in the open and over with," Victoria claimed defiantly. She was so occupied with fighting the sensations Jed's touch evoked that she was oblivious to Ali's eyebrows rising in surprise as he loosened his hold upon the sail, the *falucca* veering sharply to the right until he could get it back on course.

"Then what's the problem, Vicky?" Jed inquired, only slightly aware of the boat's movement as he tried to be patient and understanding.

"You," she erupted crossly. She wanted to send him back to his self-imposed exile in the rear of the *falucca*. How much more of his purposeful attentions she could endure, she didn't know. "What would ever make you think I'd want to marry a man like you?"

Marry? Ali thought, a grin bursting upon his face. Why hadn't either of these foolish foreigners informed him that marriage had been mentioned? That made this no more than a lover's quarrel.

"Maybe it was the way you moaned my name last night," Jed drawled, hooking his thumbs into the top of his trousers. Against the waning Egyptian sun, he appeared larger than life, more than human, and very, very male. Chuckling quietly at the impact of his words when Victoria squirmed uneasily, Jed awaited her response, certain she could not deny the truth of what he had said.

"How dare you!" Victoria finally exclaimed, seeking to make it appear that his words had offended her rather than nearly causing her surrender. "Your rude comment only proves my point. You're no gentleman. I could never wed a man of your sort," she lied, praying the quivering that shook her soul would not extend to her voice. "Vicky Kincaid? Hardly! Hayden is the one to whom I have given my heart, and I can't wait until I am *Victoria Reed.*"

Hearing her name joined with that of the consular agent was the spark that finally lit Jed's ever-shortening fuse and caused him to explode.

"So Hayden's the man you love?" he roared.

"Yes, he is," Victoria insisted, despite what it cost her.

"Then why bother to go to your parents' home tonight? Why don't we just dock in Cairo and I can take you directly to Reed, the man of your dreams?"

"But—"

"But what, Vicky?" Jed boomed, his neck corded with tension and his green eyes darkened by anger. "Surely you can't bear to be separated from him for a moment longer than need be . . . unless you're not telling me the truth."

"I am," Victoria averred. "Take me to Hayden. I'm longing to see him. I can't wait until he holds me in his arms once again."

"Then damn it, that's exactly what I'm going to do," a frustrated Jed growled, stomping over to Ali and taking control of the boat. "Just think, within a few hours, you'll be rid of me and in Reed's embrace," he taunted.

Malicious as his wretchedness made him sound, somewhere, hidden deep within the recesses of his mind, Jed nurtured the hope that if Victoria could view her two suitors side by side and compare them, she would not be so quick to settle for the Englishman. It was a gambit infused with as much risk as desperation. But the way Jed figured it, it was his last opportunity to win Vicky's heart before she disappeared into her world and he was left alone in his.

Chapter Fifteen

Darkness had fallen before Jed finally moored the *falucca* at a spot not too far from the British Consulate. Helping Victoria onto the quay, Ali darted Jed a searching look as the American jumped ashore.

"Well, what are you waiting for? Go home to your Fatima," Jed barked before the other man could speak.

"As much as I yearn to see my wife and tell her of my safe return, I do not want to desert you when you are so troubled," the Egyptian stated, his hawkish features alive with sympathy.

"You didn't mind leaving me on the bank of the Nile this morning," Jed said with a snort. "As for trouble, I won't have any once I hand *Miss Shaw* over to Reed."

"Perhaps I should go with you," Ali said indecisively. He was afraid that if he left the man to his own devices, Jed would only make the situation somehow worse. "We began this journey together. We should end it the same way."

"Listen, Ali, as far as I'm concerned, our forced partnership is over," Jed pronounced acridly. "I'm not about to tolerate your company any longer than I have to. Get the hell out of here. I've seen enough of your face to last me a lifetime."

"All right, so be it. But before I leave, there is something I must say," Ali stubbornly continued, drawing Jed aside and lowering his voice. "I thought you were a brave man, Jed Kincaid, and now I find that is not the case. Slave markets, dervishes and miles of treacherous sands mean nothing to you. Still, you fear the simple pain of the human heart. You want the woman, and yet I can see from your face you will do nothing to win her. It is a coward's action to turn away. Fight for her, Jed. Forget your trepidation and your pride."

"Go home, *fellah*, to your spouse and your shop," Jed hissed, the muscles of his jaw working in barely suppressed fury, "before I permit my temper to get the better of me and I kill you."

"You know where you can find me," the Egyptian said quietly before turning back to the *falucca* to claim Fatima's bolts of silk. Then he bid Victoria a fond if brief farewell and walked off.

Jed ran the back of his hand over the stubble-covered planes of his cheeks while he watched Ali's tall, lean frame disappear into the crowd that had begun to form at the sight of such bedraggled travelers arriving at the quay in the darkness.

He certainly wasn't looking his best, but it was Victoria with her disarrayed profusion of blond hair, disheveled blouse and torn skirt that commanded the most notice. Before she could arouse any more curiosity, Jed hired some porters, shouting orders for them to take his saddlebags to the Crescent Hotel where he kept rooms. Then he shouldered his rifle and roughly grabbed Victoria's elbow, propelling her toward the consulate.

"What do you mean Reed's not here?" Jed shouted, his black scowl meant to quell the pomposity of the aide left in charge of the consulate for the night.

"Just what I said," the new staff member replied officiously.

"Then where the hell is he?" Jed practically snarled, unwilling to see his plans for coercing Vicky into making a choice fall apart as a result of Hayden Reed's schedule.

"He's most likely at home," the aide said with a disdainful sniff, eyeing this barbaric colonial and the beauty of questionable character he had in tow.

"Well, send someone to haul his tail back here," a fuming Jed ordered, his impropriety shocking the minor official more than the rifle he had left with the guard in the vestibule.

"I beg your pardon!" the Englishman commented archly.

"You can do that later," Jed said. "Right now, go and fetch Reed. Tell him I've returned his fiancée."

"Miss Shaw?" the incredulous fellow asked in awe, as he took in Victoria's sun-reddened cheeks and shredded clothing. At her nod, his arrogance transformed into fawning solicitation. "I'll see to it right away," he replied, bowing while he backed out of the room, "and I'll have some tea sent up, shall I?"

"Yeah—I sure could do with a bracing cup of tea right about now," Jed said with sarcasm lost on the bureaucrat. "And make yourself scarce until Reed gets here," he called to the retreating figure. "Miss Shaw would like some privacy."

"Very good, sir."

After the man's departure, Victoria began to pace the room nervously. She had been shocked and put out to hear that Hayden had left his bachelor quarters and taken up residence in the house that would be theirs. But she had quickly forgiven him, supposing that the move was no more than a desperate clinging to hope, an affirmation that she would return and they would be married. However, it now dawned on her that his absence meant she would be compelled to spend more time alone with Jed Kincaid, something she hardly relished, and her pique with Hayden began to flourish all over again.

Her attitude would make it most difficult to be convincing when she threw herself into her fiancé's arms for their joyous reunion. Yet that was exactly what she had to do in order to make Jed believe Hayden was the man she truly wanted.

Would her virile rescuer watch her then as intently as he was doing at present? She felt his green eyes boring into her as she took step after step across the luxurious rug sitting upon a perfectly polished floor. Graceful and focused as he was, Jed looked like some great desert cat, hungry for prey. With trepidation, Victoria waited to hear his husky growl float across the hot, heavy air that hung between them, but to her relief, he kept his silence.

For each minute that passed without his speaking, a tiny bit of tension eased from her body and gave her cause to hope that perhaps he had seen logic and finally accepted her decision.

By the time the tea arrived, the pretty blonde was comfortable enough to perch on the edge of a damask-covered chair, though she still cast an occasional wary glance in Jed's direction. When the servant had disappeared, she chanced pouring the hot drink set before her, fighting not to allow the trembling of her hands to betray her unsettled state. There was nothing she longed to do as much as throw herself in Jed's arms, but she very civilly poured two cups of tea instead, not at all surprised when one cup remained untouched.

Oh, how she had longed for tea poured from a dainty teapot when she had set out from Khartoum. Back then, she had sworn there was nothing so wonderful as the trappings of civilization. But finding herself seated upon plush, expensive furniture beneath a crystal chandelier, with oil paintings on the wall and a fragile china cup in her hand, she discovered none of it mattered.

Jed Kincaid was what she wanted now. Even in his rumpled clothes, with his dark hair too long and a stubble of beard on his rugged face, Jed possessed a thousand times more dignity than his surroundings. There was an essential masculinity about him, and a vital, virile pride that diminished the importance of the things elite society valued. Once more, she was tempted to go to him, to bow her head and beg him to take her back, until she remembered why she could never be his. After all he had come to mean to her, it was beyond her to condemn Jed to a life of eventual unhappiness.

A soft sigh escaping her, Victoria Shaw reconciled herself to the inevitable. She would set Jed free and try to make Hayden a good wife.

Her roiling thoughts were interrupted by the sound of hurried footsteps along the corridor. Apprehensively, she stood and faced the doorway, steeling herself to do what had to be done.

At the measured tread echoing in the hallway, Jed yearned to take Victoria in his arms and crush her lips with his own, ardently claiming as his right her uninhibited response. Reed's being greeted by such a sight would settle the question of whom Vicky was going to marry once and for all. But despite the plan's bold merits, he decided against it, sensing instinctively that Vicky would hate him for doing such a thing.

With no other options he could see, Jed did nothing more than rise impatiently for the confrontation with Hayden Reed.

Suddenly the door was thrown open, and the tall, spare Englishman rushed into the room. Taking Victoria into his arms, he placed a light kiss on the top of her forehead.

Hell, that wasn't the way he would greet his woman, Jed decided in contempt. Surely a passionate woman like Vicky couldn't be satisfied with such a restrained show of devotion. Still, the sight of Victoria enfolded in Reed's embrace had him clenching his fists as well as his jaw while he waited for the diplomat to stop his murmured crooning to Victoria and to recognize his presence.

When Reed finally pulled away from her, Jed noted that Vicky was crying, huge tears cascading down the contours of her delicate face. It was only the second time he had seen her cry, and the thought that her tears could possibly be those of joy was enough to throw Jed into a frenzy.

"Reed," he said, his barely controlled voice harsh.

"Kincaid," Hayden greeted him with a tight nod. "I'll deal with you in a moment, after making certain Miss Shaw is quite all right before sending her home to her parents."

"Her parents?" Jed echoed in mocking disbelief. Hell, he'd be too busy even to think of notifying the girl's family of her return until sometime around noon tomorrow.

"Of course!" Hayden snapped, annoyed by the impudence of the man he considered no more than a vulgar ruffian. It was beneath him to lose his temper with this brash American before Victoria departed, but restraint seemed impossible in light of Jed's contemptuous smile. He decided, therefore, to dispatch his fiancée to her home with all possible haste so he could deal with the smug American as he deserved.

"Victoria, darling, you seem as well as can be expected under the circumstances," he began, his lips compressing at the sight of the shapely leg exposed by her skirt. "As overjoyed as I am at your return, I can't be entirely selfish and remiss in my duty to your parents. I shall have an escort brought around to see you safely to your father's estate so that he and your dear mother can partake of the happiness I feel."

"But, Hayden, don't you want to know what happened?" Victoria asked with distress. Suddenly she was loath to leave Jed's company, her heart bereft at the prospect of never seeing him again.

"Of course, my dear, but that can wait for tomorrow," he said with a rigid firmness couched behind a gentle tone of voice that set Jed's teeth on edge. "Besides, you must be overcome with exhaustion, and the only place for you is your own bed."

Her own bed! You don't deserve her, you fool, Jed wanted to shout, hoping that this rejection would open Vicky's eyes.

"But, Hayden," Victoria importuned, trying not to compare her fiancé with the man who had saved her life only to claim her heart.

"No buts, Victoria," Hayden insisted. He reached for the bell pull that would summon his aide. "I won't hear another

ord about the matter. Do as you're bid like a good girl, won't
ou?''

To Jed's utter disbelief, Victoria docilely agreed. This wasn't
he fiery Vicky he had known. But more than that, the anx-
ous American could not bring himself to believe she would
urn her back on him and leave this room, *still* Hayden Reed's
ntended.

Yet when the aide appeared, Victoria made no further at-
empt to protest. Eyes lowered, she bid her fiancé good-night,
eceiving a proper peck on the cheek for her efforts.

In an instant, Jed stopped her before she could follow Reed's
ackey into the hallway. Heart beating thunderously in his chest,
he knew the moment of truth was at hand.

"Aren't you going to say goodbye to me, Vicky?" he asked,
his gruff voice half jeer, half entreaty.

"Of—of course," Victoria muttered, conscious of Hayden's annoyance. Drawing close to the man she loved, she felt
as though she were being wrenched in two. But she told herself
that her present pain was for Jed's sake. She had to be strong.

"Goodbye, Mr. Kincaid," she began, studying the tips of her
ruined shoes. Given Jed's silence, she was not prepared for the
ook in his eyes when she finally raised hers to his. It was a
aunting expression, a silent dare. He never thought she'd walk
out of this room without him and into a future that included
only Hayden Reed.

She faltered for a moment, calling on every bit of courage in
order to bid Jed Kincaid farewell. Finally, she knew she had to
proceed before she broke down under the strain of what she had
to do.

"Thank you for all you have done. I truly appreciate what it
has cost you," Victoria said in a small voice. Close to tears, she
reached up to place a light kiss on Jed's cheek. Then, before she
could react to the achingly familiar sensation the brief intimacy evoked, she turned and fled amid the flutter of her tat-
tered skirt.

A stunned Jed looked at the door that closed behind her. She
really had left him forever, and all for some jackass who would
never cherish her as he would have done. Perhaps Vicky's departure was just as well, he decided in an effort to fight the
helpless rage swelling up inside him. He certainly hadn't known
her as he thought he had. She had been right, they would never
suit.

"All right, Kincaid. Let us have at it," Hayden Reed sai briskly, giving Jed an excuse to push his tumultuous emotior aside and regain his control. "You were expressly told to do n more than deliver the ransom. The next thing I know, the oa sis was strewn with carcasses and not only has Miss Shaw di appeared. but so had you, the Egyptian and the money. You' better have a good reason for disobeying orders."

"I did my job, and I did it damn well," Jed said with a laz smile at odds with the grief constricting his heart. "As for or ders, I don't answer to you or anyone else."

"You most certainly do," Reed insisted.

But before Jed could form a reply that would eradicate th Englishman's arrogance, the door swung wide, catching h attention and renewing his hopes. The figure standing at th threshold was not Victoria's, however, though it was familia all the same. At the sight of Ali Sharouk, Jed nodded. At th moment he could use a friend, and despite the harsh words wit which they had parted, Ali was just about the only one he ha in all of Egypt.

"I am sorry to be late," Ali said, entering the room briskly "but I wanted to advise my wife of my safe return."

"That's all right. You didn't take all that long. Wasn't Fa tima glad to see you?" Jed asked with a grin that caused th Egyptian to turn a darker shade. "I told you I'd handle this."

"Not trusting you, I had to come to hear what you said," A proclaimed with irritation. But regardless of his words, both h and Jed knew why he was there. It had been worry for hi friend's well-being that had driven him out into the night onc more.

"I see you two are congenial as ever," Reed interrupted im patiently, wanting only to get this over with. "I was just ques tioning Kincaid's precipitate actions near the Wadi Halfa. Hov could you have allowed him to do so reckless a thing?"

"In truth, the American had no choice," Ali lied. Then h proceeded to relate the story of Victoria's rescue, or at leas those details he thought Reed should hear, Jed interjecting oc casionally to supplement his partner's narrative.

The consular agent's eyes narrowed when the men told hin the story of Victoria's near abduction by the dervishes, an again as Jed told him what he had overheard the night at th oasis when he had crept along the sand to get Victoria water.

"Were there any names mentioned?" Hayden asked coolly, though the stare with which he fixed Jed and Ali was most intent.

"No. That doesn't mean trouble is not brewing," Jed replied.

"Then you'd best give me every detail you can remember," Hayden directed, efficiently withdrawing a pencil and paper from a nearby desk drawer. Poised to take notes, a serious Hayden Reed made an impressive official, even to Jed's prejudiced eye.

But when the American and the shopkeeper had concluded their account, he regarded them with a smirk that smacked of dismissal.

"I suppose I should commend you for your intentions in reporting this dervish business, but I can assure you, it means nothing," he stated with an arrogance born of an education rooted in imperialism. "From my experiences in this heathenish outpost, I judge this to be no more than wishful thinking on the part of the natives. There is no need to concern yourselves."

"They're building a powder magazine on Tuti Island, rifles are being run down to the Sudan, and they've taken it into their heads that they have a Mahdi, a saviour!" Jed protested.

"These people are always looking for a new redeemer," Hayden replied, his tone drenched in boredom. "As for the firearms, scoundrels constantly smuggle contraband, try as we do to stop them. And by your own account, the powder magazine is far from being finished. The Sudanese will, in all likelihood, be too shiftless to complete it. None of what you have told me means anything."

"How can you say that? I insist you pass this information on to your superior," Jed argued.

"Kincaid, you are in no position to insist upon anything. In fact, if it weren't apparent that Miss Shaw feels some sort of misplaced gratitude toward you, I'd have you and your cohort arrested for failing to simply deliver the ransom money as directed. If you had done so, I have no doubt my fiancée would have been returned long ago, without being dragged along on some wild, hazardous journey through the desert. As it is, I've half a mind to jail you both. However, since she is home safely, I will allow her father to decide what is to be done."

"Let's hope he has more sense than you do," muttered Jed.

"Mind your manners, Kincaid," Hayden ordered, "or I'
follow my first inclination. As for the senior consular agent,
will determine what, if anything, he should be told. In m
opinion, this could all be something you've fabricated to fore
stall prosecution for placing Miss Shaw in needless jeopardy
However, being a fair man, I am going to give you a choice
Leave the ransom money and go, or remain and be arrested.'

Jed and Ali exchanged glances and wordlessly got to thei
feet. Reaching into an inner pocket of his shirt, Jed withdrev
what remained of Cameron Shaw's money and threw it on
table.

"A simple thank you would have been sufficient, Reed," h
said with disdain.

When he and Ali reached the door, Jed turned around an
addressed Hayden Reed once more. "You'll find money miss
ing," he announced, his voice steely. "There were expenses
Unfortunately, I didn't think to get receipts, so you can ad
theft to my list of crimes." Then he walked away with a non
chalance that told an incensed Hayden how very little Je
feared his authority.

By the time they reached the street, Jed's barely containe
fury threatened to erupt. His rage stemmed not so much fror
Hayden's treatment as from the fact that Victoria Shaw dare
prefer such a man to him.

"Where will you go?" Ali asked quietly, his face filled wit
concern. "I'm sure Fatima wouldn't mind if you—"

"Get on home, Ali," the American growled, interruptin
him before the words began in pity were completed. Then Je
Kincaid stalked away into the night, wondering where hi
footsteps would take him before he returned to his hotel. I
spite of his weariness, he had no wish to seek his bed. It woul
seem too lonely after he had grown accustomed to having Vick
sleep by his side.

Victoria stared silently at the passing civilization of Cairo a
the small trap carried her out of the city toward her parents
estate. Despite the late hour, lights shone in occasional win
dows, but the young woman saw only dark confusion surround
ing her.

She had deliberately scorned Jed's proposal to spare him
and tonight, mere moments before, had turned her back on th

man to whom she owed so much. And how had Hayden treated her? Like an inconvenient obligation to be dispatched from sight. Hayden was, by nature, a private, reserved gentleman, while Jed was nothing if not undisciplined, but why couldn't her fiancé have shown more enthusiasm at her return? She would have thought Hayden would have been relieved to see her after nearly three weeks.

Yet despite the man's shortcomings, she *had* chosen Hayden over Jed, Victoria reminded herself. She had no right to grumble because she was weary and troubled by second thoughts. Besides, Hayden did love her, certainly he did—and in return, she loved him, at least a little . . . didn't she?

When the carriage finally stopped before the Shaw home, the query still echoed in her heart, but Victoria cast it aside as a familiar voice called out in excitement.

"Victoria? Oh, dear Lord, it is you. Every night we've waited, hoping against hope that another day wouldn't pass without your return," cried Cameron Shaw, his jubilant emotions overwhelming his banker's demeanor. Without concern for decorum, he swept his daughter into his arms. "Grace, Grace, come quickly."

"Father, you don't know how often I prayed to see you again," she murmured against his shoulder. Pleased by his blatant affection, she couldn't help but compare it to Hayden's poor example.

"I wager not half so fervently as your mother and I did," he answered, hugging her close. Rather than relinquish his hold on her, the banker carried Victoria into the house, refusing to let her down until they reached the drawing room.

"My poor child." Even as Cameron released the girl, Grace enveloped her in a warm embrace, simultaneously calling out orders to the servants. "Draw Miss Victoria a bath, prepare a tray, see that her bed is turned down, oh, and bring us some tea."

"Never mind the tea," said Victoria's father. Going to the decanters displayed on a mahogany table, he poured three glasses of amontillado. "Sherry is bloody well more soothing for the nerves. Besides, we must toast the splendid chap who rescued Victoria and brought her back to us. Kincaid, isn't that his name? Where is he, child? We owe him a large debt of gratitude—"

"Ah—well—I imagine he's still at the consulate with Hay
den."

"You were with Hayden and *he* didn't bring you home?"
Grace could hardly believe her ears.

"It wasn't Hayden's fault. He wanted to, but he had to tak
Jed's report and I didn't wish to wait for him," extemporize
Victoria. Having made her choice, she was unwilling to hea
Hayden slandered any further, especially after listening to Jed'
derogatory remarks about him for weeks. "I wanted to hurr
home and reassure you—"

"Of course you did, dear," agreed Mrs. Shaw, "and right
so."

"I still want to meet Kincaid and salute the fellow," insiste
Cameron. Handing Victoria a glass of sherry, he reached dow
to stroke her flushed cheek, all too aware of what he might hav
lost without the man's assistance. "After all, he is the one wh
restored my dearest treasure. American mercenary or not, w
must invite the man to dine, Grace."

"I doubt he would come, Father," murmured Victoria, pal
ing at the notion of facing Jed under her parents' watchful eyes
Finally home, all she wanted was to forget him and return to he
life. Confronting the choice she had been compelled to mak
was not part of her plans. "Kincaid is not very social—an
there is Ali."

"That's no problem. I'll invite them both," countere
Cameron, a man accustomed to having his way.

"But Victoria says he wouldn't be comfortable," proteste
Grace, wondering how she would entertain such an odd pair a
her table. "Perhaps you could take them to Shepheard's—"

"Nonsense. The man is a hero and deserves to be treated a
such. It is only right Kincaid and his associate come here."

"Really, Father, I don't believe Jed will accept. Such an in
vitation would only put him in an awkward position," she ar
gued weakly. It had torn her heart asunder to bid Jed a fina
farewell once. She didn't think she would have the strength t
do it again.

"Don't concern yourself," counselled Grace. "Your fathe
will do as he likes. Come upstairs. A good night's sleep in you
own bed will have you right as rain by morning."

Victoria was too exhausted to protest any further. Camero
Shaw *would* do as he wanted, regardless of what she said, bu

en, so would Jed. Turning to follow her mother, Victoria
aned forward to kiss her father's cheek.

"I will be up to say good-night," he promised, running his
and over her unruly curls. "And, in the morning, you can tell
e all about your adventures."

Watching as Grace led his daughter from the room, Camer-
n shook his head. He knew he shouldn't question the gods,
ut he couldn't help it. If Kincaid had discovered any clue as to
vhy Victoria had been taken, he wanted to know about it to
revent a recurrence, and know it he would. Besides, to meet
n adventurer with the reputation of Jed Kincaid, a man who
ould steal his daughter from the very center of white slavery,
vould be a real pleasure, even if the chap was American.

Jed's haunted steps carried him through the serpentine pas-
ageways of Cairo's *medina*. Driven by a sense of abysmal loss,
e neither saw nor cared about the exotic sights surrounding
im. No matter how desperately he tried to banish it, Victo-
ia's visage was what he carried before him, blinding him to all
lse. The dragomans and snake charmer were invisible to him,
long with the beckoning merchandise artfully displayed by the
hopkeepers. Compelling as the streets of Cairo's Arab Quar-
er were, the lovely contours of Victoria's face continued to
asily supersede the reality flanking Jed.

As he pressed onward, the American evinced the supple grace
f a caged panther. Though his physical movements were not
ampered, his emotions had been captured by a blond, blue-
yed vixen, so that Jed was held prisoner as surely as if he were
ehind bars.

Rounding one corner and then another, Jed didn't even know
vhy he was in this part of the city, where he was going, or for
hat matter, where he had been. He felt lost, alone, a stranger
n a foreign land, and for the first time in a long while, he
vished one of his brothers were close at hand.

To dispel his sense of isolation, he had gone to a tavern, but
fter one sip of whiskey, he had left. Next, he had tried Nadir's
rothel, but could not bring himself to cross its threshold.
Nothing could serve as a balm for the wounds he carried within
is heart, and so he drifted aimlessly, searching for some sort
f a cure. Yet the only palliative that would make him whole

again was the beautiful Englishwoman installed on her father's estate, and she had made it clear she did not want him.

When Jed looked up to see where his random path had finally taken him, he was not overly surprised to see a display o brassware. Cursing himself for his weakness in needing some one, he nonetheless approached the shop, stopping before it open front. Standing in the midst of tables, pitchers, trays an coffeepots, he put his hands on his hips and called out to th shop's owner, hoping to hide his despondency behind mascu line bravado.

"Ali! Ali Sharouk, get your tail out here, man!"

Momentarily, a grinning face appeared, and Ali came ou into the narrow alley that served as a street.

"I was wondering when you would arrive," the please Egyptian announced.

"Yeah, well don't get all excited about it. I'm only here o some business," Jed said gruffly. Ali was a happy man, and Je suddenly thought better of bringing his troubles to the Egyp tian's doorstep.

"I am disappointed you come to my shop simply to condu business, but what is it I can do for you?"

"Why, I'm here to...to...to pay you for that damned cof fee service," Jed fabricated, discomforted by Ali's probin stare.

"Don't be ridiculous, Jed. That is long forgotten," the bras merchant assured him.

The Jed Kincaid Ali saw standing in front of the shop wa not at all to his liking. He appeared more haggard than th Cairene had ever seen him, even during the worst of the time in the desert. Back in civilization for almost two days, Jed ha yet to shave, and while his clothing was clean, it hardly be spoke fastidiousness. His usually brilliant eyes were dulled, an his spirit weary. It was unmistakable, even to the blindest o beggars, that Jed was a human being who was feeling mos wretched.

Ali refused to take the coins the American tried to press upo him, determined he would not allow his proud friend to leav without at least attempting to help him.

"Put your money away, Jed. I've riches enough," he in sisted, pushing Jed's hand aside.

"If that's the way you feel about it, I'll be going," Jed mut tered, stuffing the money back into his trouser pocket. Though e had come to view Ali as the next best thing to a brother, Jed ouldn't see himself running to another to bemoan his ill fortune. He'd handle his own problems. Coming here had been a mistake.

"Oh, no you don't," Ali proclaimed, pulling the retreating American forward. "You must be introduced to Fatima. She vould be displeased to find you had been here, and she was not iven the opportunity of meeting the man who had saved her usband's life."

"I don't know if that's such a good idea, Ali," Jed said, ligging in his heels and shaking off the Egyptian's grasp. He vas suddenly unprepared to observe the bliss Ali and his wife njoyed, the sort of happiness that had been denied to him by he cold-hearted woman who intended to marry Hayden Reed.

"I cannot think of a better one. To deny me this is to insult ne, Jed. I would have you enter my home and be my guest."

"Some other time. I'll be back," Jed mumbled.

"It is disheartening to see a man crumble because of a voman."

"Vicky has nothing to do with my deciding not to visit for a pell, Ali," Jed lied, tipping his hat in a gesture of farewell.

"Good," Ali called to his retreating back, "because no voman, especially that one, is worth such misery."

Jed whirled around, fists clenched, ready to do battle and rove that Victoria Shaw was worth more than the whole world ut together, until he observed Ali's knowing smile.

"Damn it, man, you almost had me ready to bust up your hop all over again," Jed said with a rueful smile, walking back o stand beside him. "Clever bastard, aren't you."

"I think so," the Egyptian said smugly. "Now, come, we will njoy some refreshment and talk of things that matter."

"Don't think I came here to discuss Vicky," Jed asserted, ollowing Ali along a narrow passage to a neat whitewashed lomicile hidden in the rear of the brass studio.

"As you wish. We will talk of anything that pleases you," Ali ssured his companion, though he anticipated his friend talk-ng about nothing other than the blonde who had conquered his eart amid the blazing desert sands.

"Fatima! I have brought a guest," Ali called as he bent his ong frame in order to enter the small door leading into his ome.

After a rustling of fabric behind a heavily beaded curtain, a diminutive feminine figure appeared. Swathed in mantle and veil, she advanced with mincing steps, her black eyes glistening like polished obsidian.

So this was Fatima, Jed thought, a half smile pasting itself on his face. Why, the woman wasn't anything like Vicky at all, no matter what Ali had said previously. Besides her dark coloring, Fatima was much shorter in stature. More to the point, from what Jed could see of her under her layers of clothing, she appeared plump as a little partridge. No, he wouldn't look at Fatima and think of Vicky, Jed promised himself, until he noted the way Ali glanced at his wife, as though he would do anything for her, even those things that seemed impossible to accomplish. It was then that Jed felt a pang of envy mixed with regret, seeing in his friend's face the reflection of his own feelings for Victoria Shaw.

Following introductions, a gracious Fatima hovered around the men like a minute bird hopping from one foot to the next, as she fluffed the pillows on which Ali and Jed reclined, brought bowls of water perfumed with jasmine for their ablutions, and offered trays of fruits and Turkish delight for their enjoyment.

In her behavior, Fatima wasn't much like Vicky, either, Jed thought wryly. Certainly he couldn't envision the woman he had rescued deigning to wait on him so solicitously. It wasn't until he had pulled a flask from his shirt and held it out to Ali that Jed saw a similarity between Vicky Shaw and Ali's wife. At once the woman's dark eyes sparked angrily, signaling her condemnation of the alcohol Ali had been reaching for. Without having to speak a word, Fatima had made her displeasure known, putting Jed in mind of the spirited female he had escorted across the desert.

A heavy sigh escaping him, the rugged American theorized that women were a funny breed. As much as they might chatter and squawk, their silent glances were far more powerful when it came to keeping a man in line. Ali's abashed haste to withdraw his outstretched hand and return it to his lap before it came into contact with the whiskey only supported Jed's observation. And so did the loving nod of approval Fatima dispensed as her husband's reward.

"I'm slated to see Cookson, the consul general's aide, tomorrow," Jed informed Ali brusquely, taking refuge in masculine affairs. "Reed doesn't know. I managed to circumvent him when I made the appointment."

"Perhaps if you shave beforehand, Cookson will be more likely to believe you," Ali commented wryly. He took a goblet of water from Fatima, its top crowned with an aromatic slice of lemon.

"Don't worry, I'll clean myself up some. It's just that I've been out having so much fun the last day or so, I've been rather remiss with my grooming."

"Excuse my saying so, Jed, but from your appearance, it would seem that you and *fun* are hardly acquainted."

"Well that shows what you know," Jed grumbled.

"You're too busy having a good time to do anything about what's making you so miserable, I suppose," Ali commented with exasperation. "I've never seen a man so gloomy."

"Well, I have good cause," Jed blurted. "The Shaws had the audacity to send me an invitation to dine with them. How can I put Vicky behind me when people keep reminding me of her existence?"

"What is so wrong?" Ali inquired calmly. "The Shaws merely want to show their gratitude."

"As if I could sit there in Vicky's home, watching her with Hayden Reed, seeing her bend her head to his. I'm afraid I wouldn't have much of an appetite. I'm not accepting."

"I am," Ali said in a quiet voice.

"You were invited, too?" Jed asked in surprise. Reluctantly he had to admit the Shaws were demonstrating well-mannered cordiality in inviting Ali. Most upper-class Britons would never ask an Egyptian to their homes, much less break bread with him. Perhaps the Shaws were not as lofty as he had judged them to be. Still, that didn't solve his own dilemma. It wasn't the woman Ali loved who would be sitting beside another man.

"Well, have a good time and convey my regrets," Jed growled. "I'm staying away."

"But of course you will go!" Fatima interjected, leaving Jed little doubt as to what Ali had told her. Speaking for the first time since his arrival, Fatima's voice was high-pitched and full of Eastern melody, but her disapproval of Jed's decision was plain. "You cannot hope to win the lady if you refuse to see her. How can you decline such an opportunity," she gently scolded, flitting around Jed excitedly, "when even I, a stranger, can see that you are crestfallen? Do not be as cowardly as a runaway rooster rejected by the hen, Jed Kincaid. Instead, you must continue to strut and crow more loudly than before, displaying your fine plumage to impress your lady.''

"Now, see here, Fatima," Jed began, "I appreciate your interest, but—''

"His plumage is nothing to crow about, my dove," Ali pronounced, his dark eyes sliding critically over Jed's disheveled garments. "But perhaps Abu the tailor can be of assistance.''

"Splendid, my husband! I shall fetch him right away!" Fatima exclaimed, clapping her hands joyfully.

"Wait a minute," Jed objected, starting to rise before Ali reached out to push him back down upon the cushions.

"Not to worry. Abu is an excellent tailor. He is responsible for clothing a great many of the foreigners living in Cairo. Of course, he will not be able to provide you with evening clothes for tomorrow night's dinner, but that cannot be helped. However, with prodding, he could have your finery ready in two or three days so that you can attend other social affairs at which Victoria might be present.''

"But—" Jed began, bewilderment crossing his handsome face.

"Don't worry, Jed," Ali interrupted quickly to forestall Jed's true objections, "there will be no door in Cairo closed to you. You are the city's newest hero, the man who traveled to the Sudan to rescue Victoria Shaw. You will find yourself with more invitations than you can handle.''

"I will find myself alone in my hotel room," Jed snapped.

"No, believe me, Jed. The invitations *will* come," Ali responded, smoothly ignoring the point the nettled American was trying to make.

"But—''

"There is nothing to cause you concern. Leave it all to us," the Egyptian said with a smile. "I am afraid Fatima will have it no other way.''

Chapter Sixteen

The next evening, Victoria sat listlessly before her mirror as her mother's maid finished dressing her hair with tiny pearls.

"I fear, Miss Victoria, that you have had too much sun for your hair to be at its best," fussed the girl. "No matter how many pins I use, I doubt these curls will remain in place all evening."

"Maybe it will be a short evening." If Jed had his way, her curls would be down long before the night grew late.

To Victoria's dismay, it seemed everything anyone said or did triggered thoughts or memories of the man. Even when she sought escape in sleep, he had come to her, his evocative hands tenderly worshipping her body as he had on the bank of the Nile, filling her with inexpressible joy—until she awoke alone and wept for impossible dreams that withered beneath the harsh sun of reality.

Jed was a vagabond adventurer who had only proposed to her out of a sense of guilt, Victoria practiced telling herself. Hayden, on the other hand, had a secure future and an impeccable character. As his wife, Victoria would find herself cosseted among the highest echelons of society, not fed half-polluted water transported in uncured skins—or kissed wildly, nakedly beneath the stars.

"I believe you are ready, Miss."

"Ready? Oh, yes, for Father's dinner party," murmured the distracted Victoria. "I'll wait a few minutes, Enid. Thank you."

Who was the woman looking back at her from the glass? fretted Victoria. On the outside, except for those irritating freckles and a pinkish tinge to her cheeks, she hadn't really changed. Yet in so many different ways, she had matured. Much as it troubled her to spurn Jed's attentions, how could she do anything else, knowing eventually she would make him miserable?

"Here you are, darling. I brought you a light dinner," said Grace, bustling into the room. "Oh, you do look quite lovely."

"Thank you, Mother, but I'll wait and dine with Father's guests shortly." Preferring not to admit the identity of those guests gave Victoria a few added minutes of peace. She stood gracefully and smoothed the royal blue skirt of her gown.

"But you know a lady never really eats in public. It is much better to have a bite privately, and nibble later."

"It seems so pointless," Victoria sighed. She never would have entertained such an opinion before meeting Jed, but through his eyes, she had come to realize how much of society's behavior was a sham. "Sooner or later, Hayden will see me eat a full meal."

"Not until after the ceremony, dear, and then it won't matter, you'll already be married," explained Grace, fluttering her fan. "Now, come, the chicken and yoghurt is quite nice."

Shaking her head, Victoria realized a concession to Grace's will would delay her meeting with Jed that much longer, and so she sat to heed her mother's urging.

"Kincaid, Cameron Shaw. I am *very* pleased to meet you, sir," said the banker. Stepping forward as the butler withdrew, he clasped Jed's hand firmly in his own. Slowly Shaw's eyes measured the lanky American, looking beyond the casual beige cotton shirt and trousers to read the heart of the man displayed in his sharp gaze and confident bearing. Satisfied when Kincaid met his pointed examination without flinching, Victoria's father nodded and smiled. "And this, I presume, is Mr. Sharouk."

"I am called Ali, sir," nodded the Egyptian, resplendent in a finely woven white *gallabiya* edged with gold embroidery. Surprised at Shaw's extended hand, the Cairene recovered quickly and completed the formality of a handshake with an Englishman.

"And you must call me Cameron," urged Victoria's father. Gesturing toward the French doors, he led the men out onto the wide, shaded terrace where Grace had conceded to hold the irregular dinner party. "What can I fix for you gentlemen? Gin? Brandy?"

Jed, uncertain of Shaw's motives in inviting him, was in no hurry to accept a drink, but Ali replied quickly.

"Have you no *zabeeb?*" he asked. Jed rolled his eyes. Out of Fatima's sight, Ali was ready to indulge.

"No, but I think you'll find the Napoleon brandy an admirable substitute. Mr. Kincaid?" asked Cameron, handing Ali a snifter. "I thought we might lift a glass to Victoria's safe homecoming."

"Gin will do. Your daughter called me Jed, among other things. Why don't you do the same?"

"All right, Jed," agreed Cameron, smiling. "Victoria does have quite a temper, and while she rarely displays it unless provoked, I take it you saw a good deal of it?"

"Jed was an expert at provoking her," said Ali, the brandy loosening his tongue. "Yet he returned as much fire as he took."

"Speaking about returning, before the ladies join us, I would like to settle the matter of your fee—"

"Fee? Who said anything about a fee?" Jed didn't know whether to be offended or amused. Reed wanted to jail him and Shaw wanted to pay him for the same unauthorized efforts? What did the man think Victoria was? A piece of misplaced luggage for which you offered a reward? "I never asked for money—"

"No, but Reed gave me back forty-five hundred pounds of the ransom and I've taken the liberty of writing a bank draft to each of you for half of that amount—"

"I don't wish to be disrespectful, sir, but I didn't go after *Victoria* in the hopes of collecting any blasted reward—"

"Come, come, Jed, Ali lost money when he was away from his shop—"

"Only the few piasters for pieces my wife's cousin sold too cheaply," protested the Egyptian, keeping a close eye on Jed's rapidly reddening face.

"And Jed, you make your living solving people's problems—"

"If you mean I didn't inherit a fortune, you're right, but all the same, you can take your damned money and—"

"Jed!" interrupted Ali. "I am certain Cameron meant no offense. You did him an honorable service—"

"That you did, son, and I mean to compensate you for your help. You accepted Nabar's money for reclaiming his amulet, why not take mine, though what you returned to me was more precious?"

Because I wasn't in love with his daughter were the words Jed longed to utter, but he knew he couldn't. Instead he stalked across the veranda to stare at the burning torches leading down to the landing on the Nile.

"Look, Shaw, I didn't do it as an employee looking to earn a salary. A man does what is right because it is the right thing to do, and that's all there is to it," pronounced Jed. Turning to confront Cameron, he permitted himself a sad smile. "Besides, during the journey back, your daughter and I became friends, and for you to compensate me for that relationship cheapens it."

"I understand, and I apologize if I offended you," said the older man slowly. Jed's old-fashioned creed of right for right's sake touched a chord and he couldn't help but admire the adventurer's philosophy. No wonder Victoria had referred to Kincaid as a maverick. There were few like him. "If there is ever any way I can be of service to you, you've only to ask."

"Thank you, sir, but of course, I speak only for myself, not Ali," clarified Jed, unwilling to deny the Egyptian the reward.

"I, too, will accept nothing," concurred the Cairene. If Allah were kind, Fatima would never learn of the spurned offer. "Pay was not a part of our arrangement with Mr. Reed."

"I'll say not. It is totally out of the question even to consider paying these men," rejected Hayden as the butler led him out to the veranda. Yet he realized he would have to choose his words carefully so as not to reveal that their motive for pursuing Victoria was to avoid being jailed. As much as he would have liked to expose their true character, it would cast him in a poor light for having used such scoundrels. "They probably cheated you royally on those *essential* supplies, five hundred pounds, wasn't it?"

"Since it was your *fiancée* who was returned, and *not* your money that was spent, I wouldn't think the expenses were any of your concern," said Jed. When Hayden colored, he smiled. Maybe the evening would not be as bad as he had feared, not if he could bait Reed. "Besides, padding an expense voucher was never my style."

"No, I suppose it's not brazen enough," said Reed, smarting from the counterattack.

"Ah, ladies, how glad I am that you have finally joined us," admitted Cameron as his wife and daughter appeared, none too soon. "May I say you both look enchanting?"

At Cameron's words, Jed turned and received a glimpse of paradise. Unrecognizable as the disheveled princess he had rescued, Vicky was a stunning embodiment of beauty. The blond curls he had only seen tousled and free had been tamed into submission, drawn up to grace her head as if with a golden crown, encrusted with small pearls. Her blue gown fell softly from her shoulders to flaunt her tiny waist, baring enough of her bosom to take Jed's breath away. Still, she appeared more modestly garbed than in his memories of her naked in the moonlight, memories he had been unable to exorcize from his heart no matter how often he refused to indulge them.

"Grace, may I present Jed Kincaid and Ali Sharouk, the men who so unselfishly risked their lives to assure Victoria's return?" said the banker, interrupting Jed's reverie.

"A grandiose display that would not have been necessary had they obeyed my orders," muttered Hayden as Jed's eyes narrowed at the barely discernible words.

"Mr. Kincaid, Mr. Sharouk, I am very pleased to meet you," affirmed Victoria's mother. "Cameron and I owe you a great deal."

"Nonsense, ma'am. Becoming so well acquainted with your daughter was enough reward for me," Jed replied. As he bent to kiss Mrs. Shaw's hand, his eyes unerringly caught and held Vicky's, daring her to deny the truth of his words.

He should look out of place here in such casual attire, Victoria thought, blushing prettily at his stare. Instead, it was her father and Hayden who appeared sadly uncomfortable beside Jed's rugged masculinity. His forearms, bared by his rolled-up sleeves, displayed his muscled hardness, evoking memories she had tried desperately to eradicate.

How did he do it? In the few minutes since she had joined the others, Jed had managed to monopolize her thoughts, despite Hayden's presence. It wasn't proper, but, recalling the gentle strength with which he had held her in the desert and his solidity behind her on the camel, she couldn't take her eyes from him.

"How nice of you to say so," Grace answered gently. "Thank you, too, Mr. Sharouk. I understand from Victoria that your assistance was invaluable."

"And wasn't Hayden so very clever for dispatching them to find me?" Victoria asked suddenly. Fighting Jed's mesmerizing glance, she moved quickly to her fiancé, leaning forward to kiss his cheek. Perhaps that would ease the visible tension, she hoped.

"Thank you, my dear, but we *all* know who the heroes of this evening's festivities are," Hayden said, his jaw clenched tightly.

"We'll have no false modesty, Hayden," chided Mrs. Shaw. He was, after all, her daughter's intended, and if he came off

as more timid than the wild man standing before her husband
was it his fault? He needed a bit of consolation. "We all know
too, how very anxious you were when Victoria was missing. I
took remarkable judgment and no little skill on your part to
find just the right envoys to succeed at such an overwhelming
task."

"Indeed, quite remarkable judgment," snorted Jed in dis
gust as Victoria modestly kissed Hayden's cheek once more
Raising his drink, he emptied the glass in one swallow and
moved toward the drink table, uncertain whether to take an
other or leave.

Ali could not have been more wrong. Pursuing Vicky would
be futile. She was clearly content with her foppish diplomat
And while the choice was hers, Jed Kincaid didn't have to sit by
and watch her throw herself at the pompous fool.

"Easy, Jed," cautioned Ali quietly, coming up beside him
apart from the others. "Her eyes follow you, not Reed, and
warrant so does her heart, even if she is not ready to admit it."

When the butler announced dinner, Jed looked quickly a
Vicky, startled to see her suddenly avert her eyes. Maybe there
was something in what Ali said, he considered.

Ali smiled, pleased at his small success. He cared for Jed and
did not wish him hurt. Perhaps the meal would soothe the ruf
fled feathers of his combative friend.

"Jed, if you will sit at the other end of the table at my right,"
suggested Cameron as he seated his wife. "Ali can sit next to
you. Victoria and Hayden, you are over there."

Nodding, Jed struggled to keep his face impassive. The
seating arrangement had placed him directly opposite Vicky
unable to avoid her pert face, those freckles of hers vibrant re
minders of their days in the sun, the long hot days of desire
which, though now passed, had left him wanting her still.

"Hayden, if you will say grace," prompted Mrs. Shaw
pointedly giving the privilege to Victoria's betrothed.

"Certainly, Mrs. Shaw. Father, we thank you for the food we
are about to enjoy and the many gifts with which you have
blessed us, but, most important, we thank you for your good
ness in guiding Victoria through her many adversities. For it is
You alone who brought her safely home to her loving family,"
pronounced the diplomat. His pale eyes fixed on Jed, rather
than his folded hands, daring him to challenge this interpreta
tion of the events.

Jed, however, merely shook his head and raised his eye
brows, joining in as the others intoned "Amen."

At Grace's signal, the butler filled their wineglasses and the maids began to serve a dainty pâté.

"Now, a toast. I ask you all to raise your glasses to Jed Kincaid, whose bravery and inventiveness brought a pleasing end to a frightening chapter in our lives. What might have transpired without his involvement does not bear thinking about," said Cameron. "We salute you and Ali with the utmost gratitude."

Jed, embarrassed at the man's obvious sincerity, looked down at his plate as they drank to his efforts.

"Thank you," Victoria murmured softly over her glass, her voice bidding him to gaze at her. Surprised at the watery brightness of her eyes, he took refuge in foolishness.

"Aw, shucks, folks, 'tweren't hardly nothin'," Jed twanged. His silliness made Vicky chuckle and he was pleased.

"I daresay not," agreed Hayden, his cultured tones a deliberate contrast to Jed's exaggerated speech. "You are somewhat a creature of the desert, familiar with its ways, aren't you?"

"I suppose I've seen more of it than you have, but few men could really be at home there," acknowledged Jed.

"Yet I understand from Hayden that you are quite fond of that sandy wasteland," contributed Grace. "What can be appealing about such an arid, lifeless environment?"

It seemed a safe enough topic of conversation to the matron, who signaled the maids to serve the fish course. She was desperate for anything to draw the man's eyes away from Victoria. Why, his looks were so intimate, one might suspect the American was caressing the girl with his hands rather than his eyes. If Grace didn't know Victoria, she would have worried about what went on between them on their journey.

"In my experience, ma'am, the desert is best described as nature's imitation of a lovely woman, alluring with her promises yet dangerous with her wiles," clarified Jed. "And I'm not known for refusing such temptations."

"What an absurd notion!" judged Hayden. Startled by Jed's untoward comparison, he dropped his fish fork, sending the maid scurrying for a new one. "A woman? Don't be ridiculous."

He had never really analyzed the appeal the desert held for him before, but Jed had to concede that he loved the untamed nature of the sandy planes, a wilderness which had given him Vicky, if only temporarily. The fact that such an admission clearly shocked the blazes out of Reed made it sweeter still.

"In the early morning and late evening, the desert's beauty is unsurpassed. Against the golden sands, the blues and purples of the sky are constantly changing, transmuting its vibrancy from one form to another," explained Jed with a nod at Victoria and Grace. "Just as a lovely young girl becomes a fetching woman and, one day, a beautiful matron."

"A change in my women I've been privileged to witness," agreed Cameron, appreciating Jed's poetic insight.

"Like any female, the desert is amazingly soft and loving in her tender hours. Yet, but half a day later, she can be the ultimate virago, threatening to end a man's life with her harsh treatment," continued Jed, his eyes studying Victoria.

"Oh, come now, Mr. Kincaid, surely you exaggerate," protested Grace, flustered at the suggestive turn of the conversation.

"That's how it is with deserts," answered Jed, not missing the high spots of color in Vicky's cheeks. "Freezing cold one minute, dreadfully hot the next. Suddenly a man finds himself amid a lush, tempting haven of exquisite promise—"

"Jed!" Vicky's voice was unusually high, but the angry set to her lips and the raging fire in her eyes were familiar signs to Jed, who grinned at her. He *had* missed their confrontations these past few days, he admitted to himself, recognizing that the spark she added to his life would be worth the aggravation of pursuing her.

"Kincaid, I hardly think such a discussion is proper with ladies present," rebuked Hayden sharply. His neatly manicured hand reached out to pat Victoria's in a solicitous manner.

"I don't know what *you're* talking about, Reed, but oases are an integral part of the desert," Jed said calmly. "*I* was referring to them. What could you have been imagining?"

"But— I must have misunderstood you, sir." Realizing Jed had bested him, Hayden flushed and tried valiantly to escape the embarrassment. "Victoria, dear, did I tell you I received the confirmation of our travel plans? We depart Alexandria on the first day of October for our honeymoon."

"It will be so much cooler in England," agreed his fiancée, "*that* will truly be paradise."

"Not in *my* dreams," objected Jed, his glance lingering deliberately on Vicky's décolletage. "However, I don't suppose Hayden would consider those a matter of proper conversation, either, so perhaps I should remain silent."

"This is my home, Jed, and you are more than welcome to speak," invited Cameron, sending Hayden a quelling glance.

'I have heard you say nothing askance. In fact, I would love o hear the true account of Sheik Nabar's amulet. It's made you a legend.''

"Notoriety is fleeting," murmured Hayden. Annoyed at Shaw's willingness not only to entertain such scum as Kincaid but flatter him as well, he hoped for a quick end to the evening. However, after tonight, neither he nor Victoria need be troubled by the boor again, he consoled himself.

"But not dullness, eh, Reed? You're stuck with that for life," countered the American.

"Jed, the story," Victoria prompted. Wishing for a few minutes' peace, she missed Hayden's surprised look as her eyes pleaded with Jed to behave.

He nodded imperceptibly and launched into the tale as the servants removed their empty plates and brought the entrée of stuffed waterfowl. The night began to fly by as even Ali entered the conversation, recounting Jed's attempts to negotiate with the foreman of the quarries north of Khartoum.

To Jed's disappointment, however, as soon as dessert was finished, Mrs. Shaw rose and signaled her daughter.

"If you will excuse us, we'll leave you to your brandy and conversation while Victoria and I stroll in the gardens."

"Mother, I'd just as soon—"

"Nonsense, Victoria. You know your father prefers time for the men to talk alone."

Victoria studied her mother's firmly set mouth and nodded. Though she worried about Jed and Hayden's continued animosity, perhaps her digestion would be easier apart from her fiancé's unceasing scowls.

"Hayden," said Cameron as the women left, "tell us what the government is doing with the new appointments at the consulate."

Obediently, Reed began to explain the British position even as Jed's eyes followed Victoria out. It was no accident when, a short while later, the American excused himself, claiming he had a hankering to view the Nile from the estate's vast lawn. When Hayden rose to join him, however, Ali began a barrage of questions concerning the role of Britain in Egypt that forced the frustrated diplomat to remain where he was rather than appear rude to Shaw's guest.

Stifling a smile at his friend's clever ploy, Jed moved quickly across the grass in search of mother and daughter. Within a few minutes he had found them.

"Oh, dear! I didn't think you men would be finished so soon," Mrs. Shaw exclaimed when she looked up to see him. "We'd best get back, Victoria. We wouldn't want to appear remiss as hostesses."

"Yes, Mother," the girl replied. Unwilling to look at Jed for concern over what such a glance might reveal, she was startled to feel his restraining hand on her arm.

"It is true Mr. Shaw was wondering where you were, ma'am," Jed politely, if untruthfully, informed the matron, keeping his almost, but not quite proper, hold on Vicky. "Do you mind, however, if your daughter shows me the roses? It won't take but a minute, and she spoke of them so frequently in the desert—"

"But—"

"A moment, Mrs. Shaw, and we will rejoin you, I promise."

"I suppose it would be all right. How can I deny you such a request after all you've done for us?" the older woman said, though her reluctance was obvious. "Just don't be too long. We wouldn't want to make Hayden unnecessarily jealous," she added with a trill of laughter that did little to hide how serious she was.

The instant Mrs. Shaw's back was turned, Jed looped his arm through Victoria's and led her behind a dense planting of trees.

"The roses are that way," she murmured, trying to pull away.

"Hang the roses," Jed said, his voice grown husky and low. "You left Hayden's office without giving me a real kiss goodbye, Vicky. You owe me that much."

"I don't want to kiss you!"

"If you really loved your fiancé, you wouldn't be afraid to," Jed purred triumphantly.

"I'm not afraid."

"Prove it."

"All right, I—" Victoria began, only to have her response cut short as Jed's hard mouth descended on hers, and remained.

"Tell me again how much you love Reed," he challenged, finally releasing her from his embrace, victory imprinted on his face.

"I do!"

"You're a sweet liar," Jed said with a deep laugh before taking her arm to escort her back to the others.

All too soon after that, the evening Jed had dreaded was over and he was at the door. As he took Victoria's hand in his own o bid her goodbye, he realized such a feat was beyond even his alents. This dinner and the kiss he'd stolen had only made him letermined to change her mind about her marriage.

Ali had been right. She was a woman worth fighting for, even f the necessary combat would occur in ballrooms, formal gardens and drawing rooms. Over the next few weeks, Jed promsed himself, smiling warmly at Victoria, Hayden Reed would earn that the woman he considered his own was not.

The next morning found Hayden in a particularly foul humor as he approached his office later than was his custom. Not only had he been forced to share the Shaw carriage with Kinaid last night, but he awoke troubled by Victoria's peculiar manner during that dinner.

Initially inclined to dismiss her puzzling demeanor as a result of her abduction, he had not been prepared for her unusually assertive behavior, disagreeing with his opinions and even contradicting his wishes. Why, twice in the course of the evening, Victoria had even kissed him, inaugurating the act in front of her parents and the others and precipitating a distinct uneasiness in Hayden's breast. After her time in a slaver's mart, he would have expected her to be more readily submissive, he mused, wondering what had really occurred over those three weeks.

Seeing that Victoria had suffered through quite an ordeal, being rescued from one savage by another, perhaps it was only natural that she had forgotten herself. Still, as a rising diplomat, Hayden Reed needed a wife who would be a loving helpmate, not a free-spirited female who might raise objections to the life he had so carefully arranged—or pry into *his* affairs.

Entering his outer office, the consular agent frowned in irritation at his assistant's absence. His dismay trebled, however, when he discovered his superior, Charles Cookson, behind Hayden's own desk, shuffling through files.

"I trust you don't mind, Reed. I sent your man on an errand."

"No, certainly not, sir," acquiesced Hayden, struggling to hide his anxiety at the unexpected visit. "I do think we might be more comfortable in the chairs over here by the window."

"Nonsense, but don't stand on my account. Sit down."

Uneasy with the command, Victoria's fiancé seated himself nonetheless in one of the seats facing his desk.

"Tell me, Reed, is it your usual habit to arrive in so tardy a manner when you've no appointments on your calendar?" inquired the senior consular agent, examining the bound book on the desk.

"Of course not, sir. I—I had an early meeting this morning at the Shaw estate to learn if Victoria had recalled anything else of significance to include in my report of the rescue. Holmes should have noted that on my schedule," lied Hayden. Mentally, he made careful inventory of his excuse. He had found it essential in diplomatic circles to remember exactly which truth or variation thereof one used with whom. As with most of his tales, this was not completely untrue, simply altered slightly from the facts.

"And how is your fiancée?" asked Cookson, watching the younger man closely. "I trust she is recovering nicely."

"Yes, sir. She is still rather shaken from the events—and from dealing with Jed Kincaid, I fear. In truth, his manner is not that of a proper gentleman, even under the best of circumstances."

"Don't like the chap much, do you, Reed?" observed the senior diplomat. Fluent in Arabic and respectful of the culture in which he lived, Cookson had little use for men like Reed who considered themselves and the British way of life superior to all others.

"No, sir, I cannot say that I do," admitted Hayden, surprised that Cookson understood but relieved to speak the words publicly nonetheless. "I find the American an uncouth blowhard who delights in singing his own praises and doing little else—"

"Is that why you failed to tell me of his suspicions regarding the appearance of a Mahdi and the amassing of weapons?" charged Cookson. His voice was suddenly so sharp it could have easily flayed the skin from Hayden's back. "Well? I asked you a direct question, Reed. Answer it."

"No, sir, Kincaid never said—" began Hayden, quickly changing his words as he measured Cookson's narrowing eyes. "That is, he made some ridiculous claims about what he had seen, but in good conscience I did not wish to waste your time."

"Oh?"

"You know how one group or another of these natives is always threatening a revolt that never occurs, diminishing our meager resources with fruitless investigations of unsubstantiated rumors." Trying unobtrusively to loosen his collar,

Hayden swallowed deeply. "Why should we believe this is any different?"

"I don't know that it is, but it is not your job to censor reports meant for my office. If I decide the material is worthless, it will not reach the consul general, but that is *my* decision, not *yours!*" rebuked Cookson, his face flushed with fury. "You, Reed, are a junior officer who takes orders. Do I make myself sufficiently clear or need I write this up for your file?"

"No, sir. I understand and I do appreciate your overlooking my lapse of judgment," said Hayden, nearly choking on the subservient words.

"I haven't said I would," corrected his superior. "Yet. You will look into Kincaid's charges. I'll be in Alexandria with Consul General Malet for two weeks, and you will be in charge of day-to-day operations. I am giving you a chance to redeem yourself, Reed. By the time I return, I expect a full report, detailing the existence of that powder magazine, if it exists—"

"You want me to go to Khartoum?" Hayden was horrified at the very thought. Victoria had just returned from that hellhole and he was to go there?

"Not necessarily, but you might send a team of scouts down to learn how many guns the Mahdi has. In all likelihood the weapons are coming off some ship in Alexandria. However, Cairo cannot be overlooked."

"But, sir, there may be no truth whatsoever to Kincaid's tale, an invention out of whole cloth to make him a hero—"

"His rescuing *your* fiancée already did that," said the older man dryly. "No, I believe Kincaid's information came to us without ulterior motives."

"You would," muttered Hayden.

"Excuse me, Reed. I didn't quite catch that."

"You would like this matter closed in how many days, sir?"

"As many as it takes," ordered Cookson. Rising to his feet, he looked down at the junior diplomat, a frown marring his features. "And Reed, don't let your personal feelings interfere in this. You *might* convince me to overlook the matter of your not being alert to potential problems for the Crown if you perform this inquiry in a thorough, decisive manner."

"Yes, sir, I understand."

The words were as bitter as gall, made all the worse by Kincaid's responsibility for the situation, but, Hayden determined, the scoundrel would pay. There was absolutely no doubt of it, Jed Kincaid would not go unpunished for interfering in his life, not only on a personal level with Victoria, but on a professional one, as well.

In the pale lavender glow of twilight, Victoria smoothed the skirt of her evening gown after alighting from her father's carriage. Standing before the impressive home in the European sector of Cairo, the site of this evening's party, the elegantly clad woman was nervous. Truth be told, she had no more desire to attend this gathering than she did to return to Khartoum. Nevertheless, she unhesitatingly placed a delicate gloved hand on the arm Hayden offered her.

Waiting for her parents, Victoria realized that everything had changed woefully since Jed's audacious kiss two nights ago. Where gracing fetes such as this had once constituted an extremely important part of her life, it had come to mean nothing.

Yet to retire from society would only fuel the already-circulating gossip about what had befallen her after her abduction. There was no solution other than to brazen it out by doing what she normally would have done: chattering with the ladies, casting innocently flirtatious glances at the men, whirling about the dance floor with one partner after the next, and laughing as she circulated among the guests. These were the things that would save her parents and Hayden from the further speculation of the rumormongers. But these were also the things for which she no longer had any heart.

Bravely fixing a smile on her face, Victoria permitted Hayden to escort her, in the company of Grace and Cameron Shaw, up the few steps that led to the broad, sweeping portico fronting the Stanford home. The brilliant light shining from a multitude of crystal-laden chandeliers spilled across the threshold as the door was opened for them by a liveried servant, and the soft strains of music wafted sweetly on a gentle, evening breeze.

"You look inordinately lovely tonight, Victoria," Hayden whispered in her ear as another servant took her wrap.

Her fiancé's words might have been accepted as proof of Hayden's unflagging gallantry if the tone in which he had delivered them hadn't been edged with something less than gentility.

The man had been uncommonly reserved following Jed's coming to dine with her parents. To a stranger's eye, Hayden's behavior was socially correct, his demeanor consummately polite, but Victoria heard the iciness in his voice when he addressed her, and felt the ill humor concealed so skillfully behind his public facade.

The only thing to which she could attribute his mood was the same situation that had her on edge, causing her palms to become damp and her breathing shallow. Jed Kincaid was still in Cairo. Why didn't he go away?

Greeting her hostess, Victoria saw a few heads turn curiously in her direction. The attention she garnered was not, she supposed, a result of the pink, off-the-shoulder crepe de chine gown that clung to her breasts, waist and hips in the front before bursting into a bustle and cascade of flounces in the back. No, these people were simply theorizing about her kidnapping and speculating whether her virginity was still intact.

Trying to ignore the scrutiny directed at her, Victoria bestowed her most loving smile upon Hayden, nobly making do with the tight, impersonal curve of his mouth that she received in return. Going about in society at this point was bad enough without having to contend with Hayden's distance and Jed's continuing, unexplained proximity.

Under her father's watchful eye, she and Hayden went to converse with other young people, and Victoria breathed a sigh of relief. At least with them she felt more comfortable.

Then she saw him, coming into the ballroom from the balcony, and her traitorous heart began thundering so loudly that she was certain Hayden must hear its rapidly beating tattoo.

Jed's dark, gleaming hair had been neatly trimmed, though it was still a tad too long. His exquisite evening jacket hugged his broad shoulders, tapering down to his narrow hips, the waistcoat beneath it a tribute to his trim waist and flat stomach. The trousers he wore were slim cut, his legs encased in fine cloth that just skimmed the muscular firmness of his thighs. Even the normally staid tie that was de rigueur somehow appeared different on Jed, giving him a roguish air rather than one of respectability, as did the contrast between his stark white shirtfront and the golden tones of his sun-burnished skin.

It made no sense to her as she frantically fought to keep from staring at Jed, that she could be both glad to see her American adventurer and thoroughly appalled at the same time. More important, she wondered how she was ever going to get through an evening of surreptitiously gazing at him across the room, separated from him as much by her obligations to her parents and Hayden as she was by the people who stood between them.

To make matters worse, Jed was so devastatingly handsome that the single ladies present, and a great many of the married ones as well, responded immediately to his wickedly charming grin. They began to cluster around him like grapes to a stem, refusing to leave his side until they were plucked away.

As she watched, Jed partnered one after another through a slew of waltzes, though he never so much as asked to sign her dance card. She, who had taught him to move gracefully to unheard melodies, was one of the few women present unlikely to feel his arms around her on the dance floor. Victoria would have cried out her desolation at being so ignored if Hayden's hovering at her elbow was not a constant reminder of her status as his intended.

"Ah, so Cairo's newest hero is here," Cameron Shaw commented, finally coming to stand with his daughter and the diplomat she was engaged to marry. "The man cuts quite a figure, doesn't he?" the banker asked, carefully gauging Victoria's reaction. "No wonder the ladies flock to his side."

"They are silly as geese, the lot of them. It's to your credit, sir, that you have raised your daughter to have more sense. The blackguard doesn't belong among people of our sort. His fleeting appeal is simply that he is so different from the gentlemen with whom women of breeding are generally acquainted," Hayden proclaimed with a supercilious arch of one eyebrow.

"His appeal is that he is a manly, good-looking chap with a great deal of bravery and charm," Cameron said, emitting a snort that dismissed Hayden's opinion as rubbish. "Jed may be a diamond in the rough, but he's a diamond all the same. With a bit of polishing he'd outshine many a so-called gentleman. Don't you agree, Victoria?"

"I...I...would guess that...that..." Victoria began to flounder, wondering distractedly why her father had placed her in such an awkward position.

"Of course she doesn't," Hayden finished for her with quiet vehemence. "Victoria would never find such a crude individual attractive. Kincaid is nothing but an affront to her delicate sensibilities."

"Mmm," Cameron Shaw intoned noncommittally, his eyes moving from his uncharacteristically mute offspring to Reed and back again.

"Oh, dear, I see Mr. Kincaid has joined the festivities," Mrs. Shaw tittered uneasily, changing the trio to a foursome. "The mamas of Cairo had best be especially vigilant tonight with such a rogue set loose among their daughters. Hayden, do see to it that you look after Victoria. Though you and she are properly betrothed, Mr. Kincaid's being here is enough to make even me nervous about my daughter's welfare.''

"See here, dear, there's nothing for you to fret about. Victoria would never do anything she didn't wish to do," Cameron said to his wife. His light, soothing tone was at odds with the meaningful look he sent his adult child.

"It's what she might *want* to do that frightens me," Grace Shaw confided to her husband after Hayden escorted Victoria onto the dance floor, leaving his prospective in-laws behind.

Swaying along with the tempo, joylessly ensconced in Hayden's arms, Victoria tried in vain to feel the music. But the only thing she sensed was the emptiness building inside her as she caught an occasional glimpse of Jed standing deep in conversation with the Stanfords' beautiful redheaded niece.

Her one consolation was that Hayden, too, seemed preoccupied, caught in musings of his own so that he didn't notice how listless her steps had actually become. Or if he did, he had the good grace to remain silent about it. When the last chord sounded, a relieved Victoria sought refuge from her troubled spirits in a quiet corner.

Stationing herself in a spot where Jed was not altogether hidden from her view, Victoria was disheartened by Hayden's continued presence at her side. Taciturn as he had become, he made her uncomfortable, and she couldn't fathom why he had chosen to remain in her company rather than to seek out his acquaintances.

"You seem so far away tonight, Hayden," she said finally, looking up into his impassive face with genuine concern. How could she ever expect to make him happy and convince Jed Kincaid that she was as well, when her fiancé was so cold and distant?

"It's business, my dear, nothing for you to worry about."

"But, Hayden, as your wife I'll expect to share your burdens. We may as well start now."

"If you must know, I've been ordered to conduct an investigation of the rumors your American savior saw fit to divulge to my superior."

"That's wonderful," Victoria said with a wan half smile, visions of Jed and the journey across the desert filling her with yearning. "It might be added responsibility, but I'll feel much safer knowing the matter is in your hands."

"Oh, don't be absurd, Victoria! The whole thing is a bloody nuisance and unnecessary, as I tried to point out to Kincaid before he went over my head and approached Cookson."

"Still, it's certain to be a feather in your cap," Victoria soothed.

"It isn't wise to form opinions about subjects in which you are woefully ignorant," Hayden instructed absently.

He began searching the room for the most influential men in attendance, wanting to strengthen his acquaintance with them rather than listen to his future wife's drivel.

"Why not?" came an unexpected yet familiar voice at Victoria's elbow. "That's what most folks do, isn't it? In fact isn't that what you did regarding the information I passed along to you?"

Spinning around, Victoria saw that Jed was so close she imagined she could feel his breath caressing her reddening cheeks.

"Since you know so little about the topic, and care even less, I might do some investigating of my own," Jed volunteered, his attention centered more on Victoria than on Hayden.

"Stay out of it, Kincaid," the diplomat said tersely. He didn't need the American mucking around with the matter of the Mahdi more than he already had.

But suddenly, Hayden's thoughts turned elsewhere. His eyes narrowed speculatively as he observed Jed lift Victoria's hand to his lips, where she allowed it to linger.

Hayden would have had to be blind not to notice the sparks that flew between the two. He saw the animation that lit Victoria's previously insouciant features, just as he had noted earlier the American's bold gaze sweeping the room in search of Victoria and the girl's stealthy glances in Kincaid's direction. Though they might have hidden it during the dinner two nights ago, at this moment there existed an intimacy between Victoria and the mercenary that caused Reed to suspect they had been lovers.

The thought infuriated Hayden. He seethed at the image of his fiancée lying with Jed Kincaid. If it indeed proved so, he would bestow his name upon her as planned, but Victoria's transgression was one for which she would pay dearly once they were wed.

"It astounds me to see you here tonight, Kincaid," Hayden said, more to destroy the contented silence Victoria and her renegade were enjoying than out of any actual desire to converse with such a vulgar colonial.

"I decided to stay on in Cairo for a spell, Reed," Jed drawled, his green eyes glinting devilishly as he cast a look in Victoria's direction.

"That's not what I meant. What amazes me is finding a man as coarse as you in such a refined setting."

"Really? Then you'd better get used to it. The invitations have begun to pour in. You'll be seeing plenty of me for quite a while to come," Jed said.

"I doubt you are telling the truth," Hayden retorted, his words clipped and precise. "After all, what half-wit would sponsor your entry into polite society?"

"Oh, that was Cameron's doing," Jed replied casually, taking Victoria's hand and leading her onto the dance floor as the first lilting notes of a waltz sounded.

Victoria felt herself blushing when Jed placed a hand behind her waist and pulled her near. If she closed her eyes, she could again be dancing with him across desert sands under a blazing sun.

"Are you really staying in Cairo indefinitely?" she asked, resorting to the first question that came to mind to quell the bittersweet memory. At Jed's affirmative nod, Victoria was filled with joy. She found herself becoming lost in the depths of his commanding green eyes until the room began to fade away and there existed just the two of them.

"But why? And why are you here tonight?" she inquired softly.

"I think you know the reason," he replied, his rich, deep voice more melodic to her ear than the efforts of the orchestra.

"No, I'm afraid I don't," Victoria denied. She needed to know what he meant, but was afraid to hear it all the same.

"It's you," Jed murmured, bending his head to hers.

"How can you say that? You barely came near me most of the evening." Her voice was no louder than the rustle of silk as she searched his face for clarification, aware that his simple statement made her life very complex indeed.

"If there's one thing you've taught me, it's not to rush things," he announced. A brief chortle reverberated in the deep cavern of his chest. "And I figured this was something you would want us to ease into. That's why I waited to ask you to dance. Yet already I find myself impatient to get to the next step. Let me court you, Vicky," he entreated with sweet urgency, his hot whisper playing across her small, delicate ear.

"But I'm promised to Hayden," she protested halfheartedly, though her answer sounded as false to her as it did to him.

"Some promises were made to be broken. You don't love him. I know it, and in years to come, he will, too," Jed insisted sincerely, twirling his lovely partner in time to the music. "That makes you the only one left to convince."

"Jed, I— I—"

"Hush," he ordered with an indulgent smile. "I'm not looking for you to make a decision right away. But you can see that I'm accepted in your world, and I know you fit into mine. Allow me to court you, or at least think about it."

Victoria studied the man whose arms made her feel so secure. In the past, she had seen Jed Kincaid angry, loving, serious and playful. But never had she seen him displaying the vulnerability he exhibited as he concluded pleading his case. It was as though he had stripped away his pride to place his heart in her hands, and the sight of him almost tore her own heart in two. Although she could not instantly abandon the hopes her parents had for her in order to tell him yes, she found she could not say no. Instead, she fell into thoughtful silence, and Jed, feeling it best not to press his suit any further, did the same. Simultaneously, they gave themselves over to the music and quiet dreams.

Hayden stood at the fringe of the dance floor, his false smile hiding his true feelings. The sight of Kincaid holding Victoria much too tightly rubbed him raw, as did all of the praise he was hearing about the man who had gone to Khartoum to rescue Cameron Shaw's daughter. And to make matters worse, the girl's father, who had already spent an unconscionable time conversing with Kincaid earlier in the evening, stood smiling benignly as Victoria and the American glided by.

This public humiliation and the hornet's nest Kincaid had stirred up concerning the Mahdi prompted Hayden Reed to reach a decision. He had to find a way to be rid of Jed Kincaid, and he thought he knew just how to do so.

Cutting a path across the dance floor, Hayden tapped Kincaid's shoulder, reclaiming his fiancée for what was left of the dance.

Though Jed graciously relinquished her and kept away for the remainder of the evening, Victoria continued to feel as close to him as she had when he had held her in his embrace. No matter where he stood within the ballroom, she was acutely aware of his presence, watching him when she dared, and constantly feeling the temptation of his request. If she thought there was the least possibility she could make him happy...

Chapter Seventeen

A week later, Jed found himself leaving the most disreputable section of the *medina,* a grim smile settled upon his lips. He was getting closer; he could feel it. The realization brought a rush of blood that sharpened his senses and heightened his reflexes.

He had been annoyed, at first, to learn that Cookson had put Hayden Reed in charge of investigating the Mahdi and the gunrunning to the Sudan. But now, Jed was almost appreciative. Prompted by Reed's attitude, the American adventurer had undertaken to find out what he could on his own. It gave him something interesting to do, kept his hand in, so to speak, while he dabbled in the staid world of respectable society.

And finally his perseverance was beginning to bear fruit. Hours spent among the most scurrilous of Cairo's inhabitants had brought him into contact with two Sudanese of questionable character. They had been recommended to him as men willing to earn extra money transporting stolen firearms to Khartoum.

That they had done so before was obvious from the conversation that took place when Jed had met them, as arranged, at an outdoor café. Over pots of the thick, strong Turkish coffee so popular in Cairo, it become clear that they not only knew about the growing arsenal in Khartoum and the powder magazine being built on Tuti Island, they had been there. Boasting familiarity with trade routes that would avoid the khedive's patrols, they were eager to travel south again with Jed's fictitious shipment of guns, elated that the next batch of weapons destined for the Mahdi was not to be the last, as they had so recently and unexpectedly been informed.

In confidential tones, Jed had persuaded the pair that a new supplier had been found to take the place of the individual who had decided it was too dangerous to continue now that the British government was looking into the matter. The Sudanese had no reason to doubt the rough, lethal-looking American with the cold green eyes. He was a man likely to be involved with such a precarious undertaking.

As he had reached for his last small cup of coffee, Jed had hinted to his unsavory companions that the guns would be arriving and leaving along the usual route. That was when the Sudanese had told him of their surprise that the warehouse near the Cairo docks was still considered safe from detection. From what they had been led to believe, the British were getting close to uncovering it, which was why their operation had been marked for abandonment.

But Jed, glad to learn the approximate location for the storage of the guns, had assured them that such was not the case. Remembering what he had overheard at the oasis when he had gone to fetch water for Victoria, he advised the smugglers the only change in their routine would be the Englishman involved stepping aside. Everything else, he promised them, including the details of transport, would be very much the same.

The Sudanese were easy to convince. And though they were not so careless as to provide Jed with hard information and specific details, they had aided him in his quest nonetheless. A warehouse along Cairo's docks, how many could there be?

Now, after having made arrangements to meet with the men again, Jed was returning to his hotel room to transform himself into a presentable gentleman for a charity function at Shepheard's. As he walked along the narrow streets of the exotic city, the pungent aroma of spices and jasmine warring with less pleasant odors, Jed decided that in Cookson's absence, he was not about to share what he had learned with the British Consulate, or more specifically, with Hayden Reed. That officious fool would simply ignore what he had to say. Therefore, Jed determined to find the warehouse himself, hoping the discovery would lead him to the mysterious Englishman betraying his homeland and its foreign interests. Once the villain's identity had been established, Reed would be forced to take action.

The hulking Cairene drove his wagon, bursting with trees and shrubbery, through the gates surrounding the consular agent's

ew home. Though the house and its grounds were little more
han modest in size, there was nonetheless a constant flow of
arts and wagons arriving as the new occupant threw himself
nto renovations.

Planning a formal garden that would please his future wife
vas a tedious task, Hayden Reed had informed his neighbors.
hey no longer thought anything about the comings and go-
ngs at Reed's home, other than that the young diplomat must
ove Cameron Shaw's daughter to expend so much time and
ffort in the pursuit of her happiness.

"Greetings, *mudir*," the driver called as he stopped the
lonkey cart in the rear of the house where Hayden was wait-
ng for him. "I have brought the last of what you require."

"I'm glad that's all of it," Reed commented. "Once it grows
larker, it'll be safe to bring it into the house. But tomorrow,
ou'll have to get someone to plant some of these bloody shrubs
nd rip out others."

"And when shall my men and I return to cart away the de-
ris?"

"As soon as I can make arrangements," Reed replied, mop-
ing his brow with a pristine square of white cloth despite the
rowing coolness of approaching evening. "I don't like having
his here any longer than necessary and would have much pre-
erred it going through the normal channels."

"Things grow too perilous," the Arab said.

"Don't you think I know that?" Hayden snarled. "Even
vith my overseeing the British inquiry, the warehouse is no
onger safe. Who knows what some zealous fool in my com-
nand might find."

"That is true. But tell me, what do you know about an
American set to act as your replacement? He was put in touch
vith our two friends in the *medina,* and they feel he will soon
e seeking our contact in the warehouse."

"There *is* no replacement."

"The American?"

"I know his identity and I will deal with him," Hayden said
vehemently, icy rage swelling up inside him. "Tell the others to
nave nothing more to do with the man."

"As you say. If something should happen to this merchandise, it would anger our friends to the south. They already sent
you a warning once before when you tried to increase your
profits. You dare not fail them this time."

"I have no intentions of doing so," Hayden said. A frown
creased his normally composed features. The admonishing

threat had come in the form of Victoria's abduction. This time it would be his life the Sudanese dervishes would demand i they were dissatisfied. At the thought, sweat beaded on his pa trician forehead. "However, I hope they understand that thi is the last instance in which I can be involved."

"They are not unreasonable men," the burly Arab replied a cruel smile snaking across his face. "It will be enough fo them that the investigation you are being forced to conduct wil leave our men in place and the main routes intact."

"To be sure," Hayden agreed hastily. Though the Arab wa: supposed to be in his employ, Reed had no illusions as to whom the fellow actually served. It was a dangerous game he playe at present, and he was determined to win, Jed Kincaid be damned!

Jed woke early the next morning feeling exhilarated despite having kept late hours the night before. Polite small talk glasses of sherry, chamber music and conventional behavior did not normally quicken his pulse. Yet the handsome, dark-haired American had come to actually enjoy each affair he had attended this last week, whether ball, dinner party or concert Victoria's bright presence had transformed each otherwise drab event into something truly pleasurable.

More than that, Jed sensed her resistance to his overture: dissolving. With each circumspect conversation they shared, each glass of punch he fetched for her, each smile he coaxed from her lips, Jed patiently battered at the barriers Vicky had erected between them.

Unwilling to envision any other outcome, Jed looked forward to winning the war of hearts he waged so persuasively, just as he anticipated closing in, soon, on the circle of gunrunners and the mysterious Englishman who orchestrated the enterprise.

At first Jed had simply viewed it as his moral obligation to inform the British Consulate of the burgeoning threat in the Sudan. Then he had decided to uncover what he could when an ineffectual Reed had been charged with overseeing the investigation. But now Jed recognized that his efforts might very well bring him a benefit he had not foreseen. Should he be the one to lay bare the plot threatening Egypt, and indirectly Britain's interests in the land of the pharaohs, the Shaws would have to conclude that he was a better man than Victoria's worthless fiancé.

With renewed determination, Jed climbed out of bed. A trip to the docks called for his shabbiest, most disreputable clothing if he hoped to blend into his surroundings. Out of his wardrobe came an old, sun-bleached cotton shirt, his sturdiest, most faded, trousers, and his well-worn boots. Donning these, he completed his outfit by placing his leather hat on his head, his knife inside his boot top, and a pistol in his belt. Then he was ready. A deceptively lazy grin draped across his mouth at the prospect of finding danger and excitement within the city that had lately given him no more than an opportunity to display his manners.

Hayden's discreet inquiries and his network of informants established Kincaid's presence at the docks early that morning. Certainly someone with the American's impudent tenacity would continue his search until he discovered what he was looking for. And when he did, Hayden would be ready. Though he had a distaste for employing violence, in this instance, he would relish it.

From his hiding place in a narrow alley, the diplomat had an unobstructed view. His eyes impatiently swept the area around the warehouse used by the consulate for storing cargo it had ordered from England and the rest of the continent until it could be disbursed. Assigned the task of recording shipments and their disposal, Hayden had found it easy to occasionally hide additional illegal goods within the walls of the storehouse, and to arrange for their transport, as well. Now he'd use his power to utterly destroy Kincaid.

Almost a week ago, Hayden had begun to lay a paper trail that would implicate Jed in the smuggling. It consisted mainly of falsified receipts for shipments of questionable content and uncertain origins coinciding with Kincaid's sporadic sojourns in Cairo for this last year. In fact, heading Cookson's study made it quite simple to gather all he had to know about the rowdy American's previous stays at the Crescent Hotel.

Initially, Hayden had thought merely to cast aspersions on Kincaid so that he would no longer be welcomed in society and thus be removed from Victoria's sphere. But since the man was actively probing into the gunrunning, and was likely to appear at the spot where the rifles had usually been concealed, the American had given him an opportunity that could not be ignored. The bastard would pay for taking his woman and for putting his life in jeopardy.

Once Kincaid had visited the warehouse, the Englishman's contact inside would become expendable. Whether the man confessed his involvement or remained mute, it mattered little to Reed, for once Yosef Ahmed was dead, who would believe the American's story? With a bit of artful connivance, the murder would be blamed on Jed Kincaid. Hayden would have him arrested, and before Cookson had returned, the matter would be set to rest for good.

Given the deplorable conditions in the jails, it wouldn't be difficult for Hayden to prove the American's sudden demise while in custody was an unfortunate incident that had occurred when Kincaid had been trying to escape. And after the bastard was dead, who would dare to think he had not been guilty of the crimes the British Consulate would lay at his door?

Satisfied, Reed ran his hands along the rifle the large Arab had stolen from Kincaid's rooms after the American had left his hotel that morning, and he was hard-pressed to wait patiently for Kincaid's visit, before doing what had to be done.

Taking refuge from the afternoon sun, Victoria rested on the veranda of her parent's home. She sat dreamily, chin in hand, staring at the banks of the Nile. How extraordinary it was to think that the same waters in which she and Jed had bathed, the very ripples on the river's surface that had seen their lovemaking, had traveled northward to pass this exact location! The notion provided an irrevocable link to the past she and Jed shared. But would that history give rise to a future? She still was not certain.

Oh, she wanted Jed badly enough, so badly in fact, that she could taste his lips upon hers and feel his touch whenever she closed her eyes. But while he had recently spent time in her world, Victoria doubted her beloved, reckless Jed could ever reside there permanently. Nor, she suspected, would she truly want him to. A Jed chained by the conventions of society would not be the self-same renegade who had flaunted the rules to capture her heart in the desert. And so the question remained, was she a strong enough woman to be the sort of wife Jed would need? Think about it as she might, Victoria honestly didn't know.

Though Jed had faith in her ability to cope with the differences between them, he was blinded by his love for her. Swinging her foot in a most unladylike fashion, Victoria emitted a

gh, wishing she had even half the confidence in herself that
ed had placed in her.

She shook her head to clear it of such befuddling thoughts,
nd rose from her chair. Tonight she and her parents had been
vited to a dinner party at Lady Trenton's house in the city.
Iayden would be there, but so would Jed. If she wanted to look
er best, she had to go inside and choose something to wear,
ertainly a much easier decision to make than any that con-
erned her future.

Jed's fingers stumbled over the ends of his formal bow tie for
he third successive time. He swore softly in response and be-
an his efforts anew, remembering exactly what it was he had
lways hated about evening attire as his usually agile fingers
urned this way and that.

When he was finally successful, his was a smug reflection
hat stared back at him in the mirror. He turned to get his jacket
vhen there was a loud, angry knocking on the door of his ho-
el room.

Jed was on his way to answer the unexpected summons when
here was a fresh burst of pounding more insistent than the
irst. From the sound of it, someone was mighty riled about
omething, Jed thought, reaching out to open the door, his
ther hand ready to grab for the knife he had placed on a
earby table.

The moment the latch clicked, the door burst inward and five
olicemen, headed by the chief constable Jed had inadver-
ently punched at Nadir's brothel weeks earlier, poured into the
oom.

"Well, boys, I assume this isn't exactly a social call," a non-
lussed Jed said with a quick glance at his pocket watch. "I
ave plans for this evening, so suppose you tell me what this is
ll about."

"You'll have to come with me," the chief of police an-
ounced, his face alight with vengeful pleasure. "Our busi-
ess with you concerns the illegal shipping of stolen firearms to
he Sudan."

"I'm the one who reported that activity to the British Con-
ulate in the first place. Should Reed want me questioned fur-
her in the matter, that's for him to do, not the Egyptian
olice." Jed shrugged into his evening jacket. He had no in-
entions of allowing himself to be detained by this charade. If
Iayden thought to keep him away from tonight's dinner party,

then the Englishman could damn well come and get him per
sonally rather than sending his toadies. That way, they woul
both be absent from the table where Vicky would be dining thi
evening.

"A clever ploy, American, designed to make you appear th
innocent. But it was not a foolproof plan, especially in light o
your latest crime."

"Oh, and what's that?" Jed asked, affecting boredom as h
straightened the cuffs of his formal shirt.

"The one for which I'm arresting you, the murder of Yose
Ahmed," the constable announced, relishing the prospect o
having this foreigner in his jail cell. Kincaid would pay then fo
his past surly behavior.

"Yosef, the fellow at the warehouse?" Jed asked quickly
finally giving the Egyptian his full attention. One dark eye
brow rose quizzically as Jed tried to put this newest piece of th
puzzle into place.

"So you admit to knowing him."

"I spoke with him today," Jed acknowledged. He had bee
certain then that the watchman had been hiding something, an
he berated himself for not employing more persuasive meth
ods to draw that information out rather than playing a waitin
game. His reticence had created a situation that was damne
inconvenient.

"At which time you killed him."

"Whoa!" Jed commanded, beginning to step back into th
room as he cast subtly about for an escape route. "Talking wit
a man doesn't mean murdering him. What possible reaso
would I have for doing away with the watchman? I wanted in
formation from him, and I couldn't get that if he was dead."

"Perhaps it is that you wished to keep him from linking you
name to the gun smuggling. At least that is what Mr. Ree
thought when we found Yosef's body this afternoon."

"Reed was with you?" Jed demanded. He eyed a window o
the far side of the room that led to a balcony.

"It was he who asked for our escort when he went to ques
tion the watchman. But what we found was the man's body an
your rifle," the police chief stated, his voice cold and virulent

"My rifle!"

"The weapon used to kill Yosef had your initials carved o
it."

"Why the hell would I leave it there? Use your head, man!"

"Maybe someone entered the building and you dropped the weapon as you ran. But there will be no escape for you now, Kincaid. You are coming with us."

"Like hell I am," Jed growled, lunging at the head constable. He punched him with such force that he fell back into the men behind him. Grabbing a rifle from one of them, Jed wielded it like a club, lashing out with the broad side of the stock to slam and jab it into the group converging on him. All the while, he worked his way toward the open window, fending off blows and landing a few of his own, keeping himself so close to the Arabs that they could not fire their guns for fear of hitting each other.

Then, with the effortless grace of a jungle cat, he sprang through the air and out the window, leaving the rifle behind. A few fast somersaults saw him to the edge of the balcony, while the Egyptian police, packed too tightly at his window to fire accurately, sent shots flying all around him.

With another leap, Jed jumped to the extended roof of a patio below, and then dropped to the street, quickly rounding a corner and striking out for the Arab Quarter, a section of the city with streets so convoluted that a man might, if he was lucky, lose himself, and those who pursued him.

Going to the authorities, British or Egyptian, would be fruitless, Jed decided as he ran. What he needed was time to learn the identity of the Englishman embroiled in the smuggling. Once that was done, there was no way Reed could hope to frame him for any of the crimes with which he was being charged.

Vicky's fiancé was playing a more lethal game with him than Jed had at first supposed. To be placed in an Egyptian jail, at the hands of the chief constable who already held a grudge against him, was tantamount to being handed a death sentence. And Jed Kincaid was not about to calmly place his head in a noose of Hayden Reed's making.

As he continued his flight, Jed observed with no small sense of gratitude that the raucous shouts of his pursuers were at least growing no closer. Running for his freedom in formal attire was no easy feat. His evening dress was not only uncomfortable, but it made it impossible for him to appear inconspicuous.

The young Cairene children clamoring with glee as they saw him invade the native quarter did not help his cause, either, their excited voices alerting the authorities to every twist and turn in his evasive path through the winding streets. Yet Jed knew he had no other choice but to flee, and flee he did, swiftly and without visible pattern, hurrying through the labyrinth of the Arab sector, sometimes doubling back upon himself, using every trick he knew.

Needing to catch his breath, he slipped around a corner and ducked into a small booth in the *medina*, its wares packed away but its presence a godsend. Squatting low behind the wooden slats, Jed drew long breaths and considered his next step. But even here he was not safe, he realized as the shopkeeper came out from his private quarters to complain about Jed's invasion. Tossing a fistful of coins to the man, Jed addressed him urgently in Arabic.

"There is more for you if I get away safely," he promised, trusting greed would outweigh any civic responsibility the fellow might harbor. "The police claim I didn't pay my hotel bill."

Without hesitation the Egyptian pocketed the money and lifted the curtain between the stall and his living quarters.

"You go out through the back alley. I will send the devils the other way," he offered. "But first you pay *baksheesh*."

Thankful for the man's ready cooperation, Jed nearly lost his advantage by taking money from his pocket to oblige the merchant. Just at the police entered the street, their voices bellowing his name, he slipped behind the draping and hurried out to the rear street. His path, he discovered with a grim smile, circuitous as it had been, was true. He was but a half block from Ali's and safety.

It seemed an eternity, however, that he waited on the step, persistently knocking at the door. Standing on the street, watching over his shoulder for the police, the American could never recall feeling so vulnerable nor so dependent on others. What he would do if Ali refused to assist him did not bear thinking about, but then the door opened and Jed was inside.

"Welcome, but you need not dress so formally to visit us, Jed." The Egyptian chuckled. "We are glad to see you, even if British society *has* learned the truth and cast you out on your ear."

"They would do no such thing," disputed his wife, coming from the back room. "A handsome man like our Jed would be welcome anywhere there are women. Will you take dinner with us?"

"No, I can't. Ali, I desperately need your help. Hayden Reed has put out a warrant for my arrest—"

"Not for Ali, too?" cried Fatima.

"Arrest? For what? Spending part of the ransom he was too cowardly to deliver? It bought him Victoria, didn't it?"

"It has nothing to do with that. Reed claims I murdered a man. Half the Cairo police are searching for me." Jed's voice was tight with anger.

"And you came to me?" Ali was astounded. Usually Jed's instincts were sound, but not this time. "Don't you think they will come here after you? Once Reed sees you did not run to the Shaws, this will be his next logical stop."

"If I could hide in your shop, you could say I broke in—"

"Jed, you have seen it. There isn't a spare inch in my shop. What about one of those bars you used to frequent? They are dark and crowded, wouldn't they hide you?"

"Not when their livelihood depends on the police overlooking their illegal existences," said the American, shaking his head. It was a solution he had already considered and discarded. "I knew my going to Hayden's superior irritated him, but I never imagined he would make such trouble when I was trying to help Britain."

"You forget the woman," intruded Fatima quietly. "I suspect this Reed's blood boils hotter from his jealous anger at your courting his Victoria than it does because of any politics—"

Before Jed could reply, a sudden blast of whistles erupted in the street outside. Jed jumped to his feet and started toward the exit at the back of the house.

"I'll try not to let them see where I've come from," he promised softly. "Wish me luck."

"Check all the houses and don't miss the gardens," came the shouted orders outside as a knock sounded on the door.

"Jed Kincaid, I won't let you go, not into a trap," whispered Ali's wife urgently. She grabbed his arms and tried to direct him to the bedroom. "You saved Ali's life in Khartoum. I can do no less for you here. Stall as long as you can before you admit the police, Ali," instructed Fatima.

"Why?"

"There is no time to explain, my husband. Just remember my mother is visiting us and she is indisposed."

"You don't have to do this," protested the American, unwilling to expose Ali and his wife to the police constable's growing fury.

"It is too late to do anything else, friend," pronounced Ali.

Heavy hammering on the door halted further discussion as Jed reluctantly followed the Egyptian woman from the room.

"Sharouk! Open this damned door at once or my men will kick it in," yelled an unhappily familiar voice. "We know you are there."

Of all the police in Cairo, thought Ali sadly, why did it have to be the constable they had interrupted in the brothel, a man with a grudge? Had Allah no mercy?

"Of course I am here, sir. I am coming at once," called the merchant meekly. Spotting Jed's carelessly abandoned tie, he tucked it in the pocket of his *gallabiya* and moved to answer the angry summons, as slowly as he dared. "Do not worry, sir. I am on my way."

"From the other side of the city?" demanded the officer impatiently. When Ali unlatched the door, he entered hurriedly and surveyed the room, nodding to the two men with him. "Go through the shop and the garden carefully. Look behind every shrub and piece of brass without fail. I will search here."

"Search for what?" asked Ali, his fear of discovery lending his voice a realistic quaver. "I have no contraband in my shop."

"Don't be a fool, Sharouk. What is that to us if we are given a share in the profits? We are after your friend, Kincaid. Where is he?"

"Kincaid is no friend of mine," retorted Ali angrily. "Do you forget the trouble he made for me? Because of him I was forced to go to Khartoum where he almost got me killed. I would no more hide that villain than I would welcome a case of cholera."

"He was seen entering your house last week," interrupted the constable, his eyebrows raised. "One of your neighbors told me as much while we stood outside your door."

"More the fool I was," admitted Ali sheepishly. Suspecting what Fatima had in mind, he laid the groundwork. "Kincaid claimed to have brought payment for my coffee service and I showed him my hospitality. Instead of paying me, however, the dog insulted my Fatima, daring to remove her veil to look on her face, a privilege rightfully belonging to no man but those in her family. Because I trusted Kincaid, my wife was humiliated. Have no doubt, sir, from that day, he was no longer welcome in my house."

The policeman was torn. He had seen Sharouk and Kincaid in the brothel and they had been at odds even then. If Kincaid had approached the shopkeeper's wife as he claimed—well, for some men, that was a crime deserving of death.

"You have not seen him since?"

"At the Shaw estate, though we did not speak," snorted Ali. "It is a wonder I did not kill the American that night."

"Perhaps," smirked the constable, trying to envision the usually placid merchant in a murderous rage. "I will have a few words with your spouse, just to confirm your account."

"Since when is a woman's word called upon to substantiate her husband's?"

"It is not," appeased the police chief, "but she may remember something you've forgotten."

"She is nursing my mother-in-law, who is presently indisposed. I would hate to upset the old woman. She can be ornery," said Ali, moving toward the bedroom door, visibly reluctant. "Especially where I am involved."

"So is my own mother-in-law." The constable chuckled, relaxed in light of the all-too-common affliction they shared. Kincaid was clearly not here, but he would go through the motions to satisfy Reed. "I will be most gracious to her and your wife."

Ali opened the door to the candlelit room and saw Fatima standing in front of the chair by the window, blocking any clear view of its occupant. Uttering a silent prayer, he put his faith in her wisdom. If she were wrong, there would be no help for any of them. But she had been clever enough to position the chair in the mix of shadow from the candles and the darkness outside, so perhaps—

"Fatima, this gentleman wants to ask you about Jed Kincaid."

"That cursed infidel?" his bride of two years asked. "I have no words for a dog such as he."

Coming forward to confront the constable, Fatima was the very picture of righteous indignation. Though only her dark eyes were visible above the veil, her body was tense, her steps quick.

"May Allah steal his sight and leave him a blind beggar to live and die in the streets, drooled upon by the mongrels with whom he lies."

"Then the man has not been back and your husband has had no contact with Kincaid since he dishonored you?" He thought it highly unlikely, but it did not hurt to inquire. After all, the sprightly Fatima would be well worth fighting battles for, the constable mused.

"If my husband even *spoke* of that fiend again, I would leave him and return to my father's house," Fatima said simply.

The policeman's eyes flickered briefly to the old woman near the window, apparently oblivious to their conversation. Stooped in the chair, her body appeared misshapen, but that might have been the effect of the shadowy candlelight. With her face hidden by her veil and a shawl draped over her head and shoulders, she seemed more an object of pity than a living being.

"My mother is visiting us while my father conducts his business in Alexandria," explained Fatima, noticing his interest. "I assure you just as I care for her, she and my father would gladly take me in if ever my husband were unfaithful to me or my wishes."

"Unfaithful? Never, ever would I dream of such a thing," cried Ali, his voice convincingly agitated at what the constable might choose to reveal about their first meeting. "I am as loyal to my bride as this officer is to his wife."

"Yes," agreed the man, slapping Ali soundly on the back. "Anyone can see your husband is a man much like me. I regret having disturbed you. Good night."

Before Ali believed it possible, they were safe. He latched the door behind the constable and his men and leaned against it, drawing the first relaxed breaths since Jed had arrived.

"Fatima, you are wonderful," he praised, sweeping her into an enthusiastic embrace as she and Jed joined him. "And you are so clever to have thought of such a deception."

"It was nothing, husband," she replied modestly. "Jed, what will you do now?"

"I'm not sure. I can't help but feel that Reed is the key. True, he dislikes me for my attentions to Vicky, but the dervishes did speak of an Englishman in Cairo, and so did the men in the *medina*—"

"Wouldn't that have been the man who was killed?"

"No, he was Egyptian. Besides, his job was merely to guard the guns while they were in storage. Someone higher up had to coordinate the weapons' arrival and transport. Someone hungry for power and greedy enough for money to take the risks—"

"I suspect Reed, myself," said Ali. "But would he dare do it?"

"I think he would," confirmed the American.

"How can you prove it? Since he already has the police combing Cairo for you, it would not be difficult for him to arrange your disappearance before you can confront him."

"No, I might show up half dead and totally disgraced, but I'd never disappear. The bastard will want Vicky to admit she was wrong for being attracted to me, a common thief and murderer. He could never let her dream of my returning and clearing my name."

"If you like, I could try to reach the woman for you," offered Fatima. "You could go away together."

"Thank you, but I must see this out to the end. Besides, at this late hour, she and Reed are probably already eating dinner at Lady Trenton's," said Jed, looking at his watch. "But while Reed is busy, this particular fugitive is going to go through his office. Maybe I can find something to substantiate our suspicions."

"Will you be safe?" asked a worried Fatima. "Ali could go with you."

For a moment, Jed hesitated, aware of the trust the couple placed in him. Another set of eyes and ears, even as a lookout, might prove damned valuable. But it would be risky.

"We began this together, Jed. We should end it the same way," said Ali, sensing his friend's reluctance. "I want to come."

"And you shall. Thank you," Jed replied, clasping a hand on the Egyptian's shoulder. "I've no friend truer than you."

Ali nodded briefly, embarrassed by the sentiment.

"You will do better wearing this," interrupted Fatima, handing Jed one of Ali's *gallabiyas*. "I doubt those woman's clothes would be any less conspicuous than your Anglo garments."

"A woman beyond compare," admired Ali, squeezing his wife's hand. "My Fatima is a treasure without price."

"So you told us repeatedly in the desert," Jed called as he stepped into the shop to change clothes. "I am sorry if I ever doubted you. I do not now."

Then, all too quickly, they were out on the street, en route to Hayden's government office.

Chapter Eighteen

Victoria stood conversing with one of the other guests, fighting the urge to peer past her companion and into the ornate central hallway to see if Jed had arrived. The evening was growing late, and surely dinner would be announced shortly. These days, it was unlike Jed not to be punctual, and Victoria could hear only too well the comments Hayden would make if the man who had rescued her failed to appear before everyone went in to dinner.

An unwelcome thought suddenly flashed through Victoria's mind, disturbing her greatly. What if an impatient Jed had finally given up his pursuit of her and had moved on from Cairo? A sensation of wretchedness washed over her at the possibility, and she tried to combat it by assuring herself that there was a very logical and acceptable reason for Jed's tardiness. Exactly what that was, however, she couldn't begin to guess.

In the midst of her anxiety, Victoria was aware of one small consolation. At least she wouldn't have to deal with Hayden's increasing moodiness as well as her uncertainty about Jed. This evening, the diplomat was in a better humor than he had been of late. Her glance fell upon a flawlessly attired Hayden as he stood on the other side of the elegantly furnished room, twirling a glass of sherry between his thumb and forefinger and conversing with her mother and their hostess.

Sensing that he was the object of her perusal, Hayden raised his eyes to hers and saluted her with his glass. His smile was so full of genuine happiness that it was quite dazzling, effectively eclipsing the calculating coldness that had turned his blue eyes into veritable chips of glacial ice. Though Victoria wondered at his cheerfulness, she had no cause for alarm, until Lady Trenton stepped forward to claim everyone's attention.

"I must apologize for the delay of our evening meal," she began, with warmth and graciousness. "However, I find myself waiting for the arrival of one other guest, and it would be a shame to be seated and start without him if it can be avoided."

"Who's the person responsible for my starvation?" a retired army officer demanded with a good-natured laugh.

"That charming but naughty Mr. Kincaid," Lady Trenton replied with a rueful smile. "I assure you I will quite take him to task for keeping you from your meal, Colonel, but perhaps another glass of sherry would be acceptable while we linger just a few moments more."

"Go ahead, Colonel, indulge yourself," a smiling Cameron Shaw interjected soothingly. "I promise you'll find Kincaid interesting enough to forgive him."

"But there's no need to keep dinner if it is Kincaid who is delaying things," Hayden announced, a satisfied smile ringing his mouth. "I thought you knew."

"Knew what?" Victoria asked nervously.

"He won't be here this evening," Hayden said, managing a certain degree of nonchalance in spite of the excitement he felt.

"Not coming?" asked Cameron Shaw with a frown. "If that were the case, Kincaid would have sent his regrets."

"If he were a gentleman, he might. But then, to be fair, I suppose even a gentleman might have difficulty penning a note under the circumstances."

"What circumstances?" Victoria demanded, a handful of graceful steps bringing her to Hayden's side.

"Why, being arrested, of course," Hayden drawled insolently. "I just surmised everyone would be aware of it by now, especially with the way news travels in our little community."

"Arrested!" Victoria's mother said, her shocked voice no louder than a whisper. "Whatever for? Was he caught dallying with someone's wife or daughter?"

"Oh, no, not at all," Hayden assured her, ignoring Victoria's silent plea as he used the backs of his fingertips to needlessly smooth the lapel of his dinner jacket. "He's been taken into custody for murder, though there's more to it besides even that vile crime."

Victoria saw the room beginning to sway and everything turning hazy as she fought against the black cloud threatening to descend upon her. With sheer force of will, she managed to overcome the urge to faint, though she could not restrain herself from reaching out for her father's steadying hands.

"If any of this is true, and I have my doubts, why did you keep the information to yourself?" Cameron demanded. "It was hardly the right thing to do blurting it out like that in the presence of the ladies."

"But I assumed everyone had heard and was just too well-bred to speak of it before we dined," Hayden asserted innocently. "Lady Trenton's announcement of waiting dinner for the scoundrel took me by surprise, and when I could find my voice, I spoke without thinking. My apologies to the ladies."

"None of this is true, none of it," Victoria insisted. Her complexion, despite her weeks in the sun, had turned as pale as the ecru organza gown she wore. Still, she faced Hayden squarely and refused to be quelled by his look of icy disdain.

"I am sorry to say, my dear, that it is," he replied with an expression of sympathy that belied the triumph in his heart. The Shaw bitch deserved this and more for playing him false with the crude American. "I know you feel you owe Kincaid something. But you are completely misguided. In my opinion, he never rescued you at all."

"He most certainly did," cried Victoria. "He traveled down to Khartoum and blew up a great deal of the city in order to secure my safety."

"My dear, my dear, think about what it is you're saying," Hayden chided her. "No law-abiding man would have been able to reach you, never mind get you safely away from that devil's den where you were being held. It was only possible for Kincaid to do so because he had contacts in Khartoum, people he knew from his gunrunning operation. In fact, I shouldn't be surprised to find the whole thing had been staged simply to allow him entry into another, higher level of society where he might glean more information about exactly what the British government knew concerning his illegal activities. And your father helped him do just that," Hayden added with a reproving glance in the banker's direction.

"But you told me there was no foundation to rumors about gun smuggling," Victoria insisted.

"I couldn't speak the truth, my darling," Hayden responded, taking Victoria's hand and pressing it within his own before she snatched it away again. "How could I gamble on Kincaid learning just how closely we had him under surveillance?"

"I thought you said he was arrested for murder," the Colonel objected, forgetting his grumbling stomach in all the excitement. The knowledge that he'd be able to dine out for weeks afterward on the story that was unfolding in Lady Trenton's drawing room assuaged his hunger enough for him to want to learn every available detail.

"Yes, he was," Hayden said. "As the authorities drew nearer to arresting him, he began to suspect as much. Unaware we had already gathered evidence linking him to the unlawful transport of guns to the Sudan, shipments coinciding with his stays in Cairo I might add, he thought that he could keep his name out of this by simply murdering his confederate. But he only dug himself in deeper when we went to question the watchman and found the poor fellow's body along with Kincaid's rifle."

"A watchman, you say. What was his connection?" Victoria's father asked.

"He allowed the guns to be stored in his warehouse until they could be shipped out," Hayden said with a shrug of his shoulders.

"And which warehouse was this?" Shaw inquired, trying to reconcile what Reed had to say with his own perceptions of the American.

"Embarrassed as I am to admit this," Hayden began, knowing that at least a kernel of truth had to be included in his fabrication if he wanted it to appear truthful, "the blackguard was storing his weapons in the same warehouse that the consulate uses for its supplies."

"A rather stupid tactical error," the Colonel commented dryly.

"It was a bold move that would have been brilliant had it not been for our present investigation," Hayden lied deftly. "We would never have thought to look under our own noses for such unlawful goings-on."

"But Jed was the one who pressed for the consulate to delve into the matter," Victoria protested. "Why would he do that if he were in any way involved?"

"I don't know. Maybe he wanted to get out of the smuggling ring and couldn't. Or perhaps he fed us false information in an attempt to put himself above suspicion and send us off on the wrong track. As it was, I certainly found no use for any of the details with which he provided us. I can assure you, however, the police will be able to obtain all the specifics. They have methods for dealing with even the most recalcitrant of criminals, and they will not be shy about employing them. As for anything else I can tell you, it would merely be conjecture at this time."

"Surely you have some idea what will happen to Kincaid now," Cameron Shaw prompted in his most commanding voice.

"There'll—there'll be a trial of course," Hayden blustered.

"Just so long as there is," Shaw stated, his words echoing the thoughts of all. Everyone had heard of the terrible conditions and strange fates that sometimes befell those held in the khedive's prisons. "I'll go and see Kincaid myself tomorrow."

"Well, well, this has been a most fascinating evening," Lady Trenton interrupted, trying to salvage something of her dinner party. "All of the excitement must have sharpened everyone's appetite. I propose we continue this discussion over dinner."

"If you'll forgive me, I'm afraid I have no desire for food," Victoria said wanly.

"But, my dear—"

"Excuse me, your ladyship. There is someone to see Mr. Reed," the butler announced. "I believe he said he was the chief constable."

"Send him in," the noblewoman ordered, wanting this business conducted out in the open so she could put it to an end. Then, perhaps everyone could sit down to a glass of fine wine and the elaborate meal she had so carefully planned.

As he waited for the constable to make his appearance, Hayden wondered if the police had done away with Kincaid already. Wanting to see Victoria's expression upon hearing such news constrained him from speaking with the Egyptian officer privately. By God, he was so happy, he could be dining on camel tonight and he would think it the most enjoyable meal he had ever tasted.

"Mr. Reed," the officer called in worried greeting as he crossed the threshold into a room so richly decorated he had never seen its like.

"Yes, what is it?" Hayden inquired officiously, unable to keep from casting a look in Victoria's direction.

"In the matter of the American, Jed Kincaid, I am afraid I must inform you that—"

"Dear God!" Victoria whispered, clutching her father when she found herself unable to bear the thought of any more bad news.

"Yes," Hayden prompted, impatient for the news of the American's death.

"He has escaped."

"What!"

Victoria was conscious of no more than hearing Hayden Reed roar his anger as she slid toward the floor, the darkness that had loomed finally enveloping her and blocking out all else.

Jed stepped stealthily along the shadows flanking the ornate hallway, flattening himself against the wall wherever the soft glow of the sporadically placed lamps penetrated the murky darkness. He had stationed Ali outside with strict instructions to alert him if trouble arose.

A half grin etched itself across the American's otherwise serious face. His experience at moving undetected had begun in his youth, when he used to creep out of his mother and stepfather's house late at night. Little had he known at the time he had been honing a skill that would be useful in his chosen career. But none of his other adventures was as significant as the one in which he now found himself.

A man to whom danger was a way of life, Jed nevertheless found his heart beating rapidly as he stood stone still, hardly daring to breathe until he was satisfied no one was nearby. To be found here, in the British Consulate, would mean his capture. And he couldn't afford to be taken now, for Vicky's sake as well as his own.

After his talk with Ali, he was positive he had solved the mystery that had woven itself around him like some confining cocoon. But whom could he alert when the man he believed to be involved was, in Malet's and Cookson's absence, the very person to whom such suspicions were to be reported? What would persuade the authorities to go counter to Hayden Reed's orders? Somewhere in Hayden's office there had to exist evidence that tied him to the warehouse and the dead watchman.

Taking a slender pick supplied by Ali, Jed silently attacked the lock that kept the world from Hayden's door. With a few deft movements, he breached Reed's meager security, slipped through the anteroom and entered the Englishman's official sanctum. Here the darkness was pierced by a sole shaft of moonlight stealing into the room through a chink in the closed wooden shutters.

Noiselessly, he stole across the floor to Hayden's desk where he lit the oil lamp he had seen so many weeks before. With an expedience born of experience, Jed shaded most of the light emitted by the lamp with his hand, directing its beam onto the top of Hayden's desk.

Shuffling though papers, Jed assumed Hayden would be too clever to leave anything lying about that would provide hard and fast evidence of his illicit activities. Yet he fervently prayed that somewhere there would be a clue that would strip away his blindness, so that he could see a possible link between the minor British official and the rebel Sudanese.

Stacks of paper neatly aligned along the desk's surface produced nothing more than directives sent to Hayden by his superiors, Cookson and Malet. In a drawer Jed found files for the promotion of several consulate personnel as well as transfer requests and documents validating future postings. Nothing connected with Reed's duties seemed to reach beyond the building in which his office was located. With sagging hopes, Jed learned that another drawer yielded only a stack of announcements proclaiming Reed's recent change of residence.

The worst part of his frustration, as he shifted sheaf after useless sheaf of paper, was that it was not his fate alone hanging in the balance. It was Vicky's, as well.

A low, involuntary growl crept from Jed's throat as he thought of Vicky waiting for him at tonight's dinner party without his ever making an appearance. How had she dealt with the situation when she found out that he was a wanted man? Would she, who had already been the subject of society's scrutiny after her return from Khartoum, be able to live amid whispers and speculations concerning him? Or would she, in order to survive, simply shut him out of her world until things were settled one way or another?

The idea tore at Jed's heart and caused his breath to come fast and deep. He, who had never cared what people thought of him, was suddenly quite conscious of his reputation if only for Vicky's sake. When he came right down to it, however, his nature hadn't altered. He still possessed the savage streak that had always driven him, and he knew that he would lash out to destroy whatever stood in the way of his attempts to secure his respectability. After all, how could a man offer his name to a woman if there was a stigma attached to it?

Opening one last drawer, Jed began to explore its contents, sure, now, that he would have to break into Reed's home to find evidence enough to accuse him. Idly, his eyes moved down lists of requests for supplies and orders for the same. Large quantities of paper, ink, blank ledgers, paint, wood, rope, various foodstuffs and wines. Not only was Hayden in charge of the ordering, but the disbursement, as well. Goods seemed to be constantly flowing in from England and the Continent, stored for a few days at most, and then distributed, all at Hayden Reed's direction.

Though there was nothing ominous about such duties, something began to foment in the back of Jed's mind, and he started to read through the orders more carefully. He noted ships and dates, the expenditures for supplies, and the method of transport. He looked and searched and studied the paper again. Yet not a damn bit of it pertained to the smuggling. And then he saw it, the location of the warehouse where all of these goods were kept until they could be sent elsewhere. It was the same place that had seen Yosef Ahmed's murder. It had been in front of him all the time. Reed's consular duties gave him every opportunity to smuggle in weapons and casually send them on their way to the Sudan.

With the watchman's testimony unavailable, however, it would be difficult to prove. Perhaps that was exactly why the Egyptian had been eliminated. But the only one who could confirm such a theory was Reed himself.

Carefully replacing the papers, Jed swore that he would get the consular agent to do just that, no matter what means had to be employed. He'd go to the man's residence at once when Reed wouldn't be expecting him. And by the time he was done, Reed would have given him back his good name, a name Jed could share with Vicky.

"She's beginning to come around."

"Are you sure?"

"Yes, see how her eyelashes are fluttering?"

The voices were muted, as though they originated a great distance away. Yet through the haze that clouded her vision, Victoria could make out misty shapes close at hand, figures that she sensed were comforting and familiar.

But Victoria was in no hurry to leave the darkness behind and rush into the light. Instinct more than memory cautioned that there, in the brightness, unpleasant problems awaited. And so she was content to float amid gray brume and benumbed sensation, trying to shut out the voices that gently but insistently beckoned her forth. Finally she could ignore their urgings no longer.

"Oh, my dearest girl," she heard her mother cooing, her voice a soft ripple of sound that put Victoria in mind of her childhood.

"There, there, Grace," her father was soothing, "I told you Victoria would be fine, didn't I? We've raised ourselves quite a strong, courageous young woman."

Blinking rapidly, Victoria shifted her glance from one parent to the other. She had distinctly heard their words, yet she felt neither the least bit courageous nor strong, especially in these strange surroundings. Instead an inexplicable sorrow gnawed at her—that and pain. Tears began to gather in the corners of her eyes without her knowing exactly why. And then she remembered.

"Jed, oh Jed," she uttered miserably.

"Here, my darling, have some of the laudanum Lady Trenton's physician left for you," Grace instructed, bringing a spoonful of bitter-tasting medicine to her daughter's lips.

"For heaven's sakes, Grace!" Cameron Shaw snapped, encircling his wife's wrist and staying her hand. "You were beside yourself when the girl didn't come around, and now she's waking, you're trying to put her out again. It makes no sense to me!"

"But you heard her," Grace objected protectively, close to tears herself. "She's crying over that scandalous American. Let her drift back to sleep until she's ready to face the truth."

"The truth? Jed's being called a murderer is a lie, I know it is!" Victoria protested, trying to rise until her father's gentle hands guided her head back to her pillow. "He's innocent, no matter what Hayden has to say."

"That remains to be seen," her father maintained, his firm voice tinged with sympathy.

"I don't care what Hayden thinks, or you, or anyone else for that matter. The Jed Kincaid I know is an honorable man," Victoria insisted defiantly, nevertheless reaching for the dainty handkerchief her mother held out for her. "You don't know him as I do. Jed would never become involved with such dirty business."

"Then why, may I ask, did he run off?" inquired Lady Trenton, returning to the boudoir and overhearing the girl's remark. "I always thought there was danger lurking in that American's eyes despite the charm he exuded."

"Well, you were mistaken about Jed Kincaid," Victoria said quietly.

Weak and weary though she was, Victoria couldn't help coming to Jed's defense any more than she could help worrying about him. Why was he being charged with such heinous crimes? Had he been hurt when he escaped? Where was he now, nd was he safe? Questions flowed through Victoria's mind like elpless petals caught in the strong current of the Nile. But her gonizing queries did nothing more than turn her complexion paler shade and dull the sheen of her normally bright eyes.

"There, there, my dear. The shock has been too much for ou. But what you're reacting to, surely, is having learned that ou suffered the company of such a horrible man on your orthward journey from Khartoum. You can only be glad that e left you in peace. He did, didn't he?" Lady Trenton asked elicately, trying to uncover the source of Victoria's excessive istress.

"Of course he did!" Grace Shaw replied indignantly before Victoria could answer. Yet emphatic as the matron's reply was, he, too, had her doubts. Hadn't she seen with her own eyes the vay Kincaid had looked at her daughter?

But Victoria could not bother to defend her honor, even to he biggest gossip in all of Cairo. It was Jed who was impor- ant. Her mind searched frantically for a way to help the American who had risked his life so many times to save hers, he maverick who had been willing to join a herd in order to be ear her, the man who had taught her what it meant to be a voman. There had to be something she could do to lend assis- ance to his plight—there had to be! Suddenly a thought struck er.

"Where's Hayden?" she asked with detached calm. He could elp. He was heading Cookson's damned investigation, wasn't e? Since he was the one who started this mess, he was the one vho could stop it.

"Why—why—he's gone along home, child. After all, it is ery late," Mrs. Shaw informed her in a faltering voice.

"He wasn't concerned about me? He simply left?"

"You know how men are in an emergency," Lady Trenton aid, following Grace's lead. "They're no good at all. Hayden adn't the vaguest notion of what to do for you, so he went ome."

"With strict instructions that we were to inform him of your ealth in the morning," Grace interjected lamely, her quiet vords barely audible over her husband's snort of contempt.

"Poor Hayden couldn't leave fast enough once I had you rought to this room," Lady Trenton added, rudely interrupt- ng Victoria's memories of how well Jed Kincaid handled any risis that arose. "But then I would guess the dear man's haste o be gone was caused by the guilt he felt for upsetting you. He bviously hadn't expected you'd find the news of Kincaid's arrest and escape so unnerving. Sometimes men have no idea of just how delicate we women are,'' the socialite concluded with a sniff.

"Yes, but in his defense, I should point out that he was quite contrite, indeed,'' Mrs. Shaw said by way of comfort. She didn't bother to inform her daughter that Hayden's remorse had manifested itself only in the face of Cameron's rage.

"I'm sure he was,'' Victoria said evenly, not daring to give the slightest indication of how she had come to regard Hayden Reed. Should her parents suspect the emotions she really harbored, the plan that was beginning to form would never be a viable one.

"But Hayden's behavior is not something for you to worry about,'' Cameron stated authoritatively, tired of the way his wife and her friend were going on. "What you need is your sleep.''

"Lady Trenton insists we remain here until morning when her physician will call again to see you,'' Grace explained, giving her daughter's hand a small pat. "Your father has agreed.''

"That might be for the best,'' Victoria admitted, glad things were working in her favor. She had an idea of what the dastardly civil servant would want from her in exchange for his cooperation to clear the name of the man she loved more than life itself. Distasteful as she found the prospect, Victoria knew she would do whatever was necessary to save the man who owned her heart. Her idea could only be successful, however, if she spent the night in the city and not on her parents' estate where she had one of the servants acting as her bodyguard anytime she stepped out of doors.

"Right now I find myself exceedingly sleepy. I think I'll just lie back and close my eyes,'' she said pitifully, and gave a little moan that would make certain her father did not change his mind about his family staying the night with Lady Trenton.

"A wise decision,'' the noblewoman pronounced. "Perhaps a bit of the laudanum?''

"I'm so fatigued, I won't need it,'' Victoria replied. A dose of the potent drug now would see her intentions come to naught.

"But a weary body does not protect against an overactive mind,'' Grace chastised gently. "Consider a small spoonful.''

"There will be none at all,'' Cameron announced firmly, escorting the two older women toward the door before they could have their way. "What Victoria needs is quiet, not laudanum. I suggest we remove ourselves and give her just that.'' Usher

ng Grace and Lady Trenton through the doorway, Victoria's
ather stood at the threshold and turned to address his off-
pring.

"If you should require us, your mother and I shall be in the
ooms directly next door, my dear. As for Kincaid, don't trou-
le your pretty head about him. If he's the man I think he is,
hings will sort themselves out. And if he's not, he certainly
sn't worth your upset." Then he was gone, shutting the door
ehind him.

Victoria lay in the soft darkness, the shadows of the room
unctuated by the weak glow of a single oil lamp placed dis-
reetly in a far corner. Listening intently to the low murmur of
oices in the hallway outside, she finally heard the clicks of
loors closing along the corridor, the signal she had been wait-
ng for that everyone had retired for the evening.

Sitting up, Victoria realized she would have to be patient until
he others fell asleep and she could set out to do what she in-
ended. She settled herself on the edge of the bed, her feet
langling inches from the floor. All at once, with no warning,
. tear materialized and began to wend its way down her cheek.
Exasperated by its appearance, she brushed it away. This was
o time to be giving into emotions, the girl chided herself. She
eeded to be every bit as strong as her father evidently thought
he was. Otherwise she would have little hope of carrying out
er plan.

She refused to bemoan her inevitable separation from the
nan she loved. She would have the rest of her life to do that
fter she concluded her business with Hayden. Instead, Victo-
ia determined to use this last hour before her fate was irre-
ocably sealed to dwell on the happiness she had discovered in
ed's arms.

She didn't have to close her eyes to see his handsome visage
efore her, the exquisitely sculpted lines and planes of his
tubborn chin and clean jaw, his fine nose and broad forehead
opped by thick, coffee brown hair. But his heavily fringed
green eyes were what had held her prisoner from the very first.
She had beheld them glinting with devilment, flashing in anger, and growing dark with passion. And of late, she had seen
n their depths the unshuttered reflection of love.

Giving herself over to precious recollections, she began to
elive the numerous demonstrations of his raw, masculine
ower, his fierce protectiveness toward her, and his touching
enderness.

And, for all he had given her, Victoria would grant Jed something in return. She would give him his liberty if not his life. The sacrifice she chose to make in order to do so was a trifling thing compared with the joy she would keep hidden in her heart in years to come, a joy founded in the knowledge that somewhere Jed Kincaid lived a free man.

Commanded by her desperation to go to Hayden, Victoria rose. With icy tranquillity, her slender fingers slowly but purposefully untied the ribbons of Lady Trenton's bed jacket. Slipping out of that and a voluminous nightgown, she found her own garments and dressed, struggling quietly to fasten the back of her gown as best she could. After donning her stockings and shoes, Victoria grabbed a light cotton throw from an overstuffed striped chair, and folded it to resemble a shawl. Draping it over her hair and around her shoulders, she silently opened the wooden door of the ground-floor bedroom leading out to Lady Trenton's renowned garden.

Once she stepped from the room, Victoria kept to the shadows of the garden's high walls and searched for the gate that would lead to the street beyond. Stealthily, she placed one foot in front of the other, terrified she would be discovered prior to reaching Hayden and laying her proposition before him.

She wouldn't be afforded another chance to barter herself to Hayden for Jed's safety, she thought. She had to make the diplomat accept her proposal and assure her that the charges against Jed would be dropped, the search for him suspended. Then her all-but-disintegrated engagement to Hayden would be reaffirmed. The bargain would be sealed when she surrendered her body to him as a sign that she meant to keep her word.

Victoria was honest enough to admit that Hayden's contemptible denouncement of Jed had not been the desperate result of any love he bore her. She recognized that it had been motivated by the need to remove an obstacle impeding the golden future Hayden had ambitiously envisioned for himself. For that reason, Victoria would never be able to forget or excuse what Hayden Reed had attempted to do to Jed. Though it would make living with the consular agent all the more difficult, Victoria didn't care. She would gladly suffer that and more to save the life of her beloved American.

Finally locating a gate on the far side of the garden, Victoria emitted a breath of relief. Awkwardly, she lifted the wooden bar and pushed the barrier outward, then she slipped into the alley and shut the towering gate behind her.

Pressing close to the high walls fronting the street, she set out swiftly for the residence she would soon be sharing with a man she loathed. The European sector was quiet late at night, and Victoria anticipated no danger as she made her way along the straight, direct boulevards. Her steps almost as rapid as her heartbeat, the plucky blonde only prayed that Jed was still at large and that she was not already too late.

Soon Victoria stood on Hayden's doorstep, silently marshaling her arguments. She could not allow herself to fail in what she was about to do, and she wanted to be prepared with further incentives if Hayden thought to refuse her.

Hugging her waist in an attempt to stop her shivering, a resigned Victoria settled on exactly what she would say. She would explain to Hayden he had no choice but to accept her proposal. If the charges against Jed were not dropped immediately, or if any harm had already befallen him, she would inform her cowardly fiancé that she would never marry him. Then, Cameron Shaw's influence would be lost to him, and that was what Reed wanted, anyway, not her. It was a persuasion Victoria sensed Hayden couldn't fail to heed.

Raising her hand to knock, Victoria hesitated for one more instant while in her mind she bid Jed Kincaid a sorrowful farewell. It was, in effect, a final adieu to the love they had shared, though she knew its specter would haunt her forever. But goodbyes had to be said even if Jed wasn't there to hear them. Once she passed through this door and accomplished what she had set out to do, Victoria would never be able to face Jed Kincaid again.

Courageously, if sadly, Victoria straightened her slender shoulders and allowed her clenched fist to rap sharply on the door.

Though Victoria could have sworn she heard stirring within the house, the man she sought did not come to the door, nor did his servant, a large, burly Egyptian who frightened her most thoroughly.

Impatiently, Victoria knocked again and waited. But still there was no response. In fact, the house seemed unnaturally quiet, even the insects suddenly falling silent.

Resolved that she would not be thwarted in her attempt to help Jed, Victoria assaulted the door a third time, her banging growing in intensity and duration.

*   *   *

When the insistent knocking began for the fourth time,
Hayden looked up from what he was doing. Whoever wanted
his attention was not likely to go away, and though he certainly didn't want visitors now, neither did he need the neighbors becoming privy to activity taking place in his house so late
at night. He'd have to take care of the matter.

With a nonchalant shrug meant to belie his concern, he
straightened up from the crate of contraband rifles he'd been
inspecting. "I'll have to see to whoever that is," he said with a
nod toward the front of the house.

"Get rid of him, or I will do so—permanently," the massive
Egyptian directed.

"Just stay here out of sight and I'll do what I can," Hayden
growled, not liking his companion's attempt to usurp his authority.

On bare feet, Hayden padded into the next room and then
into the vestibule.

"What is it?" he demanded in an irritated voice designed to
intimidate any intruder and send the bounder on his way.

"It's me, Hayden, Victoria," came the reply.

Victoria! What did that bitch want at this time of night, unless it was something to do with that bloody American? Whatever her reason for coming here, Hayden couldn't deal with it
at present. The rifles had to be loaded and out of here long before sunrise. Reports had reached him of Zobeir's death, and
the British official had no desire to disappoint those who employed him, the very same people who had employed the slave
trader, as well.

"Go back to your parents, Victoria," he ordered impatiently through the closed door. "You shouldn't be here by
yourself, much less at this late hour. It's most unseemly."

"No more so than you sending me away to travel by myself
through the streets of Cairo at such an hour," she retorted.

"It's no worse than you deserve for being so brazen as to
show up here unchaperoned. If anyone sees you, your reputation will be completely beyond repair. Now, *go away!*"

"I'll pound on this bloody door and scream at the top of my
lungs if I have to. If you want to avoid a scene, let me in," Victoria insisted.

Suddenly the wooden barrier was thrown open and Hayden's hand shot out to pull her inside before she could wake the
entire neighborhood.

"Suppose you tell me what this is all about?" Hayden said harshly, glancing quickly over his shoulder into the dim recesses of the house.

"I know it was you who falsely implicated Jed Kincaid in the smuggling and the murder. And I'm aware of other things, as well."

"Oh, really?" he asked, his voice dripping with condescension. "And what else is it you think you know?"

"Why you did it," Victoria answered fiercely.

Hayden's heart skidded to a halt, but he maintained an outward show of composure. "And what do you suppose my motive was?"

"You were afraid I was going to break our engagement and marry Jed. But that isn't the case. Inform the police a mistake has been made and allow Jed to leave Cairo. If you do that, I'll wed you."

"Why should I believe that?"

"To show I mean what I say, I'm prepared to give you whatever you want right now... regardless of what that might be," Victoria stated with sincerity. "But refuse to help Jed and I'll never be your wife, no matter what happens."

Hayden wanted to laugh out loud. This was nothing to worry about. The girl had been intelligent enough to see the link between his heading the investigation and the accusations made against the American. But that was as far as her insight went. She had no inkling of his own role in the rifle running, or the murder.

Still, he had no time to attend to a strumpet willing to throw herself away in order to save the life of another man, and a crude American at that. His distaste for Victoria Shaw began to grow. She was far from being the lady he had originally thought her to be. But that in itself could be an interesting diversion, he mused salaciously. Once he got her in bed, he could treat her like the whore she was, and she would have no cause for complaint. The prospect caused his groin to tighten and his eyes to gleam. Still, that would have to wait. He had no option other than returning to his men and finishing with the rifles.

"Victoria, this conversation is absurd. I want you to go back to your parents and think about how very foolish you are," he instructed in a domineering tone.

"I know what I'm doing," Victoria said coldly, "and I'm not leaving here until the matter is settled to my satisfaction."

"Much as I might like to play your lewd little game, I refuse to take what you have to offer. I have no intention of vindicating Kincaid. As for you, you'll return to Lady Trenton's if have to take you there myself," Hayden declared. His building anger became hot fury when he had to block Victoria's path to keep her from walking past him and into the house proper.

"Not until you have exonerated Jed," Victoria maintained stubbornly. She had come too far to be foiled now. "Do as say, Hayden, or I'll still be here when my parents come look ing for me. And when they arrive, I'll charge you with all sort of things, accusations that will put an end to your career once and for all."

Hayden looked down on Victoria with barely concealed rage How dare this little bitch talk to him that way! Though she couldn't guess at it, her partial insights into his activities mean his career was already over as far as he was concerned. He couldn't chance staying here, hoping he remained above sus picion and was left in peace by the Mahdi's men. The only things remaining that were important to him were the money he had made and his life, something he would forfeit if he failed to deliver the rifles the dervishes wanted from him, rifles tha had to leave Cairo tonight.

With purposeful steps, Hayden came toward Victoria to physically remove her from the house. Once that was done he'd drag her, if need be, through the streets to Lady Trenton's residence.

Reading his thoughts, Victoria deftly sidestepped him and went running into the rear of the house, which was shrouded in darkness.

"You're not getting rid of me," she called to him just be fore she stumbled over a large, unexpected obstacle in the middle of a back room. Picking herself up, Victoria's eyes be gan to adjust to the dimness of her moonlit surroundings.

"Unfortunately, it would appear I am," Hayden said roughly grabbing her arms and pulling her to him, crushing her so tightly that she could not draw enough air into her lungs to scream. "Because of your rash and shameless actions, I'll be forced to dispose of you. What a pity."

Looking at the obstruction that had caused her fall, Victo ria was stunned to see an open crate of rifles, and in the murky corners of the room were men dressed in *gallabiyas* rising and coming toward her.

"Let me go," Victoria gasped weakly. "You'll never get away with this."

"Since you were too headstrong to depart this house of you own accord, you'll have to leave as a corpse," Hayden replied indifferently. "As for maintaining my innocence, once your body is found, your death, too, will be blamed on Kincaid. It seems he became infuriated when you rejected him for me. All of Cairo society knows he was trying to woo you. Who wouldn't believe me?"

"My parents would know that isn't so," Victoria managed to whisper, expending some of the little air left to her.

"You might be right. I'll try a different tactic. Let me see, Kincaid, furious with me for brilliantly uncovering his crimes, sought revenge by killing the woman I love. Yes, that sounds much better, doesn't it? I think it will do quite nicely," Hayden said smoothly.

He released his hold on Victoria slightly, and she deeply gulped for air until his hand covered her mouth. Horrified, the girl's eyes fell on the curved blade gleaming dully in the moonlight, held out to Hayden by his large, Egyptian confederate.

"I'll do the deed later," Hayden said with a shake of his head, "after I decide how and where it is to be done. No sense rushing these things, you know, and putting us in senseless jeopardy. For now, I'll gag the whore and tie her up until the guns are out of here. They are, after all, more important."

Victoria was dragged into a small, adjoining room. There, despite her frantic efforts to escape, Reed carried out his threat. A cloth was stuffed into her mouth and she was quickly bound to a simple wooden chair, the ropes biting savagely into her tender flesh. Then Hayden bestowed a mocking kiss upon Victoria's brow.

"Don't fret, dearest. I'll be back soon," he said with a sneer. "And then, before I close your eyes for good, you'll get exactly what you came looking for."

Chapter Nineteen

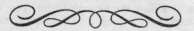

That was peculiar, thought Jed as he explored the alley behind Reed's home a short while later. The wooden gates were at the rear of the property, opening onto a garden, but even so, there was no reason they should be ajar at two o'clock in the morning.

Motioning Ali forward, Jed pointed out the unsecured entryway, but before he could tell the Egyptian of his plan to explore the grounds, they heard muffled voices within Reed's garden. As one, they pressed themselves against the gates, but after a few minutes Jed couldn't resist inching further onto the grounds, stopping when he caught sight of a wagon.

"Infidel dog! Just how many men does he think would risk this kind of cargo, even at night? Always wants extra service, but never an extra coin for it, is there?" grumbled an indistinct figure.

"He's an Englishman, what do you expect?" replied his companion. "At least this is the last load we'll be moving for him. Here, I swiped a bottle of his whiskey when he wasn't looking. Have a nip."

Then, in spite of the darkness, Jed saw the speakers. They were driving a heavily laden donkey cart, its wheels wrapped in fabric to mute the clatter. A third man rode behind, apparently to keep the precariously stowed cargo steady.

"Give me some of that," called the rear guard, coming forward as the wagon halted briefly.

Three men. He had faced worse odds a hundred times and won, considered Jed thoughtfully. If these fellows were transporting illegal guns, and he intercepted them, he would have all the evidence of Reed's guilt anyone could want. But just as Jed made up his mind to challenge the drivers, Ali caught him by the sleeve and yanked him back into the nearby shrubbery.

"Do not let haste rule your actions, Jed. If you're spoiling for a brawl, take it out on Reed, by all means. But if you want proof of your innocence, let me follow these men and see exactly what it is they are transporting and where they go," urged the Egyptian. "That way, when Reed denies everything and claims we are the insurgents, it will be possible to discredit him."

It made sense, the American acknowledged, but shouldn't he be the one to take the chances?

"Why should you risk getting involved? I could just as easily—"

"With a price on your head, you are less a free man than many a prisoner in Cairo's jails," reminded Ali. "While I—I am but another Cairene on the street after hours."

"All right, but be careful. When you've learned where they are storing the weapons, lead the police to the guns and back here. That way we can confront Hayden in front of witnesses," advised Jed, giving Ali's shoulder a quick squeeze for luck.

At once Ali slipped away, following the cart. Then that, too, was gone and Jed was alone in the garden. He meant to wait for Ali to return before doing anything, but there was no reason to wait this far from the house.

The ground underfoot was soft and spongy as though someone had been digging, he noticed, barely avoiding an uncovered pit, apparently intended for a tree leaning nearby. There was even a large excavation as if the diplomat were readying a reflecting pond. Clever bastard, Jed mused, getting the neighbors used to workmen and irregular deliveries probably dissuaded them from suspecting anything unusual.

Escaping the leafy shrubs, Jed caught his first glimpse of the house. Crouching down, he gauged its layout.

Four steps led up to a central veranda running between two short wings. When the concealing louvered shutters were open they probably revealed the main room. The bedrooms would be in one wing while the library, dining room and drawing rooms were in the other. Undoubtedly, the kitchen and servants' quarters would be situated closest to the street to keep the sounds of everyday life from the family.

Unfortunately, it was impossible to discern any flicker of light through the shutters at this distance, though it was highly unlikely that Reed would have retired so quickly. Too bad he hadn't arrived an hour earlier, Jed thought with a grimace. If his search of Hayden's office had yielded its fruit a bit sooner, he might have been able to catch the Englishman red-handed with not only the guns in his possession, but the money, too.

The money! Why hadn't he thought of that before? It was unlikely a man like Vicky's fiancé would extend credit to the buyers, so he would have been paid on the final transfer of the goods tonight. There was no possible way that Reed would have had the time to take the damning evidence out of the house . . . and no government employee, no matter how conscientious, could claim to have saved the amount of money the dervishes were rumored to be paying for weapons. All Jed had to do now was to locate the cash before the bastard hid it away.

His mind made up, the dark-haired American, newly invigorated by his insight, moved purposefully forward to examine each shuttered casement. In the far corner window, a slat of the shutter was loose near the bottom, and a few cautious tugs made it looser still, until Jed could see into the empty room.

A dim light glowed in what was apparently Reed's study. The small office seemed a strange mix of the Spartan and the luxurious. The floor was covered in an ordinary grass carpet, but an old, heavily carved mahogany desk dominated the area near the window, its grand size and intricately ornamented trim attesting to its prominence in Reed's life. What fascinated Jed, however, were the neat piles of bills in the middle of the creamy desk blotter. Five nicely ordered mounds of currency were carefully arranged in the light falling from the oil lamp.

It was all he needed to see. Not caring if Vicky's fiancé heard him or not, wanting only to get his hands on this blatant evidence of Reed's criminal activities, Jed wrenched hard on the lower edge of the shutter, his strong fingers grasping the frame and easily separating it from its hinged closure. Seconds later, he vaulted over the windowsill, landing lightly on his feet, just as Reed hurried into the room, a pistol in his hand.

"Kincaid, I hoped you would have been locked away by now, but things don't seem to be going as planned," the Englishman said with an exasperated sigh. "Still, I am the one with the gun, so this will be over for you very shortly."

"Tell me why," demanded Jed. "You're engaged to a beautiful, loving woman—"

"And you'd know exactly *how* loving she is, too, wouldn't you?" growled Hayden, angry at being reminded of Victoria's infidelity.

"Reed, whatever you're thinking, Vicky told me she loves you," lied the American, his voice firm as he inched around the desk. "I admit I asked her to reconsider, but she swore it's you she wants."

"The woman wants me so much that she offered me her body to secure the release of yours," mocked Reed. "In fact, she promised she would never so much as mention your name again if I called off the search for you. Is that what you consider love, Kincaid? If so, I'd say you were its recipient, not me."

"Vicky did that?" Jed was touched that she would have gone to such lengths for him.

"I was conducting other business at the time and couldn't immediately oblige her," Reed continued dryly. "However, what that she offered will be mine soon enough."

"Like hell it will, you lousy maggot!" goaded Jed. He was still too far from the consular agent to jump him, but a few sharp-edged barbs should take his victim's mind off his approach. "You're no more than a low-ranking civil servant who couldn't be bothered to lift a finger to help Vicky when she was abducted. Or did you engineer that deal for the money, too?"

"Say what you will, Kincaid. I have enough never to work again, over fifty thousand pounds," bragged Reed. His eyes flickered briefly toward the money on his desk and then he stepped closer as if to protect it from Jed. "This is only one installment, but what I find most rewarding is that everyone will blame you for what I've done."

"Just how do you figure that?" asked Jed. Unobtrusively he extracted a knife from his *gallabiya*, keeping it ready.

"Lady Trenton's guests were more than willing to believe you murdered the watchman, especially after your killing sprees in the desert—six or seven men, wasn't it?" asked Hayden, unaware of the tension controlling Jed's features. "It made for fascinating conversation, watching poor Victoria trying to explain the matter away and failing. It won't be any harder for them to understand that when you came here tonight to kill me, the tables were turned and you died instead when I defended myself."

"Defend yourself against this." As the words escaped Jed's mouth, he threw his knife.

Though the diplomat darted sideways to avoid the oncoming blade, it glanced off his shoulder as he fired, making his aim unsteady. The bullet went harmlessly into the garden, and before he could shoot again, Jed was on him, knocking him forcefully against the desk.

"I'm warning you, Kincaid. My men will be back any moment—"

"Let them come. I'll be ready, you bastard."

With practiced dexterity, Jed clutched the hand in which Reed held the pistol and began to hammer it against the desk while the Englishman groaned at each blow. Finally, his fingers opened and the gun fell to the floor where Jed kicked it out of reach.

Unable to hold it back any longer, Jed let his fury free. He wanted vengeance, for Vicky's sake and his own, and he would have it, but first he would make Reed squirm.

"Feeling a little nervous yet? Maybe this will help."

Jed smashed a fist into Reed's face and then punched the diplomat in the stomach, a grim smile crossing his features as the Englishman slid to the floor.

"Come on, Reed. I'll give you a fair fight. Stand up and fight back, you slimy bastard. If you manage to beat me, I'll let you leave town before the police arrive, without the money, of course," he offered. "If you lose, you'll be here to confess."

"A fair fight? With your experience? The odds are hardly ones I'd accept," said Hayden, struggling to speak through his pain. Nonetheless, he dragged himself upright against the desk. His arm was bloodied as was his lip, and his face bright red from the effort to stand erect, but his voice was more assured than Jed had ever heard it, incredibly condescending.

"It doesn't seem that you have much choice."

"But you see, Kincaid, I've a card up my sleeve," announced Reed, a curious smile lighting his face, "one that will let me leave here a rich man you won't lift a finger to detain."

"Another pistol?" guessed Jed as Reed fumbled behind his back for something on the disarranged desktop. "I took one away from you. I'll take another."

"No, not a weapon, your precious love, *Vicky,*" gloated Reed. He grabbed the oil lamp and tossed it firmly against the drapes behind the desk. "I told you she bargained for your release earlier—but I don't believe I mentioned that she was still in the house, tied up, I fear, but here all the same. Of course by the time you find her, it may be too late."

In the quickening glow of the flames licking at the curtains and the fabric wallcovering, Hayden's face had taken on a demonic cast, one that made Jed fear for the man's sanity and Vicky's life.

"Tell me where she is," he demanded, unable to stomp out
e sparks jumping across the carpet to ignite smaller fires.
You loved her once, Reed, maybe on some level you still do."

"Oh, her father was useful when I planned to stay in gov-
nment service," shrugged Reed. "Now I think I've a better
ture in trade. Of course, it will have to be far away from here,
t I've grown weary of the climate. Besides, once the Mahdi
mes to power, it won't be safe to be British."

The man was either truly mad or impervious to the danger he
d created, Jed reflected in amazement. Between the English-
an and the window, the fire had spread along the floor to-
ard the hall and the other rooms, happily devouring the carpet
d consuming the wooden ornamentation along the window
sings and the walls. Already, despite the open shutter, the
om was filled with smoke, but still Reed stood, straighten-
g each pile of currency before packing it away in a small travel
se.

"Where is she?" Jed yelled over the crackle of the burning
ood. When he got no reply, he lurched forward to clutch at
ed's shirtfront. In an instant, the American had grabbed the
plomat, holding him suspended above the flames nibbling at
e desk. "Tell me where she is or I swear I'll make this your
neral pyre."

"Oh, she's around here somewhere. I can't remember ex-
tly. You know how it is when you're under pressure," taunted
eed, delighted at Jed's dilemma. The longer the American
ent with him, the less likelihood he'd find the girl in time to
scue her. "Really, Kincaid, if you waste any more time, you
on't save your whore—"

Jed could take no more. Releasing Reed's collar, he let fly all
s muscle, every ounce of fury and disgust he had ever felt for
e Englishman, straight into his face.

Jed's fist jettisoned the man through the flames and out the
indow. Satisfied to hear the dull crack as Reed hit the marble
randa, Jed dispensed with him as an immediate concern.
ead or alive, he'd not be going anywhere for a while. Now,
here the hell would Vicky be?

The heat and the smoke were interfering with his sight, the
avy images in the overly hot air blurring his concentration and
aking breathing difficult.

"Vicky!" he bellowed, raising his voice to carry over the
apping inferno surrounding him. Without concern for him-
lf, he dashed through the flames toward the rest of the house.

"Vicky! Help me find you, damn it! Vicky, answer me!"

Opening a door, Jed found no one, succeeding only in cre
ating new drafts that encouraged the spread of the ravenou
fire.

"Vicky! Signal me if you can't speak! Make some noise be
fore it's too late," he urged. Rapidly he crossed the smoke-fille
main room and headed toward the servants' quarters.

Was it a dream? The room was so hot, as bad as the wors
days in the desert, and she had been dozing off and on, dread
ing Hayden's return, but that sounded like Jed's voice, Victo
ria thought.

"Vicky, where are you? We haven't much time, help me."

It *was* Jed, she realized, desperate to alert him to her pres
ence. In the darkened room, she wasn't certain where anythin
was, but she vaguely recalled a table off to her left.

"Vicky, the house is on fire! If it means anything, I love yo
I want to marry you, woman, but you have to be alive to sa
yes, damn it! Vicky!" Jed knew he was rambling, but his word
were the truth and he needed to say them now in case he neve
had another opportunity.

Over the din of the fire, he heard a crash. Darting throug
the dark, smoky corridor, Jed opened a door and called agair
his voice hoarse from breathing the heated, soot-laden air.

"Vicky—"

Then he found her, tied to a chair and gagged, tears runnin
down her cheeks.

"Oh, Vicky, thank God," Jed cried, kneeling to explore th
knots holding her prisoner. His entry into the room had fille
it with smoke as the fire surged into the hall. Damn it all, ther
was no time to waste. He had no knife and the flames were to
close to linger. Rising to his feet, he hesitated a minute to re
assure her. "Trust me, we'll be out of here in a minute."

Quickly he raised his leg and kicked at the shutter blockin
their escape to the street. Once, twice, finally, on the third tr
the stubborn wooden slats gave way. Hastily, Jed kicked th
remaining pieces free and returned to his beloved's side.

Lifting Vicky in the chair that held her captive, he carried he
to the window and gently lowered her outside, following a
once. Thankful to breathe the cooler, clean air of the earl
morning, he removed her from immediate danger before h
again knelt beside her and began to struggle with the cloth tie
around her head, cursing his loss of the knife. Once he ma
aged to get the gag free, all she could do was whisper.

"Jed—I was so foolish," she cried, tears sweeping the soc
from her cheeks. "I didn't realize how much you loved me."

"Hell, woman, haven't I proved over the last few weeks you mean more to me than my life?" he said indignantly, untying the rope that had bound her to the chair. "Yes, Vicky Shaw, I love you."

"And I love you, Jed Kincaid, completely and forever." Wobbly as she was, Victoria stood up and thrust herself into Jed's arms, thankful to be back where she felt safe.

And that was how Ali found them, moments later, wrapped in a tender embrace, Vicky's hands and feet still tied, she and Jed filthy with soot.

"I thought you were going to wait for me to bring the police," said the Egyptian, shaking his head. "I've sent them round to the back of the house."

"Ah, Ali," murmured Victoria. "Jed saved me, again."

"Reed was holding her prisoner inside," the American explained briefly, "and his intentions weren't honorable."

"Did you kill him?" Ali sighed. It had taken him nearly an hour to convince the police constable to go to where the men had taken the guns, only to learn that one of those he had followed was the constable's son-in-law. Quickly enough the police officer had wanted to know who had turned his daughter's husband to crime, and, though reluctant to accept the consular agent as the villain, he had agreed to accompany him to Reed's home. It would not bode well for Jed or himself if Reed wasn't alive to confess his guilt, though surely Cameron Shaw's daughter would have to be believed.

"No. At least, I don't think so," said Jed negligently. "He's on the veranda, probably not in very good shape, but I want to take Vicky home before dealing with the law. Why don't I meet up with you later at your place?"

"Please," whispered Vicky. "I couldn't face the police now, not with everyone coming to look at the fire."

For a moment the Egyptian hesitated, knowing the constable would be furious if Kincaid disappeared again, even if the charges were about to be dropped. Then he looked at Victoria's strained features and nodded sympathetically.

"Ten o'clock at the police station, Jed," he said curtly. "This time they will surely jail me if you don't show."

"We will both be there," promised Victoria, rewarding the man with a tender smile. As Ali went to join the police, she turned to Jed with a beseeching glance. "Do you really have to take me home? I don't think I can face anyone yet."

"Not your home, mine," he explained, kissing her softly, "or rather, my rooms at the Crescent Hotel. Now that I have you, I'm not in a hurry to let you out of my sight," he added kneeling down to undo the ropes at her feet. "Or out of m reach."

"You'll hear no complaints from me about that," Victori admitted, running her fingers slowly through the dark waves o his hair. "When you didn't appear at Lady Trenton's for din ner, I thought at first you had left Cairo. I only realized hov much I needed you when I thought you were gone—"

Standing, Jed took Victoria in his arms once more, inten upon showing her how far gone he was.

It was on a warm summer morning with the end of Augus approaching that Jed resisted the urge to run his finger alon, the inside of his high, stiff collar. Instead, he put his hands i his pockets with nonchalant elegance, and stood searching fo Vicky among the fashionably clad crowd gathered in the Shaws gardens.

He found her in an instant, surrounded by a small group o tittering female friends. In her exquisite off-the-shoulder whit gown that displayed her tiny waist to advantage, a sprig o rosebuds in her hair, she was the most beautiful bride Jed had ever seen. He gazed at her with tenderness, elated that she wa at long last his wife.

Looking up, as though she sensed him watching her, Victo ria sent her handsome husband a radiant, loving smile. A usual, she completely enchanted him.

How he wanted to be alone with his bride, to draw her away if for no other reason than to whisper a few loving words in he ear. But the Shaws had gone to a great deal of trouble in plan ning this wedding breakfast, and Jed decided he had best sta put for a while and appear the proper groom instead of the wild man Vicky's loveliness had him longing to be.

Coming to her side, he compromised by leaning down t place a peck on her cheek, an action that started Victoria' friends blushing and giggling all over again.

"I want to dance," he said, his liquid voice pure tempta tion.

"Knowing you, I would have thought you'd have some thing entirely different on your mind," Victoria whispered be hind her fan, decorated with the same roses she wore in he upswept hair. "It has already been a fortnight."

"Mmm, yes, but we can't do that here. The only way I'll get to hold you without your mother fainting dead away is to dance."

"There's no music," Victoria replied, lowering her eyes.

"That's never stopped us before," Jed answered smoothly, gallantly holding out his hand to her.

After a moment's hesitation, Victoria came to him and, leaning her head against his broad chest, allowed Jed to lead her where he would. Across the green lawns they twirled, neatly weaving their way through the gathered crowd, the pretty blonde oblivious to the interest their aberrant behavior aroused. All notions of decorum banished, she had no thoughts other than how fortunate she was to have found this remarkable man and made him her own.

"When you told me a small wedding breakfast, I didn't figure on anything quite like this," Jed stated. An amused twinkle lit his emerald eyes as he brought their dance to a halt amid the smiling, approving guests.

"There are only a hundred or so attendees. Mother had a mere two weeks to complete the arrangements," Victoria teased, fluttering her eyelashes in the most provocative way.

"Woman, you keep that up, and I won't be held accountable for my actions. Why don't we leave?" Jed urged, his voice hoarser than usual. "It's our private festivities I'm anticipating. Not this shindig."

"I know, but we should stay just a while longer, if only to please my parents—"

"There you are!" called Ali, hurrying to join the newlyweds. Placing a quick kiss on Victoria's cheek, he turned to shake Jed's hand. "Congratulations! Allah's blessings on your marriage. If ever there was a match that was destined it is the two of you."

"Thank you. Is Fatima here?" Victoria asked, looking around for the little figure swathed in veils that she had met at Ali's a week ago.

"No. She is too shy to attend a festivity with so many English and she begs your forgiveness. But my Fatima also wishes you happiness and desires me to invite you to a more intimate wedding celebration she will prepare for you both this evening."

"Much as we appreciate it, I think tomorrow might be a bit more convenient," Jed said, delivering a pointed look at Ali. "We had another sort of celebration in mind for tonight."

"Oh! Yes! Of course!" Ali agreed. A blush crept across his swarthy face. "Tomorrow evening it is!"

"Fine, now if you'll excuse us, Vicky and I were just getting ready to leave."

"We were?" the bride asked.

"Yes, we were," Jed asserted, his desire growing with each breath he took.

"But why?" she asked in mischievous, feigned innocence.

Lowering his dark head to hers, Jed whispered in her ear.

"And if I don't want to go just yet?" she asked, throwing him a provocative challenge designed to stir him even more.

"You don't have a choice." With that, Jed grabbed Victoria and threw her over his shoulder so that her posterior was riding high in the air. "We're going home."

"Jed, you vile beast, put me down!" Victoria giggled, beating ineffectually against his broad back. "You're shocking everyone here. I don't think they'll ever get over it."

"Lord, Vicky! If I put you down, what I'll do next will jolt your family and friends even more," he called to her with a backward glance. "Wave goodbye to your folks," he instructed, his powerful stride carrying them past the Shaws.

"Oh dear! What have we done giving our daughter in marriage to such a man?" Grace Shaw moaned. She had heard a startled gasp from her guests and looked up to discover what had caused it. "Make him stop it, Cameron, or I shall do so. First a dance with no music and now this. Victoria must be mortified. Just see how her shoulders are shaking! The poor dear is crying hysterically."

"Leave the children alone," Cameron ordered benignly. He put an arm around his wife's waist, a public display of marital intimacy in which he had not indulged himself in years. "If you'll look closely, you'll see our daughter is laughing and smiling, Grace."

"But what will others think?" she protested.

"Who gives a damn? We're lucky to have Kincaid for a son-in-law, especially when we consider what we might have been stuck with."

"Hayden," Mrs. Shaw uttered with a condemning shake of her head. "I don't know how he ever deceived us as he did. I'm glad he's in jail and will be for years to come. I suppose Jed is much better for our Victoria...if only that naughty man would learn to behave."

"If he was the type to follow the rules, he would never have gone to Khartoum, and Victoria would be lost to us. Besides that, the authorities would have received no warning about that fellow in the Sudan. Though to tell you the truth, I think those in charge still don't take the Mahdi's threat seriously enough. But that is not something to be discussed today. As it is, you and I have no cause for complaint," Cameron asserted, smiling benignly as he watched his daughter being carried off.

Jed relinquished his unorthodox hold on Victoria only when he reached the Shaws' carriage. There he lowered his bride, slowly, allowing her body to slide along the length of his before her feet finally touched the ground.

"Poor mother is aghast," Victoria said when Jed's seductive motion put an end to her fit of laughter.

"Don't worry, your father will explain. As for you, Mrs. Kincaid, tell me you don't like it when I'm incorrigible," Jed murmured, planting a half-dozen light kisses on his wife's upturned face.

"I find your behavior...admirable," Victoria admitted as Jed spanned her waist with his hands and lifted her into the carriage.

"Really? Then wait until I start misbehaving. You'll like that better yet," he promised with a wicked smile.

"Shall I?" Victoria's voice was breathless and coy.

"Without a doubt," Jed responded, totally confident. He climbed into the carriage and took the seat beside her, stretching his arm along Victoria's shoulder to enfold her in an ardent embrace.

"Jed!" she protested while the driver snapped the reins and the vehicle began to roll forward. "Everyone is still watching!"

"So?"

"Acting the adoring husband could quite ruin your reputation as a fierce adventurer," she warned, her voice playful.

"Vicky, sugar, it seems to me that with my marriage to you, my greatest adventure is only just beginning—and it's one that will last a lifetime."

* * * * *

Harlequin® Historical

WOMEN OF THE WEST

Exciting stories of the old West and the women whose dreams
and passions shaped a new land!

Join Harlequin Historicals every month as we bring you
these unforgettable tales.

Don't miss any of our **Women of the West!**